# ARK OF THE GODS

## A SEAN LIVINGSTONE ADVENTURE: BOOK TWO

# The Sean Livingstone Series

**Crown of the Pharaohs**
A Sean Livingstone Adventure (Book One)

**Ark of the Gods**
A Sean Livingstone Adventure (Book Two)

**The Spearhead of Creation**
A Sean Livingstone Adventure (Book Three)

Also available:

**Crown of the Pharaohs (Special Edition)**
Includes the prequel novella:
**Monsters, Myths, and Microchips**
A Sean Livingstone Adventure (Book Zero)

andrewdconnell.com

# ARK OF THE GODS

## A SEAN LIVINGSTONE ADVENTURE: BOOK TWO

### ANDREW D. CONNELL

EREBUS BOOKS

Ark of the Gods
Copyright © Andrew D. Connell 2018
1st Print Edition, December 2018
Published by Erebus Books

Find out more about the author and upcoming books online at andrewdconnell.com

ISBN 0-9953543-1-6

ISBN 978-0-9953543-1-9

For Ethan.

# CONTENTS

# Ras El Bar Discovery

Luminescent ripples of sunlight danced across the seafloor. Arturo Bonaforte let the current carry him over a small mound of sand. Positioned three nautical miles offshore from the town of Ras El Bar in northeastern Egypt – and 40 metres underwater – Arturo was in his element. He loved the silence of the sea. What began by diving for seashells as a child had now turned into a career, diving for his father's salvage company at the age of nineteen. After working on a cruise ship run aground in the Greek Isles, they were now taking a well-earned break. Like his father, Marco, their work was a means to fund their real passion – diving for ancient shipwrecks. Archaeology was about to run even stronger in their family, with his aunt Carla engaged to a world-renowned Egyptologist and archaeologist, Henry Livingstone.

Arturo brushed the sand aside, revealing a coral-encrusted artefact. He pulled it free with a swirl of sediment and turned it over. The slender neck, curved handles, and pointed base were distinct features of an amphora ceramic, a container used by the ancient Romans to transport wine and other goods. He shoved the amphora inside his gathering net, heart pounding with excitement.

There were mounds all over the seafloor, proving their unusual sonar readings had been accurate. This discovery would take weeks to excavate properly, but it was worth the time to do right. The wreck was of great historical importance and potentially lucrative.

A glint of light caught the edge of his mask.

One thought immediately filled his mind: *Gold!*

Arturo skimmed over the seafloor, kicking up a vortex of sand in his wake, expecting to find a trove of Roman coins. The seafloor rapidly descended, changing from sand to rock. The water darkened, but the mysterious flicker of light lured him on. He swam faster, following the drop-off until the seafloor disappeared altogether, leading him over the edge of a deep chasm.

Arturo stared in astonishment.

Twenty metres below him, a gigantic obelisk protruded from the chasm wall. The gleaming metallic surface was untarnished and reflected the surface light like a modern skyscraper.

Why hadn't the sonar picked this up? Maybe the obelisk was the reason their equipment wasn't working properly.

Arturo followed the drop-off, passing between ancient beams of wood that looked more like the ribcage of a decayed whale than the remains of a Roman galleon. The vessel must have collided with the obelisk in the distant past, scattering its cargo all over the seafloor.

He swam over the obelisk and trailed his hand along the strange inscriptions. They were unlike any form of hieroglyphics he'd seen before. Was this the mythical city of Atlantis? The idea made him light-headed with excitement. A discovery like this would catapult their family into untold success and riches. He could already see the megalith dominating headlines around the world: BONAFORTE'S OBELISK.

With his future flashing before him, Arturo kicked off for the surface.

Minutes later, he broke the surface with a burst of bubbles and ripped off his mask. Marco peered over the side with a look of concern. His tanned face was framed with dark curly hair accentuated with slivers of grey. Questing the seas had given him a healthy sun-drenched appearance, but his skin was wrinkled more than a man of fifty-five warranted.

'You were coming up fast,' Marco hollered. 'Something wrong?'

'It's amazing,' Arturo spurted, swimming to the rear landing.

Marco raced to the stern and assisted him onboard. 'You found a wreck?'

Arturo unclipped the amphora from his belt and handed it to his mother, Francesca, who was busy examining pottery shards under the canopy. 'Wow! That's beautiful.'

'*Sì!* There's a Roman galleon all over the seafloor. We hit the jackpot.'

Francesca placed the amphora beside other barnacle-encrusted relics in preparation for cleaning and cataloguing. 'Arty, remember safety first. Check your gear.'

Arturo smiled to himself. As always, his mother was the calm, level-headed member of their team and the logical voice to keep their boyish enthusiasm in check.

Marco eyed his side-scan sonar. 'So the readings were right, then?'

'Yeah, and I know what's causing the interference – a metal obelisk!'

'An obelisk,' Marco echoed.

'Yeah. Looks like the galleon crashed into it.'

'That's impossible,' Francesca said. 'It must be highly polished granite or obsidian. Probably looks like metal –'

'But there's not a mark on it. No barnacles or anything. It's like the surface repels any kind of growth.'

'If it's been underwater this long, it should be covered.'

'I know. It doesn't make sense, but it's the coolest thing I've ever seen. I need to get down there with my camera. It's covered in some kind of writing – looks like Sumerian Cuneiform, but I'm not sure.'

'That's it, I'm going with you,' Marco said, gathering his diving gear.

Francesca withdrew the underwater camera from a hard case and handed it to Arturo. 'It's charged and ready to go.' She spun him around and checked the levels on his oxygen tank. 'You have about twenty minutes left. You should swap tanks.'

'I'll be all right.'

'Okay, but keep it short, and I don't want you racing up like that again. You'll get the bends.'

'Don't wait for me. I'll follow you down,' Marco said, yanking the wetsuit up his legs.

'Be careful,' Francesca said, assisting Arturo to the rear landing.

'We're about to get rich,' Arturo said before smacking backwards into the water. The boat disappeared in a swirl of bubbles, silencing the world above. He wasn't so worried about running out of air; he could free dive to 20 metres without scuba gear and hold his breath for three minutes.

The streak of metal finally emerged from the depths beneath him.

Arturo powered on the camera just as a large shadow plunged the water into darkness. He looked up expecting to see his dad, but there was no sign of him, just open water. He positioned himself over the obelisk and took the first photo.

The flash reflected off the surface, like taking a photo into a window.

He checked the image on the LCD screen. Nothing – just a blur of white. Another shadow passed overhead, this time blotting out a portion of the obelisk for several seconds. Arturo craned his head around. The water was still empty. The shadow was too big to be his dad. What was it?

A sudden thought filled him with dread. *Shark!*

His heart leapt against his ribs. He spun around in a panic, convinced he was being circled. There were no sharks. Nothing but clear blue water. Still, something didn't feel right. He steeled himself. Just a couple of shots and he'd resurface.

He swam down to the obelisk, allowing the currents to carry him while he focused on the inscriptions. The LCD screen flickered and the camera inexplicably powered off. *What now?* He inspected the waterproof housing. No leaks. Pressing the power button did nothing. It was supposed to be fully charged, so how was it drained of energy?

He punched the housing in frustration.

Arturo felt a sudden shift in the currents. A strange tingling sensation enveloped his body.

The camera suddenly powered on by itself, firing the flash in rapid succession. Half-blinded, Arturo tried to turn it off. The tingling turned into pins and needles. He was now drifting away from the obelisk at speed, but it wasn't the currents. He was being repelled by it.

The sea grew dark and the obelisk inscriptions took on a faint blue glow.

Arturo peered topside and almost spat out his regulator in shock. A massive black disc hovered over his parent's boat. Intense flashes of light emanated from around its rim and rippled through the water like distorted fireworks. Beneath him, the obelisk resonated with an intense hum, like the two objects were communicating. The etchings glowed bright blue. The water seemed to vibrate, creating agonising pressure on his ears.

Darkness crept across his eyes and he became disoriented.

Arturo darted for their boat. He dropped the camera, but his survival instincts had taken over. He had to reach the surface before passing out. Storms of light were erupting above and below, disrupting his sense of direction. He closed his eyes and concentrated on kicking, finally breaking the surface. He ripped off his regulator and took a gulp of air. The disc was gone and everything seemed normal. He peered underwater to spy the camera sinking past the obelisk, the flash just a pinprick of intermittent light while it photographed its descent to a watery grave.

Arturo hoisted himself onto the landing. The boat was empty. No voices, just the sound of water lapping against the hull. His parents were gone. Marco's scuba gear lay on the deck as though he'd just left it. The pottery shards sat in the examination trays and his recent amphora container was shattered across the deck.

'Mama, Papa!' he screamed, peering over the edge.

There was no sign of them. It was like they'd just vanished into thin air. No boats in any direction, just the water and distant coastline. He tried the radio. It was dead. Every onboard electrical instrument was burnt out. He was stranded, alone and adrift.

Then he saw the inexplicable object heading towards the coast, dominating the skyline. It must have been there the entire time, yet he hadn't noticed it – or his rational mind had failed to perceive it.

He stumbled against the railing, staring at the city-sized alien disc floating in the sky.

# — CHAPTER 1 —

## *Resurrection*

### 16 Hours Earlier

Sean spun blindly in the darkness, clutching at the harness hoisting him through the fissure. A gust of warm air funnelled past him into the dark void below. He kicked out, hoping to find a ledge to stabilise his ascent. His foot slipped off the rocks and sent him into a spin. He tugged twice on the wire, signalling those above to stop lifting, and took a moment to gather his thoughts. His mind was still readjusting to consciousness after sleeping for thousands of years inside a cryogenic sarcophagus buried beneath the Sphinx. But things were getting clearer. He had a mission: find the Ark of the Covenant, an Isharkute power source designed to send a sample of modern-day human female DNA back in time to his alien friend Nesuk. Without it, the Isharkute would be unable to develop a cure for the affliction decimating their species, and those that did survive the last 10,000 years in hibernation would be their last generation. Neberun, the Isharkute Emperor, would do everything upon his return to save his race, even if it meant enslaving every human on the planet.

But the cure would not exist in the present until Sean sent the DNA back into the past.

The whole time-paradox thing made his head spin even worse.

Sean's friend Nocao had slept through time alongside him, one of the few Isharkute to stay on Earth. But there were others not fortunate enough to make it back with them. William Hopkins, a lifelong friend and work colleague to his dad, had sacrificed himself so he and Nocao could escape Overseer Senetep's pyramid. William had been a close friend and mentor to Sean throughout his life, often filling the void of his work-obsessed father. Caliph Aziz, the Egyptian Minister of Antiquities and originally an enemy to his family, had given his life in the end to save them in the Great Arena. Finally, Sean's dad, Henry, had been turned into a centaur by the Isharkute and volunteered to stay in the past to help humanity survive the climate change. Even though they all died 10,000 years ago, it felt like yesterday to Sean.

The memories played like a fading nightmare, one he was unable to wake from. Senetep could already be here and coordinating his attack to reclaim the planet.

Sean shook his head in disbelief...it was up to him to save the past and the future.

He tugged on the wire, signalling that he was ready to continue. A gnawing knot in his stomach reminded him he hadn't eaten in millennia. His mouth salivated at the thought of pizza, hamburgers, and chips. Junk food never seemed so good.

The fissure opened to a star-filled night sky tainted with smoke. A strong hand launched him onto firm ground. The smouldering ruins of Giza lay all around. The Great Pyramid was a pile of pulverised stone, less than half its original height, the massive stone blocks that once formed its steps now scattered across the plateau. The mighty Sphinx was no more, with only two rear legs and half a body.

'Okay, Sean, let's get that harness off,' someone said.

Sean finally acknowledged the three people who'd winched him to the surface, all members of his dad's team. First was Dylan, nicknamed the GIS guru (Geographical Information Systems specialist), who was responsible for the software, maps and geographical integration. He'd been a massive help when Sean was programming his *Genesis* star-tracking software. The other two looked familiar, but he'd only met them once, months before when he arrived in Egypt. A thickset man sat poised over the winch, and beside him, a young woman.

They disconnected Sean's harness and lowered it into the fissure, each sharing the same terrified but hopeful expressions.

'Hi, Sean. You may not remember us. I'm Lynda, this is Dylan, and Jack on winch. Are you hurt?' Lynda said, clicking open the first aid kit.

'I'm all right.'

'What happened down there?' Dylan asked.

Sean didn't know where to begin. He'd had 10,000 years to wrap his head around an explanation, but could only come up blank.

'You don't have to answer, kid,' Jack said, feverishly winding the winch. 'You've been through enough. We'll get 'em up.'

Carla was the next to emerge from the fissure. Her grim expression and bloodshot eyes sent a sudden chill through Sean's body, cementing the fact his dad had been dead and buried for millennia. But Carla was more than just a member of his dad's archaeology team, she was his fiancé. Her emotional strength and resilience were admirable considering she'd only just learnt of Henry's death.

'Who's next? William?' Dylan asked, helping Carla to her feet.

Carla shook her head solemnly.

'Henry, then,' Dylan continued, unclipping her harness and lowering it into the fissure.

Carla shook her head again, clutching the crucifix around her neck.

The team shared looks of horror and disbelief. Sean knew how much they looked up to his dad. He was more than their team leader – he was a friend.

'What happened?' Dylan snapped. 'Was it terrorists?'

'It wasn't terrorists,' Sean replied. 'But there's still one more person to bring up.'

'Who?' Jack asked.

'I'd better wind him up,' Sean said, taking over the winch.

Sean cranked the handle and brought his alien friend to the surface. Lynda's torchlight illuminated Nocao's pale, elongated head as it emerged from the fissure. His intense blue eyes reflected back at them like a cat at night. Sean locked the winch and assisted Nocao onto his feet.

The terrified trio stumbled backwards over each other.

'Don't worry, he's a friend,' Sean said. 'His name's Nocao.'

'What is it?' Jack gasped.

'His species are called Isharkute.'

Nocao greeted his startled welcoming party with the sign of the cosmos, making a thumbs-up on one hand and the outstretched fingers on his opposing hand joined the tips of his thumbs.

'It's an Isharkute greeting,' Sean said. 'It means all things in the universe are linked, including our two species.'

Dylan, Jack, and Lynda stared, mouths agape, on the verge of running away.

'They're afraid,' Nocao said in native Isharkute.

'Well, yeah. That's understandable,' Sean replied. 'They've never seen an alien before.'

Nocao assessed the cowering trio. 'If these humans lack the courage to help us find the Ark, we must move on and find others who can.'

'They can help – just give 'em a little time to adjust.'

'Adjust!'

'Sure. Remember what you were like when you found me? It took you a while, too.'

'You have a point,' Nocao replied with a smirk.

A pair of headlights cut a swathe of light across the maze of pyramid blocks and came to a stop overhead. The slam of a car door was followed by a desperate voice. 'Carla! Aunt Carla!'

'Oh no!' Carla said, leaping onto a block for a better view.

'What is it?' Sean said.

'I forgot. After everything that happened, I completely forgot –'

'Forgot what?'

'Bella, my sixteen-year-old niece. Your dad and I planned it weeks ago – to have someone your own age to hang out with on the excavation. We thought it was the perfect time to introduce you to some of your extended family.'

Sean gave Nocao a cautious look and he slipped out of view

behind a large block. His friend needed to be kept a secret for as long as possible. Bella raced down the rise of rubble, slipping and sliding to a stop in a swirl of dust. Carla jumped down and embraced her niece.

From what Sean could see, Bella was just like her aunt: fearless, confident, and beautiful. They shared the same olive complexion and dark-brown hair, except Bella's fringe was accentuated with a streak of bright red. She was dressed expedition-ready, with a splash of European style, in a khaki puffer vest, torn designer jeans, and black boots.

'Sean? Sean Livingstone!' called a voice from the shadows. 'I'm so glad you're all right.'

A man burst from shadows and threw his arms around Sean. It was Asad, the driver who'd picked him up from the airport when he first arrived in Egypt, still wearing the same chequered pullover.

'Sean Livingstone?' Bella remarked, pushing her way over to him.

Sean nodded, a little intimidated by her forthright demeanour.

'*Ciao.* I'm Bella, your soon-to-be sister-in-law,' she said, offering her hand. Her English was well spoken with a mild Italian accent. They shook hands. 'I hope you're not responsible for this mess.'

Sean was tongue-tied, surprised at how close she was to the truth. He could feel the guilt creeping over his face as he pulled his hand away.

'It's been on the news nonstop,' Bella continued. 'The Army's setting up roadblocks all over Cairo. Lucky Asad knew the back streets; otherwise, it would've been impossible to get here.'

'You should've stayed in Cairo,' Carla said, glaring at Asad. 'It's too dangerous here.'

Asad shrugged innocently. 'Ms. Bonaforte is very persuasive.'

Carla gave him a short smile.

'I heard the explosions,' Bella said. 'I tried calling you, but I've got no reception. I had to see if you were okay.'

'Where's your brother? Didn't he come with you?' Carla said.

'Arturo's diving with Papa off Ras El Bar.'

'Can we get past the roadblocks back into the city?' Sean asked.

'I doubt it – there's tanks and everything.' Bella looked around. 'Where's Henry?' Her question was met with stone-cold silence. 'Where is he?' she asked again, her tone rising with panic.

'Henry didn't make it,' Carla replied solemnly.

Bella gasped and shuddered. Her emotional response surprised Sean. How well did she know his dad? Obviously better than he thought. She'd probably spent more time with him than he had over the last few years, visiting his expeditions and travelling the world. He was overcome with a sudden pang of jealousy that reminded him of his old insecure self.

'I'm sorry,' Bella said softly.

'You knew him?' Sean asked, trying not to sound indignant.

'Of course, my aunt was about to marry him.'

'Yeah, of course,' Sean repeated.

'What about William?' Bella said in a hopeful tone.

Sean shook his head, disappointed to let her down again. Bella took an emotional breath and wiped away her tears. Sean was surprised. There was still more to discover about his dad through the people he left behind. But there were more immediate concerns, like how they were going to escape the military presence and hide Nocao.

'We need to get back to Cairo before we're arrested,' Sean said.

'Arrested!' Bella blurted. 'What for?'

'Blowing up the Giza Plateau.'

'*Che cosa!*' Bella cried, shoving Sean with two hands, almost knocking him clear off his feet.

'I didn't mean us,' Sean said, steadying himself. 'But the people who did are dead, and we'll get the blame.'

'Why are we taking orders from you?' Bella said, casting a dubious eye at her aunt. 'Who's in charge here?'

'I am,' Sean said, dusting himself off.

'Who says?' she replied sharply.

'*We don't have time for this,*' Nocao said, stepping out of the shadows.

Bella's eyes went wide as saucers at the sight of the alien now standing before her. Asad scrambled backwards, tripping over the rubble and making the sign against evil.

'A-a-aunt C-c-arla,' Bella stuttered, stumbling away, eyes locked on the weird blue figure. 'W-what is it?' Carla grabbed her before she tumbled into the fissure. 'He looks like an...an –'

'Alien,' Sean finished.

'No way,' Bella gasped, looking at Carla. 'Is it true? Is this real?'

A tremor rumbled across the plateau and the remaining section of the Sphinx collapsed in a plume of dust. Everyone jumped. Nocao held up a palm-sized crystal card and swiped over it, activating a three-dimensional hologram of the Giza Plateau. Six flashing objects were converging on the blue dot in the middle of the hologram.

'What's that? Some kind of alien phone?' Bella blurted out.

'*Your people have discovered us,*' Nocao said.

'What did he say?' Bella asked, doing a double-take between Sean and Nocao.

'We have to get out of here!' Sean said, directing everyone up the rubble-strewn slope to the car park. The rumbling intensified as they mounted the rise. Military helicopters roared over their heads, whipping up gusts of biting sand. Sean spun around, searching for another escape route. The entire plateau was now criss-crossed with searchlights. Convoys of military jeeps, trucks, and tanks approached from every direction, throwing up suffocating walls of dust.

Their chances of escape were gone, but worse, if Nocao was caught, he'd be whisked away to some hidden base, scrutinised, and dissected, never to be seen again.

Soldiers dressed in desert fatigues and black night-vision goggles materialised from the haze with their laser-sighted guns drawn. Sean raised his arms and a dozen red dots converged on his body. The soldiers surrounded everyone, forcing them to their knees.

Sean glanced over his shoulder. Nocao was surrounded by a wall of soldiers, their laser dots zipping across his body like a swarm of angry wasps. Sean leapt to his feet and cried out, 'Don't shoot him –'

*Crack!*

The butt of a semi-automatic struck Sean's cheek. A flash of stars seared into his retinas...followed by darkness.

# — CHAPTER 2 —

# Interrogation

Commander Hazim El-Amin stared with remorse at the remains of his country's greatest monuments. The magnitude of destruction was unparalleled. This was more than an act of extreme terrorism – it was war. The Great Pyramid lay scattered all around him. Stone blocks weighing hundreds of tonnes looked as though they'd been picked up and thrown around like children's blocks.

At twenty-eight years of age, Hazim was highly ranked in the Egyptian military. His handsome and youthful face made him look young for his age, and he filled out his uniform with a muscular physique.

Thankfully, his father, the late General Zayed El-Amin, wasn't alive to witness the devastation. Zayed had been one of Egypt's most respected military leaders until his unexpected death a year ago. It had taken his father a decade to return the country to a prosperous future after the fall of the previous corrupt regime. Zayed's love for Egypt and its culture was celebrated by all Egyptians. Hazim had been there every step of the way, watching and learning from his father while training in the Army. Zayed had been a strong politician as much as he was a general, but it seemed that ever since his death, Egypt had deteriorated, falling victim to riots and civil unrest.

Hazim took a deep breath, attempting to settle his growing anxiety.

His uncle, General Mohammed Nejem, was out of the country on political matters, leaving him to step up and take control of the Army until his return. Was Egypt at war? If they were being invaded, why was the government instructing him to send all their forces to the Giza Plateau? There was nothing left here, yet Cairo was a stone's throw away, with millions of vulnerable citizens.

None of it made sense.

Hazim checked his watch. Ninety minutes since the first explosion. The plateau was now crawling with Egyptian, French, and US forces, since the Egyptian Prime Minister Ahmed Ibrahim had granted multi-national military support. Surface-to-air missile launchers were entrenched around the perimeter and soldiers patrolled the rubble.

The Solar Boat Museum at the base of the Great Pyramid was miraculously intact; a small mercy in an otherwise disastrous situation. Debris had torn a hole in the side of the building, but the ancient boat inside was undamaged.

Hazim had fond memories of visiting the museum with his father.

Next to the museum sat nine massive cubes, each lowered into position by massive V-22 tilt rotor helicopters twenty minutes before. They arrived with transparent walls but had since changed to black, concealing the interior. Hazim had never seen anything like it. US soldiers patrolled the cubes, while a steady stream of personnel and equipment was trafficked inside.

Although their countries were working together, Hazim had been told surprisingly little. If his own soldiers had not reported to him that the US forces had moved the prisoners into the cubes, he wouldn't have known. Why were they in charge of the prisoners? This was his country, his jurisdiction. A rushed telephone conversation with his uncle ten minutes before left him with one very clear instruction – *Do nothing until General Ryan Maddock arrives.*

Hazim knew of the notorious US general through his father, recalling he rarely had a complimentary word to say about him. Maddock – or 'Mad-axe,' as he was more commonly known – was a cunning and stoic leader who'd earned his reputation in the Gulf Wars.

A Black Hawk helicopter swooped overhead and landed beside the cubes. Hazim straightened his jacket and marched down to meet them.

Maddock leapt out the side door, followed by a sharp-looking man bearing the rank of colonel. Both men held on to their berets as the helicopter lifted off.

'Commander Hazim El-Amin,' Maddock said with a thick Texas accent as they shook hands. 'I knew your father well. He was a fine leader. I was saddened to hear of his death.' Hazim nodded, with nothing to return in the way of pleasantries. 'This is Colonel Thomas Powell.'

The colonel removed his beret and offered his hand with an accommodating smile, sizing Hazim up with his intelligent blue eyes. 'Commander, pleased to meet you.'

'Colonel,' Hazim replied.

'I briefed your uncle General Nejem over the phone. Be aware this is a matter of global security,' Maddock said.

'Global? What happened here?'

'Our satellites picked up a power spike below the Giza Plateau that makes the Hadron Collider look like a microwave oven.'

'Your satellites?' Hazim said. 'Why are they focused on this area?'

Maddock ignored the question and headed for the cubes.

'We're in this together,' Powell said, sidling up next to Hazim. 'Prime Minister Ahmed Ibrahim has promised your full cooperation with the interrogation of the prisoners.'

'Cooperation? We haven't been near the prisoners since your soldiers moved them into the cubes.'

'Because you're not equipped to deal with them,' Maddock barked over his shoulder.

'Have you found Henry Livingstone yet?' Powell asked.

'No, but we heard reports of a strange man with pale blue skin.'

Hazim caught Maddock glancing nervously at him over his shoulder, the first chink in the general's impenetrable façade.

'Can you tell us anything about the events leading up to the first explosion?' Powell said.

'Henry Livingstone's camp was set up near ground zero. Although it was never formally announced, he discovered something beneath the Sphinx yesterday. We don't know more than that, but your satellite surveillance and swift response suggests otherwise.'

'I can assure you, we're here to help.'

'The explosives needed to destroy our monuments were considerable... If there's more attacks planned, I need to know about them.'

'You're right, Commander, and you will,' Powell said earnestly. 'What concerns us is the nuclear-sized power spike exactly twenty-nine minutes after the initial explosion – a thousand times more powerful than the Hiroshima bomb.'

'It's amazing Cairo's still standing,' Maddock said, stopping at the stairs to the first cube.

'What are these things?'

'They're an interlocking command centre that acts like a Faraday Cage, blocking radio waves and electromagnetic radiation to create a communications dead zone. When we discuss more about what's happening here, it'll be within the silence of those cubes.'

Hazim ascended the steps feeling like a child about to be told some great secret.

Inside, they were greeted by a team of military scientists. One stepped forward, his badge emblazoned with the name JAN RINZLER. His wild, dark wavy hair accentuated his horn-rimmed glasses and bulging eyes. 'Prepare to have your primitive minds blown.'

Rinzler's enthusiasm sounded crazy, rather than professional. He did a hasty round of introductions, keeping one eye on his data tablet while he ushered them ahead.

Hazim marvelled at the curious architecture. From the inside, the cubes were seamlessly joined, creating a labyrinth of rooms and corridors. They reached the end of a corridor and stood in front of a grey wall.

'We're holding the first group of prisoners in here,' Rinzler said. He placed his hand on the wall and it became transparent, revealing a starkly lit holding cell.

Hazim recognised the occupants from his soldiers' reports. Carla, Bella, and three people from Henry's team paced about nervously, speaking heatedly with each other, their voices muted by the wall –

all oblivious to the people watching them.

'They can't see us?' Hazim asked.

'Or hear us,' Rinzler confirmed. 'The opacity and viewing direction of our cubes can be controlled by electrical currents running through the structure.'

Information on each prisoner cascaded down the left side of the wall, like one big television screen. Maddock swiped a section of data into the middle of the wall and enlarged it. 'Carla Bonaforte's radiation readings are higher than the others.'

'But still within normal parameters,' Rinzler said. 'She must've been close to ground zero.'

'Hold them here. We'll question them once we finish with Sean.'

Hazim placed his hand on the transparent wall. 'What sort of glass is this?'

'It's not glass,' Powell said.

'What is it, then?'

'New technology.'

'When is someone going to tell me what's going on?' Hazim huffed.

'Right now, Commander,' Maddock said, 'but rather than try to explain, it's easier to see for yourself.'

Rinzler directed them down the corridor into a small, dimly lit room. 'Excuse the cramped quarters. I hope you all brought your breath mints,' he said with a chuckle. Nobody laughed. Rinzler nervously cleared his throat and continued. 'We're dedicating as much space to this lab as we can.' The wall slid shut, sealing them inside. Hazim squirmed, feeling a little claustrophobic with the four of them jammed together in the darkness.

'Has it attempted to communicate?' Maddock asked.

'No...but it appears to understand us,' Rinzler said. 'We just can't understand it.'

'Let me see.'

The wall in front of them became transparent, revealing a starkly lit lab full of stainless-steel trolleys and scientific equipment. Several scientists in yellow airtight hazmat suits moved around the lab like astronauts. Several overhead screens provided reams of data. One of the scientists stepped aside, revealing a pale-blue figure secured to a large metallic chair.

Hazim's breath caught in his throat. So this was the odd-looking prisoner his soldiers reported. The being was too bizarre, too deformed to be human – it had to be an alien. Although confronting, there was something noble, almost elegant about its elongated head, strange cranial tattoos, and near-perfect physique. It watched the scientists with curiosity, like they were his captives.

'Sean Livingstone says its name's "Nocao,"' Rinzler said.

'So the boy can speak to it?' Maddock asked.

'We think so, but we haven't seen it for ourselves yet. Sean's been in isolation since his capture. We're only going by what we've heard from the other prisoners.'

'Why is he in isolation?'

'He shares some of the alien's physiology.'

Maddock shot Rinzler a startled look.

'We don't know if they're implants or an infection,' Rinzler said.

Hazim was trying to keep up. The world as he knew it had changed forever. The human race was not alone in the universe. Of all the possible scenarios, he never expected the night to turn out this way – first contact with an alien species.

'Extended cranial cavity. Its brain's nearly twice the size of ours,' Rinzler said, swiping his hand across the wall, activating a set of scans and data. 'We're running DNA tests, mapping its genetic code. Overall, its physiology's similar to ours, albeit with a couple of unique traits. An extra finger for added dexterity, but probably the most interesting thing is...it's androgynous.'

'I'm not interested in gender,' Maddock said impatiently. 'I want to know its intentions.'

Nocao turned his piercing gaze to the wall, as if he heard Maddock's comment. A chill shot down Hazim's spine. The alien seemed to be staring straight through the wall at him.

'We'll start with Sean Livingstone,' Maddock said. 'Keep running the tests. I want a complete report within the hour.'

Rinzler nodded and escorted them out of the room.

'Are we being invaded by extraterrestrials?' Hazim asked, hustling to keep up.

'We're not sure,' Powell said. 'But we know they've been visiting Earth for a very long time. There's evidence of their civilisation in some of the world's oldest archaeological sites. In fact, these cubes are based on a crystal technology we uncovered at one of those locations.'

'Why haven't I heard about them?'

'Because their existence was top secret. But it seems Henry Livingstone hit the jackpot under the Sphinx. He found some kind of ancient alien library called the "Hall of Records."'

'Does that mean aliens built the Sphinx?' Hazim responded in an incredulous tone.

Maddock stopped and handed Hazim his tablet. 'You'll need to catch up on recent events if you want to be useful. It's not just Egypt. These alien artefacts are turning up all over the world. The more we dig, the more we find. We aren't the first intelligent species to inhabit this planet. But there's no doubt, Egypt was a key location for their civilisation.'

Hazim stared at the tablet, feeling like a child on his first day at school. He was about to unlearn and relearn history. He followed them into another surveillance room. Three scientists sat in front of a bank of computer screens, a lifetime's worth of information unravelling before them. On the other side of the transparent wall sat a lone teenager handcuffed to a table, a fresh purple welt emblazoned across his cheek.

The boy took Hazim by surprise. How could someone so innocent-looking be caught in the middle of such extraordinary events?

'He seems unnaturally calm,' Maddock said. 'Most teenagers would be clawing at the walls to get out...but not this one. Makes me wonder if he's still human.'

'He's definitely human,' Rinzler confirmed. 'But with some very special upgrades.'

A heat signature of Sean's body was superimposed over the

transparent wall. The discernible orange-yellow glow of Sean's body heat was visible, but down his back ran a pair of cooler blue streaks.

'What are they?' Hazim asked.

'Based on the shape, we believe they're wings. They're similar to those on a dragonfly, but appear to be folded down to a fifth or so of their actual span. The DNA structure appears to be extraterrestrial in origin.'

'Wings?' Maddock exclaimed.

'They're attached to his body on a cellular level,' Rinzler replied, magnifying the scan to focus on a pair of purple blotches at the back of his head. 'And there's some kind of organism attached to his ears. My guess is they're alien translators.'

Maddock stared at the data for a long moment, then approached the wall. 'I've fought in enough wars, and stood beside hardened soldiers as they died at my feet, to recognise the look in his eyes. We call it the "thousand-yard stare." I usually see it in men twice his age. Put me in a room full of strangers and I can pick out the soldiers, even the ones trying to act normal and forget the horrors they've seen. Call it my sixth sense. Sean Livingstone might not have seen war, but he's certainly stared down death...and survived.'

Hazim knew that look all too well. Now that Maddock had pointed it out, he could see it on Sean's face, like a veil had been lifted. But it was surprising that no-one mentioned the patchwork of scars across Sean's skin. It looked like he had seen war.

'Is it safe to enter?' Maddock asked.

'There's some residual radiation, but all within acceptable levels,' Rinzler said.

'Open the door.'

*    *    *

Sean had no idea how long he'd been handcuffed to the table. Inside this windowless room, every minute felt like an hour. Where was he? Where was Nocao? The last thing he could remember was a rifle butt smashing into his cheek. Now his face was throbbing.

The swollen lump seemed humongous at the corner of his eye and felt like it was exploding from his face. Nobody had spoken to him since he regained consciousness, leaving him to doubt the challenge ahead. He had no idea how to negotiate with leaders and governments, a skill his dad only honed after years of negotiating permits and expeditions.

A section of the wall slid open like a hidden door.

Sean straightened his posture against the handcuffs.

A broad-shouldered man in military uniform entered, his bulky frame almost too big for the door. Colourful ribbons of decoration and rank decorated his chest. His closely shaved head enhanced a brutish face locked in a scowl. Hands held in the small of his back, the man circled the room with casual menace.

Sean ignored his drilling stare, trying not to look anxious.

'Sean Livingstone,' the man said with a noticeable accent.

'Yeah,' Sean said. 'You're American?'

'General Ryan Maddock, US Marines,' Maddock said, coming to a stop on the opposite side of the table. 'Where's your father?'

'He's dead,' Sean said, a little too quickly and matter-of-fact for his own liking.

'So, let me get this straight. Since you arrived in Egypt seven hours ago, the Giza Plateau's been destroyed by a power surge stronger than any ever recorded, half of Cairo was levelled by the shockwaves, hundreds of people are unaccounted for, your father's dead...'

Sean took a sharp breath at hearing someone else say those words.

'...and we both know that's only the tip of the iceberg,' Maddock finished.

'You mean Nocao.'

'If that's what you call the alien, then yes. What do you know about it?' the general said, leaning over the table.

'That's his name. He's from a race called Isharkute.'

'Where do these Isharkute come from?'

Sean felt ashamed that he'd never asked Nocao the name of his home planet. 'Umm...a planet in the Orion system, but they lived on Earth before the last ice age, ten thousand years ago.'

'That makes them our intergalactic neighbours then.'

'Yeah, but they're more than just our neighbours...every human being shares their DNA.'

'We're related?'

'Sort of.'

Maddock narrowed his beady eyes. 'Explain.'

Sean paused. Changing a person's perspective on the world was not to be taken lightly, especially with someone as imposing as the general. But there was no way to sugar-coat it. 'They, umm... They created us.'

Maddock didn't so much as flinch, not even a twitch of his eyelids to show he'd acknowledged the comment. After what seemed like forever, he spoke in a measured, menacing tone. 'What do you mean, *created?*'

'They used to travel the universe mining rare minerals. On planets with life, they'd build workforces from the indigenous species. When they discovered Earth, they mixed their DNA with the early primates, speeding up our evolution.'

'So they engineered us as a slave race?'

'In the beginning they did, but they've changed... They –'

'How do you know so much about them?'

'That power surge you mentioned earlier was a time-travel device built by the Isharkute. It sent me, my dad, William Hopkins and Caliph Aziz back in time ten thousand years. I lived with the Isharkute before returning with Nocao.'

'And why is Nocao here?'

'To send a message back in time to the Isharkute.'

'What kind of message?'

'One encoded with female DNA.'

'DNA?'

'Yeah,' Sean said dubiously. That didn't sound so good, but he had the unshakable feeling General Maddock knew more about the Isharkute than he was letting on, almost like his line of questioning was about filling in the blanks.

'Why do they want our DNA?' Maddock asked.

'The Isharkute are dying from a collapsing genome. Since we were created from their ancestors before they became sick, we hold the key to their cure. Human DNA evolved over time to the point where some of us have a third DNA strand that our ancestors didn't. That's why they couldn't create a full cure in the past. They only have half a cure based on my DNA. Once they have the female half, it'll take them ten thousand years – until now – to cultivate it.'

'You make humanity sound like one big Petri dish. It would be remiss of us to help an alien race we know so little about, especially one this powerful. Maybe they're dying for a reason – a kind of universal natural selection. Have you ever considered that? We're not obligated to help them. I don't see why we should.'

'Because without the Isharkute, we wouldn't exist.'

Maddock grunted.

'It's true! The world was nearly wiped out by a supervolcano, but some of them stayed behind to help. They sacrificed themselves to protect the last human tribes until it was safe to repopulate the planet.'

'That's not reason enough to surrender to an alien force.'

'They're coming back for a cure, whether we help them or not.'

'We know. They've already returned.'

Sean jolted upright, ripping painfully against his handcuffs. 'What?'

'The Isharkute have been visiting us for a long time, but Nocao's the first one we've captured alive. This interrogation cell is made of a crystal based on the hull of one of their crashed ships. The pilots were deceased, but over the last few decades, we've reverse-engineered some of their technology.'

'You're talking about the alien crash in Roswell!'

Maddock's steely jaw locked in a devious grin. 'You're going to take us under the Sphinx and help us secure their source of power.'

'It's not about power, it's about knowledge. The Hall of Records is a library, a gift from some of my Isharkute friends to humanity.

It's meant to broaden our knowledge and prepare us for Senetep and Neberun's return.'

'Who are they?'

'Senetep's an Isharkute vigilante hell-bent on destroying humanity. He was arrested for rebelling against Emperor Neberun, but he escaped and jumped through time ahead of me. He could arrive at any second, start an invasion, and take over Earth for himself. But if we send the message before Neberun's fleet arrives, it shows we're willing to help them cure their sickness – the first step of trust between our species. If we don't act now, Neberun might just decide it's easier to harvest us for our spinal fluid. I've been through it, and the operation almost killed me. That's why they gave me my wings, to replace my spinal fluid and save my life. The rest of the world won't be so lucky.'

'We've researched reports from thousands of alien abductees all over the world going back a hundred years. Lumbar punctures, spinal fluid removal – that's nothing new. It's been happening for centuries, probably even thousands of years. We can deal with the public.'

'You mean cover it up.'

Maddock nodded. 'We've been doing it for decades.'

'What about dealing with millions of abductions? You can't cover that up.'

'If you help us, we won't need to.'

'What?'

'I assume the implants behind your ears are some form of organic translator?'

Sean bit his lip. He was tired of giving Maddock all the information and getting nothing in return.

'You and Nocao will show us how to harness their energy source and weaponise it. Then we'll be able to defend ourselves against them.'

Sean considered the situation carefully. He wasn't getting anywhere. Suspicions and hidden agendas within world governments were going to be major hurdles – problems he'd underestimated.

He needed to play their game for now, make them believe he was giving them something valuable. The crown was currently drained of energy and nothing more than a useless artefact. The Ark was the real source of power, and the only way to send their message. By handing over the crown, he could keep the Ark a secret until he figured out what to do. 'Their time-travel device is powered by a crown –'

'Crown?' Maddock repeated abruptly, his curiosity ignited.

'Yeah, it looks like a pharaoh's crown, but made by the Isharkute. It's energised by the same type of crystal they use to power their technology, except this one has the energy to open a wormhole.'

'And the crown's still in the Hall of Records?'

'Yeah, but you need Nocao's help. You can't just disconnect the crown from the pedestal. Shatter the crystal and you'll level more than Cairo.'

'You will assist Nocao and translate.'

'What if I say no?'

Maddock leant over Sean, casting him into shadow. 'I can lock up you for so long you'll never see daylight again, and your alien friend will be dissected into so many pieces you'll need a microscope to find him.'

Sean gulped, convinced the general was a man of his word. Maddock signalled his men to open the door. 'General, we should be talking to world governments, preparing for Neberun's return. The Isharkute are desperate. They'll do anything to survive.'

'So will we,' Maddock said with a cold finality.

The general exited the room, leaving Sean to contemplate his next move. Hopefully once he and Nocao were reunited, they could figure out a way to escape.

# CHAPTER 3

# Underground Invasion

Hazim lowered himself onto the debris-strewn bridge. It spanned a deep chasm, connecting a set of megalithic doors to the Hall of Records. The entire subterranean complex was awash with LED floodlights. Two-storey-high shelves filled with thousands of crystal shards towered around a central pedestal, the top of which pulsed with a faint blue glow. Hazim stared in awe, hands still locked on the rappel rope. He'd visited the tombs of his ancestors since he was old enough to walk, but with one glance, he could tell the hall was anything but the work of ancient Egyptian builders.

His soldiers worked alongside General Maddock's teams, analysing and photographing every detail under a ceiling of holographic stars. Soldiers stood guard over the scientists as they packed the delicate data crystals into hard cases for transport. Everyone worked in silence and with a sense of reverence, as though the hall was a sacred tomb.

Someone above tugged on the rope and Hazim let go. He stumbled over the rubble, creating a small rockslide into the chasm. The noise echoed through the hall and everyone looked in his direction. Hazim straightened and tried not to look so awe-struck.

Colonel Powell rappelled down behind him, unclipped the harness, and forged ahead. 'Everything all right, Commander?'

'If your government knew about the Isharkute, why didn't they share the knowledge with the rest of the world? We could have averted this disaster.'

'Most countries know about, or at least suspect, a lost civilisation.

The Russians, Chinese, Koreans – they've all made similar discoveries. We're just not sure how much they've pieced together yet, but we've learnt more about them in the last couple of years than we have in decades.'

'How?'

'Recent discoveries like Göbekli Tepe in Turkey and Gunung Padang in Indonesia. These ancient sites predate Egyptian culture by at least ten thousand years and point to an advanced civilisation wiped out by a global catastrophe. Geologists call it the *younger dryas*, when the warmer global temperatures suddenly reverted back to ice age conditions.'

They stepped off the walkway and approached the central pedestal. Two scientists shuffled past lugging a hard case filled with crystals.

'How does this hall compare to previous Isharkute discoveries?'

'It's like hitting a home run,' Powell said.

Hazim picked up a crystal already packed into one of the hard cases. It was smooth and clear, only slightly bigger than a credit card. 'Some kind of data storage?'

'We believe so. I know how you must feel, Commander,' Powell said.

'And how's that, Colonel?'

'We just march into your country, assume joint control of the situation, and take what's rightfully yours. I know my superiors would never allow such a thing to happen on US soil.'

'Yet you're happy to do it on ours.'

'We all have our orders, but the fact that we're working together on this proves your country's still prospering from your father's positive influence.'

Hazim placed the crystal back into the case. 'Did you ever meet him?'

'Unfortunately, no. But I have the utmost respect for him.'

Hazim was surprised by the colonel's openness. He seemed genuine. Powell leant over the central pedestal and peered into the pulsing crystal. Hazim was drawn to the glyphs inscribed inside the concentric rings radiating out from the crystal.

'Are they hieroglyphs?' Powell asked.

'No, there's nothing familiar about this hall except for...' Hazim peered up to the stars shimmering across the domed ceiling. 'Alnitak, Alnilam, and Mintaka – the three stars that make up the Belt of Orion.'

'What are you thinking?'

'They're a mirror image of the three pyramids.'

'You think the Isharkute built the pyramids as well?'

Hazim couldn't answer. His mind was racing, recounting the claims of conspiracy theorists that the ancient Egyptians didn't build the pyramids. There was one person who could set the record straight – Sean Livingstone. The boy was larger than life and a complete enigma. He had answers to questions that billions of people over thousands of years have asked: *Are we alone in the universe? Where did we come from?*

'Colonel, you should see this,' a scientist called from the antechamber.

Hazim followed Colonel Powell across the hall, noticing the look of fear and apprehension in his soldiers, some of the toughest, battle-hardened men he knew. The alien technology was unsettling to everyone and a humbling reminder that humans were far from the superior race they thought they were. Inside the darkened alcove were two futuristic sarcophagi. Their interior panels glowed like a spaceship.

'What are they?' Powell asked, peering inside the first sarcophagus.

'Some form of hibernation chamber,' the scientist replied. 'They're still active, which means the power source for the hall is still operational.'

A US soldier approached with a satellite phone. 'Colonel, it's General Maddock.'

Powell took the phone and listened for a moment. 'Yes, General, the hall's secure. The crystal retrieval should be complete within the hour. We're ready for Sean and the alien.' Powell turned to Hazim. 'They're on their way down now to retrieve the crown.'

Hazim shuddered, like an icy hand just ran down his back. Even Tutankhamen's untouched tomb with its wealth of treasures never contained a pharaoh's crown. Only ever seen in hieroglyphics, the crown was a relic of monumental and heavenly proportions – one that eluded archaeologists for thousands of years.

But the truth made Hazim nervous. It wasn't his ancestors that created the crown. It was aliens!

*    *    *

Sean guessed it had been half an hour since General Maddock left him alone. The interrogation room was soundproofed to the point that he could hear his own heart beating. His negative thoughts thrived on the silence. Could he live up to his dad's expectations? How were they going to break free and find the Ark? Hopefully Maddock's threats were just that, and Nocao was still in one piece.

Nocao's first impressions of modern humans weren't going to be overly positive and sadly echoed how they had been treated by Senetep. Sean preferred to think humanity had evolved beyond such crude treatment, but that wasn't the case.

Nocao was in real danger.

The door slid open and two stern-faced soldiers entered. They unlocked his handcuffs from the table and secured them to the chain connected to his ankle cuffs. Shackled up like a serial killer, they escorted him onto the Giza Plateau, where it was still night. The military presence had doubled. Roaming spotlights searched the rugged remains. Trucks and jeeps scoured the dunes. Soldiers raced around on foot and helicopters swooped noisily overhead.

The soldiers secured Sean to a winch and lowered him into the fissure, back into the Hall of Records. After a swift descent, he landed on the walkway between more soldiers, who unclasped his harness. The hall was now flooded with light and teeming with military. On the far side of the walkway, Nocao stood in shackles, surrounded by a circle of heavily armed soldiers. Sean drew a breath of relief. His friend was still in one piece.

'*I see you failed to convince your people to help us,*' Nocao said in Isharkute.

'Gimme a break! I've never done anything like this before.'

'*Do you have a plan?*'

'Not really. I was hoping you might.'

'*A little short notice,*' Nocao said, peering around. '*They've already taken most of the data crystals, so I assume we're here to help them get the crown.*'

'Uh-huh,' Sean replied. 'Can you think of anything –'

'Enough!' called one of the US men, stepping through the circle of soldiers. 'We can only understand one side of this conversation. What are you talking about?'

'*Is this man in charge?*' Nocao asked.

'What did he say?'

'Nocao wants to know if you're in charge,' Sean said.

The man nodded. 'I'm Colonel Thomas Powell, US Army, and this is Commander Hazim El-Amin from the Egyptian military.'

'Where's the crown?' Hazim asked Sean.

Nocao raised his hands, indicating that the handcuffs should be removed. The soldiers raised their weapons and tightened their trigger fingers.

'It's okay. Nocao understands English. He just can't speak it,' Sean said.

Powell motioned for one of the soldiers to come forward and unlock the handcuffs. Once free, Nocao pressed his finger under the control panel and the pedestal ejected a crystal card. The soldiers followed his every move through their gunsights. The card scanned his finger and he reinserted it back into the pedestal. The central core rotated anticlockwise with a *clunk*, then ejected upwards with a hiss of escaping air pressure. Bright light and vapours spilled from the opening. The soldiers stepped back, guns aimed at the pedestal as the crown ascended from its core. The slender, pearlescent headpiece was an object of incomparable beauty. Designed in the shape of the Isharkute head, it was the same motif seen all over

Egypt in every depiction of their pharaohs.

Hazim moved closer, eyes wide with fascination. Sean knew it meant more to the commander than anyone else in the hall – it was part of his Egyptian heritage. The crown came to a gentle stop, pulsing with a subtle blue energy.

'What now?' Powell asked, glancing at Sean.

'You can remove it.'

Powell walked around the pedestal, examining every inch of the crown. 'Why's it still glowing like that?'

'It's energised by a built-in crystal. Don't worry – it's safe to touch. The Egyptian pharaohs wore crowns powered like this one for thousands of years –'

'I'll do it!' Hazim said, cutting in eagerly.

Powell nodded.

Hazim placed his hands on the crown and the energy flowed over his hands. The pedestal powered off as he pulled it free and the overhead starfield vanished, leaving an empty domed ceiling. Hazim suddenly went rigid and his eyes glazed over.

'What's wrong with him?' Powell said.

'Nothing. He's feeling the energy of the crown,' Sean said. 'It's relaxing, a bit like mediation.'

Powell didn't look convinced.

But Sean was confident Hazim was going through the same sensation he'd experienced upon touching the crown, one that calmed the mind while heightening every nerve in the body, like opening a door to the universe. A moment of perfect clarity.

Nocao reached inside the crown and deactivated the crystal.

Hazim snapped back into the moment, vibrant and alert.

'Commander, are you okay?' Powell said.

'Yeah,' Hazim said, glancing at Sean like a man desperate to comprehend what just happened. He handed the crown to the soldiers and they placed it inside a steel case.

Just as they clamped it shut, a tremor shook the hall.

A shower of loose sand and dust sprinkled from the ceiling.

'Okay, let's wrap this up,' Powell ordered. 'I want every crystal packed in the next thirty minutes. Start evacuating. Send the crown up first, then the prisoners, followed by non-essential personnel.'

'I'll escort the prisoners back to the surface,' Hazim said.

Hazim and the soldiers marched Sean and Nocao back to the walkway. A stronger tremor shook the hall, this time vibrating the rubble off the walkway. The soldiers secured the crown's case to the harness and signalled for it to be winched to the surface.

'I'll look after them from here,' Hazim said to the soldiers. 'Help Colonel Powell with the evacuation.' He waited until they were out of earshot, then spoke in a hushed voice. 'What just happened to me?'

'Help us get free and I'll tell you,' Sean whispered back.

'I can't do that.'

'I know what you're feeling – I've touched the crown as well. I've felt its power. You feel like you're on the verge of understanding something that'll give you answers for everything you've seen tonight.'

Hazim nodded desperately. 'If I helped you, what would you do?'

Sean felt a weight lift from his shoulders. He'd finally made a connection. 'We need to find –'

A thunderous explosion shuddered through the hall and the entire ceiling heaved like a living beast, raining sand and dust. The walkway pitched like a swing bridge in a storm, knocking them off their feet. Huge chunks of ceiling stone crashed around the hall, barely missing the soldiers and scientists retrieving the crystals. Powell dove for refuge beneath the pedestal as a massive block crunched down in front of him, cracking the floor.

The shockwave passed and the soldiers raced back onto the walkway, forming a defensive circle around Sean and Nocao.

Powell pushed his way through to join them. 'Get the crown out of here now!'

Sean watched the case ascend into the upper reaches of the chamber and saw five fresh ropes drop through the fissure. Five black-clad figures rappelled into position and hovered near the ceiling, assessing the hall from their vantage point. They all swung around the long shafts slung over their backs. There was a sharp crackle of electricity and a flash of blue light.

A blast of energy erupted near the hall shelves.

Sean recognised the distinctive bolts – they were Isharkute staves!

The soldiers returned fire as the intruders rappelled down at breakneck speed, blasting out the work lights and plunging the hall into darkness.

Powell whipped out his radio and screamed over the noise, 'We're under attack! Repeat, we're under attack.' Frantic radio chatter crackled back at him as he retreated to the hall.

Sean and Nocao stumbled awkwardly to get off the walkway, both stuck in the middle like sitting ducks. The stave-wielding intruders picked off the soldiers around them one by one and touched down on the walkway, bullets pinging off their armoured bodies.

Hazim wrenched Sean and Nocao backwards across the bridge, away from the hall, and through the doors that *Juliette IV* initially discovered.

'Where does that go?' Hazim said, pushing them towards the shadowy entrance of the original stairwell.

'Up to the Sphinx, but it's caved in,' Sean said.

'We'll try it anyway.'

Another tremor rocked the hall, followed by a rumble of collapsing rubble. A plume of dust spurted from the stairwell and caked their faces.

'Well, it's certainly blocked now,' Hazim spat, unclipping his Beretta semi-automatic.

The battle on the other side of the hall was one-sided. Colonel Powell and the surviving soldiers were putting up a valiant fight from behind the shelves, but were clearly overpowered by the Isharkute weapons. The intruders moved with speed and purpose, already winching the crown to the surface with several more cases of crystal shards stacked and ready for the next winch.

'Are they aliens?' Hazim asked.

'They're human. You can tell by their stumpy heads,' Nocao said in well-spoken English.

Sean gawked at his friend. 'Stumpy? Did you just speak English?'

'Yes. From now on, you don't have time to waste translating.'

'How can you speak –'

'I'll explain later,' Nocao interrupted.

Sean peered into the advancing wall of smoke. The intruders were indeed human and wearing night-vision goggles, giving the impression their heads were larger than normal.

'They're stealing the crown,' Hazim said, edging forward.

Sean grabbed his arm. 'It's okay. Let it go. We don't need the crown, but we need your help.'

Two of the intruders left the walkway and approached their position. Sean peered around. They were cornered in the dark, with nowhere to escape.

'Get behind me,' Hazim said.

The intruders raised their staves. As they drew closer, Sean could see the electrical prongs reflecting off their night-vision goggles, the only chink in their bulletproof armour.

Hazim saw it too. He aimed his weapon and fired.

*BLAM!* The first intruder dropped from a direct hit right through his goggle.

The second intruder fired, blasting Hazim square in the chest with the force of lightning bolt. He slammed into the wall and collapsed between Sean and Nocao.

Sean raised his arms in surrender.

\*     \*     \*

Bella opened her eyes to a sea of glistening stars, content to stare blissfully into the heavens. The blanket of silence was comforting, like she was drifting in space. It was the perfect dream. A shooting star zoomed across the blackness, leaving a trail of rippling blue energy. It was beautiful – like something she'd capture in a painting. A soft ringing filled her ears, growing in intensity. Another shooting star appeared, this one close enough for her to feel the heat on her face. How could that be?

Bella jolted upright. This was no dream.

The walls around her shimmered like a television changing channels, from matte-grey to clear, revealing images of the burning world beyond her cube. Soldiers were running around screaming, firing at something hovering in the sky. Bolts of blue energy fired back at them.

Then it came back to her – the loud explosion, her world shaking and rolling violently. She was still inside the military holding cube, but it wasn't the same way up. The bench they'd been sitting on was upturned and several bodies lay in a crumpled heap beside her.

'Aunt Carla,' Bella gasped, crawling over. 'Please wake up!'

The soldiers gathered outside her cube and threw grappling hooks over the top. They started climbing up the outside wall. Bella realised the top of her cube was open and the outside world suddenly seemed louder. The gunshots, screaming, and explosions wracked her senses. It was harder to breathe. The panic was overwhelming. She hated being the only conscious person in the cube. This was the worst holiday ever!

Carla roused and Bella flung her arms around her.

'Are you okay?' Bella panted.

Carla rubbed her head. 'I think so.'

'Who are they shooting at? What if we're being invaded by aliens? What if –'

'It's okay,' Carla said, pulling Bella's face level with hers. 'I'll look after you. *Sí?*'

Bella nodded and slowed her breathing. 'I wish I'd gone diving with Papa and Arty.' Just saying her brother's nickname made her feel better. It's what she used to call him before she could pronounce 'Arturo' properly. He often teased her about chasing him around their family house yelling 'Arty, Arty, Arty!' Right now she needed her protective big brother more than ever.

The soldiers rappelled into the cube and got them all on their feet.

Bella was the first one lifted to the top. From above, the view was even more disturbing. Tanks and jeeps lay on their sides. Raging fires littered the ruins. Thick smoke drifted across the entire plateau. The interrogation cubes where they'd been held were separated and upended. Soldiers were picking up their wounded and regrouping amidst the disorder.

Once they were out of the cube, the soldiers hurried them through the carnage. The acrid smoke burnt their throats and stung their eyes. She stumbled and tripped, barely able to see a few paces ahead. The soldiers suddenly stopped and pushed everyone to the ground.

Terrified, Bella crouched in the shadows, anxious to know what was going on. The gunfire died down and an eerie silence befell the area. The smoke cleared, revealing an impossibly silent black stealth helicopter hovering in a clearing ahead.

The soldier in front of Bella pressed his earbud in tighter, listened for a moment, and then signalled his men to lower their weapons.

Twenty metres ahead, a group of shadowy figures emerged from the swirling dust and hastily made for the helicopter. One of them fired a blue energy bolt into the nearby debris, cracking a 50-tonne stone in two. It seemed like a warning shot, not one intended to kill. Bella glimpsed Sean and his alien friend as they were shoved aboard the helicopter, both shackled like prisoners. For some reason, the soldiers were prepared to let Bella's group escape. The helicopter lifted off and vanished into the night sky.

Bella had the feeling she was never going to see Sean again, but that was probably a good thing. He seemed like a magnet for trouble.

# — CHAPTER 4 —

# *Tjenu*

They were flying low across the desert, dipping and rising with the sand dunes like waves in a dark mountainous ocean. Their helicopter was operating in stealth mode, with no interior lights except for a faint glow coming from the cockpit instrumentation. The fires at Giza were now a dwindling match on the horizon, and as far as Sean could tell, there were no searchlights coming after them.

Nocao sat opposite him, flanked by the faceless intruders still hidden beneath their night-vision goggles. Strapped to the floor between them sat the steel case containing the crown.

'Who are you? Where are you taking us?' Sean cried across the hum of rotor blades. His question was met with silence. He eyed their Isharkute staves. 'Where'd you get the weapons?'

Silence again.

Nocao seemed unusually calm, almost unperturbed by their situation. If he was worried, he was doing a good job of hiding it.

The helicopter made a sharp descent. Sean's stomach rose into his mouth. He was convinced they were going to crash into the sand dunes, but they miraculously parted at the last second, revealing a circular hole burrowed deep into the desert. They levelled out and descended inside. Lights flickered to life down the rock walls like a vertical landing strip. Their captors withdrew their masks and night-vision goggles. Each man was of Middle Eastern appearance, none older than twenty-five.

The man next to him offered his hand. 'Sean Livingstone, my name is Malik.'

Sean was shocked, not expecting such cordiality.

Malik spoke with a hint of an English accent and the eloquence of an educated man. His youthful face was unmarked by the scars of battle – more like a man who just stepped out of an elite university, not some covert military force.

Sean kept his hands locked in his lap.

Malik nodded with an understanding smile. 'You'll have to excuse our rowdy arrival.'

'Rowdy!' Sean blurted. 'You started a war.'

'I know our actions were provocative, but it was worth the risk. Sean, you understand that time's important – the fate of the world depends on what we do before the Isharkute return. We can't sit around waiting for governments to bicker over who gets what from the Hall of Records.' Malik faced Nocao. 'And Nocao, I should apologize for your treatment at the hands of our governments. Unfortunately, they're not as educated and open-minded as some of us.'

Nocao gave Sean a quizzical look, just as stunned by Malik's obliging manner.

'I understand your reluctance to trust me,' Malik continued, 'but in time, I hope you will.'

Sean was intrigued. Malik's knowledge and empathetic demeanour had certainly sparked his curiosity, and the desire to trust him was hard to deny. Malik was the first to treat Nocao as a person and the closest Sean had come to negotiating with someone in a position of power. Sean had to remind himself that minutes before, these men were blasting soldiers into oblivion. He needed to stay vigilant and not be tricked into a false sense of security.

The helicopter descended into an immense hangar. The steel and concrete structure was the length of a football field and crammed with helicopters, desert vehicles, and pretty much any vehicle that could navigate on land, sea, or water. The soldiers freed Sean and Nocao from their cuffs.

'How do you know so much about the Isharkute?' Sean asked, rubbing his wrists.

'Please... My father's been awaiting your arrival,' Malik said, stepping into the hangar. 'He'll explain everything.'

Sean figured if the base wasn't some covert arm of the Egyptian government, then it belonged to someone with incredible wealth. To build something of this magnitude and keep it hidden required a vast influence and unlimited resources.

A lift from the hangar took them deeper underground. The doors opened into a long hallway and Malik led the way. The architecture changed as they walked. Ancient stone columns inscribed with hieroglyphics emerged from the modern structure, perfectly excavated and preserved in place. They arrived at a vaulted steel door which automatically glided open. Bombastic classical music echoed from the room beyond, like a fanfare for their arrival.

Nocao's eyes lit up.

Sean realised his friend had never heard anything like it. Grandiose horns and sweeping strings accompanied their entrance into the remains of an ancient temple. There was a mixture of old world and modern furniture. Desks, chairs, and shelves containing books and artefacts were placed sparsely around the temple, nestled between columns decorated with vibrant hieroglyphs. A sprawling glass desk dominated the centre space like an altar.

Malik motioned them inside, leaving the armed guards in the hall.

The music built to a crescendo as a man stepped out from between the columns.

Sean recognised him instantly as billionaire and entrepreneur Azar Hawati. He was immaculately dressed in a sharp suit, glossy black shoes, and a diamond-encrusted gold watch. He looked young for his age, which Sean guessed was late fifties. His slick black hair glistened like oil against his well-tanned skin and his needle-thin moustache was trimmed to knife-like precision.

Sean knew him as one of Egypt's most influential men, yet his dad always said he was more like a used-car salesman, cunning and untrustworthy.

Azar waved his hand and the music faded away. He strode

towards them, addressing them like a large audience. 'Four hundred and fifty years ago, Hernán Cortés led the Spanish conquistadors into Central America. Montezuma, the leader of the Aztecs, greeted him with open arms, believing Cortés was their god, Quetzalcoatl. In 1532, Francisco Pizarro conquered Peru. The natives believed he was the returning son of their gods. Many religions are built upon the return of their god. For the Catholics, it's Jesus Christ. The Muslims, Mahadi. The Jewish, the Messiah. Myth, belief, faith – they're the foundations for religion, but they're missing one thing...'

Azar stopped in front of Nocao and observed him with fascination. 'Tangible proof that their god ever existed. Yet here stands living evidence of that myth, proving all religion started from the same singular event, retold and reinterpreted over countless generations.'

'What event?' Sean asked.

'Alien visitation in our past.'

'How much do you know about the Isharkute?'

'I know they're the missing link in our evolution. I've collected hundreds of artefacts proving their existence, but here stands the living proof.'

'Why'd you bring us here?'

Azar drew his eyes away from Nocao and looked at Sean. 'You've played quite a role in the last twenty-four hours – changed the course of humanity. You only arrived in Egypt yesterday, but we both know you've been here much longer than that.'

'How long?' Sean asked, testing Azar's knowledge.

'Ten thousand five hundred years.'

'How do you know?'

'I've been monitoring every military communication since your arrival. I know the Isharkute are returning. They're dying from a collapsed genome and Nocao came with you to send a message with human DNA back in time.'

Sean took a moment to process what he'd just heard. Azar seemed to know everything. 'You can't just attack the military and expect to get away with it. They'll come after you.'

'They can try, but they'll never find us here,' Azar said, raising his arms.

'Why? Where are we?'

'We'll get to that shortly,' Azar said, a compassionate glint lighting his eyes. 'You look a lot like your father. I always had great respect for his work. That's why I continued to fund his expeditions over the years. I'm sorry to hear of his passing – it was a great shock to all of us.'

Sean bit his lip. Azar's mock regret was infuriating. Azar only funded his dad's expeditions to further his own knowledge, not because he respected his work.

'However, we can continue your father's legacy by helping each other,' Azar said, directing them to his glass desk. 'Please, we have much to discuss and not much time.'

A high-resolution satellite image of Egypt appeared on the desk's surface and zoomed in on the Sahara Desert. Azar swiped his hand across the glass and the photo transformed into a negative image, magically revealing the temples, houses, and streets of a city buried beneath the sand. 'The ancient Egyptians called it Tjenu, but you'll know it by its modern name, Thinis.'

Sean remembered his dad talking about Thinis. It was the capital city to some of the first dynasties and still undiscovered. His dad often said archaeology had unearthed less than 5 per cent of ancient Egyptian civilization. He believed there were pyramids and cities hiding under the sands, waiting to be found by the astute observer. Sean had spent many nights studying satellite images, trying to figure out where they might be located. It was an aspect of archaeology that fascinated him, where technology and traditional methods coalesced; a passion apparently shared by Azar.

Azar continued. 'From the ground, it looks like nothing – a few mounds and rises – but three years ago I discovered Thinis using an advanced infrared technology I pioneered. As soon as we started excavating, our ground-penetrating radar revealed something even more exciting.'

Azar swiped across the glass. 'A much larger city buried beneath the first.'

It took Sean a few seconds to recognise what he was looking at. There were interconnected causeways as wide as freeways and outlines of megalithic courtyards and buildings. It was an Isharkute capital, but not just any capital.

'Senetep!' Nocao said.

'Is that the name of the city?' Azar asked.

'No,' Sean said. 'Senetep was the Isharkute overseer for this region.'

Azar's eyes lit up. 'Fascinating!' He swiped his hand across the image and Senetep's capital was overlaid with the blueprints of his base. 'As you can see, we've built right on top, using the same layout as the original Isharkute city. Discoveries at this site led me to another in the delta where I found one of the crowns, along with the Isharkute weapons my soldiers are using.'

Sean stared at the image, trying to figure out what to say next. Azar had the resources and knowledge to help him find the Ark, but he was like a snake hiding in the grass, poised and ready to strike.

'I sense you don't trust me,' Azar said.

Sean straightened with a start. Was his face so easy to read? 'My dad's camp was attacked by Caliph Aziz, a man who reported directly to you.'

Azar sighed. 'Yes, unfortunately that's true. After your father discovered the doors to the Hall of Records, Caliph returned to my Cairo estate, ranting and raving about how the history of his ancestors was being exploited. He stole an Isharkute crown from my collection and used its power to try and stop your father.'

Sean thought about it. The explanation seemed a little too convenient, even though it fit Caliph's motivation for attacking the camp. But for now, he'd play along with Azar's games and find out as much as he could. 'Why'd you bring us here? What do you want?'

Azar looked at them, a shady grin creasing his face. 'I found evidence of an Isharkute device that could award humanity with the ultimate power. In the Bible, it's called the Ark of the Covenant.'

Sean's heart leapt and he widened his eyes in mock surprise. 'The Ark of the Covenant, like the one in the Indiana Jones film?'

'Sort of... but this Ark doesn't contain the Ten Commandments, nor is it a gift from God. Rather, it's a device from our ancestors... the Isharkute. We were given very specific instructions about how to construct the wooden box to transport it, instructions that somehow ended up in the Bible's book of Exodus: two and a half cubits long by a cubit and a half high and wide. The wooden casing was meant to be covered in gold, a metal we now understand has advanced technological properties. The same way satellites are plated in gold to shield machinery from intense solar heat and radiation, the Isharkute were instructing us how to keep the power of the Ark safely contained. Whenever it was opened prematurely, anyone near the Ark would die a horrible death. Their hair fell out and sores covered their body, much like radiation poisoning. In its raw state, this power is devastating. The ancient Israelites understood this and carried the Ark ahead of their armies. It was used to flatten the walls of Jericho, change the course of rivers, and decimate entire landscapes.'

'The Bible makes it sound like a weapon.'

'Indeed, but that's not its true purpose. The Ark's a power source designed to open a direct line of communication with a higher power, but it's not God –'

'It's the Isharkute,' Sean interjected.

'Yes. They want us to make contact with them.'

'How do you know?' Sean said, concerned that Azar knew way too much already.

Azar strode over to a stainless-steel door set between two stone columns. The door slid open. 'It's easier if you see for yourself.'

They entered an empty, square-shaped room covered in a wire mesh that glistened like a finely woven spider's web. Malik followed them inside and the door sealed shut. Azar withdrew a small remote from his pocket and pressed a button.

The room shimmered to life with billions of miniscule pixels swishing across the mesh in waves. The disorienting sensation made Sean feel like he was going to fall over. The pixels solidified and they were suddenly standing at the entrance to a cave. Sean steadied himself and looked around. Sunlight burned overhead. A cool breeze blew out of the cave and the sound of crashing waves echoed off the rock walls. Behind them, the entrance to the room had become a cliff straight down to a sprawling blue ocean.

Sean licked his lips, expecting to taste the salty air.

Azar's footsteps created small digital ripples as he walked into the cave. 'It's a combination of 3-D laser mapping and holographic projection created from an array of cameras and sensors positioned around the actual cave. I don't have time to fly around the world to every discovery, but this technology allows me to be in any place by simply walking into this room.'

'Wow!' Sean said to himself, reaching up to touch the roof of the cave. The projection tingled his skin and made his arm-hairs stand on end. Nocao forced his fingers into the cave wall and the hologram fizzled and flickered, resisting his attempts to penetrate it.

'For archaeology, this holographic chamber is the next best thing to actually being there,' Azar said. 'I can create a live uplink from the cave and direct my team as though I'm standing right there.'

'What is this place?'

'One of my excavations on the South African coast, eighteen months ago. From the pottery shards and skeletal remains, we initially thought it was a nomadic Neolithic culture... until we discovered this.' He stepped aside, revealing a mirror-smooth section of the cave wall inscribed with Isharkute glyphs.

Sean stared in astonishment, but the glyphs were only a fraction of the discovery. The entire cave wall exhibited a collection of primitive paintings and charcoal renderings depicting human stick figures, two of which had unmistakable elongated heads. *Nesuk and Rootuk!* Hybrids of all shapes and sizes were drawn in the same style, mingling and living alongside humans in depictions of everyday life.

Sean craned closer to the wall, eyes drawn to one figure in particular. The four stick legs, horse body, and torso of a man outlining the undeniable form of a centaur.

It was his dad!

Now he could see that the entire montage was arranged in

chronological order and told the story of his dad and Yeesha's tribe, from living in the caves to planting the first crops, then building the first settlements. His dad may have died thousands of years ago, but their connection felt as unbreakable and strong as ever. It filled him with the confidence to finish what his dad started. Sean wanted to touch the image of his dad, but this was his secret, not something Azar needed to know. He took a deep breath, resisting the urge to wipe his teary eyes.

'This cave wall is one big Rosetta Stone,' Azar said. 'One that retells a very important story.'

'What's that?' Sean said, standing back to appreciate the entire wall.

'The original inhabitants called this place the Cave of Myth. It documents our ancestors living alongside powerful beings and mythical creatures, but more than that, it tells the story of the Ark of the Covenant, a journey that started in Egypt ten and a half thousand years ago.'

Sean glanced at Nocao with anticipation, then back to Azar. 'Where's the Ark? I don't see it.'

Azar pointed to the bottom row of pictograms, barely visible through millennia of accumulated dirt. 'Impossible to see properly with the naked eye, these pictographs weren't fully revealed until we used infrared reflectography and terahertz imaging.'

Azar touched the hologram and the entire wall shimmered, then came alive with a wealth of previously hidden images.

'Whoa!' Sean gasped, realising they'd only been looking at half the visible artwork. He knelt for a closer look, focusing on the pictograph of the distinctive gold box. The Ark of the Covenant looked exactly the same as the one in *Indiana Jones and the Raiders of the Lost Ark*, complete with long carrying handles and a pair of golden cherubim stretching their wings over the lid.

Azar pointed to the corresponding pictographs as he spoke. 'Here you can clearly see the Ark being moved from its original resting place under the Sphinx. From there it's taken across the desert and hidden in the mountains, one of which we assume is Mount Sinai, where Moses received the Ten Commandments. Unfortunately, after that the next section of the wall has collapsed and the story skips to the end.'

Azar passed the collapsed section and pointed to the final pictograph, an obelisk with the imprint of a human hand and the Ark of the Covenant. A beam of light extended from the tip of the obelisk and connected with three stars.

Sean instantly recognised the alignment. 'That's the Belt of Orion!'

'Exactly,' Azar said. 'Those three stars are also represented in the final Isharkute glyph, the first clue that both the glyphs and pictographs were telling a similar story. Egyptian creationist myths pinpoint the Orion system as the birthplace of their gods, which, not so coincidentally, is home to the Isharkute.'

'What about the beam of light coming from the obelisk?'

'We believe the Ark is powering a beacon to communicate with the Isharkute. But with the gaps in the story, we don't know why. I believe that if we can find this obelisk, we'll find the Ark. That's why Nocao is so important. We want him to translate the Isharkute glyphs and fill in the missing sections of the wall.'

Nocao moved closer to the wall and traced the glyphs with his finger. 'Your translations are partially correct.'

'You can speak English?' Azar said in astonishment.

'Yeah – you never told me how,' Sean said under his breath.

'Over time, the biological translators in my ears trained my brain to speak the language. The glyphs describe events after Sean and I entered cryogenic sleep. Senetep's commanders, Nefaro and Vogran, sabotaged every cryogenic chamber in Emperor Neberun's fleet to stop them from waking. Since that time, his commanders have been amassing their forces, planning to coincide their invasion with Senetep's inevitable return.'

'Which is when?' Azar asked.

Sean knew exactly. The guilt weighed twice as heavy on his conscience now. 'I set the date on the pedestal for today... So he's probably here already.'

'Which means Earth is about to be invaded,' Malik said, stepping out from behind them and speaking for the first time since they entered the room.

'What about the Ark?' Azar said impatiently. 'Do the glyphs reveal its whereabouts?'

Nocao continued translating. 'After Senetep's sabotage, Nesuk realised the transmitter in the Hall of Records wasn't powerful enough to wake Neberun's fleet, so he built a new beacon capable of sending both messages: one into the past with human female DNA, the other into space to wake the fleet. After construction of the beacon was finished, the Ark was moved from the hall into the mountains to align with future events.'

'And the first event was Moses receiving the Ark on Mount Sinai,' Azar confirmed. 'But where did it go after that?'

'That's where Nesuk and Rootuk left it – the rest was up to human history.' Nocao pointed to the bottom row of glyphs. 'The last line says the Ark will be revealed after the solution of three riddles –'

'Three riddles!' Azar repeated. 'What are they?'

Nocao read ahead for a moment. 'The glyphs make no mention of specific riddles, but say that only then will the true covenant will be made.'

Sean focused on the final pictograph combining the obelisk, hand, and Ark. That had to represent the covenant, yet he couldn't shake the feeling they were missing something crucial. Why would the glyphs mention three riddles and not say anything more about them?

Malik stepped forward. 'Inviting Emperor Neberun and his fleet to Earth doesn't seem like a smart move, considering we have enough problems with Senetep –'

'I agree,' Azar cut in. 'We should be harnessing the power of the Ark to defend humanity, not using it to turn on this ancient transmitter.'

Sean couldn't stop staring at the pictograph, wondering what three riddles they needed to solve to reveal the location of the Ark. He suddenly realised his dad was missing from the last few pictographs. He traced back along the wall and found the collapsed section of wall that removed his dad from the timeline. The crumbled remnants lay scattered on the cave floor in front of him. He tried to pick up the pieces but his fingers passed straight through the hologram, reminding him that the actual rubble was thousands of kilometres away. Being so close to his dad stirred an overwhelming desire to complete his story.

'I built this base in anticipation of this day,' Azar said. 'The governments will squabble endlessly over the information in the Hall of Records and who should control the Ark's power. What we need is a neutral party. One concerned with the future of the entire planet, not just their own borders.'

It was a good pitch, but Sean wasn't convinced. 'It feels like there's something about the cave you're not telling us.'

Azar stared a Sean for a long moment, then shared a subtle nod with Malik.

'Sean, this wall is merely the tip of a very big iceberg,' Malik said. 'If you agree to help my father solve these three riddles and find the Ark, we'll reveal what we found in the collapsed section of the wall.'

Sean's mind raced with the possibilities. Was it a clue to the Ark? Maybe it was his dad. What if he was buried there? There were too many burning questions not to indulge Azar further.

'Sean, aside from finding the Ark, I'm sure you want to protect your father's legacy,' Azar said in a soft, almost-convincing tone. 'We both know he wasn't responsible for the destruction of the Giza Plateau, but that's not how the rest of the world will see it. Rather than being the torchbearer to a new paradigm of human existence, Henry Livingstone will be remembered as the man who brought about an apocalyptic alien invasion. I can place all the blame on Caliph. Isn't that something you'd like to do...exonerate your father?'

Now Sean could see the used-car salesman his dad talked about.

Sean shared a subtle nod with Nocao, indicating that they were going to keep playing Azar's game as long as they had to. 'Okay, we'll help you find the Ark and solve the riddles.'

Azar grinned from ear-to-ear like he'd just made the deal of a lifetime.

# CHAPTER 5

# Solar Boat Museum

Bella watched the soldiers scuttle about the walkways of the war-torn museum, crunching across the shattered glass like crabs on a sandy beach. She was now under military guard on the top level of the Solar Boat Museum, a modern building positioned at the base of the Great Pyramid and built specifically to display a 4,500-year-old wooden boat discovered in the same location. The boat had been meticulously restored by archaeologists and was, ironically, one of the few places Bella wanted to visit while in Egypt.

Unfortunately, this was not the kind of tour she had in mind!

The haze of smoke drifting through the museum created a dazzling effect, as though the boat was crossing through the mystical afterlife. Bella's first impulse was to sketch the spellbinding vision. As an art student, she was always looking for inspiration. Drawing helped her relax, but right now that simple distraction was impossible. Her wrists were handcuffed to the walkway balustrade and she was trembling so badly, she couldn't hold a pencil. To top things off, her precious sketchpad was sitting in Asad's 4WD, more than likely destroyed.

The US and Egyptian soldiers had taken refuge in the museum since the attack, posting guards on the myriad walkways. It was quieter now. The guns and explosions had stopped after Sean was whisked away in the black helicopter.

Bella squirmed, trying to relieve the pain in her wrists from the steel cuffs. 'Can you please loosen these?'

The nearby soldier glanced at her, saying nothing. His name

badge read: DAVIS. US ARMY. She guessed he was only a couple of years older than her. Exhausted, she leant against the balustrade's glass barrier, causing it to crack. He spun around, hand on his gun.

Bella smiled innocently. '*Scusa!*'

Davis relaxed, then suddenly stood to attention. A large angry-looking man stomped straight up the walkway towards them. His uniform was tattered and dusty and a trickle of blood ran across the bridge of his nose, accentuating his surly bulldog scowl. The soldier saluted him and stepped aside.

'Young lady, you're in a maelstrom of trouble,' the man boomed in a Texas accent.

Bella detested his accusing tone. She'd done nothing wrong and couldn't resist the temptation to stand up to him. 'Who says?'

'General Ryan Maddock, US Marines.'

'Where's the Egyptian authorities?'

'I'm in charge now.'

'This isn't even your country.'

'Don't get smart with me.'

'Where's my aunt?'

Maddock seized her wrists and wrenched her along the balustrade.

'Oww! That hurts,' she squealed.

She was now standing in Maddock's shadow, his enormous hand locked over hers like a vice. Davis peeked over his shoulder at her, a look of concern in his eyes.

'You're going to tell me everything you saw tonight or you'll never see your aunt Carla again.'

'I... I don't know much about anything,' Bella stammered. 'I –'

'Why are you in Egypt?' Maddock barked.

'Holiday. My aunt wanted me to come.'

'Why?'

'To meet Sean.'

'Why?'

'She was engaged to his dad...Henry Livingstone. I'd never met Sean before tonight –'

'Did Sean say anything about an alien attack?'

'No, I don't think so.'

'Did he mention a crown? A hidden power source? Something about the alien?'

'No...I don't know... Maybe. I can't remember.'

Maddock leaned so close she could feel the heat radiating off his face. 'Think hard. If I lose any more soldiers, I'll hold you personally accountable. You'll spend the rest of your miserable life in a cell no bigger than a toilet.'

Bella gulped. His close proximity and heavy breathing clouded her ability to think straight. She tried to remember anything that would make him back away. He squeezed tighter, crushing her wrists. She felt like throwing up – preferably all over him. At least that would make him back off.

'Did he say anything about a mission? Something he was meant to do?'

'I really can't remember.'

'Think!' Maddock demanded, hunching closer. A blood-tainted bead of sweat trickled onto the tip of his nose and wobbled precariously, threatening to drip on her.

Bella recoiled as far as she could, desperate to remember anything before that *thing* dripped on her. A detail suddenly popped into her head. 'He said the people who blew up the pyramids were dead.'

Maddock scrunched his eyes.

'General, Colonel Powell and Commander El-Amin are here,' Davis said.

Bella sighed with relief as Maddock released his hand and marched over to meet the approaching pair. Both men looked beaten and exhausted, particularly the Egyptian commander, who was clutching his chest and supported along by the US colonel.

Davis unscrewed his water bottle and held it for Bella to sip. 'You've got some guts talking to the general like that. But he means what he says. Just tell him every detail you can think of, regardless of how small or insignificant it seems.'

Bella swallowed the water with a heavy gulp and nodded. 'Can't you at least tell me if my aunt's okay?'

Davis inadvertently eyeballed the lower level of the museum. That's all Bella needed – a subtle clue to where her aunt was being held. Staying prisoner wasn't an option, so one way or another, she had to get down there. She wriggled her fingers to keep the blood flowing and was suddenly struck with an idea.

'My hands are numb.' She sighed.

Davis ignored her request.

'I just figured out a way to help the general. If you free me, I can show you.'

'How?'

'I'm an artist and really good at drawing details. I saw the people who attacked us – they wore black masks and goggles. I remember their weapons, how many there were, even what the helicopter looked like. I watched them take Sean and the alien away. Maybe there's a detail in there that can help.'

'You're an artist?' Davis said, eyeing her up and down. 'You're just a child!'

'*Bambina!? Ma che dici?*' Bella snapped. 'I'm sixteen and studying art at the Sorbonne.'

He stared at her blankly, unimpressed.

'Do you even know what the Sorbonne is? It's the University of Paris, one of the most respected universities in Europe. You don't want General Maddock to find out you put my restraints on so tight that I can't draw.'

'If you're so good, why didn't you tell the general before?'

'I wasn't thinking straight. Just a couple of minutes... Please, they're killing me.'

Davis looked at the general, who was still in deep conversation. He took a key from his pocket and unlocked the cuffs. 'Just for a minute.'

Bella nodded and rubbed her wrists – that was easier than she expected. 'If you get me some paper and a pencil, I can start drawing.'

Davis smirked and held out the cuffs. 'Nice try. Put them back on.'

'*Aspetta un attimo!*' Bella huffed. The soldier gave her a quizzical look, as he didn't speak Italian. 'I mean, wait a second. Won't it make the general happy if we can help?'

Davis glanced around at his team guarding the walkway, seemingly in two minds about helping her.

'Where could I possibly go?' she said, feigning innocence.

Davis narrowed his eyes, then waved over one of his team. He half-turned his back to her and spoke quietly to his companion. Bella's heart was fluttering like a bird inside her ribcage. Escape was either a daring sprint past all the soldiers along the walkway, or over the balustrade, a multi-level drop straight down to the ground floor.

A fresh breeze blew through the museum and the bow of the solar boat materialised from the smoke as if it were sailing towards her, beckoning her to jump aboard. It was a 2–3-metre leap off the edge of the balustrade. Easy. She just needed a bigger distraction for the soldiers, but it was impossible to move anywhere without stepping on the broken glass.

She suddenly realised, *That's it. The glass!*

Bella edged closer to the glass barrier lining the balustrade. She steadied herself and jabbed her heel against the weakened glass. The entire 2-metre-long panel broke free and sailed into the void between the walkways. There was a second of silence, then...

*Smmmaaassshhh!*

Every soldier raced to the balustrade, guns aimed into the shadows below.

Bella sprinted to the opposite side of the walkway, climbed onto the balustrade, and without looking down, leapt over the three-storey drop onto the boat. She crawled along the deck, beneath the ancient oars and open canopy, towards the cover of the main cabin. The dark wood was fragile and uneven. Gaping holes littered the deck. She kept low, avoiding the torchlights. The planks creaked precariously, but she kept on towards the cabin's pitch-black doorway. She crawled inside and suddenly found herself clawing at air before falling into a hole.

Bella landed on her back with a heavy *thud*. She lay still, the wind punched from her lungs. A cloud of dust settled around her. She stifled a cough and sat up. The soldiers were calling out, trying to find her. Their torchlights sliced between the planks of wood, creating slivers of light in the dusty air. The interior hull of the boat looked like the belly of a whale with its curved beams.

*Get up! Keep going. Find Aunt Carla.* She stood up, driven by the voice in her head.

Her back was aching, her legs trembling.

The only other time she'd been this petrified was during her entrance interview for the Sorbonne. It helped to remind her how she got through. They rarely accepted such a young student, but she'd worked for months, creating enough art to fill a gallery. Her acceptance proved how grit and determination paid off – the exact traits she needed again.

Bella crab-crawled through the dim cabin. She found an opening where a pyramid block had punched through the deck above and straight out the hull like a cannonball. The hole opened onto a support beam leading to a panel of toughened glass that sloped to the ground floor. It was a way out!

She grabbed hold of the plank above the hole and lowered herself through.

*Snap!* The 4,000-year-old wood gave way under her weight. She fell onto the support beam and bounced off it onto the glass, sliding down it to crash into the balustrade on the lower walkway.

Bella crouched in the shadows and caught her breath.

Nobody had seen her. The soldiers were still searching for her on the upper levels, giving her time to assess her surroundings. The walkway ran alongside a deep rectangular pit, the original resting place of the disassembled boat. Her aunt was at the opposite end of the walkway, handcuffed to the balustrade with a soldier standing guard.

Footfalls crunched down the walkway behind her and a torch beam illuminated the panel she'd slid down moments before.

Bella slipped over the guardrail and climbed down an old ladder into the pit.

The *thrum* of helicopter blades sounded throughout the building and a squall of dust churned through the broken windows. Bella used the distraction to race along the length of the pit. The carved walls and overhead casing stones made it feel like she was running through an ancient temple in the middle of a sandstorm. At the end of the pit was another ladder leading back up to the walkway, just a few metres from her aunt. Bella climbed it quietly and stopped a few rungs from the top, poised in the shadows.

The soldier turned away and Bella waved. 'Pssst! Down here,' she whispered.

Carla recoiled in surprise at the face glaring from the shadows, then realised who she was looking at. *Bella?* she mouthed in shock.

'What are you doing?' the soldier said, turning on Carla.

'Nothing,' Carla replied.

The soldier approached the balustrade and peered over the edge. Bella dropped out of sight, holding her breath, convinced she was about to be recaptured, or worse, shot.

The noisy helicopter passed and the dust settled, exposing her more by the second. She noticed a plank of wood teetering on the edge of the pit. The soldier jumped over the guardrail for a closer look, gun barrel aimed in her direction...

Bella lashed out with the plank... *Smack!*

A cloud of dust burst around the soldier's face and the wood snapped in two. He slumped onto the nearby casing stone, unconscious.

'Whoa... *Che culo!*' Bella gasped. She climbed up, snatched the keychain off the soldier's belt, and leapt over the balustrade.

'You're right, that was lucky,' Carla whispered. 'What do you think you're doing?'

Bella flicked through the keys. 'Getting us outta here.'

'The soldiers have been told to shoot on sight.'

'Then we keep out of sight,' Bella said, systematically trying one key after another. None fit the lock.

'It's too dangerous,' Carla whispered. 'If anything happened to you, I couldn't live with myself –'

'They don't believe us. They're going to blame everything on us.

If we don't get out of here, we'll never see each other again. They'll lock us up and...' *Click* went the final key. 'Got it!'

Carla freed her hands and kissed Bella on the forehead. '*Bravissima!*'

'Are we going back to Cairo?'

'I'll get you there, but I'll be damned if they blame this on us. I need to find out what happened to Sean – he's the only one who can fix this,' Carla said. Her eyes were filled with determination and an irrepressible sense of hope.

Before Bella could protest, her aunt had her by the hand, courageously leading her into the dangerous, unpredictable night.

# — CHAPTER 6 —

# *The Ark*

Sean was eager to ask Nocao about the Isharkute glyphs on the cave wall. Did they complete his dad's story? How did he die? Now that he'd glimpsed his dad's fate, he was desperate to know everything. Malik led them through a labyrinth of metal corridors into a sprawling multi-level laboratory. The bustling throng of scientists and technicians stopped what they were doing to watch them. Their unsettling stares reminded Sean of the bloodthirsty scientists from Senetep's hybrid labs.

'*I'm beginning to understand how you felt in my time,*' Nocao said.

'I hoped we'd be more friendly.' Sean sighed.

The laboratory was segregated into a collection of labs separated by soundproofed glass walls. They passed basic preparation labs filled with saws, micro-drills, and an array of devices designed to grind, mill, and polish rock samples. Every lab was stark and pristine.

Malik guided them through the facility.

'As you can see, we've assembled the most comprehensive archaeology labs in the world, complete with X-ray machines, electron microscopes, wet chemistry labs, furnaces for drying and melting, sedimentary labs with thousands of soil and sediment samples... All designed with a sole purpose.'

'What's that?' Sean asked.

'To study the Isharkute. Evidence of their culture has been found all over the world, not just here in Egypt. That's why we have scientists from all nations, the best in their fields, working around the clock.'

Their destination was an extensive central lab with a mezzanine level that was home to several large computer screens and worktables. The glass walls looked twice as thick and the entrance was reinforced with heavy-duty steel doors. Malik instructed the soldiers to wait outside. The doors sealed them inside with an ear-popping adjustment of air pressure. The dust-free lab housed a collection of Isharkute relics. On the nearest workbench, an activated stave was secured in a vice surrounded by sensors, feeding data into nearby computers. Another bench was lined with crystal cards, each connected to a luminous web of fibre-optic cables. Further into the lab, the crown from the Hall of Records was mounted on a glass stand.

Azar entered from the opposite side of the lab, carrying a small metallic cube. He placed it gently on a frosted-glass examination table in the middle of the lab.

'We found this cube in a section of rubble from the cave wall, but so far, my scientists have been unable to open it... In fact, we have no idea what it's meant for since we can't decipher the glyphs.'

Sean shared an excited look with Nocao. The metal cube was slightly bigger than a Rubik's cube and covered in a series of lines and circles, with one face inscribed with a line of Isharkute glyphs.

'Can you open it?' Azar said.

Sean could hear a hint of nervousness in the billionaire's voice, as if everything he'd done to this point was invested in opening this single cube. Nocao picked it up and turned it over. He set it back on the table and pressed the glyphs in a specific sequence. There was a small click and the cube unfolded into a flat cross, revealing a card-sized quartz crystal embedded in one of the four arms. The remaining three arms each had a small line of glyphs leading to an empty notch, indicating spaces for another three crystals.

'Amazing!' Azar gasped. 'We tried for weeks...countless combinations.'

'It was more than just entering the correct sequence; the cube was encoded to open with my touch and my Isharkute DNA.'

'What do these glyphs say?' Azar said, pointing to the arms of the cross.

'They indicate another three crystals are needed to complete the cube.'

'The glyphs in the Cave of Myth mention three riddles...and now we have to find three crystal keys. They're obviously related, but what are the riddles?'

Nocao carefully detached the crystal from the cross and passed it to Azar. 'The location of the Ark and beacon are encrypted on this crystal and can only be unlocked with the other three keys.'

'We've found crystals like these before,' Azar said, holding it up to the light. 'It's a little smaller than the ones we retrieved from the Hall of Records.'

'You mean stole,' Sean said curtly.

Azar glared at him.

'We should work on decrypting the information on this key in case we can't find the other crystals,' Nocao said.

'How do we do that?' Azar said eagerly.

'Transfer the data contained on this crystal to your computers. I can get to work straight away.'

'We always assumed these crystals were a form of data storage, but my scientists haven't been able to work out how to retrieve the information. We've tried every frequency to oscillate with the crystal, but nothing's worked.'

'That's because your scientists have been missing one important component...' Nocao said, holding up his hand. 'The biological interface.'

Azar's face lit up with the realisation.

Sean stopped himself from asking Nocao what he was doing. If he had a plan in motion, he was giving nothing away. It was dangerous to allow Azar too much information, but he trusted Nocao was working on a way to steal the cube and get them out of here.

Azar directed them to a worktable covered with technical equipment. He placed the crystal on the stage plate of a large modified microscope. A beam of light shone through the crystal and focused on a wide-angle lens. The attached computer monitor flashed a single message: AWAITING INPUT.

Nocao placed the tip of his finger on the crystal. 'Isharkute and human brains oscillate at the correct frequency to unlock the data.'

'A biological interface,' Azar said excitedly. 'We never thought of that.'

The monitor filled with Isharkute symbols. Azar and Malik stared in wonderment while the scientists jostled for a view around the lab's glass walls.

'As long as I hold my finger to the crystal, the data will transfer into your computers.'

'How much data are we talking about?' Azar said.

'Based on the antiquated storage of Sean's old laptop computer, infinitely larger.'

'I had a one terabyte drive. How much space have you got?'

'As much as you need,' Malik said. 'We can link this worktable directly into our mainframe, where there's 150 petabytes of storage on a fibre channel array – enough for the entire internet to be downloaded several times.'

'Is it enough?' Azar asked.

'Isharkute gauge storage capacity in more organic forms,' Nocao said. 'This crystal only holds the equivalent amount of data to a human brain.'

'Only!' Malik said, looking offended. 'Which is what?'

'About 2.5 petabytes,' Sean said, keen to reveal a fact that always fascinated him.

'But this information is compressed,' Nocao said. 'Once this transfer is complete, it will expand exponentially.'

'It'll fit,' Azar said eagerly. 'But what is it?'

Nocao assessed the stream of symbols for a moment. 'A topographical map of Earth measured from the largest mountain down to the smallest rock. It's live and continuously updated by sensors buried across the continents.'

'It's a map to the Ark!' Azar said, wide-eyed.

'Yes. Henry Livingstone knew the Ark would move locations throughout history. This map tracks the precise location of the Ark no matter where it has ended up on the planet.'

The monitors flashed with error messages emblazoned in red.

'Our network doesn't have enough bandwidth,' Malik said, waving to the scientists outside of the lab. 'Slow down the transfer until we open up more ports.'

Nocao took his finger off the crystal and the transfer stopped. Outside the lab, a couple of scientists stood at computer terminals, typing like their lives depended on it. Sean could hear Malik pacing behind him, his footsteps becoming faster by the second. The scientists finished their adjustments and waved through the window.

'Okay, we're ready to proceed,' Malik said.

Nocao touched the crystal and the monitors came alive again. Sean watched the transfer with growing anticipation, hoping that Nocao was filling their mainframe with junk data or some kind of virus. It was risky allowing Azar access to such a precise map, especially if it led directly to the Ark.

Azar and Malik watched the monitors like awe-struck children, oblivious to the fact that the speed bars were accelerating, transferring more data than they could process in a lifetime.

Nocao glanced at Sean and flicked his eyes towards the stave on the adjacent table. He did it so fast that Sean wondered if he'd imagined it. Nocao closed his eyes and the transfer bars shot into the red.

'It's too fast!' Azar said in a panic-stricken voice. 'Our network can't handle the speed. Slow it down.'

Nocao's face scrunched with concentration and the transfer bars maxed out.

The laboratory lights flickered and sparked, and then every electronic device exploded with an ear-splitting crack. Sparks showered the lab. The nearby stave blasted out of the vice and bounced off the wall on the far side of the lab. The entire complex plunged into darkness and the red glow of emergency lights kicked in.

'Now!' Nocao cried.

*Snap!* Sean's translucent wings ripped through his t-shirt, more than double an arm's length either side of him, and launched him across the lab. The blast of air alone sent equipment sliding off the worktables as he scooped up the stave: a perfectly executed manoeuvre thanks to his arena training. Nocao snatched the crystal and the cube, then raced behind the worktables.

Malik whipped out his Beretta and fired after them.

'No shooting!' Azar screamed. 'They're trapped. Get your team in here.'

Malik cursed out loud in Arabic and raced over to the lab doors. His soldiers were manually cranking them open from the opposite side, moments away from slipping through.

Nocao sided up to Sean. 'Well done.'

'You too. What did you do?'

'Overloaded their computer systems with raw data.'

'Awesome. Now, how do we get out of here?'

'Follow me.'

They crab-crawled through the lab and crouched next to the door Azar had entered through earlier. Sean went to grab the handle but Nocao wrenched him back to the floor, took his stave, and aimed at a trapdoor-sized grill beneath a nearby computer terminal. He blasted it open and dragged Sean inside. They dropped into the bowels of Azar's computer mainframe, surrounded by racks of hard drives and the noisy whir of cooling fans. Pipes and fibre-optic cabling ran through the grills under their feet. The space was high enough to stand up in and they raced ahead, twisting and turning through a disorienting maze of equipment. After shooting their way through another metal grill, they found themselves in a darkened corridor. The power was still out. Flashing red emergency lights lit the way.

'What now?' Sean asked.

Nocao checked both ways and marched off confidently. Sean did a double-take in both directions, then charged after him. 'How do you know where you're going?'

'Azar built this base on top of Senetep's capital. He made the mistake of showing us the layout.'

'You can remember that from one look?'

'Yes. Can't you?'

'No! Obviously I don't have a photographic memory like you. How do we get outta here?'

'There's a service shaft close by that leads straight up, twenty floors to the surface.'

'That's a big climb!'

'It's a warm-up compared to climbing the obelisk in the Great Arena,' Nocao said with a smirk.

Sean chuckled. 'Sure.'

The corridor lights flickered on and the limp surveillance cameras sprang to life. Nocao charged ahead at full speed. After several turns, Sean was already lost – every corridor looked identical. If they were separated, he'd never find his way out. A few paces ahead, a door shot open. Malik and his soldiers filed into the corridor, blocking their escape.

'Hand over the cube,' Malik demanded.

'Back up,' Nocao whispered over his shoulder.

Sean retreated into the previous intersection of corridors. 'Which way?'

'Go left. Then right, right, left, second right, third left, first right, and straight ahead to find the escape shaft.' Sean repeated the moves in his head, a trick he'd picked up from memorising algorithms to solve his Rubik's cube. 'And take this,' Nocao said, stuffing the reassembled cube into his hands.

A barrage of energy blasts crackled down the corridor, ricocheting and zinging over their heads.

Nocao fired back. 'Go! I'll hold them here.'

Sean covered twenty paces in one leap. He'd never flown so fast in such a confined space and concentrated hard on not missing the turns. He repeated the directions in his head as he made each turn. There were no soldiers – just a few surprised scientists he flew around.

The final turn landed him at a dead end with nothing but a door-sized metal grill. He put his hand to it and felt a breeze being sucked in through the slats. He kicked the grill and it swung open, revealing an immense circular tube dissecting the entire base.

Twenty floors above was a manhole with red flashing lights. Sean realised Nocao would never make the climb without covering fire. He flew up to the manhole and jammed the cube between the top rungs for safekeeping, then dove down and glided back into the corridor. Now he had to make the turns in reverse, but that was helped a little by the sound of an encroaching firefight. He rounded a corner and collected Nocao head-on.

'I found it!' Sean gasped, picking himself up.

'What are you doing?' Nocao snapped. 'You're meant to be on the surface by now.'

'You won't make the climb without my help.'

'You should've escaped with the cube.'

'I'm not leaving you behind.'

Nocao frowned. 'Emotions make you stubborn.'

'We're almost there,' Sean said. 'Give me the stave – I'll cover you while you climb.'

Nocao nodded appreciatively and sprinted for the tube. Sean trailed him, weapon aimed at the turn in the corridor. Multiple footfalls echoed around the bend. Malik's men were almost upon them. Nocao leapt onto the ladder and climbed furiously for the manhole. Sean flew into the tube and hovered several feet above the entrance. He had the advantage of an elevated position, but it was still going to take Nocao a few minutes to climb to the top. He steadied his aim, waiting for Malik's inevitable attack.

Seconds passed. Nothing.

Sean had a sinking feeling something bad was about to happen.

A few levels above, another grill swung open. Now he was in the lower, more vulnerable position. A small canister shot inside and clamped to the wall, quickly filling the tube with a thick poisonous gas. Rather than shoot them down and risk damaging the cube, Malik was going to gas them out. Sean held his breath, closed his eyes, and flew straight up through the cloud, careful not to breathe the fumes.

Nocao was almost at the manhole, only a few rungs ahead of the gas.

'Hold your breath,' Sean cried, flying ahead to the manhole. He rotated the release mechanism and it sprang open, bringing a rush of cool desert air into the tube. Sean threw the stave outside and retrieved the cube. They clambered free and Sean closed the manhole, trapping the gas inside. They were now standing on a rocky outcrop in the middle of the desert, the first beams of sunlight streaking over the horizon, warming the violet sky with an orange glow. A string of searchlights combed the distant desert, slowly heading in their direction.

'The military's still looking for us,' Sean said. 'What do we do now?'

'Solve three riddles and find the crystal keys.'

'But we don't know what the riddles are.'

'That's not entirely true,' Nocao said, grinning mischievously. He took the cube and pressed the sequence of glyphs, unfolding it into a cross to reveal the three empty notches and accompanying Isharkute writing. 'They're written here, on the inside of the cube. THE AGE OF WARNING BEGINS IN THE MORNING, HIDDEN FROM VIEW FROM THOSE WHO FLEW, and IN THE LIGHT OF THE SUN, TWO BECOME ONE.'

'They don't even tell us where to start looking.'

'Azar said the cube was found buried in the cave wall. That seems like the obvious place to begin.'

Sean nodded in agreement and looked around. There was nothing but sand and rock as far as the eye could see. 'We can't make it across the desert without supplies, and we just turned down our ride with Azar.'

'Then we have two choices... Be recaptured by the military or chance the driest and hottest region on the planet.'

Sean sighed. In just a few hours, the unforgiving sun would be burning overhead. 'We've probably got a better chance with the military. They just got their butts kicked by Azar, so maybe they're ready to listen. Plus, if Hazim's still alive, I reckon we can get him to help us.'

Nocao picked up the stave and fired a bolt of crackling blue energy into the dawn light. It acted like a flare. One by one the distant searchlights pointed in their direction. Sean's stomach tightened. This was their last chance to convince the military. His fingers tightened around the cube, realising that once again, he held the fate of the world in his hands.

# — CHAPTER 7 —

# *Return Of The Isharkute*

Bella stopped running to watch the helicopters circle around. Their searchlights disappeared across the desert, leaving an escape route through the pyramid blocks towards the lights of Cairo. In a few minutes, the pre-dawn shadows would vanish with the morning sun, making their escape past the soldiers combing the Giza Plateau impossible.

Carla pulled her arm. 'Come on. Stay low and keep running.'

The remains of the Great Pyramid and Sphinx had created an enormous obstacle course. One second they were crouching and crawling, the next they were clambering over the tops of huge blocks. They surfed down the bigger diagonal slabs like slides. It wasn't easy keeping up with her aunt, the expert rock climber. Distracted by how far she was falling behind, Bella mistimed the next jump and winded herself against a waist-high block. Carla doubled back, slipped down beside her, and raised a finger to her lips.

A soldier appeared on a block ahead of them, his gun sweeping over the shadows.

They crawled into a crevice and hid from view. Bella leant against the stone, forcing her winded lungs to inhale. The soldier's footfalls echoed across the debris. He jumped onto the block above them, briefly scanned their position, and moved on.

Carla waited, then crawled out. 'Let's go!'

Bella stayed in the shadows and shook her head.

'You're doing good – we're almost there,' Carla whispered.

'I don't want you to leave me in Cairo. Why do you have to come back for Sean and his *amico brutto?*'

'I haven't got time to argue about Sean and his ugly friend,' Carla said, grabbing her forearm.

'I'm not leaving you,' Bella insisted, pulling away.

'Ah, *Ragazza del Traghetto!*'

Bella chuckled nervously upon hearing her nickname, 'Ferry Girl.' It was given to her as a toddler in honour of her defiant and stubborn nature. She was only four at the time but could still remember the vacation with her family in the Greek Isles and her fascination with the large white ferries transporting tourists between the islands. Apparently, she'd whinged and moaned about not being able to ride on one. Then, on the last day, she slipped away from her parents to mingle with the crowd loading onto the ferry. Her disappearance caused immediate panic, sending her family on a frantic search through the streets and markets. Carla was the first to spot her proud and defiant face at the front of the ferry, waving excitedly as it disembarked – probably the same face she was giving her right now.

Carla sighed in resolution. 'All right. You can stay with me, but you have to do everything I say.'

'I will!' Bella said, leaping out of the crevice, eager to continue. 'What's your plan?'

Carla peered over the block. Bella imitated her. The helicopters were returning from the desert and there was a major commotion around the Army tents. Carla took out her notepad and sketched the layout of the camp, noting where the vehicles, tents, and soldiers were in proximity to each other.

'We need to get down there for a closer look to see what they found in the desert.'

'Okay.' Bella nodded. 'Let's go.'

They snaked their way through the rubble, keeping an eye on the soldiers scouring the area. The horizon was well alight with the morning sun and their shadowy cover was fast diminishing. They scrambled into position behind a large block and watched the helicopters land in the remains of the Giza car park.

Sean and Nocao appeared from the swirl of dust, escorted from the helicopter at gunpoint and straight into the nearby tents.

'He's there!' Bella said. 'Now what?'

Carla slumped down beside the block with a look of defeat. Bella knew it would be near impossible to reach Sean and Nocao without being caught. They needed to think of something.

\*    \*    \*

The military tent was hot and unbearably stuffy. As far as Sean could tell, he and Nocao had been interrogated for the better part of the day. The rays of morning sunlight had long disappeared, and now filtered through the tent flaps with a reddish, late afternoon glow. His mouth was dry and his tongue felt like it had swollen to twice its size. His constant requests for water had been ignored, but it was no surprise considering the Army's state of disorder. He had been handcuffed to the hard metal chair beside Nocao, re-explaining everything he knew about Azar, Senetep, and the Isharkute to General Maddock and Colonel Powell. Commander Hazim El-Amin hovered in the background, still looking dishevelled from the energy blast in the hall.

As a sign of trust, Sean had given Maddock the cube, knowing he'd never unlock it or access the map without Nocao and the three missing crystalline keys. Unfortunately, it hadn't garnered much in the way of trust yet. Hazim seemed to be the only one willing to listen, but even he struggled to get a word in between Maddock's booming Texas accent.

The high-tech Isharkute-inspired cubes they'd been interrogated in the first time around had now changed to a makeshift tent. Soldiers rushed in and out while superiors barked orders. From what Sean could tell, the US and Egyptian forces were preparing for an attack on Azar's base, but their disorganisation made him nervous. If Malik and his team caused this much pandemonium with a few alien staves, he could only imagine what a full-fledged Isharkute attack would be capable of.

A US lieutenant rushed into the tent and gave the general a handwritten note. He stood back and nervously waited for a response. Maddock scrunched up the note and stormed outside. 'Move the prisoners into the command tent.'

Sean and Nocao were escorted outside at gunpoint and marched through the camp. The soldiers watched the sky anxiously, as if expecting an attack. There was nothing on the horizon except the dying glare of the afternoon sun. Were they expecting Azar to retaliate? Or worse, Senetep?

The command tent was packed. The soldiers forced Sean and Nocao through the crowd of Marines, scientists, technicians, and commanding officers. Everyone was transfixed on the bank of monitors playing live news feeds from Paris. Tendrils of fire engulfed the crumbling remains of the Arc de Triomphe, casting a hellish glow down the Champs-Élysées. Hundreds of cars sat in gridlock along the famous Parisian avenue. Drivers were abandoning their cars and running from the devastation.

A distinctive flash of blue energy triggered another explosion and Sean's heart skipped a beat. *That was an Isharkute energy blast!*

BREAKING NEWS flashed across the screen and the image cut to shaky handheld footage of a tall pale-skinned being with an elongated head stalking the avenue. Terrified screams distorted the sound. Petrified onlookers stood in awe, some filming the Isharkute with their phones.

'Senetep!' Sean gasped.

The footage erratically chased an assault team as they weaved their way through the cars. A voice suddenly screamed, '*Supprimez votre arme!*' Senetep knelt in a gesture of surrender and the team closed in, surrounding him with their semi-automatic weapons.

Sean shook his head. 'I wouldn't do that –'

Senetep whipped his stave around and fired. The image pixelated and jerked violently, capturing snippets of a thunderous explosion. Nearby cars flipped over. Flaming bodies whooshed past. The camera smashed against the burning asphalt and cut to black.

A collective gasp sounded from everyone in the tent.

The news report froze on a still of Senetep and all eyes in the tent turned to Nocao.

'Oh crap!' Sean said under his breath, giving Nocao a sideways glance.

The soldiers moved closer and Sean felt the gun barrel press harder into his back. Colonel Powell pushed through the crowd, clutching the cube he gave them earlier. Powell placed it on the table amidst the wall of apprehensive faces. Maddock followed with the Isharkute stave, turning it over in his hands, admiring the glowing blue crystal. 'All that destruction in Paris started with a single weapon like this. Now that we have one, we can fight back.'

'Senetep can't be stopped with one weapon,' Sean said. 'His forces are about to attack with thousands of vessels and weapons. We need to find the Ark and activate the beacon. The Isharkute emperor is the only one who can stop Senetep now.'

'I won't commit to a course of action that invites more of their kind here.'

'You don't have a choice!'

Maddock's eyes flared. Dead silence ensued, as if every person was holding their breath in anticipation of the general's inevitable firestorm of a reply, one sure to strike with the accuracy and force of a ballistic missile. His intense stare was broken by another news report. 'Turn it up!'

A shaky handheld camera was filming the smouldering Arc de Triomphe from a distance. Helicopter gunships and tanks emerged from the smoke, converging on Senetep's lone blue figure. A volley of rockets fired towards him. Senetep picked off half the rockets with his stave, but several more were still on target.

Maddock grunted with satisfaction.

Sean held his breath, hoping the Overseer was about to be incinerated.

There was a blinding flash and forks of lightning snuffed out the rockets like candles. The camera zoomed out and captured the helicopters caught in the same phenomenon, rippling with raw electricity. They exploded and crashed into the avenue in violent fireballs. The cameraman was now screaming and running away, catching only snippets of the tanks being annihilated by the lightning.

'What the hell is that?' Maddock said.

'It's a targeted strike from orbit,' Nocao said. 'Senetep's forces have returned. By tomorrow, your entire planet will be under his control.'

Maddock leant over the table in a menacing manner. 'Your bald blue friends can give it their best shot. We're ready.'

'Are you ready for this?' Sean said, pointing to the monitors. The city of Paris was now in the shadow of a colossal disc-shaped mothership. Smaller vessels swarmed from its sides and descended upon the Champs-Élysées. 'This is it,' Sean said. 'Their invasion's started.'

Maddock watched the footage for a long moment. The realisation finally seemed to be hitting home. 'So their objectives are to attack our cities and enslave our populations?'

'I think they'll focus on other targets first.'

'Like what?' Maddock said, a hint of desperation creeping into his voice.

'Ancient monuments.'

'Monuments?' he repeated, focusing on Sean again.

'Yeah, and he'll start with pyramids and obelisks – anything that's big, old, and has been around for a few thousand years.'

'That puts us smack-bang in the middle of a goddam hot zone!'

Sean nodded. 'But there's pyramids all over the world, all the way from Java to Mexico and the Pacific islands to North America. The Chinese have hundreds. They've been burying some of their pyramids for years, planting trees on top of them, trying to hide them under man-made mountains.'

'Why would they do that?'

'Maybe they knew the Isharkute would return and did it to protect themselves.'

'Have we been keeping track of these Chinese pyramids?' Maddock said, turning to Colonel Powell.

Powell shrugged.

Sean shook his head in disbelief. 'Don't you guys have Google Earth? It's all on there.'

'We have to find the Ark and activate the beacon before Senetep destroys it,' Nocao said. 'This is your ancestors' legacy. Ten thousand years ago, they worked with the Isharkute, preparing you for this day.'

'Who stops Emperor Neberun and the rest of your people from taking over once they overthrow Senetep?' Maddock said.

'I met with Emperor Neberun,' Sean cut in. 'He's willing to listen, but –'

Maddock laughed so loud it hurt Sean's ears. 'Our ambassador for the human race is a skinny fifteen-year-old kid with wings! Does anyone else here think that's ridiculous?'

'If it wasn't for Sean, your people would've been slaughtered millennia ago,' Nocao said.

Maddock leaned closer to Nocao, eyes burning with anger.

'Wait,' Hazim said, stepping up to the table. 'Sean Livingstone does appear to be your best option. He's the only person on this entire planet that's made successful contact with the Isharkute. He's built a relationship with Nocao and knows more about their culture than any of us. Two days ago, most of us didn't even know the Isharkute existed, but this plan of his and his dad's is ten thousand years in the making. Our ancestors had a long time to think about this, so if there was another way to stop Senetep, they would have told us.'

Maddock absorbed everything he'd just heard and eased off. His scowl relaxed and the fire in his eyes flickered away.

Someone gasped out loud at the television broadcasts and everyone turned to watch. The Eiffel Tower was under attack. Huge blasts tore through the steel structure and the top half leant towards the Seine River like a wounded animal. The breaking metal beams screeched through the city and the iconic tower collapsed into the river. A wall of water crashed over the surrounding buildings and flooded the streets.

'Turn it off!' Maddock commanded.

The screens went black. There was a solemn silence.

Powell pushed the cube into the centre of the table. 'This alien box is an invaluable tactical advantage. Azar was several steps ahead of us, already searching for the Ark. Thankfully, Sean and Nocao had the courage to steal this cube and escape his stronghold...and based on that alone, we should be seriously considering their plan.'

Sean straightened proudly. It was a relief to finally be acknowledged. He understood how ludicrous it must seem for the general to make critical military decisions based on a wild, fantastic story from an alien and a 'fifteen-year-old kid with wings.' The general chewed his lip and indicated for Sean to speak.

'Can we have the cube, please?'

Maddock nodded.

Nocao pressed the glyphs in sequence and the cube unfolded, revealing the trio of empty notches and inscriptions.

'We need to find three crystal keys,' Sean said, pointing to the inscriptions. 'Each riddle is a test of some sort, and the first one reads, THE AGE OF WARNING BEGINS IN THE MORNING.'

'What does it mean?' Maddock said.

'I'm not sure. We'll know more when we get to the cave where the cube was found. It's on the coast of South Africa – I know the exact coordinates.'

'And how do you know?'

'Because it's where humanity survived a worldwide cataclysm ten thousand years ago. It's called the "Cave of Myth," but modern-day archaeologists call it the "Garden of Eden." Azar discovered the cave over a year ago, which means we need to get there ASAP. Since we stole his cube, he'd rather destroy the cave than let us gain another advantage.'

Maddock didn't say anything; his stoic, unreadable stare remained locked on the cube. After a long and considered pause, he finally looked up. 'Okay. We'll get you to these caves.'

# — CHAPTER 8 —

## *New Giza*

Senetep gazed upon the smouldering remains of the Arc de Triomphe from the safety of his hunter-craft, smiling with satisfaction. It was no coincidence that his leap through time landed him right beneath the monument. His commanders had sabotaged the control crystals in the Hall of Records prior to Nesuk finishing the time-travel device, sending him to his chosen location. After scouring the information from Sean's computer about modern-day Earth, he'd decided there was no better place to announce his arrival. The Arc de Triomphe was a human symbol of victory and military power. Human armies had marched beneath it. Reducing it to rubble was a statement: No army on Earth could stand against his forces.

Senetep took in the endless sprawl of the city against the setting sun.

Innumerable structures outlined the bustling streets, rising into the evening sky like his capital once had. It was true – humanity had spread and multiplied, just as Sean predicted, and the scope of their dominance was something to behold.

The hunter-craft rocked violently. The squad of warriors escorting him to the mothership clutched their staves. Senetep didn't recognise their faces or cranial tattoos of rank and service. They were new recruits, part of the campaign his First Commanders Nefaro and Vogran had been undertaking for the last few millennia. Most of these warriors had never seen a proper battle and only knew humans as a primitive, easily conquerable species.

That misconception was about to change.

Senetep had learnt a valuable lesson from Sean and his father: Never underestimate human determination. It was, no doubt, a trait inherited from their Isharkute creators.

Human flying machines swarmed upon them from multiple directions, buzzing like hybrid dropwings. Senetep recognised the vessels as those humans called 'helicopters.' Judging by their bulky, armoured shape, he could tell they were military grade, just like the ones that attacked him on the streets below.

The helicopters fired a volley of missiles after them.

Their hunter-craft banked hard to avoid a collision and the missiles were vaporised with overhead energy blasts.

The cabin fell into the shadow of the mothership and they flew along its gigantic underside. The immense hull arced with targeted bolts of lightning like an angry steel cloud, decimating the human retaliation.

Senetep grinned, thinking of the enjoyment yet to come.

Inside the mothership's main docking bay stood a complete regiment of 100 warriors dressed in gold armour. They snapped to attention and held their staves forward as Senetep disembarked. At the end of the docking bay stood his pair of commanders. Nefaro's wiry frame and gaunt features looked skeletal compared to Vogran's broad-shouldered, muscular physique. The warriors raised their staves in honour of their returning Overseer. Nefaro and Vogran bowed in honour.

'How many motherships did you commandeer from Neberun's fleet?' Senetep asked.

'Six,' Nefaro said, dutifully raising his head.

'What about recruits?'

'We have close to three hundred regiments,' Vogran said proudly. 'Our first targets were the Emperor's transports. We captured three annihilators, sixty squadrons of hunter-craft, and a good supply of land and air-based transport.'

'Any insubordinates?'

'Those unwilling to swear allegiance to your cause were put back into cryogenic sleep and jettisoned into space.'

'You should have killed them,' Senetep said. 'Those blind to the future should see none.'

Nefaro and Vogran nodded.

'What about the rest of Neberun's fleet?'

'The remaining motherships were directed off course and locked into the gravitational pull of a super gas giant in the Jahkut system. All remaining populations are still in cryogenic sleep, their chambers programmed on an infinite cycle, just as you instructed.'

'Good work,' Senetep said, rounding to appreciate the rows of willing warriors. 'Without Emperor Neberun's bumbling ineptitude and inaction, we can finally take this world.'

Nefaro shared a nervous glance with Vogran before speaking. 'There's a problem we must take care of first.'

Senetep sighed heavily. 'What?'

'Shortly after you were transported into the future, we learnt of a plot to thwart your dominance of this world. Henry Livingstone and Ramin's head scientist, Nesuk, built a beacon capable of waking Neberun's fleet from their cryogenic sleep. They also created a power source, which they hid in a separate location. The humans call it the Ark of the Covenant.'

'Simple. We destroy Neberun's fleet before they can be awakened.'

'We considered that option, but there's another problem. Several thousand years ago, there was a supernova in Jahkut's neighbouring system. The motherships' safety protocols must have redirected the entire fleet to a new location...and since then, we've been unable to find them. In between our cryogenic sleeps we've searched, but haven't been able to –'

'Bah!' Vogran grunted. 'We should have used tectonic missiles to destroy every continent on this pitiful planet. That would've destroyed the Ark and the beacon in one move.'

'And destroy your Overseer's capital in the process,' Nefaro shot back. 'The Ark could be hiding at the bottom of the ocean for all we know.'

'Brute force is the only way to destroy the Ark and subjugate the human pests.'

'Instead of wasting valuable resources, we've watched these humans, gathered information about their society –'

Vogran rounded angrily on his counterpart. 'With your constant talk of tactics, you sound more like Emperor Neberun –'

'Enough!' Senetep roared. 'Ranatar was right after all – the two of you combined can't fill his position. Separating the brains from the brawn seemed like a logical decision, but you're still unable to make a decision.'

Nefaro lowered his head. 'I'm sure once you see what we've accomplished, your confidence in us will be affirmed.'

'Let's see,' Senetep mused with a critical eye. 'Take me to the bridge.'

His commanders led him through the numerous passages and lifts. Vogran was keen to share his hybrid endeavours as they walked. 'I've been experimenting with a new breed of serpent hybrid, one to combat the human forces and their modern, projectile-based weaponry.'

'Sounds interesting,' Senetep replied.

Hybrid creation was one of Senetep's favourite pastimes and Vogran's enthusiasm elicited a modicum of interest. Maybe there was hope for this squabbling pair after all.

They entered the bridge and the crew turned to acknowledge their Overseer. It was Senetep's first time on a mothership bridge, but he wasn't about to let his crew know that. He'd never commanded a ship of this size. Most of the officers and pilots were recruits from the highest echelons of Isharkute command, having worked directly under Emperor Neberun himself. Senetep forced the niggling doubts from his mind and faced his crew with a confident, assertive gaze.

He was in command now.

The crew returned to their control panels and holograms. Senetep took a seat at the only chair on the bridge, admiring his 360-degree view. All the information from weapons and tactical to flight and navigation was projected holographically onto the domed ceiling above.

Senetep settled into his elevated position of authority.

Nefaro swiped his hand over a crystal pad and images of pyramids, temples, and obelisks from all over the world appeared overhead. Some were half-buried in sand, others submerged deep underwater. Less obvious structures were hidden beneath the choking vines of dense jungles. Senetep recognised the influence of Isharkute architecture in each building.

'We've completed scans of every ancient construction on the planet,' Nefaro explained. 'Although we've been unable to locate the Ark, we believe one of these structures might be the beacon.'

Senetep stared at the remnants of his culture, scattered across the world like some long-forgotten species. It enraged and enticed him all at once. Even though Henry Livingstone was dead by thousands of years, his prized hybrid had provided him a new challenge.

Nefaro continued. 'Until we find the Ark, we should destroy these structures and eliminate humanity's chances of contacting Neberun's fleet.'

'I agree, but how did you discover this plan in the first place?'

Nefaro swiped his data pad and the images changed to a series of cave walls, each covered with Isharkute glyphs accompanied by primitive human drawings. 'Beneath some of these structures we found caves, at least one on each major continent. Both languages express the same message – a warning to humanity about your return to Earth. We discovered these paintings centuries after the humans emerged from their caves and the fallout from the cataclysm had dispersed. It seems Henry and Nesuk travelled the world and spread the word, sowing the seeds for future generations.'

Senetep pointed out the last line of symbols. 'Every message ends the same way: THE COVENANT BEGINS IN THE CAVE OF MYTH.'

'We believe that's the original cave where Nesuk and Henry protected the first tribes during the volcanic eruptions. It's not connected to any of the structures and might be a natural cave. We haven't found anything like it yet.'

'That's where we'll find the clues to the Ark,' Senetep said confidently. He could feel a fire igniting in the pit of his stomach, a burning desire to tackle the task. 'Destroy all potential beacons and continue with the invasion. Secure my capital. Then, while the humans scramble to save themselves, we'll start searching for the Ark.'

Nefaro nodded and relayed the instructions to the bridge crew.

'Humour me, Commander Vogran. I'd like to see these new hybrids you've created. Perhaps we can incorporate them into our mission.'

Vogran escorted Senetep from the bridge, leaving Nefaro to coordinate the invasion. Soon they were standing on a gantry overlooking a sprawling hybrid facility. Thirty floors beneath them was an open sandpit. A door slid open and three human males dressed in black body armour were shunted onto the sand by Isharkute guards.

'This fresh catch of soldiers from the city below should provide us with some entertainment and showcase my new hybrids,' Vogran said.

The soldiers screamed abuse at the guards. Senetep didn't recognise every word, but they were a clear form of modern expletives. The guards tossed them their human weapons and closed the door. On the far side of the pit, a column of sand burst into the air and showered the men.

Intrigued, Senetep leant over the railing for a clearer view.

The soldiers grouped in a circle, aiming at the mounds of shifting sand. One of the mounds suddenly exploded in a blur of black scales, and a piercing hiss filled the pit.

Senetep spun around to follow the action over the other side of the gantry.

A gleaming black snake, as long as a fully grown terraminer, slammed into the wall with one of the soldiers impaled on its metre-long fangs. His companions opened fire. Their ammunition ricocheted off the snake's armoured scales and zinged around the pit.

Several bullets pinged off the gantry railing and Senetep recoiled, cheering with delight.

The snake reared up like a cobra and the soldier's limp body slipped off its fangs, which it then folded backwards into the roof of its widening mouth.

'Their scales are enhanced with the armoured body plates of terraminers and their fangs are based on the poison glands of cobras, a snake deadly to humans,' Vogran said proudly.

The viper hissed, spraying a shower of clear liquid from the corners of its mouth. It struck one soldier in the face and he dropped, screaming and writhing on the sand in agony. He suddenly stopped and contorted into a death pose. The last soldier clambered across the sand, firing at the viper as it circled him, closing the gap like a giant python strangling its prey. The soldier spun about, firing until his very last bullet. The wall of black scales enveloped him and his terrified scream was silenced by a *crunch* of bones.

Senetep watched the viper devour the soldiers with glee. This was exactly the kind of hybrid he would have created himself. 'How many do you have?'

'We have over a hundred fully grown vipers ready to be unleashed.'

'Impressive. You've been busy, Vogran. How did you create so many?'

'We altered the viper's reproductive organs so they can procreate on their own.'

'Hybrid procreation and breeding is illegal under punishment of death.'

Vogran nodded. 'A restriction put in place to ensure each hybrid was unique to the Great Arena. But we're at war, there's no arena, and Emperor Neberun's law is no longer enforced. We have a new Isharkute ruler, one able to make his own laws.'

Nefaro was right. Considering he was in command of the Isharkute fleet and the greater part of the Empire, it was time for him to make his own laws. Senetep let a smile creep across his face. 'Indeed. What else have you got?'

'Too many hybrids for this quick tour.'

'You'll hold onto your beard a little longer yet, Commander Vogran.'

Nefaro greeted Senetep upon his return to the bridge. 'Our

forces are in place to destroy the ancient buildings and monuments. The rest of the fleet is listening and awaiting your orders.'

Senetep inspected the hologram of Earth shimmering over the bridge. The targets pulsed with a yellow light, highlighting many of their culture's ancient sites. He strode beneath the glowing orb and looked down upon his crew.

'Today, we embark on a mission I put in motion over ten thousand years ago. You made the right decision to side with me. Emperor Neberun's laws are no longer. From here onwards, my word is your law. Serve me well and you'll be rewarded. Our Empire will return to the formidable galactic power it once was. Your first task is to subjugate these human pests. They've spread like a weed across this planet in our absence, but we'll reclaim what's ours and remind this species they're a construct of our design. They owe their pitiful existence to us. If they do not completely surrender themselves once they've been conquered, they will die. Humans shall once again be the slave race our ancestors intended them to be.'

One of the crew chanted his name. 'Sen-e-tep, Sen-e-tep, Sen-e-tep!' Every Isharkute joined in and the chant quickly reached a deafening crescendo.

Senetep relished the adulation, and then raised a hand for silence. 'Now, commence the attack!'

The crew set to work and a flurry of red dots appeared across the hologram.

Senetep stood back to watch the live visual feeds of each strike zone project across the bridge. Ancient pyramids, coliseums, temples, and monuments exploded in a fury of shattered stone – thousands of years' worth of history obliterated in an instant.

Senetep focused on the site of his former capital. The lush green jungle that once surrounded his cities was now a barren desert. Two of his three pyramids had stood the test of time. He wasn't feeling sentimental – that was a weak human trait – but it felt as though the pyramids were beckoning him to return. 'Hold fire on my former capital.'

The targets vanished from the map.

'Is there something wrong?' Nefaro asked.

'I want to govern Earth from there,' Senetep said, pointing to the immense city along the great river that bisected his capital in the past. 'What city is this?'

'They call it Cairo.'

'Prepare a landing to the south of my pyramids.'

Nefaro looked uncomfortable. 'Until we secure the human forces, it might be prudent to coordinate our invasion from orbit. After all, they do have a sizable nuclear stockpile.'

Senetep rounded on his outspoken commander. 'Are you suggesting that we're incapable of dealing with their retaliation?'

'Not at all... We'll begin landing at your coordinates straight away,' Nefaro said, rushing off to speak with the crew.

'I trust your vipers have a taste for human flesh,' Senetep said, turning to Vogran.

His commander grinned with pleasure. 'Trained since they were hatchlings.'

'Excellent! They're about to be well fed.'

# CHAPTER 9

# Escape To Cairo

Sean could hardly contain his excitement. Convincing General Maddock to take him to the Cave of Myth was his first minor victory. It filled him with optimism and boosted his spirits, proving that even when things seemed impossible, there was still hope.

'General Maddock!' cried a voice.

Everyone in the command tent turned towards the communications officer. She was hunched over her radio with one ear pressed against a headphone. 'I'm getting reports of multiple strikes... China, Peru, India, Indonesia...the Atlantic and Indian Oceans.'

Maddock focused on Sean. 'I thought Giza would've been first on Senetep's strike list.'

'This used to be his capital. Maybe he doesn't want to destroy it.'

'Or maybe he's saving it for last.'

A deep indefinable rumble vibrated through the camp, building in intensity like an earthquake. The outspread cube vibrated across the table in front of them, heading for the edge. Sean was about to grab it when...

*Crack...Craaack!*

An earth-shattering clap of thunder erupted overhead and the tent walls billowed wildly. People screamed and ducked. Soldiers rushed out of the tent, guns drawn. Nocao snatched up the cross and closed it back into its cube form.

Maddock grabbed Nocao's wrist and squeezed tight. 'What do you think you're doing?'

Nocao gave Sean a sidelong glance. '*He has the grip of a child.*'

Sean stifled a chuckle.

'What did he say?' Maddock demanded.

Sean gulped, reluctant to translate the insult. 'Nocao, maybe you should let go of the cube.'

Maddock and Nocao stared each other down, both equally determined. Nocao released the cube and the general released his grip with a self-satisfied grunt.

Powell picked up the cube. 'I'll hold on to this for now.'

'Guard it until we reach the caves,' Maddock said. 'And don't forget, you two are still our prisoners.'

'General, you need to see this!' called an anxious sounding voice.

Sean and Nocao were marched outside at gunpoint. It seemed darker than usual for so early in the evening. Sean peered up and gasped. An Isharkute mothership hung high above Cairo's skyline, casting an unnatural shadow over the city. The sight of such unfathomable power struck fear into the soldiers. Some stared in awe, while others deserted their posts in panic. Controlled lightning blasts erupted from the underside of the mothership and struck the city. The phenomenon created its own weather pattern of storm clouds around the hull, all glowing an angry orange-red from the explosions and fires raging across the city.

Waves of smaller vessels descended over the urban sprawl, unleashing energy blasts upon the defenceless buildings. The explosions were heading in their direction.

Maddock snatched up a walkie-talkie. 'This is General Maddock. We need surface-to-air missile support on the Giza Plateau. We're about to come under heavy fire and require immediate extraction.'

Sean knew it was already too late. In the few seconds it took them to retreat into the tent, Isharkute stingers and hunter-craft were flying overhead.

'*First chance we get, steal the cube and escape,*' Nocao yelled at Sean in Isharkute.

Sean nodded, realising the military were fast becoming a dead weight and blazing target. They needed to break free and finish this their own way. Colonel Powell was on the other side of the tent, still holding the cube and plotting something with Hazim on a large map.

*Boom! Boom! Boom!*

A chain of explosions resounded through the camp, getting louder with each consecutive blast until...

*Booooooom!*

A blast cleaved the tent, tearing off the roof and scattering everyone like bowling pins. The tent walls disintegrated like tissue paper and flew away. Sean was lifted off the ground and sucked into a maelstrom of sand, debris, and superheated air. Bodies tumbled over one another. Heavy cases of equipment bounced away like they weighed nothing. Sean blindly put his hands out, hit the ground, and rolled to a stop. The chaos was followed by a weird silence and a thick haze of dust. Slowly, the sounds of coughing, spluttering, and the haunting moans of the severely injured filled the air.

Sean clambered to his feet, ears ringing and slightly disoriented. Nocao stumbled from the haze, groggily searching for the cube. He kicked the debris aside and turned over several crumpled bodies until he found Colonel Powell, half-conscious and still clutching the cube. Nocao pulled it free and held it up for Sean to see.

'Put your hands up!' yelled a voice from behind.

Sean obeyed and turned to find a ghost-like figure caked in dust. It was Commander El-Amin. A dark streak of blood ran down one side of his face and his eyes stared with dogged determination over the top of his Beretta M-9 pistol. 'Carefully now, tell Nocao to put the cube on the ground.'

Behind them, Powell staggered to his feet, realising what just happened.

'Look around, Commander,' Sean said, 'and imagine what it's going to be like in an hour.'

'I don't need to imagine –'

'Then help us get to the cave. By tomorrow, the whole planet will be under Senetep's control. Every army will be conquered, with

cities and countries in lockdown. We need to get out while we can...
just a small group of us.'

'That's what Hazim and I were organising before this,' Powell
said, stumbling through the remains of the command tent to join
them.

Hazim lowered his gun. 'We can get you to the caves, but you
have to trust us.'

Sean and Nocao acknowledged each other with a simple glance.
'Okay, but Nocao holds on to the cube.'

Hazim nodded.

Powell's radio suddenly crackled to life with screams of defeat
distorted through the speaker. The military forces were overwhelmed
with heavy casualties across the city.

Three large Isharkute vessels swooped overhead, creating a
cluster of eddies through the dust and smoke.

'Are they Isharkute landing parties?' Powell asked.

'They're hybrids transports,' Nocao said.

'Hybrids... What, you mean like animals?'

'Yeah, and it's better we're not around to find out which ones,'
Sean added.

Powell's radio crackled to life again, this time with Maddock's
booming voice. 'Retreat to the desert, regroup at location alpha –'
His voice cut short as a large explosion ripped through the far side
of the camp, illuminating the haze with a column of yellow flames.

'How many men do we need?' Hazim asked.

'The fewer the better,' Sean said. 'We don't want too many people
knowing about the Ark.'

'Okay,' Powell cut in. 'First off, we're gonna need a pilot.'

'Where is he?' Sean said.

'*She's* close to Cairo, not far from here. Follow me.'

Powell led them through the chaotic camp, Hazim covering
them from behind. The burning tents created waves of intense, eye-
watering heat. Soldiers dragged the injured from the flames. Sean
imagined General Maddock rising from the flames with charred
skin and smouldering clothes, his sole mission just to stop them.

Erratic gunfire and chilling screams sounded from every direction.

The hybrids transports swooped on the camp for a second pass, this time with open compartments, dropping massive black orbs throughout the camp. Egg-shaped objects hit the ground with a dull *thud*, throwing up huge walls of sand. One landed right beside them, almost knocking all four of them off their feet.

'Keep close,' Powell said, forging through the shower of sand.

He led them into a fiery graveyard of overturned vehicles. Sean knew there were bodies inside but didn't look long enough to confirm the grisly fact. They rounded a burning truck and stopped in front of a jeep lying on its side.

'Dammit! That was our ride,' Powell said, kicking the bumper.

One of the orbs rolled out of the flames and knocked into the jeep's undercarriage, pushing the vehicle onto its roof. The orb's mirror-black surface reflected their hellish surroundings with perfect clarity.

Powell aimed his pistol at the orb and stepped back. 'What the hell is that thing? A bomb?'

Sean shrugged and looked at Nocao. 'Any ideas?'

'It's the size and colour of a terraminer egg, but it's the wrong shape.'

'Good. I hate those things,' Sean quipped.

The orb shuddered. A crack appeared from the top to bottom, and then the entire shell split in two. Embryonic fluid spewed from the egg and raced towards their feet, making all four of them jump back. The broken egg halves fell away, releasing a monstrous coil of gooey black scales.

Sean gagged. The stench was unbearable.

*Hisssssss...*

A pair of burning red eyes with slit-shaped pupils emerged from the slithering wall of scales. It was a giant hybrid snake with the flat triangular-shaped head distinctive of a viper. The snake reared up like a cobra, rising high above the jeep as it opened its salivating mouth, unfolding a pair of 3-metre-long translucent fangs.

Powell and Hazim fired at the monster snake, but their bullets ricocheted harmlessly off the armoured black scales. The viper arched back further and hissed, poised to strike.

'I don't think that was such a great idea,' Powell said dubiously.

Just then a Humvee burst through the flames, crushing the snake against the upturned jeep. The snake writhed in pain and slithered away. The Humvee door swung open, revealing an unexpected face.

'Hurry up and get in!' Bella screamed, waving them over.

Sean led the way and the four of them crammed in the back of the Humvee.

'Anyone need a ride?' Carla said, greeting them with a smirk from the driver's seat.

'I thought you two escaped,' Powell said. 'What are you doing back here?'

Carla looked at Sean. 'Finishing something Henry Livingstone started a long time ago.'

Sean smiled and nodded. It was comforting to have Carla on his side. She felt like family and made his dad feel just that bit closer.

'How'd you find us?' Hazim asked.

Bella held up a notepad with a rough sketch of the camp. 'We've been watching the camp, waiting for the right time.'

'Your timing was impeccable,' Hazim said. 'Now let's get out of here.'

'Brace yourselves. This is gonna be rough,' Carla said.

Sean pulled on a seatbelt and clicked it in place. Nocao pulled out his belt with a perplexed expression. 'Some kind of primitive restraint?'

'Yeah, but it works. Put it on,' Sean said.

Carla accelerated through the wall of burning vehicles, separating them with a metallic crunch and burst of flames. Nocao bumped his head against the roof and groaned sheepishly. He slumped into the seat and clicked his belt in place. Carla sped through the camp, swerving to avoid survivors.

Sean felt guilty, but there was no time to save any of them.

Giant vipers slithered past their Humvee with the velocity of a speeding train, twisting and coiling their bodies to flip vehicles and crush anything in their path. One smashed into the side of their Humvee and they tilted precariously onto two wheels like a stunt car. Carla corrected the steering and they crashed back onto four wheels with a jolt.

'What are you doing? Take us airborne!' Nocao cried aloud.

'Cars don't fly,' Carla said. At her words, a viper smashed into their rear bumper, lifting them off the ground. They landed hard and bounced on the rear suspension. 'On second thought –'

The rear wheels suddenly regained traction and she lost control. They smashed through a barrier and careened down a steep embankment. 'Hold on!'

A wall of stone blocks appeared in the headlights and she spun the steering wheel hard right. The abrupt turn pinned everyone against the left side of the cabin. They sideswiped the blocks with a scream of metal on stone, finally breaking free with a shower of sparks.

Sean peered out the window as the burning camp disappeared behind them. He recognised the shadowy ruins. They were heading south through the funerary complex of Queen Khentkawes towards the suburbs of Cairo. Their Humvee crashed through another barrier and onto an asphalt road.

Carla hit the brakes and smacked the glitching GPS. 'It's stopped working. I don't know where I'm going.'

Powell checked his phone. 'No signal here either... Our satellites must be down.'

'I can direct you from here,' Hazim said.

'To where? What's the plan now?' Carla asked.

'We need to fly Sean and Nocao north to Port Said, rendezvous with the naval fleet, and organise a way to get them to South Africa,' Powell said.

'South Africa!' Bella blurted.

'There's a supply depot nearby with choppers, weapons, trucks, and –'

Hazim nodded. 'I know the one – east off Al-Mansoureya Road. I'll direct you.'

Their Humvee took off with a roar. Hazim directed Carla down a maze of winding alleyways and side streets that only a local would know. Sean kept his eye on the Isharkute mothership. It was hovering over the pyramids like a giant chess piece awaiting its final, game-winning move. They turned a sharp corner, exiting onto a wider road running alongside a fenced-in field choked with US and Egyptian military vehicles. A deafening column of tanks rolled past them in the opposite direction, heading back to Giza.

Sean wished he could warn the Army that it was useless.

Nocao ducked down and hid under an army blanket. Carla pulled into the field and braked in front of the armed soldiers guarding the entrance. Powell and Hazim confirmed their identities and the soldiers waved them through. The depot was bustling with soldiers and personnel, packing trucks, arming up, and preparing for battle.

'Pull in over there, near that helipad,' Powell instructed.

Carla parked alongside a grey helicopter with UNITED STATES ARMY printed on the rear fuselage. 'All right, everyone stay here. I'm about to commandeer General Maddock's personal Black Hawk helicopter.'

'How will you do that?' Hazim asked.

'Don't worry. The pilot owes me a favour,' Powell said with a wink. He jumped out and approached the pilot. She pulled off her helmet and gave the colonel a hug, looking relieved to see him. They spoke briefly, and then she gave him something from inside the chopper. He ran back to the Humvee and opened the door. 'Okay, we're on. Let's go! Everyone into the chopper.' He threw Nocao a camouflage poncho. 'Wear this. All soldiers have been told to shoot aliens on sight.'

Nocao pulled the poncho over his head.

'That must've been some favour,' Hazim said.

'She's an old friend...plus it helped when I told her General Maddock was dead.'

'Is he?' Sean said with a little too much enthusiasm.

Powell shrugged and waved them on to the helicopter.

The pilot greeted them from the cockpit. 'I'm Captain Olivia Brasher. We're expecting some turbulence, so strap yourselves in.' She was younger than Sean expected, with blonde hair, freckly cheeks, and big blue eyes. She flicked an array of switches and the rotor blades spun to life.

'*Dio mio!* Look at that!' Bella said, pointing towards the Giza Plateau.

A metallic pyramid disengaged from the core of the mothership and descended upon the plateau. It landed directly on top of the Great Pyramid's remains, crumpling the ancient blocks beneath its weight and throwing out huge clouds of dust. Thunderous aftershocks rumbled through Cairo.

'Senetep's reclaimed his capital,' Nocao said.

Sean had a sudden sinking feeling in his stomach, reminding him of the overwhelming hopelessness he felt upon seeing Senetep's capital for the first time. But this time it was worse – the alien Overseer was threatening his world.

'Hurry up, get your belts on!' Powell said.

Hazim and Carla were the last onboard as the rotors reached full speed. The helicopter lifted off. An explosion tore through the crates beside the helipad and blasted them with hot air. Hazim and Carla were thrown out of the opposite side onto the ground several metres below.

'Wait, stop!' Bella cried. But the helicopter kept lifting.

Hunter-craft landed around the depot, dropping off squads of Isharkute warriors. Gunfire and energy blasts erupted around them like out-of-control fireworks. Hazim dragged Carla out of harm's way and waved the helicopter away.

'What are we doing?' Bella screamed, struggling to undo her belt.

'She's right,' Sean shouted, unclasping his belt. 'We can't leave without them –'

Powell locked his hands over their belts. 'We're not landing.'

Within seconds, they were flying over the depot, buffeted and rattled by more explosions. Now it was a struggle just to hold on. The raging fires of Cairo blurred beneath them as they banked hard and headed into the cover of the desert at night. Everyone stared at the distant glow with bewildered expressions. Bella was breathing so fast she was almost hyperventilating. Sean couldn't help feeling he'd failed his dad; he should have done more to protect Carla.

*Crack...*

A bolt of electrical energy struck their rotor blades and crackled through the cabin, sizzling and popping across the cockpit instrument panel. The pilot flicked the switches to save their craft from the disabling charge, but they were going down fast. Cairo's distant glow was suddenly consumed by the dunes like a monstrous black wave.

Bella screamed.

Sean and Nocao shared a fleeting glance and unclasped their belts.

'Stay in your seats!' Powell cried.

Clutching the cube, Nocao leapt into the darkness. In that split second, Sean realised he couldn't leave Bella behind. With one swift move he unlocked her belt, wrenched her from the seat, and dove out the side. Clear of the rotor blades, he released his wings and glided them onto the dunes. They hit with a *thud* and rolled across the sand as the helicopter disappeared behind a distant dune.

Seconds afterwards, a hunter-craft swooped in and fired on the downed vehicle. A tremendous explosion shook the dunes and lit up the desert like a giant bonfire. The hunter-craft circled around and returned to Giza.

Sean picked himself up and brushed the sand off his face. Nocao appeared over the top of a nearby dune. Their task now seemed more insurmountable than ever. Colonel Powell was dead. Their helicopter was a pile of twisted, burning metal, leaving them stranded in the middle of the Sahara Desert and thousands of kilometres from where they needed to be. On top of that, they had another person to worry about: Bella. She staggered to her feet, spitting the sand from her mouth, her fiery expression focused solely on him.

Sean sighed to himself. Saving the world had just got a little more complicated.

# — CHAPTER 10 —

# Senetep's United Nations

Senetep gazed upon the smouldering remains of Cairo from the command level of his new pyramid. In less than one human hour, the people of the city had fallen to their knees. He assessed the holograms of data overhead. Humanity had amassed an impressive collective of information on a global network they called the 'internet' – a testament to their advancement as a society, but also the key to their downfall.

Commander Vogran strolled around the workstations, overseeing the transmissions the command crew were intercepting.

Nefaro stood behind Senetep, proudly reeling off his accomplishments. 'In the decades leading up to your return, I've been researching human technology. By deciphering their simple software encryptions and tapping into their network of antiquated orbital satellites, I've been able to gain instant access to all their information.'

Senetep perused the endless stream of data in disbelief. Humanity's pitiful security measures afforded little protection to their sensitive information. World leaders and their secret military shelters, space programs, weapons defence systems, nuclear missiles – there was nothing that couldn't be found through their internet.

Senetep laughed to himself. He never thought it would be this easy: to have the world handed to him on a platter.

The most important data was being ingested, processed, and translated for him to read. It wouldn't take him long to learn and read the languages of the modern world, but it seemed like a wasted effort for a soon-to-be extinct species.

They were also monitoring everything humanity was broadcasting. There were dozens of languages and thousands of visual telecasts. One caught Senetep's eye – a video-feed of his new pyramid at Giza. He isolated the vision and turned up the volume. A frantic-sounding female voice accompanied the images.

'Here in Cairo, this is just one of the major landings reported around the world...huge pyramids made of metal have landed in dozens of capital cities.... Here in Egypt, this is the largest of all, twice as large as the former Great Pyramid. There's accounts of heavy fighting near the site...'

An endless row of text crawled across the bottom of the screen: London burns in shadow of invaders... Sydney harbour bridge collapses during military battle... Conflict across the US – New York and Washington fight back... North and South Korea work together, send first wave of nuclear arsenal, fail to stop invaders... Giant snakes reported in Japan, Egypt and India...

Senetep was mesmerised by the incessant information humans called 'news reports.' He suddenly realised it was the most efficient way to communicate with their entire species at once. 'Cease fire on all their communications infrastructure.'

'What about their military channels?' Nefaro asked.

'I want them to continue broadcasting their news.'

Vogran approached. 'The indigenous forces infesting your former capital have been conquered. The rest of the world will follow.'

'Good. Now bring me the world leaders,' Senetep said.

'Which leaders?' Nefaro asked. 'There's many nations, with nearly two hundred individual countries.'

'All of them!' Senetep commanded.

Nefaro nodded. 'Vogran, I'll help you coordinate an attack plan. Most leaders will be hidden and well protected, but we have everything we need to locate them.'

'I also want one of their newsmakers present when I meet the leaders. Our first interaction must be broadcast to the world.'

Nefaro and Vogran bowed and left to complete their tasks. Now that the majority of ancient sites were destroyed, Senetep could enjoy watching his forces decimate the pathetic retaliation. Humans may have the numbers, but they didn't possess a unified global force. The spread of wealth, technology, and resources was wildly uneven between nations. If humanity had worked as one, they may have put up something that resembled a resistance. North and South Korea had already released nuclear weapons in a desperate bid to protect themselves. These atomic devices were a crude and dirty response that would that would have made the world uninhabitable for millennia, and were fortunately destroyed by Isharkute defences before they had a chance to detonate. Yet they kept on coming, hundreds of fresh launches across the globe, more than enough to destroy themselves ten times over. It was amusing. They had evolved into a waring, self-serving species, more concerned in protecting their own borders than working together. They flaunted self-destruction with careless abandon, and for that alone, they deserved to be oppressed.

The bridge trembled.

Senetep looked around, expecting one of his crew to announce they were under attack, but it wasn't the bridge that was shaking, it was his leg! It had suddenly become weak and felt as though it could collapse under him at any moment.

'Nefaro, you have command until I return,' Senetep yelled across the bridge.

Nefaro nodded and returned to his duties.

Senetep shuffled off, forcing his dead leg to cooperate. He limped into the private quarters connected to the bridge, a space usually reserved for Emperor Neberun when he was in command. It was a sparse circular room with a central chair flanked by touchscreen panels. He slumped into the chair and massaged his leg. It was numb and heavy, almost a complete dead weight. Was this a side effect of his time-travelling jump? He activated a medical scanner and reclined as the sphere hovered over his body, pulsing with a clean white light. The scans completed and the results projected before him.

He leant forward, heart thumping.

The truth was devastating. The data undeniable.

The affliction decimating his species had now turned on him. The cellular degradation that ate away the central nervous system was devouring his at an accelerated rate. Senetep sat frozen in the chair, wrapping his head around the dire prognosis. If his body continued to shut down at this rate, he'd be dead within weeks. There was only one possible cure – human DNA!

Senetep snatched the sphere out of the air and crushed it in the palm of his hand. The holographic results flickered off. He hurled the remnants across the quarters and jumped up, forcing his leg into action. He stormed in circles and punched his thigh, refusing to let the affliction get the better of him. His leg regained some feeling and his initial panic shifted into more rational thoughts.

He didn't need to resort to such a drastic conclusion just yet – there were alternative steps to halting the progression. Cold therapy, slowing his body's metabolism, regular sessions in hibernation – anything except a human cure.

Faced with his own mortality, his resolve to propagate a race of pure Isharkute had never been stronger. The scourge of planet Earth would not save him. He'd rather beat himself to a pulp than poison his body with their human DNA.

Senetep paced the quarters thinking about short-term solutions. The next few days were crucial. He must be seen leading his new Empire. Once the planet was under his control and he possessed the Ark, he could consider more permanent options. In the meantime, no-one could learn of his sickness – not even his commanders.

He activated a command console and searched the ship for a cold therapy chamber. The pyramid schematics revealed one hidden behind a wall panel in his quarters.

'So, Neberun, you were using cold therapy too, you sly old beast,' Senetep muttered.

The wall panel slid open revealing a stark-white chamber. Senetep stepped inside and adjusted the temperature to the coldest setting.

The panel closed, sealing him inside. A blast of frigid air shot over him from all angles, chilling his skin, penetrating every muscle, tendon, and fibre like icy fingers. In that instant, his mind cleared and filled with an image of a spiral.

The panel slid open and he stumbled forward amidst a swirl of vapours.

A glistening layer of frost covered his arms and legs but quickly melted, leaving his skin coated with moisture. He stomped his foot, testing his troublesome leg. It felt stronger. His mind felt the sharpest it had been since his jolt through time.

Cold therapy would work for himself, but not his legions of warriors. They needed to be strong in battle, not struggling with useless limbs and failing bodies. Until an alternate cure could be found, they needed to harvest human cerebrospinal fluid, the closest remaining link between human and Isharkute DNA.

\*     \*     \*

Outside his pyramid the air was heavy with the smell of death and destruction. Senetep led his entourage of commanders and scientists down the concourse between two full regiments of warriors. The clean metal lines of his pyramid stood in stark contrast to Cairo, a shattered city now smouldering in columns of smoke. A transport vessel emerged from the haze and landed on the concourse. The captured human leaders were forced to disembark and marched towards him under warrior guard.

Senetep recognised their wide-eyed fear, the same shared by their distant human ancestors. The straggly band of thirty or so men and women, most well past their youthful prime, were lined up before him. He circled them, eyeing each leader with an air of condescension. They pleaded and bargained for their populations in a variety of colourful languages.

Senetep raised his hand, silencing the babble of voices.

Nefaro forced one of the men forward from the group. He clutched a black device with round glass on one end. 'He's called a *cameraman*,' Nefaro said, grabbing the man by the hair and twisting his head so the fresh pink-purple bulges behind his ears were visible. *'He's the only sorry one from this lot fitted with a translator.'*

Senetep took the device off the cameraman and turned it over, inspecting the archaic design. Strange that humans felt the need to name their devices, he thought, reading aloud the writing on the front: SONY.

The man glanced anxiously between Senetep and Nefaro.

*'They call it a camera,'* Nefaro said. *'It's used to capture images for their news reports.'*

*'This will transmit a message to their people?'* Senetep asked, peering into the glass.

*'I've connected the signal from his camera into every broadcast frequency across the planet.'*

Senetep handed the man his camera and indicated that he should film the line of leaders as his warriors forced them to their knees. They all obeyed except for one man. Senetep peered down at the insubordinate, a man with black skin and dressed in a tattered grey suit. His bloodshot eyes exuded a pitiful desperation.

'We can negotiate a peace treaty,' he blathered. 'Please, we can resolve this without any more fighting –'

Senetep signalled the warrior to release him and the man straightened his suit in a lame attempt to look important.

*'Who is this man?'* Senetep said, directing the question to the cameraman, his newly appointed translator.

'He wants to know who you are,' the man said.

The man batted his eyelids in surprise. 'I'm Mwai Odinga, President of Kenya.'

Senetep listened patiently and responded, *'Mwai Odinga, you are no longer president of anything. Your disobedience will be a lesson to the others.'*

The cameraman translated Isharkute into English. As soon as he finished, Vogran stepped forward, unslung his stave, and fired. The blast shredded Mwai's shirt from his chest and catapulted his body across the concourse. The remaining leaders cowered and sobbed.

The cameraman stood with his mouth agape, camera dangling aimlessly from his hand.

Senetep glared at him and he promptly lifted the camera back into position. *'It's time these former leaders hear our offer of mercy.'*

His three scientists moved to the first leader. Two held a large canister while a third reached inside with a pair of long-nosed pliers and pulled out a slimy octopus. Terrified gasps sounded from the prisoners. The creature squirmed and squelched, its tentacles grasping for a warm-blooded host. The warriors held the humans still as the scientists moved along the line, placing the organisms behind their ears. Senetep sniggered with enjoyment. Their pitiful writhing and screams were a sight to behold – the perfect message to send to the rest of the world.

He walked the line of prisoners, watching them adjust to their anatomical additions. 'I need translators who can convey my message to the billions watching.'

Even though they could understand him, none of the leaders responded. They stared up at him with fear or malevolence. Male humans were too aggressive; a female would be a better option, one with a gentle, more agreeable voice that would appeal to the masses.

Of all the females kneeling before him, only one held his stare: a fair-haired, middle-aged woman dressed in dark suit. Senetep paused in front of her. 'Stand!'

The woman rose to her feet, trembling all over the place on her strange high-heeled shoes.

'I want you to address your people.'

The woman nodded, rubbing her ears with a perplexed look.

'Who are you and what nation do you represent?'

'Belinda Kamen, I'm the prime minister of the United Kingdom.'

'I'm Senetep, your new ruler. Under my instruction, you will coordinate the surrender of your planet.'

The woman flicked her eyes towards Mwai's crumpled body. 'You can kill us, but the rest of the world won't stop fighting for their freedom. Our will can never be beaten or suppressed. However, instead of war, we'd prefer negotiation.'

Senetep realised her words echoed those spoken by Sean Livingstone millennia before. Modern humans were arrogant and overly confident compared to their ancestors. Isharkute were no longer seen as gods or creators, but a race of alien invaders. Military might, destruction, and death was commonplace in this new world. As tempting as it was, killing the leaders in front of the billions watching would have little effect and would only fuel their resolution. For this troublesome species to fall in line, they needed to witness something truly incomprehensible – a sight so horrifying it would subdue them with fear.

Senetep had the perfect solution. 'Perhaps there is something we can do for each other, but first we must talk, away from the eyes of your world.'

The warriors rounded up all the leaders and marched them up the concourse to the pyramid.

'Not you,' Senetep said to the cameraman. 'Wait here until we return.'

*    *    *

The next few hours were a pleasure to behold. Senetep watched from an overhead gantry as the human leaders experienced his new hybrid laboratories. Limbs, heads, and torsos were dismembered and reassembled across the collection of operating tables. His hybrid scientists worked diligently, hands soaked in the glistening rush of red. But this was not his usual type of hybrid conversion – these human leaders were not being merged with prime livestock, but rather the lower animals they bred, slaughtered, and looked down upon. Pigs. Cows. Goats. Sheep. Even cats and dogs. Any domestic animal that would remind human beings where they stood in the order of things.

Once the procedures were complete, Senetep appeared on the pyramid concourse. The cameraman stood in front of him, filming his every move.

Senetep peered into the glass lens and spoke in English. 'People of Earth. Your leaders have expressed their unwavering obedience. Not with words or action, but with their bodies.'

He raised his arms and a group of animals raced onto the concourse, scattering and darting in panic. The clatter of hooves and paws carried a sight of pure insanity. Sheep with human heads. Pigs crawling around on human arms. A human body with a goat's head. The leaders of the world were hybrid abominations, yelping, whining, and barking in distress. Their minds were still intact, enabling the horror to be expressed on their human and animal faces.

Senetep walked amongst the creatures and addressed the camera.

'Yesterday you were the masters. Today you are the lesser species, mere livestock. I'm open to dialogue, but it must be on the condition of your complete and total surrender. If there's one amongst you who can speak for all humanity, then come forward.'

# CHAPTER 11

# Journey To Ras El Bar

The sun rising over the Sahara Desert was a sight to behold. A deep violet sky still twinkling with stars dissolved into a palette of purple and golden hues. It was the most beautiful sunrise Bella had ever seen, but in her current state of mind, those colours were dull and muted.

For the last few hours she'd been trudging through the desert with Sean and Nocao. Destination, who knew? Somehow Sean had used the stars to guide them in the right direction. He was smart, but a little annoyingly so. How did he know so much? He was a year younger than her, had an opinion on everything, and without asking, had put himself in charge. Sure, he'd saved her from the crash with his wings – some kind of alien implant – but she couldn't stop blaming him for their situation. He wanted to fly ahead and scout for help but she'd insisted he stay...no way was she going to be left alone with the alien.

They stopped at the top of a dune and looked down at the rippling dunes of magenta and pink, spreading like a big soft blanket all the way to the horizon, silent and inviting.

'We need to find shelter before it gets hot,' Sean said, ruining her peaceful thought.

'And water!' Bella added. Her throat had been dry for ages.

Nocao squinted into the distance. 'There's a settlement north-east from here.'

Bella peered in the same direction. 'I can't see anything.'

'Your inferior eyes can't see it, but it's there.'

Bella almost hit him in the arm for being so obnoxious. 'There's nothing wrong with my eyes!' she remarked, noticing that Sean was smiling at her. 'What?'

'Nothing,' he said innocently. 'You'll get used to Nocao, he's a little –'

'Rude!'

Sean shrugged. 'You can't blame him. He's still getting used to the way we speak.'

'I didn't intend to be rude,' Nocao cut in, 'but it's a fact, human eyes are –'

'Okay, we get it,' Sean said stepping between them to quell the brewing storm. 'It's impolite to point out someone's weaknesses then compare them against your strengths.'

Nocao huffed and peered out at the desert.

Sean looked at her. 'I know you don't want me to leave, but I have to fly ahead and see what supplies I can find. We won't last a day in the desert without water.'

'Then what?' Bella replied. 'Do you have a plan after that?'

'Yeah, continue north to Point Said, find the military fleet Colonel Powell was talking about –'

'*Pazzo!*' Bella blurted in exasperation. 'Colonel Powell's dead. We stole the general's helicopter. No-one else in the military knows you're coming. You'll have to convince them all over again, and with your big-headed friend here – no pun intended – that'll be impossible.'

'She has a good point,' Nocao said. 'And it's true... I have a big head.'

Sean made a surprised chuckle, like he wasn't expecting Nocao to tell a joke.

'Bella's right,' Nocao continued. 'Now that Senetep's destroyed half the world, I doubt we can convince the military a second time. But our first riddle starts in the cave Azar discovered, almost 6,500 kilometres from here on Africa's southern coastline. We need to find an inconspicuous mode of transport capable of taking us from the top of this country to the bottom.'

Bella started to respond, then swallowed her words. Her father's boat was inconspicuous enough to circumnavigate the continent to the South African caves, but it meant sticking with Sean and Nocao for a ridiculously long journey. That was the last thing she wanted to do.

'Do you have a better idea?' Sean asked, looking at her expectantly.

Bella thought about it. They were lost in the desert. No food. No water. She had to admit that without Sean, her chances of getting back to her family were slim. And the longer she took, the harder it would be. She needed to find them before they came searching for her. 'My family's boat should be anchored in Ras El Bar,' she said, swallowing her words like poison.

Sean and Nocao glanced at each other with a glimmer of excitement.

'Is it a big boat?' Sean asked.

'Sì, Papa uses it for salvage operations. It'll be slow, but should be able to take you to the caves in South Africa.'

'Awesome! Then we just have to get to Ras El Bar.'

'One of Papa's friends drove me from there to Cairo. It took about four hours.'

'Good, but I have to fly ahead to see if I can find a 4WD or something. If there's a town, that means there's roads. We could be there by the end of the day.'

Bella's rush of excitement turned to alarm. Sean was going to leave her with Nocao. It was hard enough dealing with his piercing gaze and odd personality...now she had to spend some serious alone time with him.

Nocao pointed to a rocky outcrop to the west. 'Bella and I will find shelter there and wait for you.'

'Okay. I'll be back soon,' Sean said.

Bella lurched after him. 'Don't take too long!' she said, trying not to sound overly desperate.

'Nocao's my friend... You can trust him.'

Sean dove off the tip of the dune. Paper-thin translucent wings with the breadth of a small hang-glider shot out from the back of his torn t-shirt and carried him across the desert. They caught the morning sun and glistened iridescently like the inside of a beautiful ocean shell. Within seconds, he was a mere speck in the distance.

'I wish I could do that,' Bella whispered to herself.

Nocao marched down the dune and glanced back at her to follow. Bella hustled, keeping a safe distance between them. Her initial repulsion to his alien looks was giving way to curiosity. A lightweight bronze-coloured armour adorned his midnight-blue tunic and protected his forearms like bracers, reminding her of the armour worn by ancient Roman soldiers. His bare lower legs and arms were slender, but well defined. When the light caught his pale blue skin on the right angle, it accentuated a series of intriguing tattoos that rose up the side of his extended cranium.

By the time they reached the rocky outcrop, the sun was high and burning with intensity. Bella relished the shade. Her face felt dry and sunburnt. Nocao led her through a rocky crevice that carved a steep descent into the desert. The wind-smoothed bedrock towered above their heads and channelled a cool breeze. They followed the natural path of the stone into a cavernous fissure. It opened over their heads to the desert surface. Sunlight caught the ledges above and cast shadows across the rock face like a large sundial. Bella smiled to herself, realising that if Sean were here, he'd probably be able to tell the time just by watching the movement of the shadows. She couldn't believe that in the short time he'd been gone, she was already missing his chatter.

Nocao sat on a rock, looking content to bide his time.

Bella wandered around the fissure, checking her phone. She knew it was never going to work down here, and considering she'd lost all reception the night before, it was a poor attempt to avoid small talk with the alien.

'What are you doing?' Nocao said. His voice reverberated off the rock walls, sounding twice as loud as it really was.

'Nothing,' Bella said, shoving the phone back in her pocket.

'Then sit, conserve your energy.'

Bella frowned at him. 'Are you always this bossy?'

Nocao raised an eyebrow and pointed to the rock beside him, insisting she sit.

Reluctantly, she sat down and peered up at the shadows elongating across the cliff face, wishing they would move quicker. All the time, she could feel Nocao's piercing eyes watching her. Finally, she couldn't take the attention any longer. 'Is there something wrong?'

'You paint your face,' Nocao said.

'*Mi scusi!*' Bella blurted.

'You paint your face like your human ancestors.'

'*Sì*, I suppose I do. It's called mascara.'

'Interesting custom – one practiced by human females throughout the ages.'

'It's not that interesting,' Bella retorted. Nocao looked taken back by her abrasiveness and she felt a pang of guilt. He was attempting to make conversation. If she tried to get to know him, time might go quicker. At least he wasn't trying to kill her like the rest of his species.

'We call it make-up,' she said after a long pause. 'What about the tattoos on your head? Are they just decorative?'

'They represent my Isharkute lineage and profession. Like me, my father Horumbut was a member of the Guild of Sciences.'

'Hmm. What about Isharkute females? Do they have tattoos as well?'

'Yes... But I've never seen a female Isharkute.'

'Never?!'

'No, not even my birth mother.'

'Weird. Haven't you got photos of her or something?'

'No, I've never lived on my homeworld. That's where our females stay.'

'How do you know they have tattoos then?'

'Because all male Isharkute become life-bearers.'

Bella processed his comment, then straightened with a start. 'You're going to have a baby?'

'Yes. When I'm of age, I'll return to my home planet, enter hibernation, and become a "mother," as you call it.'

'But right now, you're male?'

'Yes.'

'Whoa, that's weird.'

'Giving birth is no different from what you will eventually do.'

Bella felt the heat return to her sunburnt face. This was an embarrassing and an uncomfortable assumption on his behalf. 'Hold on – I never said anything about having babies.'

'You don't plan to?'

'*Mi fai schiffo!*'

'Why does the question make you feel sick?'

Bella shook her head, 'I'm studying to be an artist. If you know what that means.'

'Being an artist is more important than being a mother?'

Bella widened her eyes in disbelief. Was she really having this conversation with an alien? 'To me, at this point in time, I suppose... *sí*.'

'Why?'

'I don't know... Ever since I was young I just knew I wanted to be an artist. I can't explain it.'

'Your attraction to art over motherhood is probably based upon a biological predilection to notice and appreciate colour.'

'A predi-what?' Bella said. 'I don't know the word... As much as I hate to say this, your English might be better than mine.'

'"Predilection" means to have a taste for something. I've studied many humans and discovered a small percentage who can see infinitely more of the colour spectrum than others. Millions of hues and nuances. These traits only appear in females.'

Bella remembered she'd read about such a condition during one of her school assignments. It was called 'tetrachromacy,' and had something to do with DNA and a mutation in female chromosomes.

'Normal humans have three colour receptors in their eyes, but those with a fourth are endowed with extra colour perception. My own eyes are engineered to utilise this enhanced colour spectrum.'

'So you're boasting... You see colour better than me?'

'Yes, but if you have the ability, I could help you hone your skills.

It would help you with your quest to be an artist.'

Bella laughed. 'It's not a quest. My love for art isn't just some biological advantage, it comes from within. I can't explain it and don't need to.' A shadow appeared on the cliff ledge, making Bella leap to her feet. 'Sean's back!'

Nocao jolted upright. 'Quiet!'

The shadow appeared human until it lifted its head, revealing two upright ears and a long snout. A dog's head on a human body!? The only place she'd seen something like that was in Egyptian mythology. It looked like Anubis, the jackal-headed god of the dead. The shadow swept across the stone like a hieroglyph magically come to life. First an alien invasion, now mythical gods! Could the day get any more insane?

Nocao pressed a finger to his lips and whispered, 'Don't move.'

Five more jackal-headed shadows materialised and swooped along the clifftop in tight formation, stopping every few seconds to sniff the air.

'We're being hunted,' Nocao whispered.

'What are they?' she whispered back.

'Human-jackal hybrids. Isharkute use them to track prey. They've already picked up our scent. We need to get out of here before they corner us.'

Nocao directed her to a rocky overhang where they crouched out of sight, watching the hybrids' shadows scope along the upper ledges. One of the pack pounced across the fissure. It stooped over the cliff and peered deep into the shadows, right in their direction. The creature let out a bloodcurdling cry that sounded both human and animal. The pack cried in response and their shadows suddenly vanished.

'What are they doing?' Bella said.

'They're pack hunters, working to corner us. Quick, follow me.'

Nocao crawled beneath the low-cut rocks. Bella scrambled after him, desperate to keep up. The hard stone battered her knees and grazed her hands. They were heading deeper into a maze of cracks and crevices barely wide enough to crawl through. The jagged rocks were getting darker, tighter, and far too claustrophobic. *Thump!*

'Ouch!' she cried, rubbing her head.

'Shh!' Nocao hissed.

They reached a dark slit in the rocks barely wider than their bodies. Nocao slipped through and disappeared, like he'd been swallowed whole by the stone. Bella panicked – this was definitely too claustrophobic. Her eyes adjusted to the darkness and she could see Nocao on the other side holding out his hand, waiting for her to join him. Heart pounding, she pressed through the tight crevice. Nocao caught her hand and assisted her into a void.

Bella stumbled down a small rise and stopped to let her eyes adjust to the dim light. They were now standing in a grotto, a large subterranean space hollowed through the bedrock by an ancient river. The air was damp and cool. Pockets of sunlight filtered through cracks, creating beautiful luminescent beams of light. Bella took a moment to appreciate the cavern, finally understanding her aunt's attraction to the subterranean world. It was a magical, serene space as ancient as the Earth itself.

A sharp hiss echoed through the shadows.

Bella's skin crawled across the back of her neck. 'Please don't tell me it's one of those giant snakes!'

Nocao nodded. 'Hold your breath and don't move.'

'What?'

'It hunts by smelling your pheromones. If it can't smell you, it can't see you.'

'For how long?'

'Until it passes... A couple of minutes.'

Bella glared at him. 'I can't hold my breath that –'

The hiss echoed all around them and Bella inhaled sharply. She couldn't see it yet, but could hear the rocks and pebbles being pushed aside by the monstrous viper.

*Hissssss...*

Bella went rigid in terror. She could see the tongue flicking into the air, probing for her breath. The scaly black head glided past her like the bonnet of a slow-moving car. The wall of scales knocked against her, almost throwing her off balance.

She made a pact to herself: hold her breath until she blacked out. At least she'd never know she was being devoured.

Her lungs were burning, the need to inhale a fresh gulp of air impossible to resist. It was a sensation her brother had described to her countless times. As a practicing free diver, Arturo could hold his breath for several minutes. If she'd only taken up his offer to learn the skill on their family holidays.

Now she felt light-headed. The cave swirled around her. She wobbled and steadied herself.

The snake hissed and coiled around to investigate the movement, heading directly for them.

Bella could see Nocao in the corner of her eye, his glare crystal-clear: *Don't move!*

The snake slithered through a pool of light, illuminating its hellish red eyes. The vertical black pupils focused on her in a soulless serpentine stare. Her mouth opened involuntarily, ready to gulp in a lungful of air. Just as she could wait no more...

*Booooooom!*

The cave shuddered. Columns of dust blasted through the crevices, creating a thick haze. The snake curled around and slithered back the way it came. Bella waited for the entire length of scales to disappear before taking a huge breath of dusty air. The aftershocks subsided. Nocao grabbed her hand and pulled her through the murkiness towards a sliver of light. They squeezed through the opening, back into daylight and clean air. They were in the bottom of a deep shadowy ravine.

A shadow whooshed overhead and Bella instinctively ducked.

Sean landed a few feet away holding a smoking rocket launcher, looking rather proud with himself. 'Sorry, I've never used one of these before.'

'We could have been buried alive in there,' Bella said.

'Or eaten alive,' Nocao reminded her.

Sean looked a little deflated. 'I didn't mean to cause that much damage. The hybrids were tracking you into the cave...I couldn't think of anything else to divert their attention.'

Bella felt guilty. She probably should have thanked him, or at least given him a little credit.

'You found weapons?' Nocao said, inspecting the rocket launcher. 'Crude but effective device.'

'There's a bunch of abandoned military vehicles not far from here. The soldiers were gone, but I got us a jeep and some weapons.'

'So we have a car?' Bella said, perking up.

'Yeah, but I had to drive it back. That's why I took so long.'

'Where is it?'

'Up here,' Sean said, leading the way up the ravine. A few twists and turns later, they arrived at a dead end. 'What? I must've taken a wrong turn.'

Bella placed her hands on her hips and sighed. 'I thought you knew the way out.'

'I only saw this area once from above, and that was flying at full speed.'

'So now what?'

'We climb,' Nocao said, starting up the cliff.

Bella peered up. It was at least 20 metres to the top, a climb even her aunt would find challenging.

'I'll stay close to you,' Sean said. 'You know, just in case you fall. I can catch you.'

Bella raised her eyebrow at him. Could she really trust him with such a simple task after all the trouble he'd got them in? Something caught her eye. 'Look!'

The human-jackal hybrids were coming up behind them, clawing their way along the ravine walls like a nest of disturbed spiders, darting in and out of the crags with incredible speed and agility.

She faced the unscaleable wall with new-found enthusiasm. Without looking down, she began to climb. Nocao was almost halfway up and kicking down a steady stream of sand and pebbles into her face. This was tough.

Sean hovered in the air behind her. 'That's it, keep going. A little to the left, grab the rock... Now put your foot up.' His voice grew more frantic with each new direction.

Her hand slipped off a sandy ledge. '*Aiuto!*'

Sean caught her under the arms and repositioned her a little higher. If only he had the strength to fly her all the way to the top. She caught her breath and dug her fingers into the stone. Her heart was pounding so hard she thought she heard it echo off the cliff. Nocao climbed over the top ledge to safety. Without the hazard of falling debris, she climbed faster. Bella scaled the final ledge and rolled over, panting with exhaustion.

Sean flew over her and landed next to an open-top army jeep parked on a dune. 'Quick, get in!'

Nocao jumped in the back seat and rummaged through the stash of weapons loaded in the rear tray. Bella hopped into the front passenger seat as Sean started the engine. He clunked through the gears and overaccelerated, kicking up a plume of sand from the back tyres.

'Can you drive?' Bella asked.

'I drove it here, didn't I?' Sean retorted, red-faced.

They lurched forward with a jolt and swerved haphazardly across the sand. Behind them, the human-jackals leapt out of the ravine, barking and howling at each other as they raced up the dune.

Sean swerved down the far side of the dune, wrestling with the steering wheel like a kid on a dodge-'em car, face wracked with fear.

'How long have you been driving?' Bella cried over the whine of the overworked engine.

Sean gave her a nervous, sidelong look. 'Twenty minutes.'

'Okay, let's swap.'

Sean hit the brakes and gladly gave up his seat. Bella slipped behind the wheel, put the jeep into gear, gunned the accelerator, and quickly doubled his best speed. She eyeballed the rear-view mirror. The hybrids were almost upon them, tearing up the sand dunes behind them.

Nocao snatched up a long cylindrical device from an open case. 'What's this?'

Sean read the printed case. 'RPG-22 rocket-propelled grenade launcher.'

'Sounds powerful,' Nocao said, propping himself on the rear seat and taking aim at the hybrids.

'No, wait!' Sean cried. 'I think you're pointing it in the wrong –'

*Whoosh!*

The rocket fired straight through their windscreen and decimated the dune 30 metres ahead of them. They ducked as a wall of sand showered their jeep. Seconds later, they burst through the turbulence into open desert.

'What the hell are you doing?' Bella shrieked.

'Testing your weapons,' Nocao said, sheepishly placing the smoking launcher back in the case.

'Next time read the instructions.'

The dust cloud threw the hybrids off their scent and by the time the pack regrouped, Bella had put a good 500 metres between them.

'Hey, you can't argue – it sort of worked,' Sean said.

Bella rolled her eyes.

Soon they were on a road and speeding towards Ras El Bar. Deserted cars and military vehicles littered stretches of road, but there was not a soul to be seen. Minutes dragged like hours. The desert seemed endless. Sean and Nocao weren't speaking much, their attention focused on the horizon for hybrids and Isharkute vessels. The silence was a little too overwhelming. She tried the radio. Nothing but static. That made it feel like the end of the world.

She never really thought about the end of the world before. The Rapture was predicted in the Bible, yet her Catholic upbringing didn't fit with the whole alien-invasion thing. People weren't disappearing into Heaven by the grace of God; they were being killed and abducted by aliens. The ramifications were profound. Why weren't the Isharkute mentioned in the Bible? Was there even a God? Could the Bible be a fabrication made up by humans to counteract a fear of death? It was all too much. She felt like pulling the jeep over and vomiting.

Bella took a deep breath, gripped the steering wheel, and focused on the road.

*Faith. That's it!* She needed to have faith that things would work out. Just mulling over the negative wasn't going to help the situation. Family was the most important thing now, and she needed to concentrate on finding them.

The final stretch into Ras El Bar revealed a frightening lack of human life. The bustling, resort-oriented city Bella had visited days before was now a ghost town. The wide palm-lined roads were overshadowed by empty hotels. Cars had been left in the middle of the street, doors open. Bikes lay on their sides. Food stalls stood abandoned, some still with steaming food. Sean used a map to direct her through the city, but the roads were a mess. She veered onto the sidewalk to avoid the gridlocked cars and aimed for the marina – and, hopefully, her father's boat.

Bella careered over the sidewalks and gutters, impatient to reach the rows of bobbing white boats. She screeched to a stop just metres from the main jetty and jumped out.

There wasn't a sound to be heard except for the waves lapping against the jetty. The inviting cerulean-blue water painted a deceiving portrait of the picturesque location.

Sean passed Nocao a semi-automatic machine gun.

'I hope you know which way that thing shoots,' Bella said in all seriousness.

'Here's the trigger,' Sean said, holding up an identical weapon. 'It fires out the barrel, just in case you were wondering.'

Nocao glared at them. He was having none of their humour.

Sean offered Bella a semi-automatic pistol.

'No *grazie!* I don't believe in guns,' she said, forging onto the jetty. She scooted past the empty vessels. Her father's boat was meant to be docked in port for another week, so it had to be here. Her fast-paced walk turned into a run. The boats all looked the same, abandoned and depressing. Then she spotted the distinctive blue canopy, above which flapped her father's green, white, and red striped Italian flag.

Bella leapt off the jetty onto the rear deck. 'Papa, Mama... Arturo!'

Nothing, no familiar replies. Her hope sank faster than her stomach. Then she noticed the examination tables were full of half-sorted artefacts and the deck was strewn with diving gear. Her parents would never leave it this way. It looked as though the boat had been abandoned.

Sean and Nocao jumped down onto the deck. A spear shot out of the cabin, embedding in the wooden side rail between them with an ominous twang.

'Drop your weapons!' hollered a voice from inside the cabin.

Sean nodded to Nocao and they placed their guns on the deck.

'That's it. Now don't move,' said the voice. Arturo stepped into the sunlight, loading another spear into his spearfishing gun.

'Arty!' Bella cried, swinging her arms tightly around her brother's neck.

'*Ciao*, Bella...' Arturo said, hugging her with one arm while aiming the speargun at Nocao. 'Tell Fish Head here to get off the boat before I impale him to it!'

# CHAPTER 12

# The Proposition

Azar wasn't used to feeling nervous or apprehensive. Dressed in his one-of-a-kind $35,000 William Westmancott suit, he was flying across the desert towards Cairo in his personal convoy of helicopters, en route to negotiate the deal of his life. Senetep had addressed the entire world in his recent broadcast, asking for someone to step forward and speak for all of humanity. Azar immediately knew he was that man. This was his calling. Once he was in a position of power with the Isharkute, he could use it to his advantage and continue searching for the Ark – the path to ultimate domination over Senetep, and then the world.

Rather than strap himself in with a seatbelt, he hung on to the handles, determined to look unrumpled and pristine for his arrival. A flash of light caught drew his attention to Cairo's smoky skyline. Senetep's pyramid reflected the warm afternoon sun like a beacon, highlighting their destination.

His son Malik sat across from him, staring out the open side, fingers tapping his empty holster.

'Trust me!' Azar shouted over the cabin noise. 'If we'd have brought weapons, it would've looked hostile.'

'So we're surrendering?'

'I'm negotiating.'

'If your negotiations fail, we're dead...or worse!' Malik replied harshly. 'They turned the world leaders into animals...they could do the same to us.'

'I won't fail,' Azar said. He couldn't help feeling his conviction was forced, in part to steel his own nerves rather than convince his son.

The pilots were sending constant radio messages, hoping the Isharkute would intercept them and understand their intentions were peaceful. The fact they weren't being shot down by the vessels tracking them was a positive sign.

His convoy landed at the foot of a great metal concourse leading up to Giza's new pyramid. Azar jumped out as the rotors decelerated. Malik was next, followed by ten of their best soldiers, all unarmed experts in hand-to-hand combat if the negotiations deteriorated.

Azar brushed off his lapels and straightened his jacket. He flattened his slicked hair with the palm of his hand and looked upon the alien superstructure. The pyramid was triple the size of the Great Pyramid. The original world-loved icon was now just a pile of crushed stone beneath Cairo's new tenant. The alien structure dwarfed every clandestine hangar and subterranean base Azar had ever built, with each of its four sloping faces as big as a city block. Isharkute vessels darted in and out of the open hangar near the pyramid's apex like a busy beehive.

Rather than fly straight into the hangar, Azar opted to approach the pyramid on the same concourse where the world leaders met with Senetep. This was a delicate situation and required restraint on his part – another aspect to which he was unaccustomed.

'Strange. No landing party to greet us?' Malik said.

Azar stared at the pyramid's monolithic opening at the top of the concourse. It had to be at least twenty storeys tall. 'Then we knock on the front door.'

He kicked his mirror-black shoes free of sand and started up the kilometre-long concourse. Fifty metres into their walk, an Isharkute vessel swooped onto the concourse between his party and the helicopters, cutting off any chance of escape.

'What do we do?' Malik said.

'Wait here,' Azar said, walking between his soldiers to face the aliens.

Six Isharkute warriors leapt out of the vessel and surrounded them, staves drawn. Each alien stood a good twelve inches taller than Nocao and wore long white beards braided with gold beads and gemstones. They were broad, muscular, and bigger than any of the burliest bodyguards he'd personally hired over the years; some of the strongest muscle in the Middle East.

The warriors hustled Azar and his men into the vessel and flew them up to the hangar where they were lined up and forced to kneel.

An imposing Isharkute approached. His beard hung heavy with twice as many beads. He was broader than the average warrior and carried a huge stave powered by two bulky crystals. Azar recognised him as one of the two Isharkute who stood behind Senetep during the broadcast.

The warriors forced their heads forward so that they were bowing. A pair of Isharkute dressed in bloodstained aprons stood before them and set down a cylindrical container.

Azar could feel his pulse racing against his shirt collar. He knew what was coming – a foul octopus translator was about to be attached to their heads, an unavoidable step towards communicating with the aliens. The two Isharkute moved along the line, plucking the organisms from the canister and slopping them behind his soldier's ears. The moans and writhing from his toughest men unsettled him more than the creatures themselves.

Malik was the next in line. He winced and recoiled like the others.

Azar kept his head down as the soiled aprons filled his field of vision. He closed his eyes. He could hear the squishy tentacles slap about as it was drawn from the canister, then a cold wet blob touched the bare skin behind his ears. For a second there was nothing, then it burned like searing hot needles, rapidly changing from hot to cold, clawing its way down his ear canal. His hearing became muffled and the floor swayed like he was drunk. The symptoms settled and he peered up against the dizziness.

The large Isharkute loomed over them. 'Which one of you speaks for this sorry lot?'

Azar marvelled at the instant, slightly disorienting translation. It happened in his head, somewhere between his ears and brain, like another voice beyond his eardrum.

'I do,' Azar replied. 'My name is Azar Hawati, and to whom am I speaking?'

'Vogran, First Commander to Overseer Senetep.'

'First Commander Vogran, may I stand?'

Vogran considered the request and nodded.

Azar fought the dizziness and brought himself to his feet, determined to face the commander as close to eye-to-eye as possible. 'Overseer Senetep asked for someone to speak for the people of this planet and negotiate their surrender... I'm that person.'

'What makes you worthy?' Vogran said, eyeing him.

'I can succeed where our single-minded politicians and leaders have failed. I have unlimited resources at my disposal, yet I don't govern a country or have to worry about protecting my own borders. I'm willing to assist Overseer Senetep transition humanity through the change.'

'We shall see,' Vogran said, pointing across the hangar. 'Move! But the others wait here.'

Azar avoided eye contact with Malik as he was marched out of the hangar. It would be seen as a sign of emotional weakness and give away the fact that his son was with him. Now he realised the gravity of his mistake. If it came down to a decision between Malik's life or successful negotiations, he couldn't trust himself to put family first.

He was escorted through the pyramid and delivered to a private chamber off a main control room. Overseer Senetep stood on the far side of the room, hands crossed behind his back, waiting patiently for his visitor. Between them was a wall of holograms projecting images, videos, news articles, and every piece of information the Isharkute had gleaned about him from the internet. The escorting warriors left them alone.

Senetep turned around. His pale eyes honed in on him. 'Azar Hawati... Businessman. Industrialist. Self-made billionaire. Father...'

Malik's face appeared in the holograms.

So much for keeping his son a secret!

Senetep regarded the image and another appeared – a female face Azar hadn't looked upon in ages. The woman's eternally youthful smile filled him with longing and guilt.

'Your only wife, Feyrouz Hawati, died twenty-six years ago. Since that life-changing event, you've achieved unprecedented success. This excessive wealth has allowed you to build hidden bases while amassing a network of intelligence and firepower, enough to rival the very country you supposedly serve.'

The breadth of information the Isharkute had gathered on him was intimidating. They had broken into his encrypted servers and accessed schematics and documentation on all his hidden bases.

'Yet, even with all these resources, you're not a governing power. You have no influence over your people,' Senetep said, stepping through the hologram towards him.

Azar remained silent. The Overseer was content to talk – better to let the alien reveal his cards before playing his own hand.

'You work outside the governments and usual political conventions, preferring to do what serves you. Now that your leaders have failed, it's humans with resources like you who believe they have something to offer, and that's why you're here: to claim the influence and power you believe you deserve... But are you serving yourself or your people?'

Azar was rarely lost for words, but here he stood, tongue-tied before an alien who had perceived his life's desires better than any human ever had. This wasn't the usual negotiation laced with lies to conceal true agendas. He could be honest without moral responsibility.

'I'm serving myself,' Azar replied.

'Then you're no good to me.'

'You're wrong. I'm exactly who you need.'

Senetep didn't say a word.

Azar interpreted the silence as his cue to continue. 'Any leader who puts the good of the people first will fail. Humanity is divided, and has been for thousands of years. They will never unite or submit wholly to your demands; there will always be factions that continue to rebel. I can speak for you – make them see there's no other way. I understand that sacrifices must be made. Humanity is no longer the dominant species. Complete submission is our only option for survival.'

'How would you achieve this?'

'You're a universally travelled species, knowledgeable, powerful, but most importantly, not without mercy. If the people of this world can see that then I have something to work with. They require a sense of hope; otherwise, they'll fight to their dying breath.'

'What do you want out of this?'

'Egypt was once the most powerful country on Earth. My interest in archaeology revealed your species were partly responsible for this: your culture kick-started our first civilisations and made us who we are. I want our species to work alongside each other again. Your capital here at Giza can be the dominant seat of power for the entire world. You can rule from here without worrying about the minutia. As you know, I have the infrastructure and resources to control the public while you take care of more important matters, but I'll need an area that I can work from...under your strict guidance, of course.'

Senetep strode behind him, unnervingly silent. A burst of energy electrified the air and illuminated the room with blue light. Azar recognised the distinctive hum of an Isharkute stave. He kept his eyes forward, not even daring to flinch. A crippling pain suddenly shot through the back of his legs and he dropped, kneeling on the floor like a hopeless beggar.

'Our species never worked alongside each other,' Senetep spat with contempt. 'You were created as slaves to serve us and die at our whim.'

'Forgive...my...ignorance,' Azar gasped in between painful breaths. The electrical pulses stabbed through his chest like knives. 'But...I can...still help you.'

'You misunderstood my request, Azar Hawati.'

Azar strained to listen over the pop and crackle of electrical energy.

'When I asked for someone to speak, I merely wanted a translator, someone with a familiar face that your fellow imbeciles would listen to.' Senetep brandished the electrified stave in his face. 'No human has the right to request anything from me. However, your valiant attempt has earned you a more dignified fate than your world leaders. You and your men will be the first to provide my scientists with human cerebrospinal fluid.'

Senetep disengaged his stave and Azar keeled over, gasping for air. Any chance of negotiating his way out now seemed impossible.

Azar was taken back to the hangar and reunited with Malik and the soldiers. They were loaded onto a larger transport vessel under heavy guard and flown north along the Nile River. He stared pensively across the ruins of his smouldering country; the charred remains scarred the landscape like gaping wounds. Every town and province from Cairo to the delta had been overrun and was deserted. Abandoned cars littered the roads. Boats drifted aimlessly on the rivers. There wasn't a living soul as far as he could see. Where had they all gone? The desolation sent a chill down his spine and he turned away.

They flew over the coastline towards three immense new pyramids sitting in the middle of the Mediterranean Sea. Their tips sat hundreds of metres above the waterline, with the majority of the structures hidden in the depths below. Each pyramid was fronted with expansive sea-level platforms where lines of human prisoners, several hundred deep, were being herded inside by Isharkute warriors.

Their vessel landed in front of the middle pyramid between lines of local Egyptians.

Azar felt the true weight of the Isharkute invasion for the first time. No longer just images on news reports, these were his fellow countrymen. Men, women, children, and entire families were being lined up for who-knew-what inside the pyramids. He glanced back at Malik. His face was pale with horror as the warriors marched them alongside the raucous queues. The sick and elderly were dragged away to the protestations of family and friends. The strongest men and women fought back, keeping the alien guards busy. Azar stared straight ahead, steeling his emotions against the atrocities.

Inside the pyramid's main entrance, people were being separated into groups based on age and gender and herded into dank corridors like livestock. The harsh metal interior had the feel of an industrial factory and processing plant. Steam hissed through the grilled floor. The air was hot and sticky. Azar could feel the sweat under his clothes, soaking his armpits and trickling down his back.

Nefaro led them through a maze of shadowy hallways and dimly lit chambers to arrive in a vast laboratory. Gleaming metal benches were dressed with ominous probes, saws, blades, and other alien technology. Rows of sizable glass tanks filled with luminous liquid flanked the lab walls. Bizarre, unrecognisable life forms were suspended behind the thick glass. Azar couldn't tell if the glutinous fleshy organisms were dismembered remains or deformed creatures. Nefaro finally directed them to a bench in the middle of the lab.

Four Isharkute wearing bloodstained aprons waited for them. They looked older and wiser than the warriors and their long white beards were yellowed and matted from the sinewy spray of blood and innards of previous operations.

The warriors grabbed one of Azar's soldiers and roughed him onto the bench. His desperate kicks and punches were no match for their alien strength.

Azar refrained from stepping in. This poor soul was a casualty of war and there was nothing he or his men could do to help. His battle-hardened soldiers had seen horrors like this before, but Malik wasn't so seasoned and shifted nervously. His son was more of a humanitarian than himself, a trait he'd taken from his mother, Feyrouz.

'Can't we stop them?' Malik whispered.

Azar shook his head without making eye contact.

Senetep entered the lab and stood at the head of the bench as the man was strapped face down. His shirt was torn from his body and discarded. The scientists moved their pale blue hands up and down his spine, prodding and pressing each vertebra. They found a spot and pressed their knuckles deep into his flesh. Two sickening cracks echoed through the lab as his vertebrae separated beneath his unbroken flesh. The man screamed in agony. One of the scientists withdrew a small spined organism like a sea urchin and placed it on the man's arm. The black spines pierced his skin and the soldier fell unconscious.

Azar swallowed hard, forcing back his rising nausea. It was hard to stomach such callous and brutal behaviour. They could have alleviated the man's suffering by using the anaesthetic before breaking his spine.

The scientists pulled down a pair of tubes from the overhead equipment and attached pencil-thick needles to each end.

'What are they doing?' Malik said.

Azar didn't answer. He knew the Isharkute were sick and suffering from a collapsing genome. To what extent, he had no idea, but human DNA held the cure. It was the one glaring secret of which the world was unaware. There had to be some kind of leverage in their weakness, something he could exploit before they all became paralysed lab rats.

The scientists forced the needles between the soldier's broken vertebrae, inserting the full length through his freshly bruising flesh. Seconds later, a small amount of clear liquid was sucked up the tubes and into the overhead machines. The soldier shuddered and twitched, then suddenly lay still.

'Is he dead?' Azar asked.

Senetep regarded Azar. 'Like all of you, he'll be kept in a comatose state for his cerebrospinal fluid. Your bodies produce a limited amount each day that we'll harvest for our purposes.'

Azar had seconds to come up with a plan to save them from a similar fate.

# CHAPTER 13

# The Cave Of Myth

'Don't shoot! Fish Head's with us,' Bella said, jumping in front of Arturo's speargun. Her sudden rush to protect Nocao from her brother was a surprise to everyone, and from what Sean could see, even herself.

'I don't see my resemblance to amphibians,' Nocao said, stroking his head. 'If anything, my physiology should reflect your own species –'

'Don't move!' Arturo insisted, jabbing his weapon aggressively.

Sean didn't want to mess with Bella's brother. He was at least twelve inches taller than himself and physically imposing. His loose-hanging singlet exposed a tanned, broad-shouldered and muscular physique that reminded him of an Olympic swimmer.

'They're okay, Arty. They're with me,' Bella said. She placed her hand on the speargun and forced it to the deck.

'He's one of those aliens! I saw them on the TV. They turned our leaders into animals.'

'It's okay,' Bella said in a calmer voice. 'He's on our side. His name's Nocao.'

Arturo finally looked his sister in the eye. 'They took Mama and Papa right off the boat. They're gone, Bella.'

Bella took a sharp breath and stared at her brother. Her eyes welled with tears and she started to tremble. Sean understood exactly how she felt. Her fear was like a pit with no bottom, overwhelming any sense of hope.

'They're not dead,' Sean said.

'Not yet,' Nocao added.

Sean glowered at his abrupt friend. 'Better leave the talking to me for now.'

'Why? What's going on, Sean?' Bella asked. 'Where are my parents?'

'If we could help them right now, I would, I promise... But we need to finish our mission. That's the only way we can save them.'

'What mission? Who are you?' Arturo asked, directing his questions at Sean.

'Sean Livingstone.'

Arturo did a double-take between his sister and Sean. 'Henry's son! I thought I recognised you. Where's Henry and Aunt Carla?'

'I have so much to tell you, but Sean's right, we need to get moving,' Bella said. 'Does the boat still work?'

Arturo nodded. 'Where do you want to go?'

'The east coast of South Africa,' Sean said.

Nocao placed the cube on the examination table beside the coral-encrusted relics. He pressed the sequence of glyphs and the cube unfolded into a flat cross.

'This cube can create a holographic map to the Ark, but we need three missing crystals to activate it,' Sean said, pointing to the empty notches.

'What, like Noah's Ark?' Arturo said.

'No, we're looking for the Ark of the Covenant.'

'The Ark of the Covenant!' Arturo bellowed with incredulity.

'Yeah, but it's really a power source designed to save humanity.'

Arturo shook his head in disbelief and looked at his sister. 'You believe any of this?'

Bella nodded.

'Okay, say I believe your crazy story... Our boat's not equipped to make that kind of journey.'

'Then we need to find a bigger boat,' Sean said. 'There's no-one around, so it looks like we've got the pick of the marina.'

'Your primitive vessels are too slow,' Nocao said. 'I know a way to get to the caves by the end of the day. What direction did my people take the captured?'

Arturo pointed towards Ras El Bar's sun-bleached rooftops. 'Northwest, out to sea. Why?'

'We must take this vessel in the same direction.'

Arturo shook his head. 'You're crazy! I'm not going after them.'

Bella pulled Arturo aside and they whispered heatedly. Arturo eventually stormed off and she gave Sean the nod of approval.

'What did you say to make him agree?' Sean asked.

'He knows how stubborn I can be. I told him if he didn't help us, I'd never let him forget about it, even if we were the last two people left on Earth.'

Sean smiled. 'Thanks, I'm glad I didn't have to convince him.'

Bella helped her brother load up half a dozen fuel canisters and disengage from the dock. She skipped across the deck and handled the ropes like a seasoned sailor. Sean was impressed. He sat with Nocao on the rear deck while she stood at the helm with Arturo, explaining everything while he steered them out of port. They cruised past the Ras El Bar lighthouse, cleared the shoreline, and motored across the Mediterranean Sea.

Nocao stared at the western horizon. Sean peered in the same direction, but could only see a rippling mirage of blue where water met sky. 'What is it? What are you looking for?'

'There!' Nocao said, suddenly pointing.

There was a brief shimmer in the distance. Sean squinted. 'What is it?'

Bella used a pair of binoculars to scan the horizon. 'They're pyramids!'

'Those pyramids are Senetep's hybrid facilities,' Nocao said. 'The largest is the Pyramid of Trials – that's where Sean's father was tested and turned into a hybrid.'

'Pyramids in the ocean?' Arturo said quizzically, checking the boat's built-in compass. 'I'm sure we were diving in that area yesterday when Mama and Papa disappeared. I found a metallic obelisk next to a deep ravine, but there weren't any pyramids.'

'Here, see for yourself,' Bella said, passing the binoculars.

Sean burst out with excitement, 'We're looking for an obelisk!'

'I doubt your father would place it over Senetep's old capital,' Nocao said. 'It's probably a remnant from his original complex. Ten thousand years ago when the Isharkute evacuated Earth, these three pyramids re-joined Senetep's motherships, leaving holes in the ocean floor. That accounts for the deep ravine you found beside the obelisk.'

'Does that mean they just landed there yesterday, like Senetep's pyramid at Giza?' Bella asked.

'Yes.'

'So where's everyone from Ras El Bar?' Sean asked.

'They'll be divided between the three pyramids. Senetep needs a lot of people if he's restarting his hybrid program and developing a cure for his legions. The central pyramid contains the mazes, tests, and main laboratories, while the other two are used for holding completed hybrids and livestock.'

'Livestock!' Arturo remarked. 'You mean human beings?'

'Please forgive my choice of words,' Nocao said with sincerity. 'Unfortunately, some of my kind still see you as a lesser life form.'

'Some?' Arturo snapped.

'Yes, like Senetep and his followers. But there's others, like myself, who believe you have a basic right to share this planet and live in freedom.'

Arturo calmed a little. 'What made you change your mind?'

'Sean Livingstone.'

The acknowledgment caught Sean off-guard, but he appreciated the compliment. 'So what's your plan?'

'We steal one of Senetep's vessels from the pyramid platform.'

'*Che cosa?*' Bella cried. 'That's impossible!'

'You want us to just sail right up there?' Arturo said with a look of incredulity. 'We'd be lucky to get within ten kilometres before being caught.'

'That's why we need to create a diversion.'

'What kind of diversion?' Sean asked.

'Like Arturo said, we sail right up there,' Nocao said with a mischievous smirk. He pointed to the fuel canisters. 'We place your combustible liquid at the front of the vessel and steer it straight at the pyramids. We hang a rope out the back to tow me underwater while you three jump off. When the vessel gets close enough, they'll scan for life forms and ignore it once they find no-one aboard. As it hits the pyramid and explodes, I can swim underwater to the landing platform. The distraction will give me time to steal a vessel and return to pick you up.'

There was a moment of silence and bewildered glances.

'Destroy the boat! *Che palle!*' Arturo cried.

Sean had never spoken a word of Italian in his life, but Arturo's emphatic '*What balls!*' response translated perfectly. He just couldn't work out if it was a compliment or profanity.

'I don't see what balls have to do with this plan,' Nocao said, looking quizzically around the deck.

Sean laughed.

'I hate that idea,' Bella said. 'If you get caught, we'll be left in the middle of the ocean.'

'It's crazy,' Arturo confirmed. 'This is our family boat. I'm not going to destroy it. If I knew you had a plan like this, I never would've come... I'm turning us around.'

He spun the steering wheel and the bow veered back to the port, but in the half hour they'd been gone, Ras El Bar's skyline had changed dramatically. Isharkute scout ships zipped through the atmosphere like flies buzzing over a carcass. Arturo snatched up the binoculars to survey the invasion. Nobody said a word. It was clear they couldn't return now. Arturo sighed with defeat.

Sean felt the urgency rising. Every wave they bounced over was bringing them closer to inevitable capture and death.

Nocao handed Bella the cube. 'Take this as insurance. I won't leave you behind.'

Arturo looked at Bella and the cube, then without a word, he spun the wheel and checked the compass, confirming their western alignment through the binoculars.

'So we're doing it?' Bella gasped.

'If there's one place I can look after you, it's in the water,' Arturo said confidently.

Bella nodded nervously.

Arturo raced across the deck and started preparing like a man possessed. Now committed to the plan, he was driven, focused, and unstoppable. It was easy to see why his family was so successful. He dragged a nylon rope from a storage compartment and tied it to a cleat on the rear balustrade, then sprang around the deck, assembling four piles of scuba-diving gear. He checked the air tanks. 'I only have three tanks of air left.'

'I don't need your breathing contraptions,' Nocao said. 'I can hold my breath as long as I need.'

Arturo glanced up. 'Lucky you!'

'It's not a matter of luck. My lungs have seventy-five per cent more capacity than yours,' Nocao said matter-of-factly.

'Is that so?' Arturo said, shaking his head and laughing to himself as he worked.

'Don't worry. You'll get used to the way he speaks,' Bella said.

Arturo smiled. 'Nocao, you'd make one helluva free diver!'

Sean kept an eye on the Isharkute pyramids while Arturo helped Bella into the scuba gear. A few minutes later, the three of them were sitting on the rear balustrade while Arturo gave them a quick lesson on how to use the air tank and regulator. Nocao listened in and picked up a flipper, curiously testing it against his foot.

'Looks about your size,' Sean said.

'Interesting. What is it, some kind of swimming aid?'

'Yeah, they're called flippers. They make you swim faster.'

Nocao pulled the flipper on and flapped it in the air. 'I can see how this would work. A simple but effective device. I'll use these flippers.'

'Glad we can help,' Sean said with a chuckle.

The pyramids now overshadowed the water like an ominous mountain range. They were close enough that Sean could see Isharkute vessels arriving and departing from the platforms stretching out from the south side of the pyramid. Several transports and hunter-craft were parked on the sea-level platforms.

Nocao stood up. 'That's it. We need to get off this vessel.'

Arturo stepped up to the helm and pushed the chrome throttle all the way forward. The engines roared to life, setting the boat on a collision course with the centre pyramid. He took one last remorseful look around the boat and trod solemnly back to the rear deck. They fitted their masks and breathing regulators. Arturo counted down from three with his fingers. On *one* they all flipped backwards into the trailing whitewash. Sean surfaced first, then Arturo and Bella. Bobbing in the water, they were already 30 metres behind the speeding boat.

They watched Nocao tie the rope around his waist and dive into the water. He didn't surface again.

The three of them tread water as the boat barrelled deep into the shadow of the pyramid. Several Isharkute vessels flew over to investigate and quickly left. Sean pulled off his mask and regulator to keep an eye on the boat with a pair of mini-binoculars. 'It's almost there...'

Moments later, there was a bright flash against the east side of the pyramid and a billowing cloud of black smoke.

Sean scanned the explosion with his binoculars. Thirty or more Isharkute warriors raced to the edge of the platform to watch the fiery death throes of the Bonaforte boat as it slid into the water. Ferocious blasts of escaping air and exploding tanks sent the flames a good 100 metres up the pyramid face. Sean scanned the nearby platform, an anxious knot building in the pit of his stomach. Where was Nocao? The blazing diversion was almost extinguished and several warriors returned to their watch.

Nocao suddenly slipped out of the water and hung off the edge of the platform, not far from the warriors. 'I see him!' Sean said with relief.

The boat's flaming stern was now vertical and sinking fast.

Nocao clambered onto the platform, ripped off his flippers, and skirted between two vessels as the boat succumbed to the ocean with a final blast of bubbles.

'He did it!' Sean said.

An Isharkute scout vessel lifted off the platform and skimmed across the sea towards them, creating a V-shaped plume of seawater in its wake. Within seconds, the vessel was upon them. It swerved to a complete stop, throwing up a spray of water. Nocao helped them aboard and closed the door.

Sean yanked off his scuba gear and took up the co-pilot's seat.

Nocao's fingers moved across the holographic controls with perfect dexterity. Sean was impressed. Even after 10,000 years in cryogenic sleep, Nocao didn't miss a beat.

'There's two hunter-craft on an intercept course,' Nocao said. He looked back at his passengers. 'Do you have the cube?'

Bella unclipped a pouch from her belt and withdrew the cube proudly.

'Hold onto something,' Sean said. 'This might get a little crazy.'

Arturo and Bella were wide-eyed with fascination; after all, they were riding in an alien spaceship for the first time. Nocao activated the clear-hull technology and the rear half of the vessel faded away like it wasn't there anymore. Bella gasped. Arturo pulled her towards the front half of the cabin.

'It's okay,' Sean said. 'I should've warned you. The hull's made from crystalline panels that can change opacity...sorta like a window.'

Arturo glared at him, still holding his sister tightly.

Bella pulled herself from Arturo's protective embrace and touched the invisible surface. 'It's like the Army interrogation cubes at Giza.' A blur of green-blue seawater whooshed beneath her fingers and her expression changed from fear to fascination.

Sean smiled to himself. It didn't seem that long ago when he experienced the same mind-bending revelations for the first time. Their vessel banked hard, wrenching him from his distractions. Two hunter-craft were coming up behind them, canons and harpoon nets ready to ensnare them.

Nocao plotted a course for the South African caves on the holographic map with one hand while piloting with the other.

'Can't they track us?' Sean asked.

'Not without those,' Nocao said, cocking his head towards a pile of broken crystalline shards at their feet.

Sean chuckled. 'You already hotwired it?'

'Of course!'

'Can I help?'

'Do you remember how to control the power conduits?'

'How could I forget?' Sean joked.

'Good. Let's see how fast we can go without overloading the power crystal.'

A holographic schematic appeared on the console in front of Sean. The conduits were already peaking orange-red, so he offset them into the cooler-looking blue ones. Their vessel received an immediate speed boost. The ocean's whitecaps zoomed beneath them in a dizzying blur as their speed approached supersonic, leaving the hunter-craft behind like passengers who just missed their train.

Bella stood behind Sean. 'How do you know what you're doing?'

'I've had some practice,' Sean said, eyes locked on the conduits.

The blue ocean transformed into a tapestry of verdant green fields as they flew over the Nile Delta. It quickly changed to yellow-orange over the blazing deserts of Egypt and Sudan, then back to green as they crossed the Democratic Republic of the Congo and its neighbouring countries. An entire continent passed beneath them in minutes.

Nocao slowed the vessel, bringing the blurred landscape into focus. They were flying along a rugged coastline dominated by primordial volcanic rocks and impenetrable cliffs. Thunderous waves pounded the shoreline in a shower of white. Beautiful and awe-inspiring, this forgotten corner of the world was unforgiving.

Sean became pensive, thinking how thousands of years ago, his dad lived along this coastline, sowing the seeds for a new world from the ashes of the old. His complete story was yet to be told, and hopefully their quest for the Ark would reveal his dad's final chapter.

Nocao flew them over the edge of a cliff and their vessel dipped into shadow. 'There's the cave.'

Sean shivered with anticipation. Goose bumps travelled up his arm. He was staring at the cave's entrance, a black opening tucked deep into the jagged rocks.

'We'll have to land on top of the cliff and climb down,' Nocao said.

Sean led the way outside as soon as they landed, eager to be first onto the steep path. Arturo and Bella talked excitedly as they followed, both revelling at the distances and speed they just travelled. Sean was too preoccupied to listen, his thoughts focused on what they might find in the cave.

He repeated the riddle in his head, trying to figure out what it meant: THE AGE OF WARNING BEGINS IN THE MORNING. Was it something his dad made up?

The roaring wind and crashing waves created wafts of sea mist up the cliff, making their path even more precarious and slippery. Sean reached the cave first. He waited impatiently for the others to join him before moving inside. The damp cave air enveloped them like a sodden blanket, muting the outside elements as though they'd crossed a portal into a silent underground dimension.

Nocao activated a handheld scanning device and illuminated the cave with the intensity of a dozen LED torches. The opening descended sharply and split into a network of caves and passages like catacombs. It was dank and depressing, but Sean could see how it was the perfect place to survive the volcanic storm, with enough space for Yeesha's tribe and a small number of hybrids.

'Stop!' Nocao said, lifting his scanner.

A series of sharp electrical *pops* echoed through the cave. Sean, Bella, and Arturo all jumped with fright. Sean noticed a pattern of small dome-shaped cameras nestled into the cracks and crevices, crackling and smoking like they'd just been fried by an electromagnetic pulse.

'What are they?' Bella asked.

'Alien tech?' Arturo said, poking one with his finger.

'No. They were put there by Azar Hawati to send a holographic image of this cave back to his base in Egypt,' Sean said.

'Azar Hawati, the Egyptian millionaire?!'

'Billionaire,' Sean corrected him. 'If it wasn't for his research, we wouldn't have found this cave so quickly.'

'He won't be watching this cave anymore,' Nocao said. 'Senetep's fleet will be monitoring every human broadcast and transmission. We can't afford to have our presence here broadcast straight to back Azar and Senetep.'

'Good thinking,' Sean said.

Nocao pointed to a dim wall ahead and Sean's heart skipped a beat. The Isharkute glyphs and ancient charcoal pictographs he'd seen in Azar's holographic recreation were now real. Basic stick-figure humans stood alongside a pair of taller figures with elongated heads – Nesuk and Rootuk – all in various depictions of daily life. His dad, the centaur, stood alongside them, helping with everything from fishing, cooking, and planting crops to building shelters.

Sean knelt and traced the drawings, wondering who painted them. His fingers reached the portion where part of the wall had fallen away, removing his dad from the timeline.

'What do we do now?' Arturo asked.

'THE AGE OF WARNING BEGINS IN THE MORNING,' Sean said to himself.

'What did you say?'

'Inside the cube there's three riddles. We think they're supposed to help us find the crystals. The first one says, "THE AGE OF WARNING BEGINS IN THE MORNING."'

'It's got something to do with dawn, then,' Bella said.

'The sun rises in the east,' Arturo said, turning to the cave opening. 'Maybe we missed something on our way in.'

'What about that?' Bella said, pointing to one of the smouldering cameras. It was tucked deep into a crevice above the entrance, right where they were looking.

'It's just one of Azar's cameras,' Sean said.

Arturo climbed the cave wall and reached over. He pried the camera from the crevice and accidentally cracked off a small section of the rock. 'Whoa! Look at this,' he said, rubbing away the dust to reveal an inscription of a circle with a squiggly line coming off it.

'That's the symbol for Leo!' Sean said. The discovery set his mind racing with new ideas. 'I think I get it now. THE AGE OF WARNING BEGINS IN THE MORNING refers to ten thousand, five hundred years ago when my dad and I first found the Isharkute. That's when the constellation of Leo was low on the horizon, like the rising sun.'

Arturo nodded. 'Makes sense, but how does that help us?'

Sean shrugged.

'What age are we in now?' Bella asked.

'We're living in the age of Pisces,' Sean said, glancing around the cave. 'I bet there's other symbols representing the different ages. If we find Pisces, it might be a clue to what we're meant to do now.'

Everyone spread out and searched the cave. Now that they knew what they were looking for, they quickly uncovered four more symbols, each carved into the upper section of the cave wall and hidden under thousands of years' worth of grime and soot.

'Cancer, Gemini, Taurus, and Aries,' Sean said, pointing to each new symbol. 'They're all in order, one after the other, leading up to here.' Sean was standing where the final symbol should be, right in front of the wall inscribed with Isharkute symbols and human pictographs. 'All we're missing is Pisces.'

'It should be up there,' Bella said.

'Maybe it's hidden in all these symbols and images.'

Nocao scanned the wall. 'Step back, Sean. There's something hidden behind the rock.'

Sean stood back. Nocao adjusted his scanner and pointed it at the wall. The device emitted a pulse of sound and the wall cracked in several places, then the whole thing collapsed at their feet in a swirl of dust, destroying every pictograph. Sean was horrified until he realised they were looking at the outline of a huge doorway etched into a smooth stone wall. The Isharkute glyphs were the only section of the original wall to survive and were now dead-centre of the door. Directly above the door was a previously unseen inscription made up of two curved lines intersected by a straight horizontal line.

'That's the symbol for Pisces!' Sean said.

Nocao scanned the wall. 'The original wall was a façade, built over the top to hide the door.'

Sean stepped over the fragments of his dad's pictographs and placed his hand on the wall. 'It looks like a door, but there's no handle or lever.'

Bella stood back to take it all in. 'What about that cross? What does that mean?'

'I don't see anything.'

'It's just below the Pisces symbol on the top of the door.'

Sean shook his head. 'Where?'

'You don't see that? There's a cross shape – it's really faint, but it's there.'

Nocao rubbed away the dust left over from the false wall. 'You're right. There's a cross-shaped marking painted on the stone.'

'I still don't see it,' Sean said.

'Neither can I,' Arturo said, leaning in for a closer look.

'You need enhanced vision to see what's left of the original pigments,' Nocao said, shooting Bella a sideways smirk. She smiled back, like they were sharing a private joke.

Nocao pressed the glyph sequence into the cube and it unfolded into a flat cross.

'It looks the same size,' Bella said.

'Must be the way to open it!' Arturo added.

Nocao held the cross over the marking and it snapped to the stone like a magnet. A sliver of blue light traced along the outline of the door, starting at the bottom and coming up each side simultaneously. The lines met in the centre at the top of the door and it shuddered to life, retracting into the wall with a rumble.

The four of them stood there, staring into the inky-black passage.

Sean took the first step forward.

'Wait!' Bella whispered. 'What if it's a trap?'

'We're meant to find this,' Sean said confidently.

He continued inside. The short passageway widened into a featureless circular chamber. A stone pedestal rose from the centre of the floor, adorned with a glowing crystal shard.

'We solved the first riddle,' Sean said. 'That's one of the three crystal keys!' Sean said.

He reached for the shard and paused, suddenly realising he was about to embark on the greatest archaeological quest ever – one that would test the faith of millions of people around the world.

To denounce or question someone's religion was not something to be done lightly. His hand trembled over the tiny flat shard. He was about to rewrite history.

Sean cleared his mind and plucked the shard free. Its blue glow faded.

Nocao detached the cross from the stone door and placed it on the pedestal. 'Let's see what happens when we put the shard inside the cube.'

One of the three empty slots was a perfect fit for the crystal.

Sean took a deep breath and placed the shard in position. It triggered a hologram that filled the centre of the room. His breath caught in his throat as the opaque blue image of his dad stood before him, shimmering like a ghost.

'Hello, Sean,' Henry said with a warm smile. 'If you're seeing me now, that means you've found the cube and the first of three crystals, so well done.'

'Thanks,' Sean whispered under his breath. His dad looked older and world-wearier, but there was an enlightened optimism in his eyes.

'By now you'll have learnt things didn't exactly go the way we planned – but I guess that's no surprise after everything we've been through. Hopefully for you it's only been a few days since we last saw each other. I've been living here for eighteen months, and to be honest, it feels like forever since I said goodbye to you. Pity this is only a one-way line of communication.'

Sean wanted to reach out and comfort his dad, but the hologram was only an echo embedded inside an ancient recording.

'If you've read the inscriptions on the door, then you know you have to find the Ark and activate the beacon before Senetep destroys them. The clues we've left you at your next two destinations will have been interpreted, rewritten, and changed by the cultures that came after us. But read between the lines and you'll uncover the truth. Work with Nocao – you'll need each other's help. The future of our planet relies on our two species working together. We've done it before and can do it again. It's up to both of you to lead the way –

set an example for the new world. We believe in you. I'll leave more messages for you along the way. And remember, unlike my future, yours isn't written yet.'

Sean felt like he'd just awoken from a dream. The surprise hologram had rattled his emotions, but with the promise of further messages, he was even more anxious to solve the second riddle and unlock the next key.

His dad's hologram transformed into a topographical map of their current location. It zoomed out and across the globe, finally settling on a small isolated island in the middle of the South Pacific Ocean.

'Easter Island!' Arturo said.

'That's where we'll find the next key,' Nocao said.

Sean was familiar with the history of the island. He'd been fascinated with the enormous stone heads called 'moai' since he was old enough to read. Was it fate or coincidence that Easter Island – or Rapa Nui, as it was traditionally known – was also home to an ancient birdman religion and cult? His well-concealed wings tingled with the promise it might have something to do with him.

# — CHAPTER 14 —

# *Purification*

Azar was strapped face down on the operating table, the binds so tight across his shoulderblades he could barely draw breath. Malik was strapped on the adjacent table, his shirt already torn from his body, exposing his bare back. His son was about to have his vertebrae broken and tapped with giant needles for his cerebrospinal fluid. Malik stared at him, eyes wide in terror. Azar wished he had something comforting to say in their last moments together. He should never have brought him on this mission. The Isharkute scientists huddled around Malik, breaking their gaze.

In that moment, Azar knew he only needed to say one word: *Sorry.*

Now it was too late.

A tall, spindly Isharkute entered the chamber in a hurry. 'Overseer Senetep, one of our scout vessels was just stolen from the main platform.'

Azar craned his head to follow the commotion, recognising Commander Nefaro from Senetep's worldwide telecast. His stooped and skinny body was counterbalanced by his striking pale-blue eyes.

'Show me,' Senetep demanded.

Nefaro activated a surveillance hologram of Nocao stealing the scout vessel. He slowed the footage and zoomed in on the vessel as it hovered over the sea. Nocao could be seen dragging Sean Livingstone, along with a young man and woman, from the water.

Azar wriggled against his binds for a clearer view. The young man's tanned and youthful face seemed familiar somehow. He'd never met him personally, but was certain he'd had something to do with him in the past. *That's it!* The young man was Arturo Bonaforte, the son of Marco and Francesca, owners and operators of the Bonaforte Salvage Company. They were regarded as one of the best in the business. He'd hired them when a legitimate front was needed for his ocean operations. Every member of Marco's crew, including his family, had been personally vetted and approved by himself. Although she wasn't part of the usual Bonaforte salvage crew, he figured the young woman was Arturo's sister, Bella. The netted pouch hanging from her diving belt contained the Isharkute cube. His heart thumped with excitement – this was the exact leverage he needed.

Nefaro paused the playback. 'Once the navigational crystals were tampered with, we were unable to track them,' he said sheepishly. 'We're conducting a search of the surrounding oceans and continents –'

'They're on their way to the Cave of Myth,' Azar proclaimed from his table.

Senetep, Nefaro, and Vogran spun around simultaneously. His comment had caught their undivided attention, but it was at the expense of revealing the Ark, something he'd hoped to keep to himself.

Senetep approached. 'What do you know about the Cave of Myth?'

'Let me and my men go...and I'll tell you everything.'

Senetep signalled the scientists to release his binds. 'We'll start with you first. If your information's worthwhile, I'll release your men.'

Azar hopped off the bench and straightened his collar and cuffs. 'Eighteen months ago, I discovered a cave on the South African coast filled with Isharkute glyphs and human pictographs. These inscriptions named it the Cave of Myth and detailed how a volcanic cataclysm forced your people to leave Earth. But two Isharkute remained and worked with humanity to restart civilisation. They learnt how your commanders sabotaged the Isharkute fleet so you could return and take over the world...but they put a safeguard in place to stop you.'

'Go on,' Senetep said, narrowing his eyes with suspicion.

'We found an Isharkute cube hidden within a collapsed section of the cave wall, a key that will reveal a hidden device. Humanity knows it as a religious relic called the Ark of the Covenant, but it's really a power source built to activate a beacon, one that can wake the rest of the Isharkute fleet. That's why you've been destroying ancient sites, trying to stop this transmitter from ever turning on.'

Senetep scowled. 'Where is this cube now?'

Azar hesitated, realising he'd have to admit his embarrassing mistake. 'Sean and Nocao stole the cube from my labs. The girl seen in your surveillance footage is Bella Bonaforte – she has the cube hanging off her belt. If you let my men go, I'll give you the coordinates for the cave.'

'Azar Hawati, in spite of your ineptitude, you've proven to be of some usefulness,' Senetep said.

Azar nodded dutifully. The scientists released Malik and his soldiers from the operating tables. Malik picked up his torn shirt and put it back on.

'First Commander Vogran, take a squadron of our best warriors and intercept Sean Livingstone at this Cave of Myth,' Senetep instructed. 'Retrieve the cube. Kill the others...but bring me Sean alive.'

Vogran nodded and marched out of the laboratory.

'Azar, in the meantime, you'll speak to your people, pacify the thousands awaiting processing. Many resist, preferring to die than commit to our experiments. Their defiance is arduous and time-consuming. They must understand we're their masters. They have no rights. No freedom. Their lives are no more important than the very animals they slaughter for food. Succeed in this first task, and you can have the limited freedom you requested.'

Azar breathed a sigh of relief as the guards escorted them from the lab. No human had made it out of Senetep's pyramid intact, without a tail or snout. He'd garnered a small amount of influence with the Overseer, but in the process, had given away his sole claim to the Ark. At least he was alive, and with every living breath, he still had a chance to turn this around in his favour.

'It's impossible!' Malik whispered, sidling up to him. 'What do you say to people who're about to die?'

Azar had no idea. His son was right – there was nothing he could say. There was no hope or comfort in what his fellow Egyptians were about to face. All he could rely on was his talent to make people see things his way. Over the years, he'd persuaded everyone from politicians to CEOs and archaeologists to mercenaries. His clandestine empire was built upon his innate ability to convince people to believe in him, even when his intentions were shady and nefarious. In this darkest hour, he needed to give the Egyptian people something to cling to. They needed hope.

The warriors directed them through a passage and onto a gantry high above the crowds of captured civilians. Senetep and Nefaro were waiting for them.

'You will address your world from here,' Senetep said.

Azar peered over the edge at the crowds below. 'Why have you captured so many of us?'

'It's a strict selection process – we need the finest specimens your country has to offer. The sick or physically inferior are discarded and any healthy specimens not selected for harvesting will enter the trials for my hybrid program.'

'Why is it just Egyptians?'

'Simple geography – you're closest to my labs,' Senetep said. His tone was growing impatient. 'Subdue your people with whatever lies or misdirection necessary.'

Azar had never negotiated for anyone other than himself. Yet here he was, on the threshold of negotiating the future of thousands. 'As I see it, there's only one way to alleviate the panic and disorder.'

'How?'

'By assuring them this isn't genocide; that they're not being slaughtered mercilessly.'

'I'm taking what's rightfully mine, this is genocide.'

'If you look at human history, that course of action has never gone down well. It's been the greatest causes of war and suffering. We must show them we're working towards a future of mutual understanding.'

'Not while I'm Overseer!'

Azar's mouth was dry with fear. He was pushing Senetep to the brink of his razor-thin patience. Common sense told him to back off, but there was a weakness in Senetep's physical demeanour. His right hand trembled for a moment, just like someone with Alzheimer's disease. Senetep put his hand behind his back, hiding it from view. Was it the affliction affecting his species? If Senetep was sick, then time was against him.

Azar took a deep breath and seized the opportunity. 'By my estimates, humans outnumber Isharkute at least a thousand to one. You have the firepower and technology to eradicate us, but you can't because you need us. How will your limited forces cope when there's a coordinated worldwide rebellion? Your warriors down there were only just keeping the prisoners in line when we arrived. What would you do on a larger scale? Globally, your forces must be stretched to their limits. I guarantee you, there's millions of people already in hiding, regrouping, preparing to attack. Can your warriors sustain a drawn-out fight with their sickness?'

Senetep didn't respond.

Azar knew that beneath his cool demeanour, the Overseer was bristling with anger. Dealing with a human being had to be a demoralising experience. 'I can make things easier for you, but you should show a degree of mercy.'

'Explain.'

'Instead of eliminating the sick and weak, release them. They pose no threat to you. Then I suggest you slow down the number of Egyptians being processed. If human DNA holds a potential cure, then it would make sense to sample a broader spectrum from races from all over the world.'

'I'm not wasting my resources bringing other humans here.'

'You don't have to - I can coordinate their transport using human ships and planes.'

Senetep pondered his request for a moment before responding. 'Address your people and feed them whatever false hope is necessary to placate them. We'll send the inferior specimens back to the mainland instead of feeding them to the sharks. Depending on the quality of specimens you deliver, we will return the same number of your precious Egyptians. Coordinate your deliveries with Commander Nefaro.'

Azar acknowledged Nefaro with a nod.

'Now it's time to broadcast your address to this world.'

Azar had no time to prepare. He was good at thinking on his feet, but this was the ultimate test: the immediate fate of thousands, if not millions, rested on his speech. He slicked his hair back and straightened his collar and tie. His years of operating behind closed doors were now over. He was about to become the face of hope for humanity.

A metallic sphere appeared from somewhere above and hovered in front of him. He could see his distorted reflection in the lens. He drew a deep breath and centred himself – one wrong word and Senetep wouldn't hesitate to kill him in front of the world.

'People of Earth, my name is Azar Hawati. For those of you who don't know me, I'm an Egyptian entrepreneur, innovator, and part-time archaeologist. Today, I've succeeded where our leaders failed and have successfully negotiated with the Isharkute. Overseer Senetep has asked me to speak for the entire human race. Unfortunately, their invasion and attack was inevitable, an offensive move that we forced upon them. They've been watching us for a very long time. We've become a warmongering, dangerously unpredictable species, poisoning our planet with pollution and gorging ourselves on its resources. From their perspective, our self-obsessed societies looked far from welcoming. But I implore you, as bad as things appear right now, we must lay down our arms and embark on a mission of peace and communication. The Isharkute are not here to eradicate us, but rather, study us. Over the last decade, I've funded archaeological teams that have uncovered proof of their existence. They've visited Earth countless times throughout history and paved the way for our ancestors and first civilisations to flourish. Our species are related in ways that will eventually open our minds and our understanding of life throughout the universe.'

Azar glanced sideways at Senetep. The Overseer hadn't moved. His pitch to sell out humanity was working and he hadn't overstepped the line...at least, not yet.

'To begin this new alliance, Overseer Senetep has agreed to accept a convoy from each country of their finest minds to his pyramid here in the Mediterranean Sea. Volunteers must be physically fit and ready to embrace new ways of thinking. They'll be the pioneers of our intergalactic future...in short, our saviours.'

Azar held his earnest expression as the recording sphere flew away.

'Now we'll see if your words carry any weight,' Senetep said.

Nefaro's attention was drawn to the data crystal in his hand. 'First Commander Vogran's secured the Cave of Myth, but Sean Livingstone and his companions have already left.'

*   *   *

Twenty minutes later Azar, Malik, and his men were standing at the entrance to the cave, having flown at incredible speeds in Isharkute transport vessels. Azar suddenly realised this was only his second visit to the cave since its discovery. Stepping inside, the evidence of Sean's visit presented like the aftermath of careless tomb robbers. His carefully placed spatial mapping cameras were burnt out and inoperable. The wall of ancient pictographs lay scattered over the cave floor, crumpled and trodden on. Beyond the chaos was a new circular-shaped chamber with an empty stone pedestal, unfortunately plundered of its treasure.

Azar ran his hand along the smooth chamber wall, imagining the thrill of being the first to make the discovery. He felt a pang of jealously towards Sean; the teenager was living an archaeologist's dream...his dream!

'Where have they gone?' Senetep said, following him inside. The

Overseer's formidable presence stifled the chamber.

'I'm not sure yet,' Azar said. He approached the pedestal and slid his fingers over the empty impression. 'They took a small crystal from here – the first of the cube's three keys.'

'You discovered this cave first, yet you were outsmarted by a child.'

'Maybe not entirely outsmarted,' Azar said, peering back out the passage to the cave. He slid past Senetep and looked for one of his cameras in the cave wall. 'My cameras are heavily shielded. If one of them still works, we'll have a recording of everything that happened here.'

Senetep motioned his warriors to step aside, allowing Malik and the soldiers access to the cave walls. They set to work, carefully extracting each camera from the nooks and cracks. Most fell apart in their hands, except for one tucked deep into a crevice.

'I think this one's still working!' Malik called.

Nefaro scanned the camera with some kind of crystalline device the size of a phone, instantly accessing the library of folders and recorded images. Azar shared a concerned look with Malik. It was frightening how quick the Isharkute could break through their firewalls and military-grade encryption. Nothing was secret.

'That's it,' Azar said, pointing to the top image.

Nefaro activated the file and projected it as a hologram. Sean, Nocao, Bella, and Arturo could be seen entering the cave. Nocao held up a bright light and the image suddenly pixelated, then skipped ahead in time. Snippets of scrambled, indecipherable dialogue accompanied the images. One second Sean and his friends were standing in front of the wall, the next the wall was gone and they'd moved inside the newly revealed chamber with an ethereal blue light filling the cave. Azar thought he saw Henry Livingstone hovering over Sean like a ghost. The image sent a chill down his spine, but in the same moment, another filled him with excitement. 'Stop, freeze the image!'

Nefaro paused the hologram.

The image only lasted a single frame, but it was enough. Sean and his friends were standing around a holographic map of a remote volcanic island. It was a coastline he recognised instantly.

'That's it! They're headed to Easter Island.'

# CHAPTER 15

# Easter Island

The island first appeared as a speck on the horizon, dwarfed by the sky and isolated by the ocean. Easter Island was the remains of three long-extinct volcanoes. Sean had little time to prepare before their arrival, cramming in as much information as he could read and mentally process. Their scout ship had direct access to everything the Isharkute had downloaded from the internet since their invasion, including private and government servers from all over the world. Sean had more data at his fingertips than ever before, but all he needed to know was where the next key was located. The only clue they had was the second riddle inside the cube: HIDDEN FROM VIEW FROM THOSE WHO FLEW.

Sean figured the answer was connected to the history of the island. The ancient traditions of the birdman cult were the logical place to start and surely more than a coincidence, considering he could fly.

The island's original people held a contest where selected members of the tribe would dive off the sheer cliffs and swim out to the islet of Motu Nui, braving sharks and dangerous rip tides on tiny reed mats. Contestants would hide in the island's caves, waiting to steal the first egg of the season from the sooty terns, the long-winged seabirds that nested on the rocky islet. The successful contestant would swim back to the main island and present the egg to their sponsor, usually an elder, who would win the position of tribal leader for the coming year.

Sean wondered if the tradition was a misinterpretation of an original story – a set of instructions about how to find the second crystal. As his dad said, the original message would be interpreted, rewritten, and changed by the cultures after him. He needed to read between the lines and find the truth. Could the egg represent the second crystal? Was it buried on Motu Nui? Indecipherable petroglyphs had been found all over the island from a long-forgotten writing system known as Rongorongo. Were they an encoded message from his dad?

Sean took a break and looked up. After speeding across the South Atlantic Ocean, Argentina, Chile, and the Pacific Ocean, they were approaching Rapa Nui from the east. The white tips of breaking waves were now visible, crashing against the rock-strewn shoreline.

'Where do you want me to land?' Nocao asked.

'The southwestern tip of the island – there's an old settlement called Orongo,' Sean said. 'We should start looking there.'

Nocao veered left and followed the coastline south. The majestic faces of the moai statues appeared like a race of giants. Their broad noses, deep-set eye sockets, and rectangular heads had been carved from a dark volcanic rock. Some stood in rows close to the beach, backs to the sea, facing inland as if shunning unwelcome visitors. The solemn eyes stared at them with a worldly wisdom, like the guardians of a culture that had vanished like the trees that once populated the island. Further inland, the scattered statues protruded from the green slopes, facing nothing but grass and rock from the lowest plain to the highest peak.

'What's in Orongo?' Bella asked.

'It's the ruins of the old village,' Sean said. 'Orongo was the ceremonial centre of a birdman cult. I'm hoping there's a clue to the next crystal.'

'I've heard about this before,' Arturo said. 'The Rapa Nui people used to swim out to a small island and steal a bird's egg. They did it every year until their culture was wiped out by European invaders.'

'So you're going to swim out to an island and steal an egg?' Bella said. 'How's that supposed to help us find the crystal?'

'I'm not going to swim when I can –' Sean paused, realising

Arturo had no idea he could fly. It would be weird to mention it so casually in mid-conversation. 'I, umm... I thought it might have something to do with me.'

'Why?' Arturo asked.

'Because he's the birdman,' Nocao said bluntly. 'Sean's assumption makes sense and Orongo seems like the logical place to start, considering he can fly.'

'*Aspetta!*' Arturo said, shaking his head as if waking from a dream. 'Did you just say "fly"?'

Sean nodded gingerly.

Arturo laughed in disbelief. 'Like Superman?'

'Not like Superman,' Sean replied.

'Then how?'

Reluctantly, Sean released his wings. They slipped through the holes in his t-shirt and spread out behind him, filling the cabin from end to end, shimmering like enormous silken dragonfly wings.

Arturo stumbled against the hull, mouth hanging open in awe.

Sean felt the heat rise in his face. Arturo's reaction was embarrassing, especially in front of Bella. It was a harsh reminder of how different he was now. He wasn't just an average teenager anymore – he was a freak. 'The Isharkute gave me wings to save my life,' he said defensively.

Arturo picked himself up, keeping slightly more distance between them.

Nocao turned off the coast and flew inland. The gentle grassy plains transformed into steep slopes and rugged cliffs as they ascended to the peak of Rano Kau, one of three volcanoes making up the island. The collapsed crater had formed a sprawling kilometre-wide caldera that dominated the southernmost tip of the island. One side of the mighty ridge sloped into a freshwater marsh; the opposite side was a sheer 300-metre drop onto the raging coastline.

They landed in the middle of the Orongo ruins, an isolated settlement built upon the furthest tip of the caldera. Sean led the way outside, where the gale-force wind almost lifted them off their feet. The sheer cliffs and endless expanse of deep blue water painted an incredible vista. Orongo was a village on the edge of the world.

The stone ruins were a collection of circular, windowless dwellings with low-set doors. Their soil and grass roofs gave the impression they were a natural part of the landscape. The structures were originally built for the contestants of the birdman race, to protect them from the extreme weather. Sean knew there was nothing to find inside them after they had been restored by the local authorities and visited by numerous tourists over the years. Any artefacts or valuable clues were long gone.

Sean was drawn to the edge of the cliff overlooking the rocky islet of Motu Nui and its smaller cousin, Motu Iti. Between the two islets stood the sea stack Motu Kao Kao, a pointed rocky peak jutting out of the ocean like the pitted blade of an ancient dagger.

'What now?' Nocao shouted over the howling wind.

'I should fly down there and imagine what it was like to be part of the birdman contest. It might give me an idea or clue – something we can't see from here.'

'Don't take too long,' Bella said.

'Yeah, we're like sitting ducks up here,' Arturo said.

Nocao turned to Arturo with a perplexed look. 'Your continual references to animals is unusual. I understand why you called me Fish Head – due to the oblong shape and colour of my head – but I don't see how you can compare us to plump feathered ducks.'

Sean laughed. 'It's a figure of speech. He means there's nowhere to hide up here.'

'*Certamente*, there's nowhere to hide, period! We're standing on the most barren and exposed island in the whole Pacific Ocean,' Arturo said. 'Just find the crystal!'

Sean dove off and was sucked into the gusts buffeting off the cliff face. He dove straight down until the salty mists sprayed his face, then pulled up and skimmed above the pounding waves. A kilometre out, he circled the sea stack of Motu Kao Kao like a local seabird. There was nothing on the rock except an extraordinary amount of stark-white bird poo. He flew further out and landed on

Motu Nui, peering back at Orongo. Nocao, Bella, and Arturo were now just hazy specks on the volcano rim.

Sean looked around. There wasn't much on the weathered islet, just windblown grass, craggy rocks, and a few disgruntled seabirds. They squawked at him as he inspected the weather-beaten rocks. He tread lightly, worried that he might step on a nest full of eggs. After reading about the birdman cult and lives lost in pursuit of the eggs, he couldn't shake the feeling he was trespassing on sacred ground. He soon realised there weren't any clues on the surface. The next step was to investigate the caves honeycombing the edges of the islet. He launched off, scattering a family of sooty terns.

Circling the islet, Sean spotted multiple caves set into the jagged ledges. Some were barely wide enough to crawl into, while others were gaping dark fissures. The riddle repeated through his mind: HIDDEN FROM VIEW FROM THOSE WHO FLEW. In a way, these caves fit the riddle. The birdman contestants wouldn't have been able to see them from Orongo.

Sean glided through the largest opening and landed deep inside an expansive cave. The elevated ledge was dry and protected from the swell rolling below the mouth of the cave. He waited for his eyes to adjust to the dim light before exploring further. Birdman contestants who'd made the treacherous swim often waited in caves like this for the sooty tern's eggs. Deeper inside the cave, he found a petroglyph carved into the wall. The wide face, goggle-styled eyes, small protruding ears, and long nose reminded him of a child's drawing in its simplicity. It was Makemake, the chief god of the birdman cult. Sean paused. The name seemed familiar to him, and not because he'd just read about the birdman cult. It felt like a potential clue hovering in the recesses of his mind, tantalisingly just out of reach.

Further inside, he found a sequence of petroglyphs. Above these were a collection of ancient paintings stretching across the cave ceiling, high and out of reach to visitors. The face of Makemake stared down at him yet again, this time surrounded by strange symbols and circling birdmen.

Sean was so captivated that he didn't realise Nocao, Bella, and Arturo were now all standing beside him. Their vessel was parked on the ledge behind him, their approach drowned out by the crashing ocean.

'What are you doing here?'

'You were taking too long,' Nocao said.

'Did you find anything?' Bella asked.

Nocao held a light to the ceiling, revealing the entire breadth of the paintings. There were hundreds of birdmen circling the face of Makemake, many more than Sean had seen in the darkness.

'*Bellissimo!*' Bella gasped.

'What does it mean?' Arturo asked. 'Are there any clues to the second crystal?'

Sean wished it was, but couldn't see how this was connected to the riddle. The birdmen contestants had obviously been inside these caves, so they weren't hidden from view. Where would they go from here? Maybe one of the hundreds of stone statues back on Easter Island had something to do with the crystal.

Bella pointed to a circle painted amongst the birdmen, directly beneath the face of Makemake. 'Is that an egg?'

'Eggs aren't perfectly round,' Arturo said.

Nocao followed the painting with his light. 'There's another circle below it; this one's blue.'

'Looks like Makemake's dropping eggs for the birdmen to catch,' Bella said.

'They're not eggs,' Arturo insisted.

'How do you know? Are you an expert in ancient Polynesian art?'

'No, but neither are you! Just because you go to a fancy art school in Paris doesn't mean you know everything about art.'

Nocao pointed to a third circle. It was larger than the first two and pale in colour. Sean followed the line of circles straight down. The next circle made his heart skip a beat. It was artistically camouflaged between the fluttering birdmen and encircled by a distinctive ring.

'They're planets,' Sean declared, pointing to the ringed planet. 'Look, that's Saturn.' Further down the painting was an even larger sphere with a red eye. 'And this one has Jupiter's storm.'

Nocao illuminated the line of planets emerging from the painting. They were all there. Mars, Earth, Venus, and finally, Mercury. The birdmen petered out after Mercury, leaving blank, unpainted rock.

'Where's the sun?' Bella asked, rubbing her hand over wall.

Sean wondered if this was his dad sending him a clue. The painting couldn't be that old – probably a few hundred years at most. His dad would have visited the island thousands of years before to hide the crystal. It didn't add up. He tried to think the same way his dad did. How would you send a message through time, one that was bound to be changed or misinterpreted? It had to be simple, yet something unique to them and hard for anyone else to understand. Something that could eventually become the legend of the island. This painting had too many coincidences not to be a message. His dad knew he loved astronomy, but how would a simple map of the solar system help? Why was there no sun?

Nocao scanned the wall, flicking between infrared and X-ray. No false walls or hidden compartments. Nothing. As far as Sean could tell, there was only the natural volcanic rock.

'What are you looking for?' Arturo said.

'Are we missing part of the painting?' Bella added. 'There should a sun, right?'

Sean followed the line of planets back up to the face of Makemake. Suddenly it came to him, as if the god spoke directly to him. 'That's it! I know why Makemake sounds familiar.'

Bella and Arturo looked at him expectantly, waiting for him to continue.

'It's a dwarf planet in the Kuiper Belt, I know it from astronomy. This is a map of our solar system.'

'No kidding!' Arturo said. 'Lots of ancient cultures associated their gods with stars and planets. I don't see how it helps.'

'This painting suggests the ancient Rapa Nui people knew about the dwarf planet, but that's impossible because it can't be seen by the naked eye and wasn't discovered until 2005. The astronomers who found it named it Makemake because they found it during Easter...that's its connection to Easter Island.'

'How did the Rapa Nui people find the planet if they couldn't see it?' Bella said.

'They didn't.'

'Then how did they know about it?'

'My dad,' Sean replied. 'It's the clue we've been looking for.'

'That's not a clue, it's just an interesting fact that doesn't lead us anywhere,' Arturo said.

Sean sighed, admitting it didn't immediately help them.

'What if it's like the other cave and there's parts of the painting we can't see?' Bella said.

'You're right,' Nocao said. He adjusted the parameters of his scanner and the image changed wavelengths, suddenly revealing the missing sun and a line of Isharkute inscriptions. It was like shining ultraviolet light on invisible ink.

'Wow! Look at that,' Sean said.

'You can thank me later,' Bella remarked.

Nocao translated the inscription. 'Makemake stands on Earth as he does in the sky. His original name will point the way.'

'That's the clue to the crystal,' Sean said.

'Sí, but what's Makemake's original name?' Arturo said.

Sean's crash course on Easter Island before their arrival didn't mention an original name for Makemake. There wasn't much known about the deity because the Rapa Nui culture had been deliberately erased by European settlers. Other than being the creator of humanity and a god of fertility, Makemake was predominantly the chief god of the birdman cult, represented by a man with a bird's head. Sean examined the alignment of planets, following each one until his eyes met Makemake. He thought about the name, not as a god, but a planet. If his dad had left an astronomy clue, this had to be it. Then it came to him – the answer was so obvious. 'I've got it! Before planets are officially named by astronomers, they're given a number.'

'What's its number?' Nocao asked.

'I can't remember – access it through your scanner.'

Nocao entered the information. 'Here it is! Before the planet was named Makemake it was designated with the number 136472.'

'Is that a code for something?' Arturo said.

'They sound like coordinates,' Bella added.

'There's not enough numbers – you need degrees, minutes, and seconds –'

'That's for human coordinates,' Nocao said, keying the numbers into his device. 'But the numbers work for Isharkute coordinates... and point to a position on the northeast of Easter Island.' He held up his device for everyone to see the flashing point on the map.

Sean was bursting with confidence. It was evident the crystals could only be found if human and Isharkute worked together. It was obviously a safeguard put in place by his dad and Nesuk all those millennia ago, avoiding premature discovery by archaeologists and explorers who visited the cave before them.

Nocao flew them back to the island using the new coordinates and landed beside Ahu Tongariki, the largest assembly of moai on the island. The fifteen nonchalant statues stood side-by-side in a straight line, silent custodians of the next crystal. He directed them up a rock embankment onto a platform of stone called "ahu." The large rectangular stones that formed the base of the ahu were monolithic in size, a scale of construction Sean had only seen used by the Isharkute.

Sean's stomach churned with anticipation. The moai towered over them, several storeys in height and weighing tonnes. He placed his hand on the eroded volcanic stone. Up close, the details in the stonework were more apparent. The moai's slender arms and hands cradled its stomach with spindly, alien-looking fingers. He counted the fingers, almost expecting there to be six digits instead of five, but the moai clearly represented the human form. The statues hadn't always stood in these exact positions after being toppled by civil wars and tsunamis.

He saw Bella standing in front of the next moai, hand on the stone just his, looking up in awe at the weather-beaten face.

Sean found himself unable to take his eyes off her. His pulse quickened and his palms became sweaty. In all the chaos, he'd forgotten how beautiful she was, but more than that, she was a kindred spirit, captivated and enthralled by the ancient moai just like him.

'Hurry up!' Arturo cried.

Bella caught Sean staring at her. '*Cosa?*'

'Nothing, let's go,' he said, spinning around to hide his embarrassment.

'These are the exact coordinates,' Nocao said, stopping in front of the largest moai, an 86-tonne behemoth – the biggest erected on the island.

'Of course, we should have guessed,' Bella said. 'It's under the biggest one here.'

'What now?' Arturo said, pushing against the moai. 'Do we have to move it?'

Sean walked behind the statue, inspecting its heavily weathered surface. There were ancient markings and tattoos etched into the stone, but they were so worn and covered in white lichen that it was hard to decipher their original form. Nocao's scanner suddenly emitted a loud continuous beep.

Sean sprinted around the moai. 'Did you find something?'

Nocao looked out to the sea. 'No, but someone's found us!'

# — CHAPTER 16 —

# *Betrayal*

Sean felt panic rise through his body like a volcano about to erupt. The pair of approaching Isharkute vessels grew larger by the second, swooping across the ocean, creating massive plumes of seawater in their wake. Sean struggled to think straight. They were so close to finding the second crystal, but they'd run out of time.

'It's a scout vessel and hybrids transport,' Nocao said.

'Oh great!' Bella cried. 'I hate those giant snakes.'

'We need to come back for the crystal,' Arturo said.

'No!' Sean said sharply. His growing desperation was impossible to hide. 'We're so close. If we leave now, we'll never get near this island again. The crystal's somewhere around this moai. We need to keep searching.'

'Okay, let's stop talking and start looking,' Bella said.

Sean flew over the top of the moai while everyone scoured the platform. He ran his hands over the rough volcanic stone. There were no markings or evidence of any hidden compartments.

'There's nothing here,' Sean shouted.

'Nothing here either!' Arturo called back.

The scout vessel whooshed overhead. Sean ducked and watched it circle higher up the mountain. The hybrids transport landed on the nearby coastline and lowered its side panels to the sand. Two giant crabs crawled out sideways, kicking up half the beach with their powerful legs. Their blood-red shells were the size of tanks and just as armoured. Their eight legs blended into a mesmerising yellow at the tip, creating the impression they were super-hot. The crabs froze, and in unison, eyestalks protruded from their shells like a pair of periscopes. They raised their enormous pincers and snapped at the air, sending an unsettling clacking sound over the island.

'Hybrids!' Nocao shouted. 'Get back to the vessel. Now!'

'What about the crystal?' Sean said, landing beside him. 'It must be under this moai.' He gave the immovable statue a token push.

'We're not waiting around to be turned into crab food,' Arturo bellowed, pulling Bella towards their vessel.

'Arturo's right,' Nocao said. 'We don't have any weapons. We have to think of something else.'

'Sean, hurry up!' Bella shrieked.

Sean knew they were right, but he wasn't willing to give up yet. He looked back at the crabs, zigzagging left and right towards them. Although their legs carried them with lightning speed, they couldn't run in a forward direction to their target. Their unique sideways running style presented an opportunity.

'I've got an idea!' Sean called after them.

Before anyone could protest, he launched towards the beach, baiting the crabs away from his friends and into the waves. The crabs barrelled through the surf with an explosion of seawater, furiously clacking their pincers up at him. One of the crabs arched back on two legs and exposed its underside. Sean couldn't believe what he was seeing. There were six human arms reaching out for him, and between them all was a human face, fused within the fleshy underbelly of the crab. The tortured-looking face appeared to be screaming at him, yet there was no noise coming from his mouth. The six arms pulled open the crab's belly, releasing a pair of gooey tentacles.

'Urgh!' Sean gagged. Could this thing get any uglier?

He flew higher, barely evading the impossibly long tentacles latching out for him. He peered towards the island, making sure his friends were safely in the vessel, and then flew towards the row of moai. He lined up with the largest statue, baiting the crabs to follow as he swooped in and hovered in position. If he timed his escape just right, the crabs would crash into the statue and knock it over, doing the hard work for him and revealing what was hiding underneath. Hopefully it was the second crystal.

The crabs criss-crossed the beach towards him, pincers snapping and clacking. Sean suddenly noticed two Isharkute approaching from the transport, staves aimed in his direction...

*Boom!*

The first energy blast ricocheted off the moai behind him, tossing him through the air in a whirlwind of stinging debris. Ears ringing, he somehow managed to stay airborne, but the near-miss had cost him.

The crabs were coming in from both sides.

Seconds from impact.

Sean shot straight up, leaving the crabs to slam into each other at full speed. The impact flipped one onto its back, leaving it struggling helplessly, trying to right itself with its impossibly short legs. The other crab was knocked into the first moai in the line. The massive statue teetered on its side for a moment, and then toppled into the next one like falling dominoes. One by one, the moai toppled with earth-shaking thuds and rolled off the platform.

Sean watched with a heavy heart. There was nothing he could do to stop the unfolding destruction – just another historical monument he helped to destroy. *This is becoming a bad habit!*

The upright crab lurched after him, snatching at his feet.

More energy blasts zinged over his head.

Sean dipped low and flew along the line of collapsing moai. He caught up to the final three statues still in the process of toppling over. He held his breath, closed his eyes, and darted around the final statue. A crab followed as the moai toppled off the end of the ahu, pinning half its legs to the ground with a heavy crunch.

Sean circled around and landed on the platform, hiding from the Isharkute between the fallen statues. He had a short time to figure this out. There was an indentation in the megalithic blockwork, previously hidden by the moai. He rubbed away the compressed dirt and gravel, uncovering a partial cross-shaped indentation in the stone. His heart leapt. He'd found the access point for the second crystal.

Nocao landed their vessel between the fallen moai and his friends joined him.

'Here! This is it,' Sean said.

Nocao opened the cube and set the cross into the indentation. Sean stood back, expecting an instantaneous reaction. Nothing happened.

'It didn't snap to the stone like it did in the cave,' Bella said, touching the cross to make sure it was positioned correctly. She rubbed away more of the dirt, uncovering a well-worn glyph etched into the ancient blockwork. 'Look! It's their god Makemake again.'

'Makemake stands on Earth as he does in the sky,' Sean said, repeating the Isharkute transcription from the cave.

Bella picked up the cross and repositioned it, lining up the empty slot for the second crystal with the glyph of Makemake's face.

The entire platform clunked and shuddered. This time everyone stepped back in anticipation. Their cross ejected from the ahu atop a cross-shaped stone plinth that rose and stopped at chest height, revealing the second crystal embedded in its centre cavity.

Sean plucked the crystal free and placed it on their cross.

The crystals powered up and projected a new hologram of his dad. Henry opened his mouth to speak just as a blast ricocheted off the pedestal, showering them with shattered stone and sending the cross flying. Arturo tackled Bella to the ground, shielding her from the explosion as Sean and Nocao dove for cover.

The Isharkute warriors hid amongst the fallen moai and fired again.

'Get back to the ship,' Sean cried over the incoming blasts. 'I'll get the cube!'

Nocao helped Arturo and Bella to their feet. Arturo grimaced and clutched his crooked shoulder.

Sean made sure they were safe before swooping off the ahu. He scooped up the cross with one hand and it transformed back into a cube. He circled overhead, drawing the Isharkute warriors away from his friends. The fallen statues had created a maze of stone – the perfect opportunity to lure the unsuspecting warriors into a trap. He whipped over their heads and dove between the statues. Energy blasts tore holes in the statues behind him. He landed on his feet and raced around the corner, skidding to a stop just metres from the hybrid crab still caught beneath the 30-tonne moai. The creature snapped and yanked against its trapped legs. After several loud pops and sickening cracks, the crab wrenched itself free, leaving three twitching legs under the moai.

The maimed creature hobbled towards him, pincers snapping.

Sean left it to the last second and shot into the air.

The warriors rounded the moai expecting to find him, but were confronted by their hybrid crustacean. The first warrior was snatched up in a pincer and snapped in two. His companion fired, taking out two more legs. The crab collapsed and floundered after him with its dying energy.

Sean left the chaos and flew back to his vessel.

Halfway across the grassy plain, a barrage of energy blasts vaporised the air behind him, singeing his heels. Sean peered over his shoulder and found another Isharkute chasing him. He recognised the heavy-set alien in his gold-plated regalia – it was Commander Vogran. A distinctive *clack clack clack* echoed up the hill. Vogran stopped running and looked back towards the beach. The other crab had righted itself and was racing sideways up the hill. Vogran turned his weapon on the hybrid and fired, suddenly finding himself in a battle against the crab.

*Lucky break!* Sean thought, diving for his escape vessel.

He raced inside to be confronted by Bella.

'Have you still got it?' she blurted out.

Sean held up the cube, but she didn't even glance at it. She seemed more relieved that he'd made it back in one piece. Nocao punched the thrusters and they accelerated over the ocean, putting as much distance between themselves and Easter Island as possible.

'Did you see Commander Vogran?' Sean said.

Nocao nodded. 'Strange, he ran straight past our vessel and started shooting at you. He was piloting the first scout ship that landed further up the volcano. He could have intercepted us earlier, but for some reason, he let us go.'

'That means Senetep's not far behind.'

Nocao reached out for the cube. 'Then we need our next destination.'

Sean handed it over, eager to hear his dad's next message. Nocao unlocked the cube and Henry Livingstone materialised in front of them, smiling proudly.

'Congratulations, Sean and Nocao, on finding the second crystal. In the next location, you'll find more than just the third and final crystal...we've left some things to help you. By now we're guessing Senetep will be hot on your tail, so you're going to need every advantage. Your next journey is the shortest yet, so keep moving, you're doing well. Once you've collected all the crystals, you'll have the power to unlock the Ark. You're almost there. See you again soon.'

Sean was a little disappointed that his dad's message was so short, but now wasn't the time to be sentimental or disappointed.

Henry's image transformed into a map of Guatemala, a small Central American country jammed between Mexico's southern border with Honduras on one side and El Salvador on the other. The map zoomed into the dense jungle to focus on a point near the northern border.

Nocao input their new coordinates and they sped off across the Pacific Ocean, leaving Rapa Nui to its new inhabitants. 'Now we must tend to Arturo's dislocated shoulder.'

Arturo was sitting up the back of the vessel, his pale face wracked with pain. His left shoulder bulged awkwardly and he cradled the affected arm. Sean hadn't heard a peep from him since they left the island, testament to how tough Arturo was. Nocao opened a panel and pulled out a metallic box full of containers, tubes, and stainless-steel instruments. He opened a small container and rubbed a cherry-coloured salve between his hands. He sat beside Arturo, gently placing both hands on either side of his dislocated shoulder.

'What's in the fancy box?' Arturo asked. 'Some kind of alien first aid kit?'

Nocao didn't say a word. He was focused on his hands, gently pressing and manipulating the tendons and bones beneath Arturo's skin.

'That feels better already... What are you –'

*Pop!* The shoulder popped back into position with a surprisingly loud noise. It made everyone jump except Nocao.

'Eww!' Bella cried, covering her mouth in disgust.

Nocao rubbed more ointment over Arturo's shoulder and closed the kit.

Arturo tested his shoulder and lifted his arm with ease. 'Unbelievable!'

'The salve will repair your torn and stretched tendons over the next few minutes – something that would take your human-based treatments months to remedy.'

'Wow! Isharkute medicine's amazing. I wish human medicine was this advanced.'

'In some ways, your ancestors were more advanced than you. They were in touch with the Earth around them, the natural remedies that existed in nature. Your modern society is so focused on technology, you've lost your connection to nature.'

'Is that why your species is so advanced, because you have a connection to both?'

'In some ways, yes. Our technology's advanced compared to yours, but our obsession with nature and the benefits of implanting other biological species to improve our own bodies was taken too far. It led to the affliction decimating our species.'

Nocao returned to the flight controls.

Arturo turned his attention to Sean. 'That was some smart moves back there. Who trained you to fly like that? I've never seen anything like it.'

'*Che forte*, you're so quick!' Bella said.

'A bird-man hybrid called Nasir. He trained me for the Great Arena, taught me how to read the air and use the currents.'

'I thought all hybrids were monsters.'

Sean didn't know what to say. He certainly wasn't a monster.

'*Scusami*,' Bella said, seeing his embarrassment. She quickly realised her mistake. 'I didn't mean you're a... Well...you know.'

'It's okay,' Sean said. 'Being able to fly's something I'm still getting used to myself.'

'What's the Great Arena?' Arturo asked.

'It's the ultimate survival contest, kinda like the colosseum in Rome. Except we weren't fighting gladiators, we were fighting hybrids.'

'Like those giant crabs and snakes?' Bella said.

'If you can imagine it, we fought it. Every monster from every mythology was trying to kill us.'

'Unbelievable!' Bella gasped.

Arturo laughed. '*Sei serio?*'

'Yes, Arturo, Sean is serious,' Nocao cut in. 'Under Sean's guidance, we were victorious over fifty-six teams, the most the arena had ever held. He chose the hybrids and came up with the strategies to win. I'll play the visual recording of the final Great Arena battle.'

The holographic map hovering in the middle of the cabin flickered off and was replaced with a visual recording of the Great Arena. Nocao controlled the angle and zoom, homing in on Sean mid-battle.

Sean was aghast. He had no idea such a recording existed. At first glance, he didn't even realise the lightning-fast speck zipping over the platforms and tips of the obelisks was himself. Nocao skimmed through Sean's highlights, from saving Caliph and riding the pegasus, diving for Nasir after his wings were shot by Krasun, to his arena-winning defeat of the monstrous shredder bug as it crashed into the pool beside the legendary kraken.

Bella and Arturo sat frozen in their seats, gawking at each other in shock.

'*Mamma Mia!*' Bella gasped. 'Sean, you're like *Percy Jackson!*'

'Or like a mutant from the *X-Men!*' Arturo added.

'I'm no hero,' Sean said, half-laughing, not so impressed with the mutant jibe. They both seemed in awe of him now, making the embarrassment he felt earlier more of an uncomfortable awkwardness. He wasn't sure which was worse – he just wanted to be normal.

'While we were on the island, Senetep sent another transmission to the world,' Nocao said.

'What did he say?' Sean asked.

'Senetep didn't say anything – the message was from Azar Hawati.'

'Azar!' Sean gasped. His stomach dropped with the sudden and terrible feeling that their escape from Azar's base was coming back to haunt them.

The final moments of the Great Arena cut to footage of Azar standing beside Senetep and his commanders. Nocao let Azar's speech play all the way through. The hologram finished and disappeared. Sean couldn't believe everything he'd just heard.

'"Pioneers of our intergalactic future!"' Sean said, mocking Azar's closing words. 'Is he joking or what?'

'He's lying. He's not trying to help humanity,' Arturo said.

Bella nodded. 'Sí. What does he really want?'

'He wants the Ark,' Sean said. 'But he can't find the Ark without our key.'

'That's why he's joined forces with Senetep – to find us!' Nocao said.

'That's right, and then the Ark!'

'Well then, we just have to make sure we find the Ark and turn on the beacon before they find us,' Bella said, sounding more determined than ever.

\*   \*   \*

Senetep returned to his private quarters during the journey to Easter Island. He needed a fresh round of cold therapy to reduce his increasing tremors, but unlike his pyramid at Giza, the annihilator had no cold chamber, so he made do with sprays and salves – a short-term solution that alleviated most of his symptoms.

He watched the holographic map as they approached the tiny spot designated as Easter Island.

With a single command, he had the firepower to obliterate the island and wipe Sean Livingstone from existence. He entertained the idea. The human teenager had been a persistent annoyance since the Great Arena, but it was hard not to admire his inventiveness and tenacity, surprising traits for such an inferior species. It would be far more satisfying to capture the child for his own amusement than to kill him.

Senetep straightened, squeezing his arms and legs to increase the blood flow.

Content that his body was free of shakes and twitches, he left the privacy of his quarters and strode onto the annihilator's main bridge. Nefaro stood with Azar, Malik, and his soldiers, overseeing their approach through the main viewscreen. His human passengers looked in awe of the expansive bridge. It was of a scale and might that dwarfed any of their military vessels.

'Where's Vogran's advance scout party?' Senetep asked. 'Why haven't we heard from him?'

'We're scanning the island now,' Nefaro said.

'Commander Vogran's scout vessel and hybrids transport are located on the northeast of the island. Adjusting our approach to match,' announced one of the bridge crew.

The annihilator pulled up and hovered over the coastline, casting the entire beach into shadow. A squad of warriors escorted Senetep, Nefaro, Azar, Malik, and his soldiers down to the remains of the battle. They walked between the scattered moai and found the legless remains of a hybrid crab with a dead warrior slumped in its massive pincer. Pieces of another unfortunate warrior littered the area.

Senetep kicked away the dismembered forearm at his feet with contempt. 'If Commander Vogran's failed me, he'll wish he was in pieces too.'

'If he's alive, I'm sure he has succeeded in his plan,' Nefaro said.

They walked up the ahu and stood around the stone plinth. Senetep examined the empty indentation and missing crystal. 'Why are we still one step behind this human child?'

Nefaro didn't respond. He knew when to keep his mouth shut, unlike the human meat beside him.

'Overseer Senetep,' Malik interrupted. 'If you give me and my soldiers access to our vehicles and resources, we can help you track Sean Livingstone.'

The unsolicited voice cut through Senetep's patience. How dare this meat speak to him without permission?

Malik mistook his silence as an invitation to continue. 'We've captured him once and can do it again. My men are highly trained war veterans and experts in tracking. We can anticipate his actions and beat him to the next location. With your permission, we – arghh –'

Senetep had Malik by the throat, choking his next word into a desperate gasp. He forced the weak, purple-faced human to his knees.

'Your son shows no respect for his master,' Senetep said, turning to Azar.

Malik focused on his father, his desperate eyes pleading for help. The human soldiers moved in, but Azar waved them back, knowing exactly how that would end. Senetep tightened his grip until Malik's windpipe reached the breaking point, then turned to Azar, enticing him to respond. How far was Azar prepared to go to achieve his goals? Would he watch the death of his son at the hand of his master and still be loyal? This was the ultimate test.

Azar stood his ground, but Senetep could see through his thin veneer of emotions. He was trembling and sweating, pulse thumping in his neck. His dogged and determined eyes filled with tears. The man was fighting every human emotion not to intervene.

Malik's eyes rolled back and his body went limp.

Senetep held tight until Malik's pulse fluttered and disappeared. He tossed him off the ahu and faced Azar. 'Good to see you imbeciles are learning some respect.'

Azar's eyelids twitched ever so slightly and a bead of sweat trickled down his brow. He looked like a man pushed to the brink of his own sanity. Senetep snickered.

Vogran emerged from the fallen moai and stepped over Malik's body. His golden pauldron and beard were splattered with chunks of white crab flesh. Several deep cuts marked his arms and legs as though he'd just stepped out of battle.

'Having trouble with your hybrids, Commander Vogran?'

'Not at all. They were a necessary distraction.'

'Were you successful?'

Vogran nodded proudly. 'While they were busy finding the crystal key, I placed a locater node on their scout vessel. I'm already tracking them to their next destination.'

'Well done. Return to the annihilator – we'll continue tracking them from there.'

Senetep spied Azar staring at his son's crumpled body. Considering how emotionally attached humans were to each other, it was probably an error to kill Malik at this point. Azar still had much work to do for him. Surprisingly, even though Azar was caught in such an unguarded moment, his eyes didn't reveal any malice or revenge, but rather a determination. Could a human be this cold and rational after witnessing the death of his only child? If so, Azar was the right human to bring about the subjugation of his own species. He had proven himself useful, but as soon as that usefulness expired, Azar would be killed.

# CHAPTER 17

# El Mirador

The lush, impenetrable jungles of Guatemala was one of the last corners on Earth truly untouched by civilisation. But Sean knew that wasn't always the case. Hidden beneath the canopy of green leaves and choking vines were the remains of ancient Mayan cities. Some of the steep pyramids were still visible. Their grey stone tips poked out through the treetops, hinting at the majestic culture that once thrived here.

Sean turned his attention to the holographic map. The coordinates for the next key were smack-bang in the middle of the thickest jungle, an ancient Mayan city known as El Mirador. There were no roads, paths, or landing strips, and the nearest settlements were a five-day trek on foot.

Nocao flew them over the highest tree-covered peak for several kilometres. Basic wooden platforms built by archaeologists and sightseers weaved around the grey blocks making up the tip of the mountain. 'The coordinates are beneath us, right in the middle of that mountain.'

'That's not a mountain, it's a pyramid,' Sean said, peering down through the trees.

'It's too big to be a pyramid,' Bella said.

'Those blocks on top of the mountain are just the tip of the pyramid. Archaeologists call it La Danta. Some say it's the largest pyramid in the world.'

'How?' Arturo asked. 'It doesn't even look as tall as Egypt's Great Pyramid.'

'It's the largest by volume – over 2.8 million cubic metres of stone.'

'How do we get inside?' Bella asked.

'That's a good question,' Sean said. 'Nocao, can you scan for openings and shafts?'

Nocao adjusted the scan and the hologram created an X-ray of the mountain, highlighting every shaft and chamber in red like a cross-section drawing. One immense chamber was set into the lower third of the pyramid and connected via passages to three smaller chambers at higher levels.

'Wow!' Sean said. 'Did the Mayans build this?'

'They built the cruder stone façade sitting on top of the original Isharkute structure,' Nocao said. 'I can isolate the different stone.'

As soon as he did, the two distinct pyramids became visible. The original was built from megalithic stone blocks, while the one on top was stacked with millions of smaller irregularly cut stone blocks.

'That's amazing!' Bella said.

Arturo nodded eagerly. '*Si!* If Papa had that kind of scanning tech, our salvage operations would be so much easier.'

Sean pointed to an intersection of shafts. 'There's a point here where one of the Isharkute shafts meets up with a Mayan shaft. It's the link between the two pyramids and our way in, but it's buried under half the mountain.'

'I'll adjust the scan to focus on the surrounding soil and sediment,' Nocao said. As soon as he did, a tunnel materialised through the mountain, snaking its way to emerge at the surface, 100 metres above the target.

'There's our way in,' Nocao said. 'It appears someone tried to dig their way in years ago. The tunnel is highly unstable, but appears to be our only way inside.'

Bella shook her head. 'Looks dangerous. Don't you have a laser gun or something to blast an opening through the mountain?'

'This is a scout vessel – we don't have weapons of that magnitude on board. Only annihilators can move that much rubble. This shaft's our only way in.'

'We have to climb down there,' Sean said.

'I wish Aunt Carla was here,' Bella sighed.

Sean couldn't agree more – this was a job for an experienced cave explorer. Nocao set their vessel down in the shadows of the jungle canopy. After Easter Island's brisk sea air, the Guatemalan jungle was hot and muggy. The short trek up to the tunnel opening left Sean, Bella, and Arturo in a sweat and pulling at their sticking clothes.

Nocao weathered the heat better than any of them and forged ahead, monitoring the ground with his scanner.

Sean kicked at the dirt, exposing a layer of heavily weathered stone blocks. In some areas, the rough pyramid blocks were hardly buried, while in other places, they were lost beneath the soil and dense foliage. From the ground, it was impossible to appreciate the scope of the pyramid hiding beneath their feet, presenting to the casual observer like the remains of an ancient village. This was probably why La Danta had remained undiscovered for so long.

Nocao climbed over the exposed root of a giant Kapok tree that looked like the tail of a dinosaur and dropped into a shady hollow littered with decomposing foliage. He snatched at something in the undergrowth, and without warning, hurled it over their heads with a shower of leaves.

Sean glimpsed the glistening black scales and ducked. 'Whoa!'

Bella screamed as the snake flopped on the ground and slithered away.

Nocao craned his head over the tree root. 'Something wrong?'

'Next time you're about to throw something deadly, you might want to warn us first,' Sean grumbled.

'That was a non-venomous species,' Nocao said, noticing Bella's terrified expression. 'But I see your point. Next time, I'll give you fair warning. Here, I've found the entrance.' He kicked at the dirt and it collapsed into a deep hole.

Bella peered into the web-infested opening. 'What else's in there?'

'My scans identified multiple species of arachnids, scorpions, and beetles, and several colonies of ants,' Nocao said without skipping a beat.

Bella frowned. 'You're not helping.'

'It's better if we don't know what's down there,' Sean said. 'Why don't you go first?'

Nocao climbed into the shaft without hesitation and led the way. The gnarled tree roots twisted their way downwards, creating a natural ladder upon which they descended. Sean didn't look into the cracks and webby crevices lining the shaft walls, knowing that the sight of one giant spider would send him climbing out at light speed. His hand passed through webs as thick and sticky as fairy-floss. As his eyes adjusted to the dim light, he started to make out shapes moving in the shadows. A huge, metre-long centipede crawled over his fingers and he ripped his hand away, almost losing his footing.

Bella was making all sorts of terrified whimpers from above. Arturo whispered down to her, 'Keep calm. Remember, these insects are more afraid of you than –'

'Impossible!' she hissed back.

Sean agreed with Bella on this one.

The damp soil and large roots gave way to drier earth and sturdy rocks, where only the deepest-rooted trees penetrated. The subterranean world was quiet and still. The natural light from the opening was long gone and they were guided by Nocao's solitary torch. Crouched one after the other in single file, it was crawling room only.

Sean's heart thumped in his ears and seemed to be the only thing he could hear now. He felt the claustrophobia closing in, suffocating him.

There was no flying out of here.

No quick escape.

The surface became soft and tacky under their hands. Nocao stopped and spun around, illuminating the spider silk lining the tunnel.

'It's a giant spider web!' Sean gasped.

'I believe you call this larger arachnid species "tarantulas,"' Nocao said. 'Don't worry – their silk isn't used like a web to catch prey. It keeps their habitat clean.'

'*Va bene*, but what happens if we mess it up?' Arturo whispered from behind. 'They're gonna get angry.'

'Their venom's less toxic than a bee sting.'

'I don't care!' Bella cried. 'I hate spiders.'

'Then keep moving,' Nocao said, crawling on.

Everyone crawled at double speed now, but the faster they moved, the more entangled they became. Sean scratched at his face, pulling the tough silken strands off as quickly as he could. Nocao stopped abruptly and shone the light back on them. From the corner of his eye, Sean could see a blur of big hairy spider legs resting on his own shoulder, then noticed the bristled black fangs and eight glistening eyes. It was a massive tarantula! The spider arched back, raising its front legs, spreading out wide enough to cover Sean's entire face.

Sean froze, utterly petrified.

Nocao lashed out, knocking the spider through the web wall. The sound of scurrying legs surrounded them and the entire silken-covered wall pulsed like a living organism. There were hundreds of tarantulas, all scurrying around behind the web.

'We're in the middle of a nest,' Nocao said. 'Crawl!'

Nocao ploughed ahead, ripping his way through the silky strands. Sean stuck close behind, eyes half-shut. He could feel the spiders moving under his hands, caught between the silk and earth. He imagined them latched onto him, crawling over his back, looking for bare flesh to sink their inch-long fangs into. Bella and Arturo crawled over his heels, screaming at him to crawl faster.

Nocao dove through a final silk wall and disappeared over the edge.

They all clambered after him and tumbled down a steep decline, landing on top of each other in a large chamber. Sean jumped up and frantically brushed his body, pulling the web off his clothes. Bella and Arturo danced the same horrified Get-Them-Off-Me! routine as several tarantulas dropped to the earth and crawled away.

'Urgh, they're all over me!' Bella cried, hopping around, trying to brush off her back.

Nocao calmly picked off the remaining tarantulas and within a few moments, everyone had calmed down, realising they were clear of the nest.

'I can't believe you're not scared of spiders, Nocao,' Sean said.

'I'm surprised you still are after the hybrids you've encountered.'

'I'll take a giant hybrid crab with tentacles over tarantulas anytime.'

'Interesting,' Nocao mused. 'The human fear of spiders seems to be totally irrational.'

The chamber opened into a cavern dominated by a section of the Mayan pyramid. The sloping wall was covered in a well-preserved stucco frieze depicting deities from Mayan mythology. The frieze was made from a smoothed lime plaster and painted with bright colours that jutted out like two-dimensional hieroglyphs. An oppressive tangle of roots draped down like monstrous tentacles, ensnaring the beautiful artwork and devouring the pyramid within the ever-growing mountain. Sean knew that on any other day, this would be an amazing archaeological discovery, but the entrance they were looking for was somewhere behind the wall. Several sections had been chipped away where previous treasure hunters had tried to find an opening into the pyramid.

'Where's the entrance?' Arturo asked.

Nocao scanned the wall and pointed to the stucco relief of a long serpent with plumes of feathers sprouting from its head and tail. The snake encircled a large collection of reliefs decorating the wall, turning to face its own tail with an open mouth. 'It's the Mayan god Kukulkan,' Nocao said, reading the results from his scanner. 'Kukulkan is known as the "Feathered Serpent."'

'Is it a hybrid?' Bella asked.

'It might've been,' Sean said, remembering he'd seen similar creatures in the Great Arena. 'Maybe that's where the myth started.'

'What was the final riddle again?' Arturo asked.

'IN THE LIGHT OF THE SUN, TWO BECOME ONE,' Sean said.

They all stared at the wall, trying to make sense of the intricate collage of patterns, shapes, animals, and human figures imprinted in the plaster. Sean knew the proper meaning would take Mayan experts days to decipher – time they didn't have.

'Each riddle has had to do with astronomy,' Arturo said. 'They're aimed at you, Sean. You're the budding astro-archaeologist.'

'IN THE LIGHT OF THE SUN, TWO BECOME ONE,' Bella repeated. 'It sounds like an eclipse.'

'You're right, it does!' Sean said. 'But I've been thinking it refers to Venus. The planet's also known as the "Evening Star" and "Morning Star." Ancient cultures used to think it was two separate stars because it was visible just after sunset, then would disappear until just before sunrise...but when it's at its brightest, it can be seen with the midday sun.'

Arturo nodded eagerly. 'That makes sense...two become one!'

'The Mayans were obsessed by the cycle of Venus. They thought it was more important than the sun. They timed their wars, crops, and even their human sacrifices around it.'

'Simple. We just need to find Venus, then!' Bella said. 'What's the Mayan symbol for it?'

'It's there!' Nocao said, climbing over the frieze to a symbol wedged between Kukulkan's mouth and tail. 'The symbol for Venus is a cross with four circles on each corner, representing the complete star.'

'That's it!' Sean cried, high-fiving Bella and Arturo.

Nocao transformed the cube into a cross and held it up to the symbol. They were the same size. It snapped to the stucco frieze like a magnet and the entire section of wall inside Kukulkan's body retracted into the pyramid wall and parted. The soil and dust settled, revealing a perfectly smooth red granite slope, the outer casing of the original Isharkute pyramid. The outline of a door was etched into the granite with a cross indentation positioned dead-centre.

'Hah!' Arturo shouted.

'You did it!' Bella cried, throwing her arms around Sean.

Nocao removed the cross from the frieze and placed it on the Isharkute pyramid. The crystals glowed and the granite slab retracted silently into the pyramid. Five metres into the outer casing, the door swivelled and slid back to sit flush with the passage wall.

'Amazing!' Arturo said. 'Look at the stonework. This place is indestructible.'

Sean led the way into the pyramid as Nocao removed the cross from the wall. The polished surfaces were pristine, without a hint of dirt or dust anywhere, as if the entire pyramid had been sealed airtight. The passage descended into the centre of the pyramid. Crystals embedded in the walls illuminated ahead of them like modern sensor lighting. The ceiling stepped higher the deeper they went, transforming into a massive void of corbel-vaulted blocks. It reminded Sean of the Grand Gallery in Giza's Great Pyramid, where each massive block jutted out over the one below to support the ceiling above.

The passage opened into a wide circular chamber with a domed ceiling. Another three passages entered into the chamber, making four in total. From a quick glance, Sean guessed each was aligned to a cardinal point. A granite plinth ejected from the mirror-smooth floor, stopping at waist height in the centre of the room, presenting them with another cross-shaped indentation.

'This is it – the last one!' Sean said confidently.

Nocao placed the cross onto the indentation and the core of the plinth ejected another twelve inches higher, revealing the final crystal embedded inside.

Sean plucked it free and gave everyone a tentative look. 'Here goes!'

He held his breath and set the crystal in place upon the cross. Four rectangular pedestals silently rose from the floor, each facing one of the passages. The domed ceiling shimmered to life in a cloudless night sky, brimming with a universe of a billion vibrant stars. A bright band of magical light weaved through the centre of the heavens.

'*Bellisimo!*' Bella gasped.

'The Milky Way,' Sean said. 'It really is a spiral galaxy.'

'I've never seen stars so beautiful.'

'They're a hologram,' Nocao said.

'It's an underground observatory like the Hall of Records,'

Sean said. He was impressed – Nesuk and his dad had built their own version in perfectly polished granite. 'No wonder the ancient cultures had such an obsession with the stars.'

The four pedestals locked into place and emitted holographic controls with Isharkute glyphs. A final hologram illuminated above the central pedestal.

Sean's heart lifted at the sight of his dad.

'Congratulations, Sean and Nocao, for making it this far. Your completed cube is now the final key to unlock the Ark. Unfortunately, I can't tell you exactly where it's hidden, but I can point you in the right direction. Looking at your history, we know it moved since Nesuk, Rootuk, and I buried it on Mount Sinai. That was inevitable – it had to be found there in order to begin the story of Moses and the Ten Commandments. We're currently scavenging whatever resources we can find to build a cryogenic chamber to prolong Nesuk's life. He'll outlive me and Rootuk by centuries and will keep an eye on the Ark long after this pyramid's been sealed. After many discussions, we've agreed that Nesuk will direct the course of the Ark towards the town of Axum in Ethiopia. With a bit of luck, it's still there.

'One thing I can tell you for certain is the location of the beacon. It's hidden inside an underwater monument near the island of Yonaguni, not far from the coast of Japan. Sean, I'm pretty sure you're familiar with this place – there was a lot of debate between archaeologists and geologists as to whether the Yonaguni Monument was a natural rock formation or the traces of an ancient culture. I guess that's just another debate we've put to rest.'

Sean smiled to himself.

'We deliberately built the Yonaguni Monument on the coastline when it was still above sea level, but over the millennia it's been conveniently hidden by rising sea levels. You'll need scuba gear to reach the opening. It won't be easy, but once you find the Ark, you'll know how to get inside. Going forward from here, this pyramid contains a wealth of equipment and information to help you on your journey.'

Henry paused with a pensive, slightly sad expression before continuing. 'Sean, you'll find this is where my journey ends. Hopefully my final message can give you some closure.'

The hologram faded away, leaving Sean emotionally drained and hungry for answers.

Bella squeezed his arm gently. 'Are you okay?'

Sean took a deep breath and nodded.

Nocao examined the four control panels. 'These panels control the pyramid. There's two storage chambers below and a mausoleum in the chamber above us.'

'Mausoleum!' Sean said. His emphatic response echoed off the walls and amplified in volume. Everyone looked at him. 'Which passage?' he asked in a quieter voice.

Nocao pointed the way.

Sean nodded, heart pounding against his ribs. He gingerly approached the imposing corbel-vaulted entrance. This was a hard finality. The holographic messages had created the feeling his dad was still alive, almost as if he was taking the journey with them, but this final revelation had destroyed that comforting illusion.

Bella started after him and took his hand. 'Do you want me to come with you?'

Sean was tempted to say yes, but he needed one last moment alone with his dad. 'Thanks – I'll be all right. Just give me a few minutes.'

Bella nodded and let go of his hand.

Sean entered the passage, feeling more confident knowing that Bella cared about him. The passage ascended for 50 metres, then turned 90 degrees on a steeper incline towards the centre of the pyramid, finally opening into a vast darkened chamber. The crystalline lighting flickered to life, highlighting two granite sarcophagi dominating the centre of the room. One of the sarcophagi was an adult-sized box, but the other was double the height and width.

Sean could tell with one glance that was his dad's sarcophagus.

Numerous offerings were piled around the base. There were

sealed urns, a collection of potteries, offerings of food, and bunches of flowers. His footsteps caused the delicate, millennia-old petals to drop from their stems and disappear into dust.

Sean placed his hand on the cool granite. 'Hey, Dad.'

'Hi, Sean,' his dad replied in a warm, comforting voice.

Startled, Sean stepped back. His dad was standing beside the sarcophagus in an automatically activated hologram. He was considerably older, with grey hair and deeper-set wrinkles. His horse half seemed thinner, almost undernourished, and was covered in long-healed scars.

'If you're thinking that's me inside the sarcophagus, then you're right. I'm not so keen on having such a grandiose burial, but Yeesha and her tribes are insistent. Over the years, I've come to realise we had to bury every hybrid as securely as possible. The reason hybrids like me became myths and legends was because evidence of our existence was never found – something we're ensuring will happen again. Every hybrid on Earth will eventually be buried and sealed inside pyramids and structures like this. Over the last two decades, Nesuk, Rootuk, and I travelled the world, collecting every abandoned Isharkute vessel, weapon, and piece of technology we could find. We stored it all here to ensure it was found at the right time, to help you on your final quest for the Ark.'

Henry paused. A solemn look creased his brow. 'I'm one of the few hybrids left. You'll notice how much I've aged since you saw me in the last hologram. It's been about twenty years. In my first hologram, I said it felt like we'd been separated for years, but for me it was only a matter of weeks. Now it feels like an eternity since I saw you last.'

Sean's chest was heavy with emotion. He felt the same way, except for him, it was only minutes since he'd watched the previous hologram.

'But don't despair, Sean. I've lived a full life and achieved everything I set out to do. I expect you'll do the same in your time. We're both fortunate to play a pivotal role in the evolution of human civilisation, even though we lived ten thousand years apart.

You'll find hundreds more recordings stored on crystals inside this pyramid. I've documented everything we've done, filling in the gaps of humanity's forgotten history. You know where the beacon is – now all you need to do is find the Ark.

'But remember, many people look upon the Ark as a covenant between God and man, and in essence, this belief still holds true. The Ark represents a truth and connection to our origins, to a greater knowledge and understanding of the universe. It's an awakening for humanity. I couldn't imagine anyone more suited to guiding the world through these tumultuous changes than you. I believe in you. I love you, son.'

Henry smiled as his hologram faded, eyes glistening with tears.

Sean wiped the tears from his own eyes. He stood in silence for a long moment, staring at the space where his dad had stood. A colourful bracelet in the pile of offerings caught his eye. He leant down and picked it up. It was a friendship bracelet, just like the one Yeesha made for him millennia before. He knew in his heart this was from her, a gift through time and a symbol of their everlasting friendship. The sound of shuffling feet made him spin around. Bella was standing behind him.

'How long were you standing there?'

'A little while,' Bella said sheepishly. 'Your dad seems really nice. I wish I'd met him.'

Sean smiled and glanced at the bracelet.

'What's that?' Bella asked, noticing the delicately woven band.

'A gift from a friend.'

'Who was she?'

'Her name was Yeesha. She was a slave to the Isharkute, about the same age as me. She helped me when things got tough...which was most of the time. When I left with Nocao to come back to the future, she stayed with my dad and helped her tribe.'

'She must have been special, then...' Bella said in a soft, slightly probing tone.

Sean looked up with surprise. Were his emotions that obvious and easy to read?

'Sorry, I didn't mean to pry,' she said quickly, cheeks flushed with embarrassment.

Sean relaxed. He didn't consider it prying – she seemed genuinely interested in his personal life and emotional wellbeing. He had to admit, he was growing more interested in her as well.

Arturo rushed into the chamber, panting heavily. 'You're never gonna believe what we found at the bottom of the pyramid. It's incredible!'

# — CHAPTER 18 —

# *Pyramid Assault*

Arturo raced back through the control room, leading Sean and Bella down a stretch of steep passages into the core of the pyramid. After what seemed like a kilometre of running, they chased Arturo into a huge open void, puffing heavily and staring at the astonishing sight. Standing before them was a cavernous hangar packed with Isharkute hunter-craft, stingers, transport and scout vessels, and row upon row of smaller land-based vehicles. Sean was shocked. This was more than he ever imagined. His dad and Nesuk had salvaged every abandoned piece of Isharkute technology they could find and stored it in one place. Hiding everything away from humanity ensured history remained the same while giving them a fighting chance for the future.

Nocao stood at a control panel, assessing the inventory. 'Combined with the armoury above, there's enough equipment to start a proper resistance against Senetep.'

'There's an armoury as well?' Sean gasped.

'*Sí* – the other passage from the control room takes you there,' Arturo said, puffing slightly. 'It's the chamber above this one. There's enough weapons to equip an army.'

'Wow! This is unbelievable.'

'I told you,' Arturo said, grinning wildly.

Sean wandered into the hangar, admiring the rows of pristine vessels. Excitement swelled in his chest. They were still one step ahead of Senetep, and now armed with a major advantage that was bound to catch him off-guard. There was more stored here than they would ever need for themselves. It was a gift from his father to the world – a means to fight back.

'Now we just need to find the Ark of the Covenant,' Bella said. 'Your dad said it was somewhere in the town of Axum in Ethiopia.'

'*Sí*, probably in a warehouse full of boxes,' Arturo quipped.

'What warehouse?' Nocao asked in a serious tone.

Sean chuckled. 'Arturo's not serious. He's referencing *Raiders of the Lost Ark*. It's a movie.'

'Then this movie can help us.'

'Not really. *Raiders* is just entertainment, you know...a work of fiction.'

Nocao shook his head. 'Why do humans waste so much time with fiction? I don't see the point of a made-up story.'

'We get enjoyment from it.'

'But it's not real.'

'I know, but it's like a distraction from real life.'

'I don't see how immersing yourself in fantasy is productive.'

'If I'd never played *Mythic*, then I wouldn't have been able to create the teams for the Great Arena. We wouldn't have won.'

Nocao nodded. 'But playing the game was like training. I don't see how other forms of fiction help.'

'It opens a door for us to reflect upon ourselves,' Bella said. 'We express our feelings, thoughts, and desires through books, movies, music, paintings, and all forms of art. It connects us on an emotional level.'

Nocao still looked perplexed.

'Nocao's a member of the Isharkute Guild of Sciences,' Sean said. 'He's never studied art.'

'Then you're the science nerd and I'm the *alternative* art student,' Bella said, making air quotation marks with her fingers.

Nocao smiled, but still looked confused. 'We should focus on the Ark.'

'Arty and I were brought up Catholic,' Bella said. 'We know about the Ark from our religious studies and going to church.'

'*Sí*. I've always been fascinated with finding artefacts from the

Bible,' Arturo said. 'Noah's Ark, the Holy Grail, the Ark of the Covenant. I tried to convince Papa we should use our salvage company to search for them in between jobs. In Axum, there's a church called St. Mary of Zion where a solitary monk is appointed to guard the Ark for the rest of his life.'

'Oh, yeah! I've read about that,' Sean said. 'Doesn't every monk guarding it go blind?'

'*Sì!* And they have unnaturally short life spans. If the nominated guardian doesn't name a predecessor before he dies, then the monks have to vote for a new guardian.'

'That's horrible,' Bella said. 'Why do they go blind?'

'Because whatever the monk's guarding is powerful enough to poison and kill him,' Sean said. 'Does this sound like the power source Nesuk left for us?'

'Yes. If there's even the slightest breach in the gold casing, then the Ark's power will leak,' Nocao said. 'That's why anyone exposed to it will become sick.'

'Maybe the box built to carry the Ark was damaged somewhere in the past,' Sean said. 'Arturo, what else do you know about Axum?'

'The main church has been destroyed and rebuilt several times, but the Ark is rumoured to be kept in the sanctuary chapel. It's a smaller domed building beside the main church. But we have to be careful – we can't just walk in there and take it. Christian Ethiopians believe they have a duty to protect the Ark. There's over twenty thousand Orthodox Christian churches throughout the country and each one has a wooden replica of the Ark called a *tabot*. They even have processions where priests bring out the *tabots* for the public to see.'

Sean found it hard to reconcile why such a priceless and sought-after artefact like the Ark was guarded by a lonely monk in a simple chapel. There had to be some kind of higher power watching over it. The entire hangar suddenly rumbled, as if God himself reached down to answer his thoughts.

'Is that an earthquake?' Sean said.

'I can't scan the pyramid from here. We need to get back to the central chamber,' Nocao said, heading for the passage.

Halfway back, another earth-shaking tremor rocked the pyramid, throwing everyone against the walls.

'That doesn't feel like an earthquake,' Arturo said.

'More like a bomb blast,' Sean said.

They all sprinted the rest of the way back to the main chamber. Nocao activated the pyramid sensors and scanned the surface hundreds of metres above. A hologram revealed Senetep's annihilator hovering over the jungle with dozens of hunter-craft and stingers circling the pyramid mountain.

'Senetep!' Sean said, feeling an icy surge of terror shoot through his chest.

'How'd they find us so quick?' Bella asked.

'They must have tracked us here,' Nocao said. 'The only time they were close enough to plant a homing device on our vessel was on Easter Island.'

'That's why Commander Vogran let me get away so easily,' Sean said.

'Too late to worry about that now,' Arturo said, pointing to the hologram. 'Look!'

The annihilator fired a missile into the mountain, obliterating the entire top quarter in an instant. The force stripped the blocks from the Mayan pyramid and uprooted trees in a dark umbrella of debris that showered the lower jungle.

'Brace yourselves!' Nocao yelled, grabbing hold of the pedestal.

The shockwave descended through the pyramid, growing in power like the whole world was about to explode. Sean reached for Bella's hand as the tremors hit, rocking the chamber with the force of an atom bomb and knocking everyone to the floor. Hairline cracks appeared in the granite blocks as the pyramid creaked and groaned like a wounded animal. The tremors settled, leaving them sprawled on the floor, stunned and nervously expecting another shockwave.

Sean helped Bella to her feet. 'We have to get out of here!' she said. 'They'll bury us alive.'

'Senetep's not trying to destroy the pyramid – he's trying to get inside,' Nocao said.

'Doesn't feel that way,' Arturo said.

'I have to agree – he destroyed half the mountain,' Sean added.

'The only reason we're still talking is because Senetep wants to capture us alive,' Nocao said.

'You're right,' Sean said, examining the hologram. Half the mountain was gone, along with huge sections of the Mayan pyramid. The gaping hole revealed their perfect red granite pyramid, bare to the world for the first time in over 10,000 years. A squad of hybrids transports descended upon the fresh pyramid face, releasing packs of human-jackal hybrids. They raced across the surface, sniffing and hunting their way towards the open entrance.

'They're coming inside!' Bella shouted.

'*E allora!* Close the entrance,' Arturo said.

Nocao accessed the pyramid control system, highlighting every door and passage throughout the structure. The outer door flashed red. 'There's debris blocking the opening. I can't close it.'

'Hurry up!' Bella shrieked.

'I can close the inner doors – that'll slow them down.'

'Do it!' Arturo cried.

A *thud* sounded down the passage as the first door closed higher inside the pyramid, and then the entrance into the control room sealed shut with a metre-thick stone door.

'While they're trying to get inside, we can take what we need from the lower chambers and get out of here,' Sean said.

'How do we get the vessels out of the hangar?' Arturo asked.

'The hangar entrance is located at the base of the pyramid,' Nocao said. 'The only problem is it's buried under the rubble of the Mayan pyramid and the weight of half the mountain.'

'Can't we open the hangar door and blast our way out? We've got enough firepower with all our weapons and ships.'

'That could work,' Nocao said, working the holographic controls. 'I'll open the hangar door from here.'

'You guys should get down to the hangar and pick our escape

vessels,' Sean said. 'I'll head to the armoury and grab whatever I can.'

'I'll show you the way and give you a hand,' Arturo said.

'I'm coming too,' Bella said.

'No!' Arturo said sharply. 'It's too dangerous. If Sean and I get cornered by those hybrids, we'll have to fight our way out. Go with Nocao.'

'I can fight!' Bella said, giving him a strong sisterly shove.

'*Sí*, but you're not coming with us,' Arturo argued. There was no debating with his stern tone. Bella glared at him and stormed off with Nocao to the hangar.

Sean was impressed by Bella's fearless enthusiasm. 'Your sister's pretty brave,' he said as they raced down the passage to the armoury.

'Too brave,' Arturo grumbled, glancing sidelong at Sean. 'If something happens to me, you need to look out for her. She's pretty picky with her friends, especially boys. But she likes you.'

Sean's heart skipped a beat. What did Arturo mean? Did she like him as a friend, or something more? The situation seemed a little weird considering his dad was meant to marry her aunt. That would've made them family, and right now they were the closest thing he had to a family.

They ran inside the armoury, a square chamber the size of a warehouse. Hundreds of staves were stacked neatly in racks, while damaged ones were heaped on the floor in shoulder-high piles. Sean raced between the racks and found a collection of staves with large crystals and double-sized forks. He snatched one up and twisted the grip activator. The power crystal hummed to life and the forks snapped open, crackling with electricity. The stave was still as powerful as the last day it was used.

'That one looks good,' Arturo said.

'I've only seen royal guards and overseers use staves like this. It's powerful enough to blow a hole through solid stone walls.'

Arturo picked one off the rack and swung it about confidently. 'I like it. How do you use it?'

Sean gave him a quick demonstration. 'Twist the centre grip to activate the forks, aim, and push the button on the grip to fire.'

Arturo repeated the action and charged up the stave. The power vibrated up his arms and illuminated his broadening smile with a blue glow. *'Fantastico!* Let's get started on that hangar wall.'

They loaded up as many staves as they could carry and raced down the passage. Inside the hangar, the entire northern wall had slid aside, revealing a mass of tangled roots, stone, and sediment. It was going to take some serious firepower to blast their way through. Two robust scout vessels were now parked in line with the exit, both double the size of their previous vessel and equipped with built-in weapons. Nocao and Bella anxiously waved them over. Sean and Arturo proudly threw down their collection of weapons upon joining them.

'Why two vessels?' Sean asked.

'It's safer if we split up,' Nocao said. 'I'll fly ahead and draw Senetep's smaller vessels away. You take Bella, Arturo, and the cube. I've programmed the coordinates for Axum into the navigation systems, but you can override the autopilot if you need to take control.'

'I don't know how to fly it,' Sean said with concern. 'I've only watched you.'

Another explosion rumbled through the pyramid.

'That wasn't a missile,' Nocao said, analysing his scanner. 'They've broken through the first door. One more and they'll be inside the control chamber.'

'Then Senetep gets everything my dad collected,' Sean said, suddenly realising the gravity of the situation.

'Even worse...from the control room, they can close the hangar door and lock us in.'

'Than why are we standing here talking?' Arturo said. He activated his stave and started firing on the root-infested wall.

Bella watched her brother and picked up a stave. Without a word of instruction from anyone, she imitated Arturo's actions and began firing on the sediment. Sean was surprised at how well she handled the weapon's kickback. Embarrassingly, she did it a little better than him.

'This is fun!' she cried, firing off shot after shot.

Sean and Nocao joined in. A growing pile of soil, splintered roots, and blocks from the Mayan pyramid crashed down in front of them. Shafts of natural light streamed into the hangar. Beyond the growing hole, a vibrant splash of green jungle teased their freedom.

Sean noticed something in the corner of his eye. The hangar door had started sliding back into place, an immense 1,000-tonne slab of impenetrable stone that threatened to seal off their opening.

'They're closing the hangar door,' Nocao called. 'Focus your shots on mine.'

The four of them concentrated their firepower on a single area. It didn't take long for a substantial shaft to appear. Bigger chunks of debris collapsed into the hangar and they were bathed with warm sunlight.

'That's big enough,' Nocao cried, heading for his vessel.

'Wait!' Sean shrieked, chasing after him. 'We can't just leave everything in this pyramid to Senetep. My dad spent twenty years collecting all this to make us stronger against Senetep, not weaker.'

Nocao slowed and looked around the hangar. 'You have a point. What do you suggest?'

'We should try contacting Carla and Commander El-Amin. He might be able to coordinate an attack with the Guatemalan government and retake the pyramid.'

Nocao nodded. 'That's a good idea. It might also divert some of Senetep's forces from us. As soon as we're clear of the pyramid, I'll make contact.'

'I still think we should stick together. I don't think I can fly that –'

'You can do it,' Nocao said, placing a reassuring hand on Sean's shoulder. 'I'll see you at Axum.'

Nocao boarded his vessel and took off through the hole, shooting across the jungle like a silent bullet. Isharkute vessels swarmed after him like angry bees.

'It worked!' Arturo said.

The closing hangar door crept across the edge of their escape shaft, eclipsing the daylight.

'Quick, we have to go!' Sean said.

He climbed aboard their vessel and sat hesitantly in the pilot's seat. Now he really felt the pressure. If the autopilot didn't cut it, he'd have to fly it himself. He familiarised himself with the holographic controls, trying to remember how Nocao used them. Bella and Arturo sat behind him as the door slid shut. The ignition button flashed under his fingertip, awaiting his touch.

'What are we waiting for?' Bella said.

'*Sì, sbrigatevi!*' Arturo said.

*Hurry up!* translated in Sean's mind with blunt urgency. With a deep breath, he pressed the button and they rocketed towards the shaft. Their vessel rolled sideways to squeeze through the gap and zoomed across the valley, clipping the tops off the trees.

'Whoa!' Arturo cried. '*Che forte!*'

Sean wasn't so impressed. He couldn't shake the nagging feeling of déjà vu. The last time he and Nocao fled from Senetep's forces in a pursuit across the globe, things didn't end so well – in fact, they almost destroyed the world.

## — CHAPTER 19 —

# *Battle Plans*

Sean was anxious about piloting the vessel, that was obvious. His eyes were wide as saucers and his hands trembled over the controls. Bella wished she could help him in some way, but aside from his visible nerves, he seemed to be managing okay. He activated the clear-view technology and the rear cabin became transparent. Bella peered over the edge, still getting used to the illusion that half their vessel just disappeared. The red granite pyramid was now in the shadow of an immense, elongated vessel the size of several aircraft carriers. There were rows of what appeared to be cannons or laser guns along its length, all of which were pointed at them.

'Is that Senetep's ship?' Bella asked.

'Yeah, it's called an annihilator,' Sean said. 'But don't worry – I'm about to put as much distance between us as possible.'

The annihilator veered after them, casting a shadow over the entire valley. Squadrons of smaller vessels departed from its underside and swooped over the jungle.

'Why did Nocao have to leave us with the biggest one?' Arturo whined. 'Look! Now there's more of them.'

Sean took one glance at the squadrons bearing down on them. 'Marauders!'

'What are marauders? Hybrids?'

'No, they're warrior transports. The Isharkute equivalent to a Black Hawk helicopter.'

'Can't we go any faster?' Bella said.

'Only if I override the autopilot,' Sean said, peering back through the hull. The marauders were catching up fast. 'All right... Hold onto something.'

Sean turned off the autopilot and the vessel jolted abruptly, knocking Bella and Arturo to the floor. He carefully corrected their trajectory.

'I hope you're better at flying than driving,' Bella said, sharing a concerned look with Arturo.

'I hope so too,' Sean said with an audible gulp.

A hologram of Nocao materialised beside the viewscreen map. 'If you're going to fly yourself, meet me at these coordinates.' The revised destination flashed with a green dot, marking a point on the Yucatan coastline almost 1,000 kilometres north of their position.

Sean gingerly pushed the accelerator and they burst ahead of the squadron. The sudden shift in speed made Bella feel dizzy. Mountains and valleys whooshed by in a surreal blur, almost like they were inside a virtual reality simulation. Their vessel rolled and swerved like a supersonic missile, then suddenly veered too close to a cliff. Sean over-corrected, jolting them about the cabin. 'Sorry about that.'

'At that speed, you need to anticipate your course more accurately,' Nocao said.

Sean huffed and shook his head.

Bella sympathised with him. Nocao's brash manner was frustrating at the best of times, and it certainly wasn't helping now. She placed her hand on Sean's shoulder and whispered into his ear, 'Don't worry, you're doing fine.'

Sean relaxed his shoulders and took a deep, determined breath.

Their ride smoothed out and she took a deep breath herself.

Sean glanced at Nocao's hologram. 'When are we contacting Hazim?'

'I'm scanning all human communication across Cairo now,' Nocao said. 'Luckily for us, Senetep's kept some of your satellite infrastructure intact.'

A discord of garbled voices sounded through their cabin, each one talking over the other. Nocao fine-tuned the noise, isolating and focusing on specific conversations that mentioned the name Hazim El-Amin. The cacophony thinned out and a sequence of Isharkute glyphs appeared across their console, transforming one by one into a phone number.

'This is Hazim's satellite phone number. I've encrypted the connection so we can't be monitored. Just press it to call.'

'Can you do it?' Sean said, glancing at Bella. 'It's hard enough flying.'

Bella pressed the hologram and the number dialled. After several rings, the call was answered. 'Commander Hazim El-Amin speaking. Who's this?'

'Commander, it's Bella Bonaforte.'

There was a moment of silence on the other end. 'Bella! We thought you'd been killed.'

'I'm fine. Is my aunt Carla okay?'

'She's fine. In fact, she's with me and Colonel Powell right now. I'll put you on speaker phone.'

'*Ciao*, Bella!' Carla cried down the line.

'Aunt Carla!' Bella cheered.

'Bella, it's a relief to hear your voice. I'm so glad you're okay. After we found the helicopter crash site, we feared the worst. Is Sean with you?'

'Yes, and we found Arturo.'

'*Ciao!*' Arturo said, joining in the conversation.

'*Ciao*, Arty!'

'Commander, we've collected all the crystals for the cube and we know where the Ark is,' Sean said.

'Well done. You're making better progress than us,' Hazim said in a tone that sounded more downbeat. 'We're regrouping our forces around Cairo, but to be honest, things aren't looking good. We're stretched to our limits.'

'I've got a plan – one that helps both of us.'

'At this point, we're open to any help we can get. Explain.'

'We've discovered a pyramid buried under a mountain in El Mirador in Guatemala. It's full of Isharkute weapons and vessels hidden by my dad. Send as many soldiers as you can. Senetep's busy chasing us, so he's only left a small force to protect it. If you take control of the pyramid, you can use what's in there to fight back.'

'Sean, this is Colonel Powell speaking. Good to hear you're alive and well.'

'You too!' Sean replied.

'Organising soldiers to take control of the pyramid in Guatemala won't be easy. General Maddock's still in command here. He doesn't know you're alive and we'd like to keep it that way. He's busy regrouping troops for an attack on Senetep's pyramid at Giza. I need to stay here and work with him - keep him as far away from you as possible.'

'I can organise transport for Carla and myself to Guatemala,' Hazim cut in. 'I'll take a small special-ops squad that can work alongside the Guatemalan government. We're at least half a day away, but we'll do our best to take the pyramid.'

'Sounds good,' Sean said, taking a tentative pause before speaking again. 'Carla, I thought you should know...my dad's buried there, in the mausoleum above the control room.'

There was silence on the other end of the connection.

'If you're going there, I thought you'd like to know,' Sean finished softly.

'Thank you, Sean,' Carla said.

Bella recognised the emotion in her aunt's voice - a timely reminder that to her, it had only been a day since she lost her beloved Henry.

'You all look out for each other. I'll see you when this's over,' Carla said.

Bella wiped the tears from her eyes. '*Sí, certo*. We will.'

'God be with you,' Arturo said.

'And you too,' Carla replied.

The phone call ended. Everyone sat in silence. The conversation had left Bella emotional, like her heart had been pulled out of her chest and stomped on. She wished she was by her aunt's side to give her the love and support she needed.

Alarms sounded and a blaze of red dots pulsed across the holographic map, snapping everyone from their thoughts. Multiple missiles were homing in on their vessel.

'Look out!' Bella screamed, catching sight of them through the rear hull.

Sean slammed the accelerator all the way forward. The sudden burst of speed sent Bella and Arturo tumbling over the transparent section of the hull. The disorienting illusion of rocketing through midair made Bella feel nauseous. She quickly crawled back into the front half of the cabin onto visible floor. Sean looked like he was in a trance, staring ahead, hands riding the controls with superhuman precision. How could he fly at such incredible speeds? The missiles were a distant speck now, but Sean kept accelerating, causing their vessel to shudder.

'Don't overload the power crystal,' Nocao warned.

Sean didn't even glance at Nocao's hologram. He was so focused on flying that Bella wondered if he'd even heard the instruction. The vibrations were getting worse.

'You lost them,' Bella assured him. 'Slow down a bit.'

'*Tutto'aposto.* Give yourself a rest,' Arturo said.

Sean decelerated and followed the course of a wide, gentle river. He slumped back into his chair and caught his breath. Bella watched him with concern. The short burst of intense concentration had taken its toll. His hands were trembling and his forehead was lathered in sweat. More red dots suddenly flashed across the scanner.

'What are they?' Bella asked.

'More Isharkute.' Sean sighed in exasperation. He eyeballed Nocao's hologram. 'I thought you were supposed to get rid of these guys.'

'Every Isharkute vessel's been ordered to intercept you.'

'Oh, great!'

'Keep going,' Nocao ordered. 'Fly low – the natural rock in the region will help mask your crystalline hull from more missile locks.'

'I can't keep this up. We're still hundreds of kilometres away from our rendezvous,' Sean said. He dragged the holographic map higher, revealing an extensive labyrinth of caves and grottos beneath the surface. He double-checked the map and stood, peering out the viewscreen. 'I've got a better idea.'

Bella pointed ahead to the edge of a massive waterfall. 'Wow! Look at that.'

'That's what I was looking for,' Sean said.

The river suddenly vanished beneath their vessel in a dense white mist. Raging waters plummeted down a vertical 200-metre drop, showering the lower jungle in a fine spray. A near-complete rainbow arched from one side of the river to the other. Bella stared in wonder as they flew through the iridescent colours. *It's so beautiful.* What a shame they were experiencing the most amazing places on Earth under the worst imaginable circumstances.

Sean turned their vessel to face the wall of crashing water and the delicate rainbow faded from sight. He enlarged the hologram, showing the entrance to the caves located behind the waterfall.

'What are you thinking?' Arturo asked.

'If we fly through the caves, they'll never be able to find us. We'll just look like part of the rock.'

'Won't it be harder to fly through caves?' Bella asked.

'Not when I can set it to autopilot. It'll just fly us out.'

'Don't go into the caves,' Nocao said. 'Even I won't be able to track you. If you get cornered or lost, you might never find a way out.'

'I'll stick close to the surface. It'll be all right,' Sean said, forging ahead.

They flew through the torrent of cascading water. Bella peered up through the transparent hull as the water pummelled their vessel, making her feel like a child staring out the window in a giant car wash. The incandescent shower was abruptly replaced with dark rock as they passed into a gigantic cavern. Their vessel emitted a blue laser that scanned the void ahead. They skimmed between huge stalactites and stalagmites that looked like giant teeth, devouring them into the bowels of the Earth.

Sean worked feverishly on their escape route, but it was proving more difficult than he first let on. He tapped repeatedly on the hologram, searching for a way through the endless maze of caverns. Every route was coming up as impassable or a dead end.

'You still have time to turn around,' Nocao said.

'I'll find a way,' Sean said, determined to the point of sounding stubborn. 'There – I've got it!'

Sure enough, he'd found an exit shaft. It was over 100 kilometres away and close to the coastline where Nocao had set their rendezvous. Sean reactivated the autopilot and their vessel accelerated into the darkness. They rocked, rolled, and swerved through the tightest of cracks and fissures. Bella's stomach was in her mouth. The autopilot left it to the very last moment to correct itself, giving the impression they were about to collide with the cave wall with every manoeuvre. She couldn't watch.

'We're on our way,' Sean said proudly, relaxing back into his seat.

Nocao's hologram began to flicker and disappear. 'You're about to pass through the Earth's crust into the upper mantle.'

'Is that bad?' Bella said.

'The changing composition of the rocks will disrupt your navigation and communications –'

Nocao's voice turned to static.

'Nocao, can you hear me?' Sean said.

Bella quivered. The isolation and creeping claustrophobia was almost unbearable. It felt like the weight of the world was crushing down on them. Arturo's pale and horrified expression only amplified her feelings of terror.

'We're too deep for a signal,' Sean said, expanding the map. The tiny blue dot representing their vessel was so far underground, there was no visible surface. Several red dots appeared across the hologram and trailed them deep into the Earth. 'Damn! Senetep's marauders must've tracked us into the caves.'

'You said they wouldn't be able to track us down here,' Arturo said angrily.

'I thought they couldn't,' Sean said innocently.

'Don't worry about that now – just keep focusing,' Bella said. The last thing they needed to do was panic and argue.

'What sort of weapons do we have?' Arturo asked.

Sean skimmed through their onboard arsenal. 'Six seismic charges, two homing missiles, a fully charged laser array, and one fire extinguisher.'

Arturo laughed. 'Fire extinguisher? What'll we do with that – shoot them with water?'

'It's not what you think,' Sean said. 'Last time Nocao and I were shot with one, it suffocated our vessel in foam resin and we crashed.'

'They're getting closer,' Bella said, pointing at the dots tracking them. 'Can we go faster?'

'Not on autopilot.'

'Then take us off autopilot,' Arturo insisted. 'This cave's big enough to navigate yourself.'

The cave opened into a subterranean void so vast that their scanning lasers couldn't find the edges in places. Their vessel cast little light into the darkness, like a candle in an empty hall. Bella hated the endless indeterminable black. The sooner they made it back to daylight, the better.

Sean sat up straight and switched off the autopilot.

Building-sized stalactites appeared without warning and Sean steered around them like they were flying through an upside-down city. Bella couldn't stop trembling. The scale of Earth's interior was awe-inspiring and intimidating. She'd never imagined such places even existed. Distant pinpricks of light appeared deep in the cavern, like car headlights trailing them in the night.

'I think I see them!' Bella cried.

'All right, hold onto something,' Sean said. 'I'm going closer to the bigger rocks.'

They swerved closer to the stalactites, almost shaving the sides. Bella squinted, unsure if it was better to watch ahead or behind – both angles were just as terrifying. A hellish red glow appeared ahead. 'Where's that light coming from?' she said.

Sean rolled their vessel through a tight fissure and they shot into an enormous lava chamber. Molten rock spewed at them like an angry subterranean god spitting upon a puny intruder. Glowing flecks landed on their hull and stuck like mud.

'Whoa! Maybe we'll need the fire extinguisher after all,' Bella said.

The marauders trailed them into the chamber, zipping around the fountains of exploding lava close enough that the Isharkute pilots were visible through the windscreens.

'I'm gonna fly us low over the lava. When we're close enough, drop two of the seismic charges,' Sean said, nodding his head at the pulsing button on the panel next to her.

Bella gulped. 'You want me to do it?'

Sean was too occupied to respond. His hands were locked on the flight controls, attention focused on navigating the chamber. She didn't want to be burdened with such responsibility, but there was no time to question his decision. They descended sharply and skimmed across the searing terrain. A tumultuous lake of magma filled their viewscreen, bubbling and exploding around them without warning, each mini-eruption a one-way ticket to fiery doom.

Bella felt a tickle of sweat race down her back.

'Now!' Sean hollered.

Bella punched the button and two football-sized charges dropped into the lava.

'Hold on to something,' he cried, jamming the accelerator all the way forward.

Bella and Arturo tumbled towards the rear of the cabin as their vessel rocketed high into the chamber. The lava lake erupted in a fountain of white-hot magma, instantly vaporising the Isharkute vessels. Sean veered them hard away from the chamber ceiling as the dark rock was splattered with glowing blobs of lava, creating a beautiful galaxy of molten rock.

'You did it!' Bella said.

'There's our exit,' Sean said, pointing to the fissure ahead. 'It's a direct shaft back to the surface.'

'Are we inside a volcano?' Bella asked.

'Yep,' Sean replied, flying them into the main volcanic vent.

The walls were smooth from previous eruptions, their path to the pinprick of sunlight a straight flight upwards. Bella sighed with relief. The end was in sight, but they weren't leaving the sleeping volcano so peaceful. Their destructive influence deep in the chamber had awoken the powerful forces of nature. They passed through the volcano's main vent and shot high into the atmosphere. Poisonous gases were being ejected from every crevice and the dark volcanic cone turned bright yellow. A world-shattering explosion annihilated the peak and sent a cloud of cinders and superheated ash roaring after them.

Nocao's hologram shimmered back to life. 'What's going on?'

'Nothing! We're on our way,' Sean said.

Nocao went quiet for a moment and assessed the data. 'There's a volcanic eruption to the south-east of my position. Volcano Atitlán! Has that got something to do with you?'

'Sort of,' Sean replied sheepishly.

'You're too far south – our meeting point's north of there.'

'We'll be there in a few minutes.'

'I can't wait for you. Sending new coordinates for the North Atlantic Ocean,' Nocao grumbled. 'No more detours this time.'

'Okay, sorry,' Sean said. He adjusted their course to match and sat back.

They circled the lake at the foot of the volcano, which was now in the throes of erupting, spewing lava and ash over the surrounding jungles. Bella watched with a heavy heart. She felt guilty for creating such devastation. The eruption disappeared on the horizon and they flew north over the ocean. Nocao's vessel appeared on the scanner and within a few minutes, they were flying alongside him. At that very moment, sirens sounded throughout the cabin and a new red dot appeared on the map, closing in on their position.

'What's that?' Arturo said.

'Tectonic missile!' Nocao cried.

'Not again!' Sean gasped. 'This didn't end so well last time.'

'You have the cube and the coordinates. You know where to go. Leave and don't come back for me. I'll catch up with you when I can,' Nocao said.

'Wait! What're you doing?' Sean said.

Nocao made a simple gesture with his hands that made Sean stand up from his chair and call out in desperation, 'No!'

Nocao gave Sean a smile and terminated the communication. His vessel turned away from theirs and flew on a direct line with the missile.

Bella was overcome with a grave feeling. 'What's he doing?'

Sean eyed the hologram. 'He's put all his energy into his shields... He's going to knock the missile off course before it detonates.'

Bella stared at the two converging dots.

'What are you waiting for?' Arturo said. 'Get us out of here!'

Sean's hand hovered over the accelerator, reluctant to commit his friend to face the missile alone.

'Do it!' Bella whispered.

Sean gave her a fleeting glance, eyes filled with tears. He slammed the accelerator and they tore ahead, placing hundreds of kilometres between them and the impending explosion. Nocao's dot suddenly disappeared from the map. An invisible shockwave chased them across the ocean and slammed into their vessel, throwing them into a violent spin and pinning them against the wall. Sean fought his way back to the controls. He corrected their trajectory and slumped back into the chair with a vacant, devastated stare.

Nocao was gone.

# — CHAPTER 20 —

# *The Covenant*

Sean was lost in his own thoughts during the flight back to Africa. He felt hollow and numb. Bella and Arturo did their best to console him, but they couldn't alleviate the emptiness eating away inside him. His dad, William, and now Nocao. Anyone close to him was dead. If he'd only listened and not gone into the caves. Nocao might still be alive.

'Sean, we're here,' Bella said gently.

Sean took a deep breath and tried not to think about his friend. He needed to be strong and unemotional, like Nocao would be under the same circumstances. At least until this was over. He sat up and looked upon the flat, sunburnt plains of Ethiopia. The small unassuming city of Axum was nestled in the middle of nowhere, untouched by the events shaping the rest of the world. The autopilot flew them north of the city, over the dome of the church of St. Mary of Zion, to land on the outskirts of Axum's famous stelae park, home to a collection of massive, obelisk-like monuments.

'You sure you're okay?' Arturo said, placing a friendly hand on his shoulder.

Sean nodded.

'We're sorry about Nocao,' Bella said. 'If he was here, you know he'd want us to keep going.'

'You're right,' Sean said, feigning a smile.

He appreciated their thoughts, and for now, they gave him the strength to continue. He ejected a crystalline scanner from the console, collected the cube, and led the way outside. The ancient stelae loomed high over the park and looked very different from the obelisks found in Egypt. Each one was topped with a curved headpiece shaped like a half-moon. The front of the stelae were decorated with carvings of windows and doors, creating the impression of multi-storey buildings.

'I've seen these stelae before,' Arturo said. 'We used to have the Obelisk of Axum in Rome. I was young, but I remember Papa took me to see it a couple of times before the Italian government returned it to Ethiopia. He hated the fact that we'd stolen it as war booty in the 1930s...said it was a slight against our nation.'

'I don't remember it,' Bella said.

'You were too young. It was dismantled and returned to Axum in the mid-2000s.'

'Is that it?' Sean said, pointing to the largest stela in the park.

'No, that's King Ezana's stela. Legend says the Ark of the Covenant's power sliced the stelae out of granite and erected it here.'

'Why do they look like buildings?'

'I think they're grave markers for underground burial chambers.'

Sean spotted the dome of the church of St. Mary of Zion over the treetops and headed off. Their footsteps echoed through the empty street. There were no voices in the distance, no cars or motorbikes – nothing to indicate there was a single living soul left in the town. A pack of dogs raced past them, growling and salivating like wild animals. Bella's face went white and she pointed to the road. The dogs had left a trail of bloody paw prints across the asphalt. The road leading up to the church was strewn with abandoned cars and bicycles. Cars were littered with bullet holes, their windscreens shattered, doors left wide open. An empty pram lay on the steps leading up to the church doors.

'*Dio mio!*' Bella gasped.

The lack of human presence was more unsettling than the aftermath itself. There were no bodies – just splatters and pools of dried blood. Axum had been deserted for days, enough time for the dogs to start fending for themselves. It appeared this fight had taken place before the Isharkute even invaded.

Sean led them around the church to the adjoining chapels. 'In 2014, the Ark was moved from the old chapel into a new one. We should start looking there.'

The new Chapel of the Tablet was a modestly-sized, underwhelming box of a building. The dull stone-clad walls stood two storeys high, with barred windows and topped with a domed roof and cross. The old chapel stood beside it, similar in design but slightly smaller. A simple wrought-iron fence enclosed the two structures from the rest of the town. They entered the chapel courtyard through a section of flattened fence. The paving was littered with rubble and streaked with tyre marks, showing where the intruders rammed their way through.

'Look!' Bella gasped, peering over her shoulder. The pack of dogs had doubled in size and stood along the fence line, growling at them. 'What do we do?'

'Don't run,' Arturo said calmly. 'Keep walking towards the chapel.'

Their snarls seemed to elicit a warning: *Don't enter the chapel!*

Sean understood the chapel was the holiest of holies for every Ethiopian Christian, the fervent, self-appointed guardians of the Ark. There was an unearthly, spiritual presence in the air, reminding him they were trespassers on hallowed ground. Strangely, the dogs didn't pass beyond the line of the perimeter fence.

The chapel walls were riddled with bullet holes. The main wooden door was splintered and hanging precariously on one hinge. They stooped beneath it and entered the chapel. The interior was a surprisingly lively space with bright red carpet and yellow walls. The middle of the room was dominated by the inner sanctum, a solid floor-to-ceiling box painted with colourful Biblical scenes separated into panels, like a graphic novel of the Bible. It started with the birth of Jesus Christ and progressed through his life to the Last Supper, crucifixion, and resurrection. Several Old Testament stories were also depicted, including the story of Moses receiving the Ten Commandments, and the details about the Ark of the Covenant being brought to Ethiopia.

Three of the sanctum walls were inset with a central window, closed off by ornate wooden shutters. Carved into the framework above the closed shutters was a cherub with no body – just an angelic head with wings.

*Cherubs would make one freaky hybrid,* Sean thought.

They rounded the sanctum and found the entrance. The wooden door sat ajar, revealing an empty interior. Whatever had been housed inside the sanctum was gone.

Sean stared at the stone floor, numb with shock. They were too late!

An old Ethiopian man dressed in black and white robes suddenly appeared behind them. He was extremely thin, with a gaunt face and straggly grey beard. His haunted eyes were clouded with milky-white cataracts, a tell-tale feature of a guardian of the Ark.

'Are you the monk assigned to protect the Ark?' Sean said.

The monk nodded.

Sean motioned Bella and Arturo to lower their weapons and continued in a respectful tone. 'What happened to the Ark?'

The monk approached them, his blind eyes assessing them as though he could see straight through his affliction. *'Who are you?'* the monk asked in his native tongue.

The Ethiopian dialect translated perfectly through Sean's Isharkute implant. 'I'm Sean Livingstone. These are my friends, Bella and Arturo.'

The monk approached Bella and raised his gangly fingers to her face. She recoiled.

'It's okay,' Sean assured her. 'I think he needs to see who we are.'

Bella closed her eyes, hiding the monk's unsettling gaze. She grimaced as he examined the contours of her face. Once the monk was done, he moved on to Arturo, and then Sean.

*'You're just children!'* the monk said in a surprised tone.

'What did he say?' Bella whispered.

'He said we're children.'

'Speak for yourself,' Arturo said.

'He just means we're young,' Sean said.

'Young compared to those who came before you,' the monk said in English, his sudden change of language taking them by surprise.

'Who came before us?' Sean asked.

'Their leader was called Malik.'

'Malik Hawati!' Sean said. 'Azar's son.'

'His men ransacked our town. They created chaos and panic. Our people fled after they left, fearing others would come in search of the Ark.'

'If Malik didn't find the Ark, then where is it?'

The monk shuffled to in front of Sean and stared right at him, as if peering into his soul. 'The search for the Ark must be a selfless quest. Why do you seek its power?'

Sean knew everything hinged on answering the question correctly.

There was only one answer, the truth.

'To save the world.'

'What makes you think you can control the power of the Ark?'

Sean withdrew the cube. 'Because we have this.'

The monk's hands were drawn to the cube. He caressed the inscriptions with care, and then moved over Sean's hand and along his forearm. Sean was tempted to pull away, but the monk's firm grip was working up his arm to his shoulder. The monk touched his wings, causing them to quiver. Sean was a little embarrassed. He'd never let anyone touch them, not even his dad.

The monk lowered his hands, his wrinkled expression stricken with awe. 'Have you heard of the Nephilim, Sean?'

'I think so. Aren't they from the Bible?'

'Weren't they fallen angels?' Bella said, cutting in. 'Disgraced in the eyes of God.'

'Not exactly,' Arturo said. 'The book of Genesis says the Nephilim were the offspring of the sons of god and the daughters of men.'

The monk nodded. 'The Nephilim represent a covenant between us and a higher power.'

'Don't you mean God?' Bella said.

The monk scratched his beard in consternation, and then

shuffled past the chapel door into the glaring sunlight. Outside, the dogs were still guarding the perimeter fence. They were no longer snarling and stood watching them with curiosity. The monk led them across a paved area to the old Chapel of the Tablet.

'Where's he taking us?' Bella asked.

'Maybe the new chapel was built as a decoy to lead people away from the Ark,' Arturo said.

The monk directed Sean through the red curtains draped over the entrance. Bella moved to follow, but the monk blocked her from entering. 'I'm sorry. Women are not permitted inside the chapel.'

'What?!' Bella said.

'We're not leaving my sister out here,' Arturo said.

Sean poked his head through the curtain. 'With the fate of the world in our hands, I think we can bend the rules a little.'

'I don't discriminate,' the monk said, 'but I didn't make the rules. They've been passed down from one guardian to the next.'

'God doesn't discriminate – only people do,' Bella said.

The monk considered their comments and lowered his hand.

'Thank you,' Bella said, nodding respectfully.

The inside of the old chapel was dark and foreboding, compared to the first. Dark green tarpaulins hung from the ceiling and a skeleton of scaffolding scaled the interior walls, making it look more like a worksite than a chapel. Shafts of light from the upper windows created pools of light on the stone floor. There were no colourful paintings or decorations, and the air was thick with a musty smell. The monk weaved his way through the construction material like he had 20/20 vision. As the sole guardian, he'd walked this path a million times. The monk pulled back the tarpaulin covering the inner sanctum and directed them inside.

The empty interior was the size of a lift. The monk pushed them against the walls, away from the centre of the sanctum. He pulled a crucifix from his robes, inserted it into a hole in the wall, and turned it like a key. The floor shuddered and dropped away, creating a set of stairs leading deep beneath the sanctum. The monk descended into the darkness.

Sean followed first. Soon he was in the same dark world as the monk, unable to see anything. He grasped the wall to guide his descent, testing each new step with his feet.

The monk stopped at the bottom of the stairs and waited for them to assemble in the darkness. He struck a match against the stone. The flickering light caught his milky eyes, giving him an ominous, zombie-like appearance. He lit a torch hanging on the wall and passed it to Sean, then disappeared into the long dark tunnel.

'What's going on?' Bella whispered.

'Hopefully he's taking us to the Ark,' Arturo whispered back.

'There's only one way to find out,' Sean said, starting after the monk.

The tunnel was hewn straight out of solid rock and covered in more Biblical paintings. From what Sean could tell, they depicted the history of the Ark through the ages. They hustled to catch up to the monk.

'The Ark's journey is almost complete,' the monk said over his shoulder. 'After one thousand years of Judaism and two thousand years of Christianity, the people of Axum are staunch followers of the Old Testament. None of them have ever seen the Ark, but they are believers. The Ark's journey began with Moses receiving the Ten Commandments on Mount Sinai. It was carried by the Jews as they wandered the desert, and helped them in their wars with Edom and Midian. The Ark was carried ahead of the army and cleared a path of any enemy that stood in their way with jets of flame, burning snakes, and scorpions. When they passed into the land of Canaan, the Ark parted the waters of the River Jordan to give them safe passage. The Jews conquered this land and brought down the walls of Jericho by marching the Ark around the city and blowing their trumpets.'

Sean followed the story on the tunnel wall. The monk's tale kept in perfect time with the passing images. His story sounded rehearsed, as though his years spent as guardian of the Ark had been preparing him for this very moment.

'How does it do all this?' Bella asked.

'The Ark is a physical manifestation of God on Earth,' the monk said. 'There's no greater power than this.'

'Looks like a dangerous weapon, not a holy relic,' Arturo said.

Sean noticed several paintings displayed the Ark surrounded by columns of cloud and fire. Some showed the bearers carrying the Ark in midair, its power lifting them right off the ground. 'Why's the Ark surrounded by clouds?'

'This is God's presence on Earth. By day the Ark was surrounded by pillars of cloud, at night, this turned to fire. When the Philistines stole the Ark from the Jews, it caused pain and suffering amongst their people. To touch the Ark or look upon it at the wrong time of day would cause immediate death.'

Sean couldn't believe all these terrifying side-effects were intended by his dad and Nesuk. The device must have been damaged at some point – that would explain its uncontrollable power.

'How did the Ark end up in Axum?' Arturo said.

'Queen Sheba, the ancestral queen of Ethiopia, visited King Solomon in Jerusalem three thousand years ago. During her stay, Solomon shared his great wisdom and converted the queen to Judaism. On her return to Ethiopia, Queen Sheba bore the king a son, whom she named Baina-lekhem, more commonly known as Menelik. When Menelik was twenty years old, he visited Jerusalem to meet his father. Afterwards, he returned to Ethiopia, accompanied by the firstborn sons of several Israelite nobles . Menelik soon learnt these men had stolen the Ark of the Covenant from Solomon's Temple. Fearing heavenly consequences, Menelik prayed to the Ark and it parted the seas for his people, creating safe passage back to Ethiopia. Menelik reasoned that because the Ark had saved his people instead of destroying them, it should stay in Aksum. The Ark has been here ever since.'

'Why didn't Solomon come after the Ark?' Sean asked.

'He tried and failed. When Solomon returned to Jerusalem, he kept the theft a secret and ordered a copy of the Ark of the Covenant to be placed in the Temple.'

The monk finished his story and the tunnel came to a dead end.

The smooth tunnel butted into a jagged stone wall as if the builders just dropped their tools and left the tunnel unfinished. The final painting depicted an Ethiopian monk and an Isharkute dressed in elegant robes.

Sean's heart skipped a beat. It was Nesuk! The two figures were depicted in a long tunnel, with Nesuk pointing towards a rock wall: the same dead end they were currently facing.

'Three hundred years ago, the guardian of the Ark was visited by a messenger with pale blue skin,' the monk said. 'He helped construct this final hiding place and said that one day a young man with wings, a Nephilim, would come to Axum in search of the Ark. If he was worthy, he would carry the key to open the final seal.'

'Nesuk was still alive three hundred years ago?' Sean asked in surprise.

The monk's wrinkled brow lifted with surprise. 'Only the previous guardians knew his name. How have you heard of the messenger?'

'He's an old friend. This isn't the first time he's helped us –' Sean said, cutting himself short, realising Nesuk's full story was too much to explain right now.

'I don't get it,' Arturo said. 'If Nesuk had the Ark three hundred years ago, why didn't he just use it to activate the beacon before Senetep arrived?'

'My dad hid the Ark, understanding it would be found and moved around. He would've organised Nesuk to return when the Ark was settled in Axum, concealing it so only we could find it. Dad didn't want to disrupt the established course of history.'

'Nesuk predicted another of his kind would arrive with you,' the monk said.

'Nocao,' Sean said with a sudden pang of remorse.

'Where is he?'

The guilt swept over Sean. He'd pushed the tragedy to the back of his mind, but the loss came surging back. He was lost for words.

'Nocao sacrificed himself so we could get here,' Bella said.

Sean gathered his thoughts and focused. 'What do we need to do?'

The monk stepped aside, revealing the final painting of a figure holding up a glowing cross and walking through a wall of solid rock. It took Sean a few seconds to realise the figure had wings – it was him!

Sean touched the unfinished stone blocking the end of the tunnel, half-expecting it to slide back and reveal the Ark. It was solid and immovable. He pulled out the cube, entered the sequence, and the cube transformed into a cross.

'Only you can pass,' the monk said. 'But remember...the true Ark is a covenant between humanity and a higher power.'

'Higher power. You mean the Isharkute?'

'It's called many things, but you should look upon it as enlightenment and a deeper connection to the universe. Once you understand what the covenant means, you'll know what to do next.'

The crystals on the cross were now glowing brighter than ever, creating a warm tingling sensation that travelled up his arm and made him feel giddy. He held out the cross, just like in the painting, and stepped forward. His hands disappeared straight through the rock, followed by his forearms and elbows. He stopped short, the tip of his nose just inches from the stone. With one deep breath, he closed his eyes and stepped all the way through.

A wave of energy fizzled over his body as he stumbled into a void beyond. He found himself standing at the top of a short flight of steps descending into a dark chamber.

Behind him, he could see Bella, Arturo, and the monk stuck in the tunnel, unable to see or hear him through the holographic rock. Arturo hit the wall and called out, but his voice was silenced by the illusion. Isharkute technology built into the tunnel walls had created a hard hologram of the wall he'd just walked through, one that could only be passed with the completed cross.

Sean's stomach flipped at the thought of what he was about to find – the Ark of the Covenant, the most sought-after religious artefact from history, not to mention the deadliest!

He descended the steps into the chamber, holding the cross in front of himself for protection. In the centre of the chamber was a large cylindrical container fed by pipes and conduits. Sean approached with a cautious step. A stone plinth ejected from the floor in front of him. It had no controls, only an indentation on the top that matched his glowing cross.

Sean held the cross over the indentation and it shot out of his hand, locking into place. He took a nervous step back.

Rivulets of blue energy transferred from the cross, down the plinth, and spread across the floor, branching into hundreds of miniature pathways like the blueprints of some ancient plan, all converging to create a glowing ring of light around the cylinder. An ear-splitting hiss shot through the chamber and the cylinder ascended, releasing misty tendrils across the floor.

Sean jumped back as the ghostly fingers grasped and swirled towards him. He fought the urge to race back up the stairs.

The mist dispersed, revealing a golden box. The Ark of the Covenant!

It looked just like the Ark he'd seen in books and movies. Sean stared in awe, feet locked to floor, reluctant to take him forward. It was a surreal. This was the actual relic from the Bible. The Ark was the size of a large chest, gilded entirely in gold and flanked by two long carrying rods. The lid was adorned with a pair of golden cherubim, facing each other, the tips of their outstretched wings meeting over the centre of the lid. Was it coincidence he had wings like the cherubim? Maybe they were originally hybrids like himself. In the Christian Bible, cherubs were also said to have four faces: one human, the others a lion, ox, and eagle. This combination of man and animal was a common theme in religion and mythology.

Sean took a tentative step forward, his heart pounding so hard it felt like it was going to jump out of his chest. A low hum reverberated through the chamber and charged the air with electricity.

It made the hairs on his arm stand on end.

'What now?' Sean whispered to himself. 'Do I touch it?'

The monk said once he understood the true meaning of the Ark and its covenant, he'd know what do. There was no way of carrying the Ark out by himself. Was he supposed to open it? Just touching it could cause instant death, but how else was he going to learn about this so-called covenant?

There was no option but to open the lid and peek inside.

A flicker of light caught his eye, right between the tips of the cherubim's wings.

Sean stared intently, waiting for it to happen again, wondering if it was just a glint off the gold casing. He leant a little closer. A tiny spark of electricity ignited between the wing tips. Was the Ark attempting to power up?

Sean reached out, mesmerised by the miniature bolt of energy. He wasn't even sure why he was doing so, but before he could withdraw his hand, he was struck with a blinding flash of white light.

# — CHAPTER 21 —

# *Deadly Doublecross*

Sean's first thought was *I'm dead!* The intense pain and flash of light disappeared in the same instant, leaving him hovering in darkness. A gentle blue light appeared overhead, dancing and rippling all around him. He was deep underwater and travelling fast, but he wasn't swimming – rather, being propelled by some invisible force.

A sprawling stone structure emerged from the depths, comprised of flat terraces, sharp right angles, and odd-shaped megaliths. The formation rose from the craggy rocks of the ocean floor. Sean was looking at the Yonaguni Monument, the submerged rock formation off the coast of Japan and the hidden beacon designed to awaken the Isharkute fleet.

He zoomed straight towards an eroded face carved into one of the walls. The shadowy eyes stared back at him through the water. The invisible force controlling his body ripped him away at the last second, whipping him between the structures in a disorienting blur. He entered a crevice between two monolithic blocks and whooshed down a tunnel, eventually bursting free of the water to fly through the dry interior.

It was an impossible path to remember, but he sensed every twist and turn was being etched into the back of his mind. The final tunnel opened into a circular chamber dominated by an immense obelisk. He flew around it once, then down another tunnel into a smaller chamber, slowing to hover over an imprint of a human hand recessed into a central stone plinth.

Without any conscious effort, his hand reached out and nestled into the indentation.

An intense glow consumed his hand, separating his mind and body. His consciousness hurtled straight up, passing through Yonaguni's stone ceiling and then the ocean, bursting into the open sky and accelerating like a rocket into the upper atmosphere. The speed was exhilarating. The ocean disappeared far below, obscured by a shield of flaming light as he passed through Earth's final barrier.

The turbulence cleared and he was thrust amongst the heavens.

Sean stared in wonder. He'd never seen the stars so clearly.

In the serenity of space, Sean suddenly realised that he was the key to activating Yonaguni: the covenant between humanity, the Isharkute, and the universe. The Ark had empowered him with an energy only his body could withstand. His unique sequence of DNA was the crucial element – the key that prevented him from being killed by the Ark, like so many before him.

All this information was instantly present in his thoughts, implanted by the Ark.

With his body left behind on Earth, Sean's consciousness journeyed beyond the solar system into the furthest reaches of the universe. Space wasn't the black void with tiny stars he was accustomed to seeing from Earth; it was brimming with vibrant nebulae in a divine spectrum of colours. Suns, planets, and galaxies whizzed by in infinite splendour. His trajectory suddenly changed to veer in line with a specific star. He passed into the star's outer system and slowed to hover near a crimson-coloured planet and its grey moon.

Nestled between them was the Isharkute fleet. Hundreds of dormant motherships hung in the silent vacuum of space, awaiting a signal to be awakened.

The image began to fade.

Sean was being pulled back to his mortal body by the call of a female voice. 'Sean... Sean... Can you hear me? Sean... Wake up, *ti prego!*'

Sean forced his eyes open to find Bella and Arturo hunched

over him. Their terrified expressions quickly changed to relief. Bella hugged him tightly. 'We thought you were dead.'

'I found the Ark!' Sean gasped. 'I know what to do.'

'Shh!' Bella whispered. 'Not now.'

'Sean, thank God you're okay!' Colonel Powell said, kneeling beside him. 'I was about to get the medical team to evac you out of here.'

Sean looked around. The chamber was crawling with military personnel. A team of scientists dressed in silver hazmat suits crowded around the Ark, scanning it with scientific instruments in preparation to lift it off the pedestal. A squad of US soldiers stood guard around the scientists, hands on their weapons.

Sean had a bad feeling. Something wasn't right. Bella and Arturo were too quiet. Colonel Powell seemed on edge and kept looking between the soldiers and the tunnel back to the chapel. Sean gingerly stood with a little support from Bella and Arturo, still disoriented from his universe-hopping experience. 'How long was I unconscious?'

'An hour or so,' Arturo said.

'How'd you get here so fast, Colonel Powell?' Sean asked. 'We said we'd contact you when we found the Ark.'

Powell glanced at the soldiers standing over them and spoke in an odd, unconvincing tone. 'We couldn't wait. Securing the Ark is now our top priority.'

Sean got the sense Powell wasn't telling him everything. He peered around the chamber. The monk was standing at the top of the steps under military guard. 'The monk's harmless. You can let him go – he's been protecting the Ark for the last few years.'

'He's free to go once we leave,' Powell said. 'Is there anything our scientists need to know before moving the Ark?'

'Sure, don't open it! And don't touch it if the lid sparks.'

'But otherwise it's safe to move?'

'I think so.'

Powell nodded and left to speak with the scientists. After a brief conversation, Powell was promptly escorted from the chambers by two soldiers. Sean shared a concerned look with Bella and Arturo as they were ordered to follow.

'How'd you get into the chamber?' Sean asked over his shoulder.

'Shortly after you walked through the wall, there was a big earthquake,' Bella said. 'Then the wall just disappeared like it was a hologram. We found you unconscious in front of the Ark.'

'Forty-five minutes after that, Colonel Powell and his soldiers turned up,' Arturo said.

They followed Powell up the stairs, through the heavily guarded chapel, and trod over the torn red curtain that previously hung over the entrance. Three Black Hawk helicopters were parked in the courtyard. Colonel Powell turned around to face them.

'What's going on, Colonel?' Sean asked.

Powell didn't answer. He wasn't his usual confident self and seemed somewhat intimidated by the soldiers. Sean suddenly noticed the colonel's holster was empty. Why was he unarmed? Just as he thought that, the soldiers turned their weapons on Powell and pushed him towards them.

'I'm sorry,' Powell said. 'I couldn't say anything before now.'

'What are you talking about?'

'Somehow General Maddock overheard our previous conversation. He knows all our plans. I was arrested, then ordered to come here and use our friendship to secure the Ark. Now that it's complete, I'm a prisoner – just like you.'

'Mission accomplished, then,' Arturo grumbled.

'I didn't have much of a choice. It was either play along or be sent to solitary confinement for who knows how long. I was hoping I could figure out a way to warn you before I got here. At least together, we might be able to make Mad-axe see reason.'

'Mad-axe?' Sean asked.

'It's Maddock's nickname. He earned it during the Gulf War.'

'Why, what did he do?'

'You're probably better off not knowing.'

Sean nodded. 'Probably. What about Carla and Hazim? Have they been captured too?'

'I saw them leave... They may have made it in time, but I haven't heard anything.'

Their conversation was drowned out by the throbbing blades of a massive tilt rotor helicopter. It flew over the trees lining the courtyard, thrashing the branches with its downdraft and sending whirlwinds of dust towards them. The impressive vehicle touched down in the middle of the courtyard.

'What sort of helicopter's that?' Sean shouted over the noise.

'V-22 Osprey,' Powell replied. 'Heavy transport vehicle, here to collect the Ark... It's now General Maddock's helicopter of choice after we crashed his last one in the desert. Considering I was responsible for stealing that vehicle, I'm in about as much trouble as you.'

'Really?'

'No, not really,' Powell said with a wistful grin. 'You're on a whole different level of trouble.'

'But we're the good guys!' Bella said.

'Try telling that to the general.'

The Osprey's side door opened and General Maddock leapt onto the pavement. The downdraft flapped his tattered uniform and whipped the dust off his shoulders. His left sleeve was torn off at the shoulder, displaying his bulging bicep wrapped in a blood-soaked bandage. He marched towards them in full bulldog-scowl mode, his scrunched-up face covered in cuts and scratches, looking like he'd just crawled out of a pit fight.

'Sean Livingstone!' Maddock boomed. 'For a scrawny fifteen-year-old kid, you don't disappoint. When you're not blowing up half of Cairo, you're travelling the world discovering priceless relics. Where's Nocao?'

'He's dead,' Sean said.

Maddock snickered. 'Good. That's one less conehead I need to worry about.'

Sean clenched his fists, keen to punch the general on his big broad nose.

'You're a heartless monster!' Bella gasped.

Maddock grinned as the Ark was marched past them.

The Ark's new custodians were neither priests nor devout believers, but faceless minions hidden beneath silver hazmat suits. The reverence humanity once held for the Ark had been replaced with fear, greed, and misunderstanding. Sean relaxed with the knowledge that the real power of the Ark wasn't being whisked away to a secret facility – it had been imbued within him. All he needed to do was escape and find his way to Yonaguni.

A squad of soldiers escorted the scientists across the courtyard and up the ramp into the Osprey.

'What are you doing with the Ark?' Sean asked.

Maddock laughed. 'That's classified. However, I can tell you I'm not using it to turn on your hidden beacon and invite more Isharkute here. This is humanity's battle. We'll win...or die trying.'

'That kind of mentality will be the end of humanity,' Sean said. 'In case you haven't noticed, we're not on our own anymore. We live in a bigger universe now.'

'This ball of dirt's big enough for me.'

The general's obstinate nature reminded Sean of Senetep.

The soldiers strapped the Ark into the Osprey's cargo hold and the ramp retracted, concealing the golden treasure within its metal belly.

'You can't control the Ark,' Sean said. 'Your soldiers and scientists will die trying. You don't understand what its power means.'

'And I suppose you do?'

Sean wondered what to tell him. The general would never believe that he was now the Ark *and* the covenant. It sounded far-fetched, even to himself. Besides, the general hadn't trusted him so far, so there was no reason to try and convince him now. The truth would only complicate their situation and lessen their chances of escape. They were better off alone. Sean kept his mouth shut, pretending to be lost for words.

Maddock made a satisfied snort and headed for the Osprey. 'Don't worry, Sean – we have our best people working on it. We'll figure it out.'

'You have what you want. Why don't you let us go?' Sean yelled.

'You're far too valuable an asset to let go,' Maddock called over his shoulder. 'Oh, and thanks for the heads-up on El Mirador. With the Ark and the pyramid under our control, we'll have the firepower to bring Senetep to his knees.'

'What are you going to do with us?' Bella cried.

Maddock ignored her and continued over to the soldiers waiting by the Osprey.

'It's no use trying to bargain with him,' Powell said. 'We're under military arrest. We'll be sent to separate bases for interrogation and imprisonment.'

Sean watched Maddock speak with his soldiers, doing his best to read their lips, but they were too far away. One of the soldiers answered a satellite phone and handed it to the general. Sean's stomach dropped with the terrible realisation. 'If the general's been using satellite-based communications, Senetep will know everything. He would've tracked you here –'

'How's that possible?' Powell cut in. 'Our comms employ a 256-bit encrypted network. You think the Isharkute can decipher it?'

'They would've deciphered your codes within minutes of invading. When Nocao contacted you about El Mirador, we used an Isharkute-encrypted signal that couldn't be hacked or traced. Didn't you ever wonder why Senetep left our satellites intact?'

Powell's face went pale. 'Our entire military – everything we've done has been an open book.'

Sean nodded. 'I'm surprised Senetep's not here already.'

Powell rounded on the nearest soldier, checking his rank and name. 'Private Lockman, you've been listening to our conversation – you know what's at stake here. An Isharkute attack is imminent, you need to warn the general.'

The private glanced at his comrades. They wore brave faces, but there was a discernible glint of uncertainty in their eyes. None volunteered to inform their hot-headed general.

'I recognise some of you,' Powell said. 'You're good soldiers and I respect that you're obeying orders, but if you don't tell General

Maddock, I'll be forced to go over there and tell him myself.'

Private Lockman stood his ground, hand locked on his M-27 assault rifle.

Powell stepped past him, only to have the gun barrel pressed in his back.

Lockman tightened his trigger finger. 'Stop right there, Colonel, or I'll be forced to shoot.'

'Then you'll have to shoot!'

'You know the colonel's right,' Sean said, stepping closer. 'We have to evacuate before Senetep gets here.'

'It's already too late,' Bella said, pointing over the tree line.

A dark swarm of Isharkute vessels were descending on the outskirts of Axum. Behind them loomed Senetep's annihilator, casting an ominous shadow over the landscape.

'Get them to the helicopters!' Maddock screamed across the courtyard.

Private Lockman and his squad hustled Sean's group to the waiting Black Hawks. Their rotors were only just starting up.

'We'll never take off in time,' Sean said quietly to the colonel. 'We have an Isharkute vessel around the corner that's safer and faster than your helicopters.'

'What about the Ark?' Powell asked under his breath.

'We don't need it anymore.'

The colonel shot him a perplexed look. 'What do you mean? I thought –'

*Whoosh!*

The first wave of hunter-craft swooped in with a hail of energy blasts. The three Black Hawks exploded in a succession of intense fireballs, sending a maelstrom of burning shrapnel across the courtyard. They shielded themselves from the blast of scorched air. Flaming shrapnel screamed past, careening off the pavement. The soldiers took aim at the Isharkute vessels zipping overhead, but their bullets just ricocheted off the alien armour.

The gunfire was unrelenting and deafening. Bella dropped to her knees, hands clasped tight over her ears. Arturo knelt over his sister, shielding her from the deadly fray.

General Maddock scrambled to resume command in the chaos.

Every soldier was scattered around the courtyard and firing back at the Isharkute. The Osprey was damaged and unable to take off, leaving the Ark caught in the middle of everything.

Sean tapped Powell on the shoulder, nodding towards an escape route by the rear of the chapel.

'All right – lead the way!' Powell shouted.

Sean raced through the war zone. Bullets pinged off the pavement as he leapt over the smouldering remains. Once his group were safely behind the chapel, he flew over the wrought-iron fence bordering the chapels.

'What are you doing?' Bella said.

'Escaping!' Sean replied, helping her over the fence.

'*Cretino!*' she said, punching his arm. 'I can see that, but you left the Ark behind!'

'We don't need it.'

'What do you mean?' Arturo said, jumping down. 'How will we turn on the beacon?'

'I'll tell you when we get out of here.'

'Better make it quick,' Powell said.

Several hunter-craft landed around the church and chapels. Squads of Isharkute warriors leapt out and continued the assault on foot, closing in around General Maddock and the Ark. Sean crouched out of sight and raced along a low stone fence past the church of St. Mary of Zion. He could see the tip of King Ezana's stela looming over the trees, marking their destination. The battle between Maddock's soldiers and Senetep's warriors echoed through the empty streets.

Sean raced around the final corner and stopped abruptly. The road to their vessel now glistened with fresh blood. It took him a moment to recognise the mangled, chewed-up carcasses lying ahead of them. It was the pack of dogs from earlier. Sean took a step back, removing his shoe from the sticky crimson puddle. Bella covered her mouth with a sickened gasp.

A dozen large jackals with blood-drenched snouts emerged from the shadows of the surrounding trees. One by one they stood on their two legs, revealing their human bodies and large clawed hands dripping with blood.

'What the hell?' Powell said.

'They're hybrid pack hunters,' Sean said. 'Half-human, half-jackal – like the Egyptian god Anubis.'

Powell instinctively reached for his empty gun holster and sighed. 'Damn! What do we do?'

More hybrids stepped into the sunlight, sniffing the air, closing in a circle around them. Sean glimpsed their vessel. It was only a couple of seconds away if he flew, but he'd be leaving his friends. If they tried to run, they'd be torn to shreds, like the unfortunate dogs. The hybrids edged closer, staring intently, snarling. The largest hybrid raised his head and released an unsettling, childlike cackle.

Bella huddled behind Sean.

A sleek Isharkute vessel flew overhead and landed in the middle of the crimson road.

'What's the bet that's Senetep?' Powell said.

Sean dreaded the thought of facing the Overseer again. In Earth-time, it had been 10,000 years since their last encounter, but to Senetep and himself, it was only a few days since they stood before Emperor Neberun arguing the fate of humanity.

The vessel gangway descended into a pool of blood.

Sean's confidence crumbled away. His legs trembled beneath him like he'd just run a marathon. He steeled himself, preparing for the worst. But Senetep wasn't the first to appear on the gangway. The shiny black shoes, smart suit, and gold watch could only belong to one person: Azar Hawati, the scheming traitor who'd sold out the world in pursuit of his own power.

Four warriors followed Azar onto the street. He casually sidestepped the dog remains, keeping the soles of his shoes free from the deep pools of blood.

The hybrid jackals parted, allowing Azar and the warriors into the circle.

Azar slicked down his needle-thin moustache and raised an eyebrow. 'Sean Livingstone, you certainly don't disappoint. The Ark of the Covenant, arguably the greatest archaeological discovery of all time...and we have you to thank for it.'

'You should try discovering something yourself,' Sean retorted. 'It's way more satisfying.'

'Don't concern yourself, Sean. I'm quite satisfied. I prefer others do the dirty work.'

'Yeah, like me and my dad.'

'Please don't put yourself down. You've exceeded my expectations today – your father would be proud.'

Sean snickered. How dare he talk about his dad as if they were friends? Azar was nothing more than an unseen investor in his father's Giza excavation. He always had a secret agenda and never really supported his dad, just his own devious needs.

'I see you've picked up some friends along the way,' Azar said.

'So have you,' Powell said, glaring at the Isharkute warriors. 'Shame you picked the wrong side.'

Azar frowned. 'Who are you?'

'Colonel Powell, United States Armed Forces.'

'Colonel, I'm the only one with the foresight to appreciate the bigger picture. Our world leaders had it all wrong. We no longer hold sole claim to planet Earth... In fact, we never did. We must work with the Isharkute if we're to survive.'

'You're just a puppet,' Sean said. 'You don't have any real power. Once Senetep's done with you, he'll rip you apart in his labs. Next thing you know you'll have four legs, a tail, and be licking his heels.'

'We'll see,' Azar said with a cunning grin. 'Unlike yourselves, I have greater control in my future than you may think. But don't worry – it seems Senetep has something rather exciting planned for all of you.'

Sean knew *exciting* wasn't the word. *Terrifying* would be a better description.

# — CHAPTER 22 —

# *Closure*

Carla squirmed in her seat. The military helicopter certainly wasn't built for comfort. Its interior fuselage was a long open space with two rows of seats facing each other. Hazim sat across from her, one ear pressed against his satellite phone. Sitting alongside them were fifteen of Hazim's best soldiers, all combat-ready with camouflage fatigues, night-vision goggles, and heavy weaponry. Travelling from Cairo to Guatemala was an uncomfortable multi-hour flight. In that time, she'd experienced the various forms of military transport. The first leg of their journey across the Atlantic Ocean was aboard a C-17 Globemaster III, an aircraft the size of a commercial passenger plane but stripped of padded seats and other in-flight luxuries.

After landing at a naval base in Puerto Barrios on the eastern tip of Guatemala, they transferred into their current vehicle, a CH-47 Chinook. Hazim assured her it was one of the fastest military helicopters available, but she couldn't get past the name. It reminded her of a plump feathery bird.

'How fast can this chook fly?' Carla hollered over the thudding twin rotors.

'Three hundred and fifteen kilometres per hour,' Hazim said with a laugh. The stoic soldiers didn't find her comment as amusing. 'You confident to rappel into the jungle?'

'*Sí!* I'm a rock climber. I've probably done it more times than you.'

'Fair enough,' Hazim said. 'How's your crash course on Isharkute going?'

Carla opened the laptop with a weary sigh. 'I spent the first few hours of our flight memorising the translations until I was seeing double. But there's hundreds of incomplete glyphs – I don't know if I can help you.'

'You're doing fine. Stay confident.'

'Where did you get this information?'

'Earlier today, this email was sent to the governments of the world. It contained the translations you've been studying, plus schematics on Isharkute weapons and crowns like the one we found in the Hall of Records. Someone knows more about the Isharkute than we do, and they're trying to help.'

'Sound like Azar Hawati. He's the only person with the reach and resources to acquire this kind of information, and now he's working with Senetep. How can you trust him? This is probably an attempt to mislead us.'

'For now, it's the best we've got. We're planning to take control of Isharkute technology – we need to know how to use it.'

'I wish you weren't counting on me. I'm not a symbologist or linguist. A couple of days ago I didn't even know the Isharkute existed; now I'm trying to learn their language in a few hours. It's impossible!'

'As long as you know the basics, we'll get by,' Hazim said. He stood to address the soldiers. 'Okay, we're coming up on El Mirador. The F-15's are splitting off for their first flyover. Get ready.'

Carla peered out the window. A flutter of nervous butterflies flew through her chest.

The pair of F-15 fighter jets that escorted them from the Puerto Barrios naval base veered off with a thunderous boom.

Carla was feeling the emotional pressure. This mysterious pyramid in the middle of a remote jungle was Henry's final resting place. There'd been no goodbyes, no funeral, and nothing to prepare her for this final moment. His death still felt surreal. It was only a couple of days since they held each other, felt the warmth of one another's touch. Now her beloved was alone, dead and buried for 10,000 years before she was even born.

The helicopter descended and Carla grasped the seat. Suddenly the treetops were metres from the window, rushing past in a green blur. The soldiers readied themselves and clipped the rappel ropes on to the cabin.

Carla pulled on her combat helmet and drew a slow deep breath to settle her nerves. This was no harder than some of her toughest climbs, plus she was well equipped for the mission. During the two flights to El Mirador, she'd cherry-picked essential survival gear from the military supplies, everything from a water bottle, extra rope, utility knife, and thermal blanket to gloves and knee pads. The one thing she didn't feel comfortable with was the Beretta M-9 tucked into her holster. Hazim had insisted she take it, even though she swore she'd never use it.

The helicopter banked hard and Carla glimpsed the majestic red granite pyramid towering over the jungle. Her heart raced. Henry was close now.

The F-15's circled the pyramid's apex and strafed the surrounding jungle with machine-gun fire. Her view was obscured as their chook banked again, rolling turbulently from side to side, descending with speed into the leafy canopy. They suddenly levelled out and hovered over the jungle. The rear gangway opened and the cabin filled with a gust of humid air.

The soldiers hurled the two ropes outside and rappelled down in pairs. Hazim directed Carla towards the gangway. 'After you!'

Carla attached her harness and peered over the edge. Far below, the soldiers were already spreading out into the jungle. She shook her head in disbelief, wondering how she went from rock-climbing archaeologist to soldier in a couple of days. She kissed the crucifix hanging around her neck, gripped the rope, and leapt off, plummeting 20 metres in a matter of seconds.

Hazim touched down beside her and waved the helicopter away. The soldiers made a series of silent hand gestures, directing everyone towards the pyramid.

The jungle was dense and hot. The trees were alive with bird calls and monkey screeches. Every few paces, hidden creatures would slither or scurry off through the undergrowth. It was a tough, twenty-minute trek up a steep incline before they reached the first clearing with a view. Carla stared in wonder at the soaring red granite pyramid. The perfectly smooth face emerged from the landslide of rubble piled up around its sides. The remainder of the original Mayan pyramid was now scattered over the kilometre-wide valley below.

'Anyone see a way in?' Hazim asked.

The lead soldier scanned the pyramid through a pair of binoculars. 'There's an opening one hundred metres up the pyramid face, looks like an entrance passage. No hostiles in sight.'

'That's easily a forty-five-degree angle climb up a smooth surface,' Carla said. 'Even with all our equipment, I doubt we'd make it.'

'And we're sitting targets if we try,' Hazim said. 'Is there another way in?'

'There!' the soldier said, pointing to the lower third of the pyramid still buried under sections of the Mayan pyramid and obscured by knotted vines and roots. An Isharkute vessel emerged from a dark crevice and took off after the F-15's. 'Looks like the entrance to a landing bay or hangar.'

'That's our entry point,' Hazim said, removing his sweat-stained jacket. 'Could be the hangar Sean was talking about.' He glanced at Carla. 'You okay to keep going?'

'Sí – it's all downhill from here. Let's go!'

The soldiers set off at speed, not slowing their pace one bit to accommodate her. Carla considered herself super-fit, but these Egyptian soldiers were setting a new standard in athleticism. They were used to the heat of the desert and cut effortlessly through the entwining jungle, gunsights always targeted, their focus never faltering. It was a tough march, but she kept up.

Halfway through the valley, they stopped under the shadow of the pyramid to drink and refill their water bottles in a small stream.

'We haven't seen any Isharkute apart from that vessel,' Carla said. 'Do you think they abandoned the pyramid?'

'I doubt it. They're probably guarding it from the inside.'

The lead soldier signalled everyone to move. The final approach was a steep half-kilometre climb up a treacherous heap of collapsed stone, fallen trees, and loose soil that could give way without warning. Carla was in her element now. She kept pace with the team, even overtaking a couple of the soldiers as they neared the top. They assembled on a ridge overlooking the entrance to the hangar. Carla found it hard to believe that the Isharkute pyramid was yet to be fully revealed. How far down did it go? It must have taken the Mayans forever to build over it. Three Isharkute warriors paced the length of the opening, staves in hand.

'Doesn't look too heavily guarded,' Hazim said, assessing the area through his binoculars. 'I can't see any more warriors inside yet. Let's take these three out from flanking positions.'

The soldiers nodded and split into two groups.

'What do we do?' Carla asked.

'Wait. They'll take care of the Isharkute guards, and then we can move in.'

Carla didn't argue the point – the further she was away from the killing, the better. The two groups descended through the tangle of vines to opposite ends of the hangar, then held their positions as a soldier from each team took aim at the nearest warrior. Carla held her breath, waiting for the inevitable.

There was no sound, just the visual kickback as the snipers took their shots. Both were precise headshots and the warriors dropped in unison. Before the third Isharkute even realised his companions had collapsed, he was taken out as well.

Carla turned away. Even at a distance, the brutality of war was distressing. She waited, wondering when it would be safe to look back. 'Do we go now?'

'Not yet. We need to wait for the all clear.'

Carla peeked over the ridge. The soldiers snuck inside the hangar and vanished into the shadows. Seconds played out like minutes. The sound of gunfire rang from the hangar in short controlled bursts. Bright muzzle flashes and electric-blue energy blasts illuminated the darkness, but it was all over in a matter of seconds.

'Did they do it?' Carla whispered.

Hazim scanned the opening with his binoculars. One of their soldiers emerged and gave them the thumbs-up. 'That's us. Let's get down there.'

They scrambled down the ridge and raced past the monolithic stone door into the hangar. Carla's eyes took a moment to adjust. As the shadows cleared, her heart skipped excitedly. There were hundreds of Isharkute vessels and weapons, all stockpiled and ready to go. Their haul was a game-changing blow to Senetep's forces.

'The hangar's secure,' the lead soldier announced. 'There's a passageway on the far side, looks like it leads to the upper pyramid levels.'

'Well done. Post some men here while we secure the rest of the pyramid,' Hazim said. 'We also need to find a way to shut this hangar door.'

The soldier nodded and organised his men into squads.

'Amazing,' Hazim said, taking a moment to appreciate their find. 'I can't believe Sean's dad collected all this stuff for us.'

'*Lo so!* It's incredible,' Carla said.

Several soldiers took up positions along the hangar entrance. Carla followed Hazim and his squad into the main passage, a long straight incline into the centre of the pyramid. Their movement activated crystalline lighting recessed into the floor. The lead soldier turned around a corner and suddenly opened fire. Carla clasped her ears and crouched as stray bullets pinged off the walls. Hazim and his soldiers swarmed around the bend and joined in, leaving her alone at the back of the line. In between the gunfire, she could hear the screeches and yelps of dying animals.

The gunshots finally ceased and Hazim returned. 'You might want to prepare yourself,' he said, giving her a hand up.

Carla rounded the corner and was confronted with a sight of pure carnage. A pile of hybrid bodies, still smoking from their bullet wounds, littered the passage. They looked human except for their jackal heads and clawed hands. Carla slipped the gun out of her holster and tiptoed around the terrifying corpses.

'I thought you said you'd never use it!' Hazim said.

'I changed my mind.'

'Make sure the safety's off,' he said, indicating the safety switch.

'Oh, yeah!' Carla replied with a sheepish grin. 'I forgot about that.'

She flicked it off and kept the gun aimed at the floor, concerned she might accidentally shoot one of the soldiers if something surprised them. The passage led directly into the main chamber, a circular room topped with a domed ceiling similar to the Hall of Records. The soldiers spread out and guarded the passages into the chamber.

Carla and Hazim walked between the four stone pedestals.

'These look like they might be control panels,' Hazim said, running his hand over the smooth granite. His touch inadvertently activated the system. The overhead dome came to life with a hologram of the pyramid and the four pedestals projected holographic screens with Isharkute glyphs.

'And you just worked out how to turn it on,' Carla said. 'Bravo!'

'Must be the pyramid control room. See if you can figure out how to close the hangar.'

Carla took a deep breath. The moment to prove herself had arrived sooner than expected. She examined the four screens, noting each faced a specific passage. Some glyphs looked familiar, others she'd never seen before, but the obvious ones were starting to make sense. 'I think each one of these panels controls a different section of the pyramid...and I'm pretty sure this panel operates the hangar. This glyph means "door".'

'Try it,' Hazim said.

Carla pressed the glyph and the overhead hologram zoomed in to focus on the hangar door, which flashed red and began to close. She breathed a sigh of relief. The hologram zoomed out again, showing the pyramid layout. It was a simple design, with two larger chambers below theirs and one above.

'Good work. What's in the chamber above the hangar?'

Carla took a moment to decipher the glyphs. 'I think this says "weapons," or "armoury".'

'What about the chamber above this one?' Hazim said, pointing to the final chamber.

Carla's stomach tightened. She didn't even need to translate the glyphs, as there was only chamber unaccounted for...the mausoleum. 'That's him!' she whispered to herself.

'What did you say?' Hazim asked.

'It's a tomb.'

Hazim nodded as if he'd been expecting this moment. 'We've secured the pyramid. We can take over from here if you want some time alone.'

'Thank you, I do.'

'Do you want us to accompany you?'

Carla shook her head. 'No, I'd like to do this alone.'

'Be careful,' Hazim said, unclipping his walkie-talkie. 'Here, take this. If you need anything, just press the button and talk. My men will be with you in seconds.'

Carla nodded in thanks and crossed the chamber. The soldiers guarding the passage stood aside to let her pass. Her emotions swelled inside her chest with each new step, her mind oblivious to any dangers lurking ahead. She entered the mausoleum, shivering with uncertainty. Her presence activated the ancient lighting and two granite sarcophagi appeared from the darkness. One was human-sized, but the other was double the proportions and large enough for a horse or bull. It was similar to the mysterious 100-tonne stone boxes found in the Serapeum at Saqqara, an underground complex located in Lower Egypt that she'd visited several times with Henry.

Offerings were piled around both sarcophagi, like those usually found in a royal tomb. There were long decayed flowers, exquisite jewellery. Urns and pottery filled with food and wine. From the choice of items and care in which they were laid out, she could tell it was done with great affection for the deceased. Everything was covered in a fine layer of dust, some of which had been recently disturbed. She knelt and found a fresh shoeprint. Sean had stood in the same spot!

Deep in her heart, she knew Henry was buried in the large

sarcophagus. She took a moment to remember him, affectionately placing her hand on the cool stone. As she did, the room was filled with a heavenly blue light.

'Carla, I was hoping you'd make it,' Henry said.

She clutched her crucifix and stood back, heart pounding. His voice was coming from the ethereal light. She peered around the sarcophagus and her breath caught in her throat.

Henry's face beamed back at her. 'Don't be afraid, I'm not a ghost. This is a holographic recording I made just for you.'

He stood much taller than usual, dressed in a long tunic that hid the lower half of his body. He'd lost weight, but he wasn't skinny. His sinewy muscles were marked with old scars and scrapes. Aside from a few grey flecks in his beard, his face hadn't changed all that much. His eyes were still imbued with the warmth and spirit she'd fallen in love with. It was an older version of the Henry she knew – as if he'd lived a lifetime since they last saw each other.

'I know what you're thinking... I look a little different. Well, for me it's been a few years,' he said with a grin. 'I wish I could see you... hold you, but it comforts me to think you're seeing this.'

Carla stepped out and reached for Henry's face. Her fingers passed through his cheek with a gentle fizz of energy. She stared into his eyes, hoping for a reaction, but he stared straight past her, his ancient recording unable to respond.

'Do you remember the first time we met?' Henry continued. 'It's a reoccurring dream I've had so many times since we've been apart.'

Carla took a couple of steps back to stand in Henry's line of sight. It helped make the hologram feel more real. 'We met on a Friday afternoon,' she said to herself.

'It was late, the Cairo Museum was preparing to close,' Henry continued. 'I remember rushing through the main doors as the lines of tourists were leaving for the day. I wasn't in a great mood after a week of battling government officials for permits and visas. It was one of those days where it all felt too hard. I knew the museum would clear my head and bring perspective. I was wandering past the display cases on the first floor when I caught sight of an angel.

You were standing in the perfect position, sunlight catching your hair with a golden glow...a sight from heaven. I was intoxicated and instantly drawn to you. I knew I had to talk to you, but it was unlike me to act so impulsively. You glanced at me and continued admiring the silver sarcophagus of Sheshonq II.'

Carla smiled to herself, recounting the moment just as vividly.

'Do you remember what I said?' Henry asked, pausing as if waiting for her response.

Carla nodded. 'You said, "Beautiful, isn't it?"'

'Then you asked me in your Italian accent if I worked in the museum, pretending not to recognise me.'

'Sí,' Carla said, laughing. 'I was teasing you. I knew exactly who you were the moment you walked through the museum doors.'

'I was tongue-tied and embarrassed.'

'You were, and I told you not to let fame go to your head,' Carla added.

'I followed you as you moved along the cabinet, studying the jewellery and ornaments from the tomb of Psusennes. Your hair was tied up in a ponytail and I couldn't take my eyes off the slender curve in the back of your neck. Your skin was a perfect olive complexion, and then I caught a scent of your perfume. It was subtle, enticing, and reminded me what it was like to be close to someone...feelings I'd avoided since Julie's death. In that moment, I was entranced... and have been ever since.'

'I remember blabbing on about Pierre Montet, how he deserved more credit than most Egyptologists acknowledged,' Carla said.

'You told me that Howard Carter was known all over the world for discovering Tutankhamen's tomb, how the boy king's treasures were beautiful, but it was just one tomb. Pierre Montet unearthed three intact royal tombs just before the Second World War, but was overlooked by the world for his discoveries. The treasures were just as astonishing, if not more than Tutankhamen's.'

Carla smiled to herself. Henry's recollection of their meeting was so thorough, it reminded her of the little details she'd forgotten.

Henry continued. 'I had nothing of value to offer to the

conversation, even though I knew more about the treasures than anyone – except for you, of course. In that moment, I realised I knew more about the lives of long-dead Egyptians than my own.'

'Then I asked you out to dinner,' Carla cut in.

'Then you asked me out to dinner to discuss the treasures of Montet further. My life has never been the same since.'

'Me too,' she whispered.

'There's so much more to tell you, but I'm guessing right now you don't have a lot of time. You must do everything you can to contact Emperor Neberun and help Sean on his final quest. I've left everything in this pyramid to assist you.' Henry pointed to his sarcophagus. 'In the top corner of my sarcophagus, you'll find a crystalline data card.'

A small blue light illuminated in the exact spot he was pointing at and a small crystal shard was ejected from the granite.

'If you wave this card over any control panel, it will change the Isharkute glyphs into English. It helped me a lot when I built this pyramid with Nesuk.'

Carla kissed the card. 'Thank God!'

'It's also encoded with the rest of my story. When you're ready to hear it, all you need to do is place it on one of the holographic projection panels. Good luck, and remember that I love you...and have done so for the last ten and a half thousand years.'

'I love you too,' she whispered.

Henry's hologram dematerialised, leaving Carla staring into the shadows. She looked down at the card and held it tighter, taking solace that one day, she would learn everything. Their journey wasn't over yet; Henry had given her something to look forward to.

Hazim's voice crackled through the walkie-talkie. 'Carla, you need to get back here right away. We're receiving a distress transmission from Nocao.'

Carla spoke into the walkie-talkie. 'I'm on my way!'

# CHAPTER 23

# The Spearhead Of Creation

Sean tried to remain positive, but their situation was grim. Every living soldier from the battle at Axum had been rounded up and moved aboard the annihilator's main hangar. They were huddled in a large circle patrolled by Isharkute warriors who were ready to fire their deadly staves at the slightest sign of insubordination. After stealing the Ark, the Isharkute unleashed a fury of energy blasts, destroying Maddock's V-22 Osprey, the two chapels, the church of St. Mary of Zion, and half the town. The smouldering remains of Axum lay far behind them now, the loyal monk buried somewhere beneath the rubble.

Sean felt guilty, as if he'd failed the monk. Even though he'd discovered the Ark and unlocked its secret, he might never have a chance to activate the final beacon.

The hangar stretched on forever, with the height and breadth of a cargo container ship. The moans of the wounded echoed through the cavernous space. Some of the injured soldiers propped themselves up and nursed their wounds, while the worst lay sprawled on the floor in pools of their own blood. The sight gave Sean the chills, reminding him of Senetep's hybrid labs.

He knew that far worse was yet to come.

Bella, Arturo, and Colonel Powell stood by Sean while General Maddock hovered around the edge of the circle, tending to the wounded and watching his alien captors with contempt.

'What will they do with us?' Bella whispered.

'I don't know,' Sean whispered back.

Another tortured moan sounded from an injured soldier.

Bella turned away. 'They're dying. I don't understand why the Isharkute didn't just leave them behind. Why'd they bring them?'

Sean forced the horrifying reality from his mind, knowing all too well what Senetep's hybrid labs were capable of. The Overseer could make use of any body part, providing it was fresh enough.

On the far side of the hangar, Azar stood hunched over the Ark of the Covenant, busy reading the ancient Hebrew inscriptions, assessing every detail, feverishly taking in as much of the relic as he could before handing it over to Senetep. Nefaro stood over him, watching his every move like an adult would a child.

There was a shudder through the hangar as the annihilator came to a stop and landed. The sprawling hangar doors opened to the orange glow of the afternoon sun. They were back in Giza, parked in the shadow of Senetep's monolithic pyramid.

Nefaro directed the warriors to separate Sean from the group. Bella intervened and grabbed his arm. 'Where are they taking you?'

A warrior smacked her away and she fell to her knees, clutching her face. Arturo and Powell leapt to her defence. The warriors turned on them, their merciless pale eyes focused to kill.

'Stop!' Sean cried, leaping between them.

The warriors raised their staves at him and a nervous tingle rippled down his back, his wings itching to lift him out of trouble.

'Enough!' Nefaro bellowed, waving the warriors back. 'If any prisoners die, you will personally explain why to Senetep. He wants them alive, and where possible, whole. Especially this one,' Nefaro finished, pointing his spindly finger at Sean.

Sean helped Bella back on her feet. Her eye was already puffy and a trickle of blood ran from her brow. The sight ignited a deep, burning conviction to protect her. He was tired of seeing the innocent treated so unjustly. 'Don't worry. I'll think of something and come back for you.'

'Promise?'

Sean nodded. 'I will...or I'll die trying.'

Bella touched his face affectionately, eyes glistening with tears.

She pulled his face closer and tilted her head, lips ready to meet his. He closed his eyes and waited for the kiss. Her warmth breath touched his lips, then...

...Sean was yanked away. They stared into each other's eyes as he was forced from the group. Bella straightened and wiped the blood from her brow, looking stronger and more confident than she had just moments before. He gave her a subtle nod.

Now he just needed to live up to his promise.

Azar followed Nefaro and his entourage as they left the hangar, keeping as close to the Ark as possible. His relentless determination to possess the Ark was surprising. Sean wondered if he still had a plan in place. It was possible Azar had only aligned with Senetep to secure the Ark, regardless of the moral and human cost. Azar had previously hinted about a weaponised use for the Ark.

Inside the pyramid, Nefaro separated Sean from the group and led him up to one of the highest levels where they entered an expansive private quarters. It had to belong to Senetep, but the Overseer was nowhere to be seen. A sombre, ochre-tinted light spilled through the open floor-to-ceiling windows and there was the distinct taste of smoke in the air. The view was vastly different from his previous visit to Senetep's quarters. There were no lush jungles – just the smouldering remains of war-torn Cairo. No pieces of art or weapon collections, just empty floors and blank walls. Of all the differences, one made Sean draw a sigh of relief: there were no deadly slitherquills!

'Leave us,' Senetep's voice boomed through the space.

Nefaro dutifully left the quarters. Sean looked around, wondering why there were no warriors to prevent him from flying out the windows.

A sudden hiss cut through the unnerving silence and a sliver of white light dissected the nearby wall. Vapours swirled through the opening as the walls parted. Senetep emerged from the luminous void, the bare skin on his arms and head steaming like he'd stepped straight out of a freezer. The only time Sean had seen the Isharkute in similar sub-zero temperatures was in the stasis chambers beneath

Ramin's pyramid. The extreme cold halted their cellular degradation.

'Sean Livingstone!' Senetep said, wiping the condensation off his forearms. 'You're a resilient pest, scurrying about like a cockroach, avoiding being squashed.'

Sean wanted to respond with something just as scathing, but he held his tongue, knowing the Overseer was lethally impulsive. Senetep strode to the centre of the room with a slight limp. He might have been hurt, but Sean couldn't see any visible injuries. It had to be the Isharkute affliction. His weakness gave Sean a morbid sense of satisfaction.

'The crown only had enough energy for one trip through time... How did you get here?'

Sean didn't need to tell him anything and drew out the silence before responding. 'We put the crown's remaining energy into a pair of cryogenic chambers and slept our way here.'

'Who was the other?'

'Nocao.'

'Where's Nocao now?'

Sean swallowed the lump in his throat like a bitter pill. 'He's dead.'

Senetep crossed his muscular arms with a contented breath. Sean noticed the faint purple blotches on his forearms, the tell-tale bruises of the Isharkute affliction. He suddenly realised why Nefaro was ordered to leave and why no warriors were guarding the room. Senetep was keeping his illness a secret!

'You're sick!' Sean said.

Senetep stared with contempt. 'My entire species is in various stages of cellular decay.'

'If you're using a cold chamber, you must be really sick.'

'The travel through time sped up my affliction.'

Sean sensed one last chance to reach a truce. 'You need human DNA more now than ever.'

'Not anymore,' Senetep said, narrowing his eyes. The final wisps of vapour twirled off his skin as he activated a holographic map of the universe between them. 'There's a myth, one handed down since the first generations of Isharkute...that our ancestors created every form of life throughout the universe.'

Sean stared into the expanse of galaxies, convinced Senetep's delusions of self-importance had grown as large as the universe itself.

'A hundred thousand years before I arrived on this planet, my ancestors travelled the stars, seeding planets and solar systems with life. This vessel was known as the *Spearhead of Creation*. It contained the materials and blueprints for life itself.'

A red line tracked through the hologram of stars, bouncing off one system to the next, intersecting entire constellations.

'Over the millennia, my culture has come to consider the *Spearhead* a myth, a creationist story to explain our existence. But I believe the *Spearhead* is real and is still out there, travelling the universe, proliferating and sowing the seeds of life for all eternity. I've spent decades researching, tracking the rate of evolution across thousands of worlds, but there were too many possibilities, too many variables to gain any useful data. I needed a clue – a place in the universe to start looking. Something came to me during my jump through time, courtesy of your ineptitude –'

'You're welcome,' Sean said flatly.

'It seeded the spiral image in my mind. It was a revelation. Once I applied that to my data, it created a path. One that extends to the furthest reaches of the explored universe.'

The hologram zoomed out to take in the billions of stars. The red line now revealed a uniform pattern that started in the centre of the universe and spiralled outwards – beautiful, elegant, and simple in design. Sean recognised the shape, the perfect example of the Golden Ratio, also called the Golden Number or God's Fingerprint, the magical number of 1.618. Leonardo da Vinci called this design 'the divine proportion'. The mathematical enigma could be found everywhere: in art, architecture, music, and nature. From spiral galaxies to hurricanes, whirlpools to seashells, even down to the aspect ratio of a human DNA spiral, the proportions of the Golden Ratio were an underlying constant to the structure of things within the universe.

Sean had first come across the Golden Ratio when he was studying the dimensions of the Great Pyramid. The surface of the four sides divided by the surface of the base equalled the famous 1.618. It was no coincidence that ancient Egyptian and Greek architecture was so pleasing to the eye, as both cultures had incorporated the mathematical ratio into their designs. Now Sean was seeing it in a whole new light, an ancient spacecraft that travelled the universe in a spiral that replicated the Golden Ratio.

'One point six one eight,' Sean said to himself, staring at the spiral.

Senetep straightened. 'You're unusually sophisticated for a useless slab of meat. The clue to finding my ancestors was inside every living thing. Once I knew where to look, the *Spearhead* revealed itself to me.'

Sean noticed the flashing red dot at the end of the line, indicating the vessel's proposed location. 'What if it wasn't your ancestors who sent it out there? It was so long ago, the *Spearhead* could belong to another race that existed before yours.'

Senetep laughed. 'In the end, it doesn't matter. It still contains the data to wipe my biological sequence clean and reset the Isharkute genome. Once I've taken control of the *Spearhead of Creation*, I'll eradicate entire galaxies of life and start again.'

Sean suddenly realised how delusional Senetep really was. He wasn't just talking about eradicating humanity, but all life, everywhere. He was on the verge of becoming destroyer and creator – or in another word, God.

'I would've left this pitiful excuse of a planet already if it weren't for Neberun and his human sympathisers. Their weak constitutions threaten to poison every Isharkute with the kind of emotional decision-making that makes your species so flawed and predictable. They must never be allowed to wake from their cryogenic sleep. Once I've established communication with Neberun's fleet with your precious beacon, I'll direct them into the nearest star, cleansing the filth of humanity from my species. Now, I'm going to ask you once. Where's the beacon?'

Sean was numb with shock. How could he respond without betraying every living thing in the universe?

'You know I have ways of making you talk,' Senetep said. 'I can pull you and your friends apart piece by piece, keeping you conscious through the entire ordeal. It's effective, but not that entertaining. I can't think of anything more tedious than waiting for a dismembered head to talk.'

Sean blurted out a nervous laugh. 'You've almost developed a sense of humour in the last ten thousand years.'

Senetep smirked and loomed over him. 'One last time: Tell me where to find the beacon.'

'I don't know.'

'Of course, just the answer I was expecting. You were impressive in the Great Arena. Better than I expected and far more effective than your father, even after all the resources I poured into him. That's why I think it befitting to continue the tradition, but this time with a few changes.'

'Another arena?'

'Emperor Neberun's Great Arena now rests at the bottom of the ocean, but I have something far more dangerous...a subterranean labyrinth littered with traps of cunning design and ravenous hybrids. It was first built when my capitol sat upon the area you now call the Giza Plateau. It was to be a larger, grander version of my Pyramid of Trials.'

Sean knew about a legendary labyrinth rumoured to be buried beneath the sands at Hawara, 90 kilometres south of Cairo. Ancient accounts of the hidden structure had been handed down through the millennia by authors like Strabo and Herodotus, both of whom claimed to have visited the site before it was lost to antiquity.

'You and your friends will be sealed in the labyrinth. There you will watch them die horrible deaths one by one. However, if you tell me where to find the beacon, I'll deny myself this small pleasure and spare you from my latest hybrids.'

Sean was facing an impossible, no-win situation. Senetep was preying on his emotional side, hoping he'd put his friends out of harm's way. But the second he gave away the Yonaguni beacon, he would unravel everything his dad and Nesuk had put in place. Their sacrifices would be for nothing.

He had no choice but to condemn his friends to the labyrinth. At least they had a fighting chance. Their only hope was to find an escape route and reach Yonaguni. It was a long shot, but it was all he had.

'I really don't know,' Sean said. 'Even if I did, I wouldn't be able to turn it on because you've got the Ark... Either way, you've won.'

'Have it your way, but you're not going into the labyrinth with the same advantage you had in the Great Arena.'

Senetep pressed a button, opening the door to the quarters. Commanders Nefaro and Vogran entered. Vogran hovered behind Sean while Nefaro paced in front, brandishing a long curved knife. None of them said anything. Sean felt the increasing thud of his heart against his chest.

Senetep nodded and Sean suddenly found both his arms locked in Vogran's grip. He struggled desperately, but the commander was a vice of immovable muscle. Nefaro reached over Sean's shoulder and grasped his left wing, stretching it over his head at an awkward angle.

A sudden sting shot through his shoulderblade, followed by a rush of intense heat.

Nefaro stepped back, the severed wing dangling from his hand. He threw it to the floor and moved to Sean's other shoulder.

Sean was in shock. He couldn't breathe. His pounding heart felt like it was going to explode. His right wing was cut off and callously discarded before him. He stared, aghast, his back burning. There was no blood, just a clear glistening liquid oozing from the stumps of his severed wings.

He was never going to fly again.

# — CHAPTER 24 —

# A Timely Message

Carla sprinted down the passage to the pyramid control chamber, anxious to hear Nocao's distress call. The last time she'd heard from Sean and Nocao, they were splitting up to escape from Senetep and recover the Ark. Hopefully, they were all okay. She raced past the soldiers to find Hazim standing in the middle of the chamber watching a holographic transmission from Nocao.

Nocao was in a dark confined space surrounded by flashing red lights. He spoke in a low, breathless voice. 'Carla Bonaforte, I'm sending this message to you in the hope that you've taken control of the pyramid at El Mirador. Sean escaped, but I crashed and now I'm stuck on the bottom of the ocean with less than three per cent oxygen. My vessel's energy crystal's been damaged. I have just enough power to send this message, then I'll divert the rest to life support. I've encoded my coordinates into this message. They can only be unlocked with your DNA signature. Place your hand on one of the control panels and it will scan you.'

The transmission ended.

Carla followed Nocao's instructions and the panel scanned her hand like a photocopier, sequencing her DNA into a stream of Isharkute glyphs. A small crystal shard ejected from the plinth and Nocao's hologram continued.

'Carla, I'm glad you made it. You should see a small crystal card sticking out of the panel you're standing at. It's encoded with my coordinates. Take it to one of the vessels in the hangar, wave it across the instrument panel, and it will initiate the autopilot to my location. I look forward to seeing you soon.'

Carla pulled the clear crystal card from the panel. It was no bigger than a USB thumb drive.

'I'm coming with you,' Hazim said. 'I'll bring two soldiers.'

'Okay, but we're leaving now.'

Hazim called over his lead soldier. 'You're in charge while we're gone. As soon as we're free, close the hangar door and don't let anything else inside.'

The soldier eyed the panels. 'We don't know how to operate this alien tech.'

Carla waved Henry's card over the control panel and every Isharkute glyph transformed into English.

'How'd you do that?' Hazim said.

'A little present Henry left for me,' Carla said with a smile. 'Let's go!'

They ran back to the hangar. There were Isharkute vessels of all shapes and sizes to choose from. Carla avoided the bulky ones and picked one of the smaller stealthier-looking vessels. They climbed inside and sat in the two pilot's seats. The interior was no bigger than a van and as sleek and streamlined as the exterior hull. There were no flight sticks, switches, levers, or anything to start or control the vessel.

'The Isharkute aren't big on controls, are they?' Hazim said.

Carla waved the crystal across the blank panel and the holographic controls materialised in front of them. A translucent map superimposed over the windscreen with two flashing dots, one showing their current position in Guatemala, the other Nocao, deep in the middle of the Atlantic Ocean. The vessel powered up and lifted off silently.

Carla peered out the windscreen. 'Amazing! I didn't even feel us take off.'

The hangar door slid open and they flew straight over the jungle, leaving the pyramid far behind them.

'This thing can move!' Hazim said with exhilaration.

Four new dots appeared on the map, each converging on their position.

'What are they?' Carla said.

The dots suddenly multiplied and moved twice as fast.

'They look like missiles,' Hazim said. He pointed to the Isharkute glyphs flashing over the map. 'What does all this mean? You should try your magic card.'

'Oh, yeah!' Carla said, swiping Henry's card over the panel. The glyphs transformed into big bold letters: ALERT, HOSTILE INCOMING!

'We're under attack,' Hazim said, assessing the Isharkute readouts on the incoming vessels. 'It's a squadron of F-22 Raptors.'

'Aren't they supposed to be on our side?'

'They're US fighter jets, unmatched in speed and performance. They think we're Isharkute. We're in trouble unless we can get this thing off autopilot.'

Carla glanced at the map. The missiles were seconds from impact. There were too many screens and controls to make sense of anything in the time they had left. Hazim grabbed the holographic control stick and their vessel jerked violently. A new message appeared: INITIATING REMOTE FLIGHT MODE.

'What did you do?' Carla said.

'Nothing!' Hazim said, throwing his hands up in the air. 'I just touched the controls. I don't know how to fly this thing. How do I change it back?'

'Too late!' Carla said, clutching her crucifix.

The missiles were upon them. She shared a final look with Hazim and held her breath, expecting to be obliterated from the sky.

'I'll take over from here,' Nocao gasped as his hologram appeared before them. 'Hold on to your seats.'

Their vessel made a sudden barrel roll and the missiles whooshed past, narrowly missing their fuselage. Carla dug her fingernails into her seat. They dove towards land and flew between the cover of the mountains.

'I was monitoring your approach and noticed you were in trouble,' Nocao gasped, sounding like he was on his last breath of air. 'You're being attacked by your own forces. I'm opening a line of communication with your jets so you can call them off.'

'*Mio Dio!*' Carla said. 'I thought you were running out of power.'

'I am. This is using up my reserves.'

'How will you survive?'

'I'm good at holding my breath,' Nocao said with a grin. 'But don't take too long. Opening communications now.'

'US Air Force, this is Commander Hazim El-Amin of the Egyptian Armed Forces. Please call off your attack – we're on your side. We've taken control of this vessel and a pyramid full of Isharkute weapons and vehicles.'

There was no response, just a small crackle of radio silence.

'You think they heard us?' Carla whispered.

Hazim nodded. 'Please confirm with your superiors – we've been working with Colonel Powell from the US Army. We have a joint forces division out of Cairo.'

'Commander El-Amin, this is Lieutenant Colonel Rene Hochholzer, commander of the twenty-sixth fighter squadron. You're to surrender your vessel immediately. We'll escort you back to the Naval Air Station in Key West, Florida.'

'We can't deviate from our course. We're on a rescue mission.'

'Surrender your vessel, Commander El-Amin, or we'll open fire again.'

'Lieutenant, we've taken possession of information and equipment that can turn this war in our favour. Please confirm with Colonel Powell.'

Silence again.

Carla shared a concerned look with Hazim and whispered, 'What do we do?'

Hazim muted the communications channel so the lieutenant couldn't hear them. 'Colonel Powell must've been caught by General Maddock, which means he knows what we're up to.'

'We led the military straight here.'

'Maddock would've contacted the closest US air force base to Guatemala and ordered them to secure the pyramid before us.' Hazim pointed to the swarm of dots converging on El Mirador. 'And those aren't fighter jets – they're heavy cargo and troop transport helicopters.'

'Even if they secure the pyramid, it'll take them months to figure everything out without us.'

Hazim's eyes lit up. 'You're right! Between Nocao and your translator crystal, we have the ultimate bargaining chip.' He reactivated the communications. 'Lieutenant Hochholzer, we know your mission is to take control of the pyramid, but you're too late. We've already captured it. You'll spend days trying to blast your way inside, and if you manage to make it that far, you'll spend the next few weeks trying to figure out the Isharkute technology. By that time, the world will be completely overrun by Senetep's forces. We know how to use their technology and we're willing to help, but only if we work together. If you get Colonel Powell or General Maddock on the line, we can figure this out.'

'There's no way to confirm your story,' the lieutenant responded. 'All communication with General Maddock's forces in Egypt has ceased.'

'That means they're captured. You need to make a decision now, Lieutenant.'

There was silence again.

Carla shook her head and muted the comms. 'This is taking too long. Nocao, if you're still listening, can you speed us out of here or something?'

'I could,' Nocao gasped. 'But wait – give them a little longer.'

Hazim nodded. 'He's right, sounds like they're talking to a third party. That's what all the gaps in the conversation are.' He opened the comms again. 'Lieutenant, have you made a decision?'

'I've received new orders directly from the president to assist you on your mission.'

'Yes!' Carla whispered, fist pumping in the air.

'We'll meet you back at the pyramid soon. We have to finish a rescue mission in the Atlantic Ocean.'

'Do you need an escort?'

'I'd say yes, Lieutenant, but I doubt you can keep up.'

'You're on, Commander!' Hochholzer said spiritedly.

With a thunderous crack, their vessel broke the sound barrier and left the F-22's hundreds of kilometres behind in a matter of seconds.

'Whoa!' Hochholzer cried over the transmission. 'See you when you get back.'

The last tip of land disappeared in the blink of an eye and the sprawling deep blue Atlantic filled the horizon.

Carla glimpsed their speed on the instrument panel. 'Thirteen hundred kilometres an hour,' she called out in surprise.

'Incredible!' Hazim called back.

They were almost upon Nocao's dot on the map. Their vessel angled downwards and they dove through the surface with barely a shudder. The sunlight dimmed the deeper they descended until they were in complete darkness. Carla had never been this deep underwater. The thought of all that crushing pressure above made her nervous. There was no escape if something went wrong. It was the main reason she never went diving, even though her family business revolved around it. She preferred heights and open air. Give her the most dangerous cliff or mountain to climb...anywhere but here!

The viewscreen emitted a new message: INITIATING CLEAR-HULL.

'What's that?' Carla said.

'Enjoy...the view,' Nocao gasped, sounding even more tired and breathless.

Their vessel emitted a headlight, illuminating the craggy rock face of an imposing underwater cliff. The interior of the cabin faded away, giving Carla and Hazim a perfect 360-degree view of the surrounding depths.

'Oh my!' Carla said.

Hazim reached out and touched the invisible wall. 'Amazing, the hull's still there!'

Carla tried to appreciate the undersea wonders as they descended into the depths. They passed bizarre deep-sea creatures with bulbous eyes that looked more alien than fish. Nocao's vessel finally appeared from the darkness, resting precariously on a rock ledge. The autopilot directed them overhead and there was a loud *clunk* as the two vessels locked together. They shot straight up with incredible speed and catapulted through the surface with an explosion of frothy seawater.

Their vessels separated and bobbed in the water. Nocao stuck his head outside, took a gulp of air, and gave them a thumbs-up. Carla waved back, glad to see him alive and breathing. Nocao dove into the ocean and swam over to their vessel.

'Just in time,' Nocao said, pulling himself inside. 'I ran out of oxygen ten minutes ago.'

'Wow!' Carla said. 'I didn't know you could hold your breath that long.'

'Neither did I, until now,' Nocao said, seating himself in the pilot seat. He took one look at the instrumentation and turned to them. 'How did you translate this into your language?'

Carla held up the crystal card. 'A little gift from Henry.'

'Clever,' Nocao said, his hands flying across the panels.

'What are you doing?' Hazim asked.

'Locating Sean's vessel.' The holographic map reappeared over the windscreen and zoomed in on the town of Axum in Ethiopia. 'Here it is, but there's no life signs aboard. Before we were separated, I activated his vessel's visual recorder. This will show us everything that's happened since then.'

'Just like a dashcam recorder!' Carla said.

A live video stream from Sean's vessel materialised showing the flaming ruins of Axum. Nocao swiped across the image and changed the angle, bringing into focus a horrible mess of bloody remains strewn across the street.

Carla gasped and turned away. 'Please, tell me it's not them.'

'They're not human,' Hazim said.

'They're canine,' Nocao affirmed, reversing the footage through the last few hours. He slowed the playback to normal speed and found Sean, Bella, Arturo, and Colonel Powell surrounded by Isharkute warriors. A smartly dressed man stepped out of an Isharkute vessel and approached them.

'Azar Hawati!' Carla said, suppressing a surge of anger. The group had a short discussion, then Sean and his friends were escorted under guard into the vessel and flown away. 'Where'd they take them?'

'Senetep's capital at Giza,' Nocao said.

'Did they find the Ark of the Covenant?' Hazim asked.

'I thought it was supposed to be in Axum,' Carla said.

Nocao nodded. 'It was, but they might have abandoned their search when they were discovered.'

'We have to go after them.'

'Carla's right – without Sean we can't find the Ark,' Hazim said. 'It's the last chance to contact your Emperor's fleet for help.'

'I agree, but we can't do this alone,' Nocao said. 'We should return to the El Mirador pyramid and prepare your soldiers. I'll teach them how to fly the vessels and use our weapons. Then we can attack Senetep at Giza and rescue Sean.'

Carla couldn't stop worrying about her niece and nephew during their return flight. She was scared to ask Nocao what might become of them after seeing what Senetep did to the world leaders. She felt as though they were her responsibility since their parents were captured.

'This is Commander Hazim El-Amin,' he announced over the communications. 'We're approaching El Mirador now in an Isharkute vessel. Hold your fire, I repeat... Hold your fire!'

They flew over the treetops and circled red granite pyramid. The area was teeming with soldiers like a disturbed colony of ants. A full regiment of military helicopters were parked outside the hangar entrance and squads of soldiers were spreading into the jungle, securing the perimeter. Pairs of fighter jets thundered by as more military helicopters arrived, dropping off surface-to-air missile launchers hanging from their fuselage.

'Looks like our message got through,' Carla said.

Hazim straightened his uniform. It was the first time she'd seen him nervous. The pressure of uniting military forces from all over the world now rested on his shoulders.

'You'll do fine,' she assured him.

Hazim took a deep breath and nodded. 'We've got some work to do.'

They landed outside the main hangar, drawing a huge crowd of US and Guatemalan military. The soldiers surrounded their vessel, their semi-automatic rifles aimed at the door.

'Nocao, it might be better if you stay inside the vessel until I brief them on the situation,' Hazim said.

Nocao took one glance at the wall of stone-faced soldiers. 'I understand.'

'All right, let's meet our guests, then.'

Carla nodded and followed Hazim outside.

'Welcome. I'm Commander Hazim El-Amin from the Egyptian Armed Forces,' he said confidently. 'This is Carla Bonaforte, our most valued advisor on the Isharkute.'

Carla was humbled that he thought so highly of her. Hazim explained the situation involving Sean, contacting the Isharkute fleet, and their impending attack on Senetep's forces. He spoke with authority, retaining a warmth and compassion the soldiers could relate to. They appeared invested and enthusiastic, ready to follow his lead. Carla could see why he was so respected amongst his countrymen.

'But we wouldn't have made it this far without Isharkute help,' Hazim said. There was a groan of concern and discontent from the soldiers. 'I'm asking you to put your prejudices and preconceptions aside. My friend's name is Nocao and I assure you, he's a friend to all of us.'

Nocao tentatively emerged from the vessel.

The soldiers gripped their weapons a little tighter, trigger fingers sliding into position.

'Starting immediately, Nocao will teach you how to operate the Isharkute vessels and weapons inside the pyramid.'

The soldiers stared in silence, hands poised on their weapons. Carla understood their hesitancy, being the first time most of them had seen an Isharkute in the flesh.

'I understand – most of you are reluctant to trust him,' Carla said. 'A few days ago, I felt the same way. But their invasion doesn't represent the intentions of their entire species. Senetep's the leader of a radical group of Isharkute whose main goal is to overthrow humanity and stop our species working from together. You'll come to learn the Isharkute were an important part of human civilisation millennia ago and without them, we wouldn't be here today.'

'If they're not here to conquer us, then why are they here?' called one of the soldiers.

'Because they need our help,' Carla replied. 'Nocao, maybe you should explain.'

Nocao nodded. 'We're suffering from a degrading genome. The affliction has decimated entire generations, and mine may be the last.' Nocao rolled back his sleeve and showed them a series of purple bruises along his forearm. 'Humans and Isharkute share a similar genetic code. Our cure resides in the DNA of every human being on this planet, so it makes no sense to eradicate you.'

Carla stared with surprise at Nocao's bruises. She had no idea he was sick.

'Once you get what you want, what's stopping you from joining Senetep?' another soldier shouted.

'Because I'm going to help you destroy him,' Nocao said.

The soldiers glanced at each other. Some of them shrugged, others nodded.

'Good! Let's get started. We need pilots and soldiers,' Hazim said, 'as many as you can spare. Bring them to the hangar and we'll get to work straight away.'

The squads dispersed and organised their forces.

'Well done, both of you!' Hazim said. 'I'll head to the hangar with Nocao and start the training. Carla, I'd like you to coordinate everything from the pyramid's control room. Familiarise yourself with the communications, defence systems, and anything else you can find. Let's see if there's an inventory of vehicles and weapons.'

'*Sí!*' Carla said.

Hazim checked his watch. 'Let's aim to leave at fourteen hundred hours. That gives us two hours to prep. Is there any way we can monitor Senetep's transmissions, find out exactly where Sean and everyone are being held?'

'Show me the card Henry left for you,' Nocao said.

Carla handed it over and he keyed in a sequence of glyphs then handed it back. 'These are the frequencies you need to monitor to listen in on Senetep's communications. Hold the card over the pedestal and it will activate the channels.'

'Okay, let's get started,' Hazim said, marching towards the hangar.

Carla pulled Nocao aside. 'I didn't know you were sick. How bad is it?'

'I don't know. The rate of degradation is different for all Isharkute. All I know is it's accelerated since I woke from my cryogenic sleep.'

'Does Sean know?'

'No, I didn't want to tell him until this was all over.'

Carla watched him walk away, amazed how Nocao's thoughts and actions seemed more human than alien. He genuinely cared for Sean. It filled her with the hope that their species could eventually live together.

# — CHAPTER 25 —

# *Labyrinth*

Sean wasn't cold, but he couldn't stop shivering. He was in such a state of shock that he couldn't even tell how much pain he was really in. All he could think about was his severed wings being kicked across the floor by Senetep. The hunter-craft landed with a jolt and the Isharkute warriors shoved him outside. They were in the middle of the desert, sand dunes in every direction.

Any chance of escape was now impossible.

The warriors forced him down a rocky escarpment and into a dark crevice cutting into the desert. Huge piles of freshly dug sand and rock were heaped around area, showing the site had only just been excavated. Deeper inside, the craggy stone walls transformed into a passage of monolithic blocks, formerly preserved beneath the desert for thousands of years. Isharkute warriors lined the passage and stood guard outside a 20-metre-high rectangular opening, beyond which waited a dank, unsettling gloom.

Sean's shoulderblades twinged as if his wings were still attached. A searing pain shot up his spine, like someone just pressed a hot iron to his back. It jolted him back into the moment and he suddenly realised where he was standing.

This was the entrance to Senetep's labyrinth!

The warriors pushed him over the threshold and an immense stone door rumbled to life, descending to seal him inside. One of the warriors threw a flaming torch at his feet and the door closed with an ominous *thud*, echoing through the labyrinth like rolling thunder.

Sean's eyes adjusted to the dim flame. He was standing in a massive underground chamber constructed with the same gargantuan stone blocks from the passage. What was he supposed to do now? It was like awakening from one horrendous nightmare and being thrown into another. Something moved through the shadows, making him stumble back against the wall in fright.

'Sean! It's okay, it's me,' Bella said, stepping into the torchlight. 'Are you all right?'

He couldn't answer. His legs and hands trembled uncontrollably. Even the sound of her voice couldn't pull him from the horrors of his recent ordeal. He'd just been mutilated. There was no other word to describe it. An intense nausea churned in the pit of his stomach. He wanted to vomit.

'Sean, what happened?' Arturo asked, emerging from the shadows.

Sean stared at them, unable to speak. His emotions were bursting, yet he couldn't even bring himself to speak. His shock was completely debilitating.

Bella reached for him. 'Sean...it's me... Bella.'

Gently, her hand found his. Bella's compassion swept over him and calmed the anguished screams deafening his thoughts. His breathing slowed and the knot in his stomach eased.

'What's wrong?' she whispered softly. 'What did they do to you?'

Sean let his muscles relax a little. Considering a part of his body had just been hacked off, he wasn't feeling intolerable pain. Strangely, it felt like his wings were still there, giving him the same tingling he felt before flying. He mustered all his strength to respond. 'I'm okay.'

Bella stared at him with wide, disbelieving eyes. She could plainly see he was far from okay.

Now his vision had fully adjusted to the darkness, he could see everyone behind her: General Maddock, Colonel Powell, Arturo, and a squad of ten to fifteen US Marines.

General Maddock pushed through the group. 'Sean, what are we doing down here? Is this a prison?'

'It's a labyrinth.'

'Labyrinth?' Maddock boomed. 'Like a maze?'

Sean nodded.

'I don't get it. Why drop us in a maze? Why don't they just kill us?'

'Because that wouldn't be anywhere as entertaining,' Senetep said as his life-sized hologram materialised behind them. 'I've created twelve checkpoints inside this labyrinth. Reach one and you'll be awarded with weapons. If you survive to the centre of the maze and find the exit, I'll spare your life. But for those of you who don't make it that far, I have a simple request: die slowly – the bloodier the better.'

'You know where you can shove your request,' Bella said under her breath.

Senetep sniggered. 'That kind of spunk might keep you alive a little longer. I want Sean to witness your suffering – to see the futility of his stubbornness and realise that the information he's protecting, I'll have. One way or another. In case you haven't already realised, he's the reason you're down here. Maybe you can convince him to talk. In the meantime, my hybrid scientists have drawn inspiration from your human mythologies. Their creations await you within my labyrinth. If these horrors fail to change Sean's mind, then maybe your dying screams will.'

The hologram dematerialised.

Maddock grabbed Sean by the collar and slammed him against the wall, crushing the stumps of his severed wings. Sean squirmed in agony. It felt like there were daggers in his back. 'That conehead already has the Ark of the Covenant, so you'd better be protecting something important!'

'I am,' Sean wheezed.

'That's enough,' Powell said, pulling Maddock away. 'From here on, we work together!'

Maddock shrugged Powell off with a disgruntled huff.

'Anyone got any ideas what to do next?' Powell asked.

Sean realised everyone was looking at him for their next instruction, not Maddock or Powell. Like it or not, he was calling the shots now. 'Reach the first checkpoint, survive as long as we can, and find another way out.'

'You think there's another way out?' Bella asked.

'But mazes only have one solution, and that'll lead us straight back to Senetep,' Arturo said.

'That's true,' Sean said. 'But Senetep built this maze ten thousand years ago. Since then, it was adopted by the pharaohs and used by the Egyptians. They might've changed sections he doesn't know about. There could be cave-ins and other places to escape.'

'How big's this labyrinth?' Maddock asked.

Sean was well-read on Egypt's legendary labyrinth thanks to the many books his dad sent him. 'There was a Greek historian called Herodotus who wrote about it in the fifth century BCE. He described it as a huge temple with three thousand rooms, paths, courtyards, and chambers.'

'Three thousand rooms!' Maddock cried. 'We go in, we'll never come out.'

'It sounds worse than it is,' Sean said, remembering an image he'd used on his computer as wallpaper for a few months – a seventeenth-century drawing of the labyrinth created by a scholar named Athanasius Kircher, one of the first people to claim he'd deciphered Egyptian hieroglyphics. His translations were published in the book *Oedipus Aegyptiacus*, which people believed to be correct at the time. Even though his translations proved wrong, his work paved the way for later scholars, many of whom called him a pioneer in the serious study of hieroglyphs. The one thing about Kircher that intrigued Sean more than anything else was his sketch of the labyrinth inspired by Herodotus's description.

Sean knelt and drew a large square in the sand. 'The maze is in the centre of the labyrinth. There's supposed to be twelve courtyards around it, each one with a different layout of rooms, passageways, and colonnades.' He drew another twelve squares around the middle, criss-crossing the lines and boxes to give the impression of the scale and complexity.

'Senetep said there were twelve checkpoints,' Powell added.

'Yeah. I reckon the twelve checkpoints are in the courtyards.'

'Then we secure the checkpoints,' Maddock said. 'Arm ourselves with as many weapons as we can carry and see what we find in that maze.'

Sean was surprised by Maddock's reaction. For once, the general wasn't arguing with him – he was actually agreeing with him.

Powell edged closer to Sean and whispered, 'Outstanding work.'

Sean nodded, feeling a major burst of confidence. It was just what he needed to help take his mind off his severed wings.

'How do you know so much about this stuff?' Arturo asked.

'I read a lot,' Sean said. 'I was a bit of a nerd at school. I didn't play much sports like the other kids – I was usually on a computer in the library or building something in the robotics lab. Good for knowledge...not so great for a social life.'

Powell laughed. 'Or girlfriends!'

Sean shrugged. He couldn't help himself from glancing at Bella. She was already watching him with an amused expression. He felt his face go red-hot with embarrassment.

'Don't worry,' she said, smiling. 'While you were studying in the library, I was painting in the art room. Didn't give me much time for boyfriends.'

In that instant, Bella won him over. Only a couple of days before she was blaming him for everything and now she was sticking up for him. They were more alike than he realised.

Maddock picked up the flaming torch and entered the labyrinth. Half of the Marines marched ahead of the general while the others followed Sean and his friends. Thirty metres in, the passage opened into a grand space dominated by evenly spaced stone columns. They stood like the petrified tree trunks of a prehistoric forest and disappeared into the hovering darkness, the ceiling so high their torchlight failed to illuminate it. The soaring columns reminded Sean of the great hypostyle hall in Karnak.

Sean kept his eyes on the shadows, half-expecting something to leap out and attack them. It was unusually quiet. The columns eventually opened into an empty central square.

Maddock waved the torch around. 'Isn't this supposed to be a checkpoint?'

Everyone turned to Sean. 'I'm not sure,' he said.

'You said each courtyard was a checkpoint. I don't see any weapons.'

'What about that?' Bella said, pointing to something in the shadows above them.

Maddock raised his torch. The flames illuminated a barred crate full of weapons hovering 10 or so metres over the middle of the courtyard. On the one side of the crate was a blinking red light.

'How do we get it down?' Maddock said.

'Easy – Sean, you can fly up there, open the crate, and throw down the weapons,' Powell said.

Just hearing the word 'fly' sent a phantom pain shooting down Sean's back. He envisioned his severed wings again, trampled on and kicked aside by Senetep.

'What's wrong?' Bella asked.

Sean suddenly realised he'd been standing there, reliving his traumatic experience while everyone waited for his response. 'I can't fly anymore.'

'What?!'

Sean swallowed the lump in his throat. 'Senetep cut off my wings.'

Bella looked at his shoulders and gasped. 'That's horrible!'

'Bastard!' Arturo said. 'If I get my hands on him, I'll tear him limb from limb.'

A bloodcurdling moan echoed from the shadows. It sounded like someone being strangled, gasping for air. Maddock swung the torch around, but the light barely illuminated beyond the first row of columns. Arturo pulled Bella near. Maddock spun around, waving the torch at the impenetrable darkness. The moan sounded again, this time echoed by growls, grunts, hissing, and the sound of approaching footsteps.

'Whatever they are, we're surrounded!' Powell said.

A humanoid figure staggered out from between the columns. His milky-white eyes and dragging feet were just like a zombie. It was an injured soldier from the battle at Axum. His US Army fatigues were caked in dust and dried bloodstains. His shirt was torn open and a large scar ran down the length of his chest.

'Stand down, soldier!' Maddock bellowed.

The soldier ignored the command and shuffled blindly into the courtyard.

'He's not a soldier anymore,' Sean said. 'He's a hybrid.'

'I said, stand down!' Maddock said, holding his position.

Everyone else stepped back.

The soldier lumbered to a stop and swayed on his feet. He was holding a crystalline card with a blinking red light. Sean could see it was an Isharkute control card, blinking in unison with the light on the crate above.

'Senetep wants our first fight to be hand-to-hand,' Sean said, pointing to the blinking card. 'He's holding the trigger to release the crate.'

'Well, let's give 'em a fight,' Maddock said, waving the torch in front of the soldier's expressionless face.

The soldier's lips curled back, baring his teeth. He opened his mouth and a sharp hiss filled the air. His jaw widened more than humanly possible and suddenly collapsed downwards with a bone-cracking snap. Two yellow eyes appeared down the soldier's throat and he suddenly arched forward, spitting a snake out of his oesophagus like a massive tongue. Maddock jumped back. It snapped at him and reared up over the soldier's head, flattening its neck like a cobra and hissing aggressively.

Bella screamed.

'We need those weapons,' Maddock said, glancing up at the crate. 'Marines, on my count, we're gonna take down this unholy creation.'

Several Marines surrounded the hybrid-soldier. The snake coiled around the soldier's head, keeping an eye on them.

'Three...two...one!' Maddock screamed, waving the torch at the snake's head.

They pounced on the soldier and tackled him to the ground.

The snake struck one of the Marines with blurring speed, plunging its fangs deep into his neck. He screamed, then stiffened with a convulsion of muscle spasms. Maddock whacked the snake with the torch, creating an explosion of cinders. The snake released the Marine's limp body and arched up, fangs dripping with blood. Maddock tossed the torch aside, seized the snake with two hands, and ripped. Soldier and snake separated with a sickening squelch and both went limp. Maddock tossed the carcass aside and pried the crystal card from the soldier's dead hand.

Now Sean could see why the general had earned the nickname 'Mad-axe.'

Maddock held the card aloft and pressed the blinking button. The crate released a stash of weapons into the middle of the courtyard, clanging and bouncing around on the stone floor. The noise attracted more hybrid-soldiers from the shadows. They lumbered out from between the columns, each one a unique and monstrous creation. There were clawed hands and taloned feet, crocodile tails, muscular gorilla arms, and jackal and lion heads, all stitched onto the remains of the unfortunate soldiers in a Frankenstein-inspired nightmare.

There was a crude, rushed look to their hybrid changes and paled in comparison to the mythical creatures Sean had seen in the Great Arena.

Sean dove in and snatched the nearest stave. In one quick action, he powered it on and fired an energy blast to ward off the hybrid-soldiers. His shot ricocheted off a column, throwing up a flash of dust and debris. Bella and Arturo took the other two staves while the Marines armed themselves with various knives, swords, spears, and close-range weapons.

Maddock picked out two curved swords and clanged them together. 'Now this is old school fightin'! I feel like Russell Crowe in *Gladiator*.'

Sean laughed to himself. General Mad-axe was nuts!

The hybrids leapt at them in a fury of claws and teeth. Bella fired first, taking down a jackal-headed soldier. The Marines kept a solid defensive circle, parrying back the onslaught with their weapons. A burly hybrid-soldier with a crocodile head and tail dove to the floor and cleaned up several Marines with one swipe of its massive tail, breaking their main line of defence. Maddock jumped in, slashing wildly with his dual swords, but the blades bounced harmlessly off the hybrid's scaly snout. The croc-soldier launched upright, bearing down on the general with its teeth-filled maw.

Maddock raised his swords to impale the hybrid down the throat. 'Come on, you ugly son of a –'

Sean blasted the hybrid-croc off its feet, leaving the general hanging mid-sentence.

Maddock gave him a sidelong nod – the closest Sean would ever come to receiving a personal thank-you from the general. Arturo and Bella fired at the remaining hybrid-soldiers, sending them back into the shadows.

Their group raced on, aiming into the shadows, and passed the final row of columns to be confronted with an immense stone wall.

'It's a dead end!' Maddock said, turning on Sean. 'What now?'

'The courtyards should be connected by a door or passage. It must be somewhere along this wall.'

'Spread out, find the entrance,' Maddock ordered.

Four Marines split into pairs and disappeared in opposite directions. Seconds later, a whistle sounded from the darkness and they found the Marines assembled around the entrance of a rectangular passage. Sean led the way through, the blue energy glow of his stave lighting the way.

After several paces, the passage opened into another massive space.

The next courtyard was circular in design and comprised of twelve descending levels like an ancient Greek amphitheatre. There were no columns or pillars supporting the incredible stone ceiling. Each level was a waist-high step down into a central circle. A collection of staves were piled in the middle at the lowest point, but they could bypass it altogether by running around the top level to the next exit.

'Looks easy enough,' Arturo said.

'Let's get down there, Marines. Secure those weapons,' Maddock said.

'Wait!' Sean said. 'That's a low-lying position that's hard to defend.'

'I see that, but I need my men armed with weapons like yours,' Maddock said, pointing to his stave. 'You three kids are currently the best shots with those things – that's the only reason you're still holding them.'

Sean glanced at Bella and Arturo. Between the three of them, they were the only ones armed with staves, while the Marines were stuck with basic handheld weapons. Sean knew better than anyone that most hybrids couldn't be defeated with blades alone. A little extra firepower was necessary.

'You're right – we need the extra staves,' Sean said. 'We'll defend you from up here.'

Maddock nodded. 'Colonel Powell, stay with them. If anything happens to us, keep going. Do what you can to get Sean out of here.'

'Understood,' Powell said enthusiastically.

Maddock jumped down the first level and looked up. 'You three: apart from us, shoot anything that moves!'

Sean, Bella, and Arturo nodded and steadied themselves.

The general followed his Marines into the centre of the courtyard, leaping down each successive tier like they were racing through an army training course. They slowed down upon reaching the lowest level and tentatively approached the pile of weapons.

'This seems too easy,' Arturo whispered.

As if on cue, the central portion of the courtyard floor suddenly ascended like a lift. Maddock and his men rode the rising stone column. Three Marines were caught on the edge and fell aside, dropping back to the lowest level.

'We should've seen that coming,' Powell said.

'Get ready!' Sean replied, aiming at the courtyard. He eyed the exit. It was still open. They could still escape if they needed to.

The central column carried Maddock and his Marines high above the courtyard, looking like it was going to sandwich them against the ceiling. But it clunked to a stop at the last second, leaving a couple of metres above their heads.

'How will they get down?' Bella said.

Sean was more concerned with the newly revealed cavity at the base of the column. It had brought something up from beneath the courtyard which was now lurking in the shadows. Monstrous features emerged briefly and disappeared. Hairy spider legs, glistening black fangs, the wet snouts of three giant dogs, and finally, a towering scorpion's tail. None of them appeared at the same time, but rotated out of the shadows, one after the other.

'What the hell is that thing?' Powell asked.

Sean couldn't tell if it was one giant hybrid or a group. Without warning, the twelve levels of the courtyard slanted downward, creating an inescapable slope towards the column. Sean lost his footing, landed on his butt, and slid down the smooth surface. Bella, Arturo, and Colonel Powell skidded down the 45-degree slope beside him. They all hit the bottom at the same time and rolled across the stone.

Sean jumped to his feet, aiming into the cavity in the base of the column.

Six glowing red eyes glared down at him from the darkness. The creature snorted, blasting him with a hot foul-smelling breath. A stream of thick saliva pooled on the floor before him.

Sean had enough time for one final thought.

*I'm gonna be eaten!*

# CHAPTER 26

# Survival Of The Fastest

Three enormous black snouts emerged from the column, snarling and drooling saliva all over Sean's shoe. It was a three-headed dog, just like the Cerberus from Greek mythology. Sean's first instinct was to fly out of danger, but without his wings, he stumbled backwards onto the incline he'd just slid down. A wall of stained canine teeth and pink tongues rushed at him until it was all he could see. He held up a futile hand to fend off the snapping mouths.

Energy blasts erupted from overhead and the trio of dog heads retreated into the column, whining and whimpering.

'Here!' Maddock shouted from the top of the column.

The general peered over the edge, stave in hand, a proud-looking smirk plastered across his face. Sean never thought he'd be so pleased to see Maddock's bulldog smile. His men threw down a fresh haul of staves for Colonel Powell and the Marines.

Arturo helped Sean to his feet. 'You okay?'

Sean nodded.

'What now?' Powell asked.

'This is a test. We have to pass it before moving to the next chamber.'

Four jet-black spider legs emerged from the column, each as tall and thick as a flag pole. A massive spider crawled out and arced up like a funnel web, its two impossibly long fangs glistening with venom. The arachnid was more than capable of a lethal bite – it could impale all of them along a single fang and still have room for more.

Bella shrieked.

Bad move. The spider crawled after her, hissing so hard it blew the venom off its fangs. Bella jumped back as the deadly spray saturated the floor in front of her. The Marines stepped in, blasting away. Everyone joined the fight, hammering the spider with energy blasts, but their shots just rippled across the spider's armoured underside.

'Aim for the eyes,' Powell cried.

They aimed for the bulbous clump of eyes on top of its head. One blast hit a fang and partially severed it, leaving it swinging on a sliver of sinewy flesh. Furious, the spider crawled out from the shadow of the column, revealing the rest of its body. It wasn't three separate hybrids, but one horrific creation all joined at the abdomen. Part spider, dog, and scorpion, the monster was the ugliest hybrid Sean had ever seen. It scuttled about, each creature vying for dominance. The dog heads snapped at the spider legs and scorpion pincers, like a dog chasing its own tail, each part unaware it was the same creature.

The scorpion side rounded on Sean's group, pincers snapping, salivating mouthparts clacking for a tasty human morsel. The stinger towered overhead, nearly as high as the column Maddock and his Marines were firing from.

'Look out!' Sean screamed.

The stinger struck with incredible speed and impaled the Marine standing beside Arturo. It lifted him into the air and flung him across the courtyard.

'These weapons are useless against this thing,' Powell cried, waving them around to the far side of the column. For the moment, they were out of view of the hybrid. 'It'll pick us off one by one before we give it a scratch worth itching.'

'We need to find its weak spot,' Sean said.

'Si! But where?' Arturo said.

'What about the middle, where the monsters are joined?' Bella said.

'You're right. That's it!' Sean said, impressed with Bella's thinking. She would have done well in the Great Arena.

'Aim for its middle,' Powell shouted up to Maddock.

The general acknowledged with a wave and ordered his men to focus their fire. The courtyard alighted with energy blasts, flashing off the stonework like lightning. The hybrid barked, hissed, and snapped at the column with so much force, the entire courtyard quaked. Rivulets of sand showered from the ceiling. For a moment, Sean thought the entire structure might collapse upon them. The dog heads appeared around the column, two barking at Maddock and his men, the third sniffing the floor, tracking their scent. The rest of the creature writhed and scuttled to avoid the onslaught of energy blasts.

The scorpion tail stabbed at the upper reaches of the column, carving huge divots out of the stone. The Marines stood their ground and intensified their fire. Sean was impressed at how quickly the Marines had mastered the Isharkute staves.

The hybrid spun around in a frantic circle, creating a blur of spider, scorpion, and dog. The dog heads suddenly raised up and howled in agony, then crashed to the floor. The scorpion's tail stiffened and slumped against the column. Two-thirds of the hybrid was almost dead. The spider stabbed its legs into the stone, attempting to haul itself onto them.

'Get back!' Sean cried.

Too late – the spider knocked one of the Marines to the floor. Before he could raise his stave, the giant fang came down, stabbing straight through his chest, cracking the stone floor and instantly silencing his bloodcurdling scream.

Bella turned away with a horrified gasp.

Powell grabbed her arm and directed them around the column to safety. The cavity that brought the hybrid into the courtyard was now clear, allowing them to see inside for the first time. It was a hollow circular space, similar to the inside of a chimney. The floor glistened with pools of dog saliva and deep scratches pitted the stone walls. Nestled on the far wall was a blinking red light.

Sean's heart leapt with excitement. 'That must be the control switch to lower the column and reset the courtyard.'

Powell nodded and their surviving Marine moved inside the cavity.

The spider rounded the column, struggling to drag the weight of its half-dead carcasses. Limp tongues hung from the lifeless dog heads, leaving big streaks of saliva on the stone. The scorpion's pincers were shot to pieces, barely able to rise off the floor.

The Marine raced across the shadowy interior and punched the red light. It turned blue. The courtyard rumbled and the column began to descend.

'Get out of there!' Powell cried, backing up.

The spider dragged itself across the opening, trapping the Marine inside. He tried to shoot his way past the tangle of giant legs. The spider hauled itself into the cavity, unaware the closing gap was about to guillotine it like a lift moving between the floors of a building. The Marine was trapped. His scream echoed across the courtyard as the column severed the spider in two and levelled with the courtyard floor. The surrounding slope transformed back into the concentric tiers.

'Well done, everyone,' Maddock said, re-joining them. 'Except we're losing too many Marines.'

'From now on, we stick together no matter what,' Sean said.

'I hear you, kid,' Maddock replied.

They climbed up the tiers and Sean led them through the passage to the next courtyard. He suddenly stopped and teetered on the edge of a metre-high drop-off. The courtyard below was a square-shaped pool of dark, eerily still water. The only way across was on the square tiles chequerboarding the width and length in a ten-by-ten pattern. Each tile looked about 5 metres wide and within jumping distance of one another. There was no visible exit, but the central tile had a pedestal with a blinking red light.

Powell peered over the edge. 'God knows what's under that water.'

'I don't see an exit,' Maddock said.

Sean pointed to the centre of the pool. 'We will once we activate that red light.'

'Nobody jump to another tile until everyone's caught up,' Sean said. 'We're better facing whatever comes out of this water as one. The second we split up, we weaken our team.'

Maddock nodded. 'It'll be a squeeze to fit us all on a single tile, but you're right.'

Sean jumped down onto the first tile and waited for everyone to join him. He watched the water. There wasn't so much as a ripple on the mirror-black surface. It made him even more nervous. Once they were all together, he continued onto the second square, then the third and fourth. They were one leap away from the blinking light and still hadn't encountered anything. Sean paused on the edge of the tile, hesitant to make the final jump.

'What's wrong?' Powell asked.

Sean stared at the black water, convinced something was waiting to snatch him. It shouldn't have been this easy. He took a step back and sprang across the water as Bella moved into position, next in line to jump. Sean reached out to help and noticed flashes of light deep in the water. At first he thought it was the energy from their staves reflecting off the surface, but it was emanating from the depths of the pool. 'Wait a second!' he shouted.

Bella stepped back.

The flashes intensified in brightness and frequency, like an upside-down thunderstorm with plenty of lightning but no thunder. Sean's tile vibrated.

'Sean, get off there!' Bella cried.

Sean's feet were suddenly inundated by water. His tile was sinking fast. Without thinking, he made a running jump back to the previous tile. By the time he landed and turned around, the pedestal with its blinking red light was almost submerged beneath the water.

'What about the button?' Maddock said.

'Damn it!' Sean cursed. He couldn't believe he'd been so stupid. *Why didn't I press the button? I was right there!*

'Here, hold this,' Arturo said, handing his stave to Bella.

'No!' Bella shrieked as her brother dove into the water.

'Stupid...but gutsy,' Maddock said. 'Let's give him some covering fire.'

The Marines lined the edge of the tile, weapons aimed into the depths. Every few seconds the flashes illuminated Arturo's distorted shape through the water, swimming furiously for the blinking light.

Sean felt incredibly guilty. This was his fault. Bella would never forgive him if anything happened to her brother. Arturo was now too deep to see, even amongst the brightest flashes.

Bella screamed after her brother, 'Arty!'

She jumped back as a tentacle swirled up from the depths, its translucent form rippling with biological energy. A wall of tentacles suddenly surfaced around the tile, writhing and curling high over their heads. Luminous hues of blue, green, pink, and yellow reflected off the water and filled the courtyard with a beautiful but terrifying incandescence. The tentacles swayed over them, poised to strike. Several tiles away, the creature's slender mantle broke the surface, a massive elongated head that flashed like a neon sign rising from the pool.

'What the hell is that?' Maddock shouted.

'It's some type of kraken...a giant squid!' Sean yelled back.

The kraken rotated, revealing two enormous eyes.

Bella dropped to her knees and screamed at the water. 'Arty!'

Sean wished he could help her, but swimming wasn't his strength. He wouldn't be able to hold his breath for a third of the time Arturo had been gone. How long could Arturo hold his breath? He must have been down there for two or three minutes. Even if he survived this long, how would he get past the tentacles?

'Look out!' Powell cried.

The tentacles struck in waves, cracking at them like electric whips. One of the Marines was caught around the waist. The kraken's energy rippled over his body, paralysing him, and then the tentacle flicked him across the courtyard where he bounced off a tile and splashed down in front of the kraken's mouth. A swarm of smaller tentacles emerged from its head and pulled his body into its snapping beak.

The Marines blasted several tentacles in half. The limp appendages flopped onto the adjacent tiles and lost their glow. The injured tentacle stumps whooshed back into the water and the kraken rose higher, the tip of its mantle close to hitting the courtyard ceiling.

Everyone jostled for a safer position, shooting with growing desperation and panic. Another Marine was ensnared and thrown into the air, then another.

A tentacle latched onto Maddock's leg. He gave it a futile punch as it flipped him off his feet and onto his back. He fought against the disabling shocks racing up his leg, then aimed his stave high and fired. The close-range blast obliterated the tentacle and showered him in luminous goo.

Sean glimpsed something between the wall of tentacles that made him pause. An exit to the next courtyard was opening. Then, as if by magic, Arturo surfaced on the tile beside it, panting heavily.

'Look!' Sean cried, pointing to Arturo. 'He did it!'

'Arturo!' Bella screamed, jumping high with excitement.

Arturo waved everyone over to join him.

'Clear a path,' Powell commanded. 'We're gettin' outta here after all.'

They blasted an opening through the tentacles and leapt across the tiles. Maddock struggled to keep up with his partially paralysed leg, the severed tentacle still hanging from his thigh. Sean was surprised the general could walk at all considering that the other Marines had been completely incapacitated by the shocks. The tentacles retreated into the water and the kraken's head submerged in a surge of bubbles, losing its glow as it disappeared. The water became still and dark again.

Bella leapt ahead onto Arturo's tile and hugged him tightly. 'I thought you were dead.'

'Anch' io!' Arturo gasped. 'I've never held my breath that long. I thought my lungs were going to burst.'

'Stop congratulating yourselves and keep moving,' Maddock said, limping past them.

'A thank-you would've been nice,' Bella huffed. 'He just saved our lives!'

'We're not out of here yet.'

'*Odio quel bruto!*' she hissed.

Sean laughed to himself; he hated the brute too.

They were one tile away from the exit when the water erupted in a maelstrom of light. The kraken's mantle shot up and crashed into the ceiling, blocking their exit. A wall of tentacles burst out of the pool, spraying everyone with water. The Marines opened fire, but the tentacles were faster and more elusive than before, as if the kraken was anticipating their actions. One of the Marines was caught and swung overhead, where his scream was silenced with a crack of paralysing electricity. His limp body was thrown into the kraken's snapping beak and devoured in a surge of frothy blood-red bubbles.

Sean couldn't turn away – as horrific as it was to watch, it gave him an idea. He spun his stave around, crystal end first, like the point of a javelin, then leant back and hurled it straight into the kraken's beak. The creature chomped down on it, unaware of the explosive crystal.

'Everybody get down!' Sean yelled, dragging Bella down by the shoulders.

Maddock remained on his feet, shooting wildly at the tentacles, that war-crazed Mad-axe look in his eyes again.

Sean peered over his shoulder. The stave was being devoured, just as he'd hoped. With every snap, the kraken was working the power crystal into the corner of its beak. Three more chomps... two...one...

*Crack!*

The crystal shattered with a muted explosion. The unfortunate creature weathered most of the blast inside its head, killing it instantly. The shockwave knocked Maddock of his feet and he landed on his butt in the middle of the tile. The tentacles flopped into the water. The kraken went dark, teetered, and then collapsed across the courtyard. The mantle crashed through the far wall and created a gaping new hole – a lucky break considering the dead sea monster was blocking their original exit.

'We could blast our way through the carcass,' Powell said.

Sean eyed their new option. The kraken's mantle was now a bridge into a dark void beyond the courtyard wall. 'We might avoid the labyrinth if we go that way. Could be our best chance to escape.'

'You're right,' Maddock said, ripping the tentacle flesh off his leg. 'Lead the way.'

Sean climbed over the mushy remains of the kraken's face and onto the mantle, and then turned to help Bella up. Her shoe squelched into a half-destroyed eyeball. 'Urgh! I'm never eating calamari again.'

Sean made his way across the slippery mantle and through the remains of the partially collapsed wall. A second wall appeared through the haze of settling dust, constructed from colossal slabs of stone and towering several storeys high. The top of the wall didn't even touch the ceiling, which was so dark and distant that it looked like a starless night sky. The wall led to three gargantuan openings, each veering in different directions, beckoning them into the darkness.

'It's a way into the labyrinth,' Sean said.

'You said we'd avoid the labyrinth this way,' Maddock said, jumping off the kraken's mantle.

'I said we *might* have a better chance of escaping. At least this shortcut bypasses other courtyards and gets us straight into the final challenge.'

'Which is what? What's in there?'

Sean stared into the shadowy passage, recounting Senetep's introduction: *My hybrid scientists have drawn inspiration from your human mythologies.* There was a well-known Greek myth that immediately sprang to mind: the legend of Theseus and his journey into the maze to defeat the minotaur. Once he'd killed the monster, Theseus famously escaped the maze by retracing a ball of string he'd unravelled along the floor upon entering. The key difference here was they didn't want to come back the same way – they needed to find another way out of the maze.

'Well?' Maddock asked.

'Senetep said his hybrid scientists drew inspiration from our myths. There's only one monster I can think of that's found in a maze.'

'A minotaur,' Bella said.

'Half-man, half-bull,' Powell confirmed. 'We've all heard of that before. After everything we've seen, he doesn't sound so bad.'

'Let's find out,' Maddock said, pushing ahead.

'Wait!' Arturo said. 'We can't just walk in there and hope to find a way out. We need a system so we don't get lost.'

'Like what?' Maddock said.

'We use the right-hand rule. Keep a hand on the right-hand wall at all times, and always turn right at intersections. If it's a dead end, we'll just loop around, but always keep a hand on the wall. It'll take longer, but this method will eventually get us out of here.'

'You sure it works?' Powell asked.

'I used it to get out of the famous Villa Pisani maze. It's supposed to be one of the hardest mazes in the world to solve. I spent a very long afternoon using the right-hand method, but it worked.'

'We'll start in the right-hand passage, then,' Maddock said.

Sean and Bella kept to the middle of the group. Arturo walked alongside them, his hand running along the wall. He was now everyone's guide. They rounded the first corner and the silence became as thick and impenetrable as the walls. The passages weren't just turning at right angles, but also diagonally, which made their previous route impossible to remember. Several intersections and turns later, they were deep inside the maze and completely disoriented.

'Whatever happens, keep your hand on that wall,' Colonel Powell whispered. 'If this thing surprise attacks, we may need to retreat.'

'*Sì, sì!*' Arturo whispered back.

They arrived at another intersection and turned right, this time entering a dead end. They looped around and followed the next right. After a couple more turns, they faced another dead end. Now all they seemed to be doing was retracing their own steps. Every wall and every corner looked the same, but Sean had faith that Arturo's right-hand system was working, albeit taking a while. Without it, they would've been lost after the first few turns. They entered an intersection of six passages and the Marines stopped abruptly, aiming at the darkness ahead.

'What is it?' Bella whispered.

'I don't know,' Arturo whispered back.

'Shh!' Powell whispered.

A scraping sound echoed out of the surrounding gloom, like something being ground against the stone walls. Sean craned around, trying to pinpoint the direction of the noise. It sounded like it was coming from all six passages. He gripped his stave, ready for action. Bella backed up against him, aiming in the opposite direction. An aggressive snort suddenly echoed off the walls, so close that Sean expected to be hit with spittle. The heave of cavernous breathing followed. It sounded angry and determined, like a bull poised to charge.

'Where's it coming from?' Bella whispered.

'I don't know,' Sean said.

There was a sudden rush of footsteps, but nobody in their group was moving. Each pounding step was powerful and heavy, coming from every direction.

The silhouette of a man with the head and horns of a bull materialised in the murky passage to their right, soaring over them, four times the size of a normal person with horns scraping along the wall. The minotaur barrelled through their group. Desperate screams and frantic energy blasts filled the passage. Sean and Bella scrambled into the nearest passage, peering over their shoulders at the chaos. Marines were being picked up and thrown around like dolls. One of the men shot the minotaur in the shoulder and it spun around with a roar, impaling him against the wall on one of its immense horns.

'Arturo, keep your hand on that wall!' Maddock screamed over the fray.

But Arturo already had two hands on his weapon, staring in awe at the creature.

Sean knew there was no time to follow the wall back way they came – too many dead ends.

Colonel Powell shepherded Arturo through the chaos to join them. General Maddock followed, firing a volley of blasts at the monster in a last-ditch attempt to protect his Marines. The minotaur blocked each shot with its metallic wrist bracers, sending them ricocheting down the passages. The Marines were being stomped on, skewered, and hurled through the air, but fought bravely in the face of a battle already lost.

The carnage made Sean sick to his stomach.

'Come on, General, let's go!' Powell hollered.

Sean placed his right hand on the wall and took the lead, dashing into the shadows. They rounded a corner, then several paces on, they rounded another. The sounds of battle were becoming a distant echo. Maddock trailed at the back of the group, puffing and panting louder than the minotaur. After a straight stretch, they turned another corner. Several paces in, the passage finished with a dead end. Sean turned around, bumping shoulders with everyone still heading in the opposite direction.

A loud snort resonated through the passage.

Sean froze mid-stride, hoping it was the general.

The scrape of horns across stone echoed overhead.

Sean was blasted with a snort of hot, foul-smelling breath. The silhouette of the minotaur loomed over him, a dead Marine hanging from one of its horns. He raised his stave and stumbled back into Bella.

'Mio Dio!' she gasped.

Everyone scrambled back into one another, cramming against the dead end like sardines. This was it. No way out. Death seemed inevitable.

Unfortunately for himself, Sean knew this wasn't the end, but the beginning of a new nightmare. Even if the minotaur tore him limb from limb, Senetep could reactivate his remains and keep him alive until he revealed the Yonaguni beacon. After everything he'd done, every plan his dad had put in place over the millennia, Senetep had ultimately won!

'This can't be it,' Sean whispered to himself.

'It's not. This ain't over yet, kid!' Maddock said, pushing to the front of the group. 'It's time to give this deformed bull an attitude adjustment.'

Sean admired the general for facing death on his own terms – he wished he was as brave. The minotaur lumbered forward, pounding the passage walls with its fists and snorting powerful bursts of spittle across the stone.

Powell moved alongside the general, peering over his shoulder at Sean. 'We'll hold this beast as long as we can. If there's a chance to get past, take it!'

The minotaur rushed forward, arms wide to scoop them up. Maddock and Powell lit up the passage with energy blasts. The minotaur deflected the shots with its bracers, sending them into the distant ceiling. It roared in anger and hammered the walls, shaking the entire passage.

'The maze is going to collapse!' Bella gasped.

A sound like thunder rolled across the ceiling and a shaft of light opened directly overhead. Several large blocks fell from the opening and crashed off the maze wall, smashing to the floor between them and the minotaur in a swirl of dust. A dazzling beam of sunlight spotlighted the passage.

The minotaur grunted and shielded its eyes, retreating into the shadows.

Three rope ladders unfurled from the hole and dangled in the light. Sean squinted up at the opening, but all he could see were the silhouettes of people waving at them to climb the ladders.

'Let's go!' Powell said, pushing Sean, Bella, and Arturo ahead. 'You three first – we'll cover you.'

They dropped their staves and launched onto separate ladders. Their enthusiasm caused the ladders to swing and spin uncontrollably. It took them a few seconds to settle and figure out how fast they could climb without losing control.

A blast of hot air suddenly scattered their ladders.

Sean stopped on the next rung and stared in horror. Bella was dangling directly in front of the minotaur's glistening black nostrils, swaying in rhythm with each monstrous snort. She seized the rungs in terror, staring right into the soulless bovine eyes.

Energy blasts erupted from below.

The minotaur roared and swung its head, catching Bella's ladder on its horn. She was flung high into the air and came down on its horn, impaling her through the stomach. Her chilling scream pierced Sean's heart like an ice-cold bullet.

'Bella!' Arturo shouted, reaching for her.

A well-aimed shot blasted through the hole above. The minotaur stiffened and collapsed against the wall, a gaping wound carved into the back of its head. It shuddered and a large drool of saliva ran from its mouth. Bella clutched the bloody horn protruding from her lower body with a look of disbelief. The minotaur spluttered its final breath and slumped down the wall, taking Bella with it.

Sean and Arturo started down their ladders after her.

'Keep climbing, you two!' Maddock ordered. 'I'll bring her up.'

Bella screamed as Powell and Maddock carefully pulled her off the horn. Maddock placed her over his shoulders like a fireman's rescue and climbed the ladder.

Sean continued climbing. Between every rung, a million thoughts raced through his mind, flitting between elation and panic. He reached the top and was yanked into the daylight by Nocao.

'Nocao!' Sean panted, throwing his arms around his friend. 'How'd you –'

'I'll explain later,' Nocao said, prying himself free from Sean's embrace. 'We need to get everyone out.'

They were in the middle of the desert, surrounded by a ragtag team of soldiers from various nationalities and armies. Two hunter-craft and half a dozen stingers were parked nearby, manned and guarded by soldiers with Isharkute weapons – the spoils of the El Mirador pyramid.

Carla pushed through the group and gave him a hug. 'Sean, I'm so glad you're okay.'

Sean hugged her back, relieved to see her alive and well.

Arturo and Powell climbed out of the hole, then turned to help Maddock.

Carla's horrified gasp cut the air like a knife.

Bella emerged from the darkness, draped lifelessly over Maddock's shoulders. Everyone helped lift her to safety and lay her on the ground. Arturo supported her head as Carla put pressure on the wound, stemming the steady crimson ooze. Bella was ashen-faced and soaked in blood. Sean knelt next to her and gently squeezed her hand. Her purple lips managed a weary smile and she passed out.

'Hurry up!' Nocao said. 'Get her aboard the transport.'

A roar echoed from the labyrinth.

General Maddock was half out of the hole when his ladder was ripped from its metal pegs and pulled across the sand, taking him back into the labyrinth. Everyone dove onto it, grasping the rungs as Maddock disappeared into the hole.

'Climb!' Powell cried, skidding to a stop on the edge, both hands holding the ladder.

Sean peered inside the hole to see the general clinging desperately to the ladder with one hand. Below him, the minotaur writhed and screamed, insane with rage. It was still alive! Maddock gripped the ladder with two hands and looked up. He was at least twenty rungs from the top and struggling to get a foothold. His eyes met Sean's and glazed over with the hopeless realisation he wasn't going to make it.

'Don't stop!' Sean screamed. 'Keep going!'

Maddock didn't even attempt to climb. 'Turn on that beacon, kid.'

Sean nodded, accepting the duty and responsibility being passed on to him. In the next instant the general was gone, swiped out of existence by the minotaur's hand. The ladder went limp and everyone tumbled backwards.

Sean stared into the shadows, realising it was now a race to Yonaguni. He was about to save the world, but all he could think about was Bella.

# CHAPTER 27

# *Perfect Shadow*

Senetep stormed across the pyramid control room, blaring orders at the crew monitoring the situation. The Isharkute technicians scrambled to keep track of the vessels. Azar watched the unfolding chaos with a sense of satisfaction. It was an embarrassing defeat for the alien leader. Sean and his friends had been rescued from right under his nose and were now escaping across the desert.

Commander Nefaro pushed one of the technicians off his control panel and took over. 'Why can't we track them?'

'They're using an encrypted cloaking frequency,' the technician said.

Senetep knew that was something only an Isharkute could do, which meant Nocao was alive and helping the human resistance. He rounded on Commander Vogran. 'Why are you still standing here? Take a squadron, find them, kill them, and bring me what's left of Sean.'

Vogran marched out of the control room, waving several elite warriors to follow him.

Senetep hovered over Nefaro, waiting for a result. Azar noticed beads of sweat forming across Nefaro's blue brow.

'You had ten thousand years to prepare for this, yet this insignificant band of human rebels have outsmarted us with our own vessels?'

'We weren't expecting Henry's hidden pyramid –'

*Whack!*

Senetep backhanded Nefaro and sent him sprawling across the

floor. 'You should've anticipated this. Your ineptitude makes Henry Livingstone look like a superior tactician. Maybe I'm better off looking to Azar and his pitiful resources – even they could do a better job!'

The insult gave Azar a sudden burst of inspiration, an ingenious tactical move to claim the Ark, overthrow Senetep, and avenge Malik's death. The plan unravelled in his mind like it had been there all along, sitting in his subconscious, just waiting for the right trigger.

Azar spoke up. 'I have a faster, foolproof way of finding them.'

Senetep turned to him, face alight with anger. 'If you're wasting my time...'

'When I discovered the Cave of Myth, I also uncovered a global network of hidden Isharkute sensors. Henry Livingstone and Nesuk put them in place to monitor the Ark over the millennia. We could use the extra power from the Ark to tap into this network and enhance the signal. In theory, you could monitor every millimetre of this planet in real time. Not only would you find Sean instantly, but if you modified the technology to scan for specific power signatures, you might be able to find the beacon and destroy it.'

'Without one of these sensors, your plan's useless.'

'I have one in my labs.'

Senetep's frown eased into a new look of interest.

'We only need one sensor to access the global network,' Nefaro offered in a cautious tone, picking himself up from the floor.

Senetep seized Azar by the throat. 'Why didn't you tell me about the sensor before?'

Azar gripped Senetep's forearms. He couldn't breathe. The building pressure made his eyes feel like they were going to burst from their sockets. How was he expected to answer? He forced the remaining air from his lungs, struggling to whisper through his crushed larynx. He could feel his rapid pulse terminating in his neck – there was no blood reaching his head, no air into his lungs. The corners of his vision dimmed. Senetep was choking him to death, the same way he'd killed his son. Malik's face filled his mind until it was all he could see.

When he was on the point of unconsciousness, Senetep released him.

Azar resisted the dizziness, determined not to fall to his knees. He straightened his suit and gathered his thoughts, determined never to bow before the tyrannical alien again. 'I didn't become a billionaire by playing it safe,' he said hoarsely. 'To succeed in life, a person must be the ultimate tactician: outsmart their adversaries, learn their weaknesses, and exploit them. I've always been one step ahead of my competitors, ready to sacrifice anything to survive.'

'Like your son, Malik,' Senetep said dryly.

Azar shuddered on the inside. An icy hatred had gripped his heart, tighter than Senetep's cold blue hand could ever hold. The surge of raw emotion made him acknowledge the grief he'd been harbouring. The pain of losing Malik had bored a hole so deep and wide through his soul, it threatened to suck him in. He regretted standing by as Senetep choked his son to death. His inaction would haunt him forever. Malik could never be replaced, but at least his plan would exact some retribution.

'If you bring the Ark to my labs, we can use its energy to power the sensor.'

Senetep nodded and limped from the control room, leaving Nefaro to coordinate the details.

Not long after, Azar was forced aboard a hunter-craft and flown across the desert with Senetep, Nefaro, and a platoon of warriors guarding the Ark of the Covenant. The relic was literally within his grasp. He used the brief journey to consider every detail of his plan. It would be tricky to pull off on his own, but not impossible. Hopefully the skeleton crew of scientists and armed guards he'd left in place to keep his base operational were still at their posts.

These last remaining scientists were also responsible for sending the world governments every piece of information he'd gathered on the Isharkute, a backup plan that would have been automatically initiated when he didn't return to his base twelve hours after his initial meeting with Senetep. Even though his intention to possess the Ark was a self-serving quest for power, he wasn't ready to leave humanity in the dark if he failed. It was an anonymous gesture of goodwill to the world.

Azar directed the Isharkute pilots to land on the far side of a rocky ridge jutting out from the dunes, one of the many secret entrances to his base. Azar jumped out. The sand spilled over the sides of his $3,000 shoes, reminding him how far he was from his comfort zone. He performed his best work in offices and boardrooms, not outside in the elements.

He led them to a natural-looking rock wall.

Senetep rounded on him. 'If this is a ploy to waste my time, I'll rip your head from your neck.'

Azar shifted one of the rock ledges aside, revealing a numeric keypad and fingerprint sensor. He entered an eight-digit code and scanned his thumbprint. A door-sized section of the wall jerked inwards and descended into the ground, revealing a metal passage burrowing deep into the desert.

'This is one of the back doors into my base,' Azar said, entering. He slipped off his shoes and poured out the sand, much to everyone's irritation.

'What are you doing?' Senetep groaned.

'I hate sand. The benefit of building an airtight base beneath the desert is that you can keep the sand out, but most importantly, one can keep it from their shoes.'

Azar stepped back into his shoes.

Once everyone was inside the passage, the door sealed shut behind them. A warrior jabbed him to move along. Azar directed them into his base, a self-satisfied grin creeping across his lips. He was pushing his luck, but this close to the end, it was gratifying to antagonise Senetep at every opportunity. It was hard to believe the Ark of the Covenant was being carried inside his base by the enemy. His ultimate objective was almost complete. Azar picked up the pace, his confidence rising with each step. This was his domain, and soon he'd be in control.

Deeper inside the base, the modern architecture merged with ancient stone columns, once preserved beneath the desert for thousands of years.

'Do you recognise this stonework?' Azar said, stopping in front of a monolithic column displaying perfectly interlocked joints.

'It's Isharkute,' Senetep said.

'The ancient Egyptians called this city Tjenu. It was built upon a much older city, one that stood here millennia before.'

Senetep traced the column's joint with his six fingers. 'This architecture was unique to my capital. It was powerful, austere, unadorned with useless flourishes.'

Azar sensed a hint of remorse in Senetep's voice. *Good! You have feelings after all...my revenge is worth the sacrifice.*

They arrived at the heart of the base to find two armed guards stationed by the steel doors protecting his library, their automatic assault rifles already raised in defence.

'Lower your weapons,' Azar ordered.

His guards obeyed and stepped aside, keeping their eyes on the Isharkute intruders.

Azar entered his code into the control panel and scanned his fingerprint. The doors parted, revealing his personal headquarters – a combination of library, control room, and glass-walled laboratories – the nerve centre of his entire base. He breathed a silent sigh of relief. He'd made it this far. *Not long to go now.*

'Stay here,' Azar said to his guards. 'Once we're inside, don't let anyone else through these doors.'

Senetep was intrigued by the combination of human and Isharkute architecture. He stopped for a moment to examine the exposed steel beams and glass-and-concrete walls built around his original columns.

Azar hustled them to the far end of the library and entered the central passage dividing his labs. A pair of scientists were still working. They stopped what they were doing and stared in shock at Azar and the blue-skinned visitors carrying the golden Ark.

Azar waved the scientists into the passage. 'Follow me to Laboratory Three. We're going to initiate program *Perfect Shadow*.'

The scientists looked at each other and nodded nervously.

'What's *Perfect Shadow*?' Senetep asked.

'The code name we've given to the Isharkute sensor system.' Azar said, giving his scientists a sidelong nod. Understandably, they both wore perplexed expressions since the code name was for another program entirely. He just hoped they had the nerve and foresight to play along with his plan. Azar knew every step from now on was a bonus. Senetep hadn't sensed his deceit – at least, not yet!

After several long passages they entered Laboratory Three, a tall, hexagonally-shaped room with steel doors set into the eight walls. The middle of the lab was dissected by a floor-to-ceiling power conduit humming with 582 megawatts of energy from the nuclear reactor beneath the base.

The scientists set to work, typing commands into the conduit's computer interfaces.

Senetep and Nefaro entered and the warriors positioned themselves around the lab, placing the Ark down beside the conduit.

Azar felt a tickle of sweat on his forehead, sitting just inside his hairline. He prayed for it not to run down his face. The slightest sign of nerves or anxiousness was bound to give him away.

'This doesn't look like a laboratory,' Nefaro said, eyeing the conduit.

'You're right, it's a power substation used to designate and route power throughout my base. The adjoining laboratories require the extra power consumption.'

'We've wasted enough time,' Senetep said with growing impatience. 'Show me the sensor!'

Azar nodded to his scientists. The first scientist typed a command into his workstation and one of the steel doors slid open.

'Bring the Ark through here,' Azar said, leading the way. He paused momentarily in the rim of light framing the doorway. It scanned him in a flash and he entered, quickly sidestepping as a holographic version of himself continued into the room. It was precise in every way: identical suit, shoes, gold watch, right down to his hair and moustache – a complete digital representation of his current appearance based on the scan from seconds before. This was the first beta build of *Perfect Shadow*. His hologram technology was no longer restricted to objects and environments. This experimental program was an attempt to recreate a holographic human, indistinguishable from the real thing.

The rest of the holographic chamber was a recreation of one of his labs, incorporating the same technology he'd used to show Sean and Nocao the Cave of Myth.

Azar backed out of sight and a wall panel materialised in front of him, hiding his physical body from the Isharkute. He held his breath, hoping Senetep hadn't noticed the transition between himself and his hologram.

Senetep entered the chamber and peered around. For one terrifying moment he stared right into Azar's real eyes, but from Senetep's perspective, all he should be able to see was a wall. The Overseer seemed unaware of the shift from reality to hologram and moved on. Nefaro entered, followed by the warriors carrying the Ark. Azar waited. He needed all of them to enter before escaping back to the control room. His holographic-self was only programmed to stand at a podium and repeat pre-recorded speeches – something that would instantly reveal the ruse.

Azar's holographic-self turned to face the aliens, his eyes making no contact with theirs, looking straight ahead. 'My name is Azar Hawati. I welcome you here today...'

'The sensor?' Senetep asked.

Azar's digital self continued speaking, completely ignoring Senetep's question '...this is our first shareholder meeting for the year and...'

Senetep and Nefaro shared looks of puzzlement, and then turned back to the hologram. Senetep reached for Azar's neck, only to have his hand pass straight through the hologram with a fizzle of energy.

Azar jumped through the holographic wall panel and raced out of the chamber. 'Now!' he screamed.

The scientists sealed the door shut, locking the Isharkute inside.

'Override the hologram's safety protocols and amplify the electrical current into the chamber.'

'By how much?' asked one of the scientists.

'Full power.'

The scientists glared at him in unison, eyes bulging with incredulity. That amount of energy would electrify the Isharkute into a burnt crisp. Azar was flush with panic and excitement. They were on the verge of taking back planet Earth, the closest humanity had come since Senetep first arrived at the Arc de Triomphe in Paris.

'Well?' Azar said, snapping the scientists from their stares. 'Do it!'

The pair set to work, rapidly typing the override commands into the system. Azar observed a nearby monitor with a live video-feed from the chamber. There was no need to turn up the volume. Senetep's furious expression and muted screams said it all. The warriors created a defensive circle around him and raised their weapons.

'Hurry up!' Azar cried. 'If they fire their weapons in there, they might damage the Ark.'

The scientists typed with blurring speed, their faces red with concentration, foreheads dripping with perspiration.

Azar's heart pounded so hard, he swore someone was pummelling his chest. Beads of sweat raced down his back, soaking his shirt. The stress of every boardroom battle he'd ever faced was nothing compared to this. His entire life, everything he'd achieved, had boiled down to this single event – his last chance to claim the Ark and avenge Malik. *Come on. Hurry up!*

He checked the video-feed.

The warriors forced their staves through the holographic walls, creating temporary holes in the visual matrix to reveal the real chamber. Nefaro pointed out a clump of power conduits running along the actual chamber ceiling.

'How long?' Azar cried.

'I'm there!' the first scientist said, raising his hands in the air.

'Okay...one second... Ready!' the second scientist said, finger paused over the Enter key.

Azar eyed the monitor. The warriors aimed their staves at the conduits. 'Quick, do it!'

The scientist pressed the key and took a nervous step away from his workstation.

The steady hum of accumulating electricity vibrated through the lab as the system built up the charge. The workstation monitors came to life as the green safety bars steadily climbed into yellow, then orange...the red DANGER ZONE taking forever to reach.

Azar gnashed his teeth with anticipation.

The warrior's staves clicked open, preparing to fire.

Azar checked the power indicators. The rising bars finally tipped into the red, then suddenly rocketed towards an overload. 'Come on!' he cried.

A burst of electricity rippled through the lab. Sparks flew from the surrounding equipment and the lights flickered. The unbridled energy electrified every holographic emitter inside chamber, turning it into a death trap. Azar stared, awe-struck. The Isharkute were locked to the chamber floor, lightning-sized bolts of electricity crackling between the emitters, the gold-plated Ark, and their bodies. It scorched their skin and made their armour smoke, like mosquitos caught in a giant bug zapper. The surge of power reached a crescendo and shorted out the system.

The lab plunged into darkness.

Azar stood dead still, listening over the sound his drumming heart. Nothing but silence. The emergency lighting flickered on, illuminating the lab with an eerie red light. The video-feed was dead. There was no way the Isharkute could be alive, but he still needed to stand over Senetep's charred remains and see for himself.

'Open the door.'

'They're dead,' said one of the scientists.

'We shouldn't have a problem then. Open it!'

Reluctantly, the scientists positioned themselves on both sides of the door and cranked the manual release handles. The door parted with a grind of metal, releasing a thick waft of foul-smelling smoke. Azar covered his mouth, blocking the stench of burnt flesh. The scientists coughed and spluttered as they continued winding. With every turn the door opened a little more, gradually revealing the horrors inside.

The gap was now wide enough to step through and the scientists stood back.

Azar held his breath and proceeded inside. The Ark of the Covenant stood amidst the carnage, unscathed in gleaming gold. There were bodies everywhere, blackened and unrecognisable. Contorted arms and legs jutted out at weird angles, all smouldering in a thick haze of death like a sculpture from hell. Azar stepped over the corpses, determined to find Senetep.

He could barely breathe though the reek.

The trail of corpses led him to the far end of the chamber where the smoke hung the thickest. It wouldn't clear until the air filtration systems came back online, yet for some reason, it was swirling past him like someone just opened a window. Then he noticed a gaping black hole in the chamber wall. The damaged panels curled out, as if the blast had torn it open from within the chamber. One of the Isharkute had shot their way out.

*Crack!* A set of stave forks snapped open, illuminating a scorched, seething face. Senetep!

Azar didn't even have time to blink.

A flash of energy and he was flying backwards through the chamber, over the Ark and into the previous room. He slammed into the wall and slumped to the floor, unable to move. His empty lungs were unwilling to suck in life-saving air and his heart was still and heavy like a stone.

Azar's wide-eyed death stare was focused on the chamber doors. His fading vision captured the Overseer emerging from the chamber, and with his dying thought, he knew Senetep had beaten him.

# — CHAPTER 28 —

# *Frozen Negotiations*

Sean pushed through the soldiers crowding the hunter-craft and knelt beside Bella. Her complexion had changed from ashen-grey to blue. He squeezed her hand. It was cool and unresponsive. She'd lost so much blood. Carla and Arturo knelt opposite, staring gravely at Bella's lifeless body. Like him, they were fast losing hope.

Nocao rummaged through an onboard compartment, yanking out all manner of Isharkute devices and throwing them across the floor. He pulled out a cylindrical stainless-steel container and held it up proudly. 'Standard medical kit for all hunter-craft.'

Nocao moved next to Bella and opened the container. He dipped his hand inside and pulled out a gooey, dark-red substance that looked like a massive blood clot.

'Clear her clothes, I need to see the wound.'

'What are you doing?' Carla said, peeling the sticky, blood-soaked shirt from Bella's skin. The deep hole in her abdomen was barely oozing blood now.

'This plasma salve seals wounds and replenishes blood.'

Arturo grabbed Nocao's wrist. 'Wait a minute! She doesn't have Isharkute blood – how do you know it'll work?'

'It's an active organism that adapts to the host, human or Isharkute. It matches any blood type and accelerates dermal repair.'

Arturo kept a firm grip, looking nervous and uncertain, more afraid of the unknown than if the salve really worked.

'It's okay,' Sean said. 'I pretty much used it every night after my arena training.'

Arturo sighed and released Nocao's hand.

Nocao forced the tips of his fingers inside Bella's abdomen, making sure the salve penetrated deep enough. He shoved several more wads into the wound and wiped the remainder over the outside. His actions looked brutal, almost careless, but Sean knew this was standard Isharkute medicine. No antiseptic. No stitches or instruments. Everything was tactile and hands-on.

'That's it?' Arturo asked.

Nocao nodded.

Everyone waited in silence. Sean watched her intently, waiting for an eyelid to flicker or a finger to twitch – any sign she was okay. Even the battle-hardened soldiers stood over them, waiting with bated breath.

Then, like magic, Bella's wound pulled together, as if invisible hands were operating on her. The severed skin gelled and healed, leaving only a faint scar. Her cheeks flushed with colour and her chest started moving up and down.

Sean felt her squeeze his hand. Bella's eyes fluttered open. Arturo and Carla helped her up and showered her with hugs and kisses, but she didn't let go of his hand the entire time.

'How do you feel?' Nocao asked.

Bella glanced at the crimson salve on Nocao's hands and turned to Sean with a smile. 'Better.'

Sean wanted to sweep her into his arms and kiss her. He'd never experienced such intense emotion for anyone other than his family, not even Yeesha. He cared for her...a lot! *Is this love? Whoa! Did I just think that?* The thought resounded so loudly, he was convinced Bella heard it. Heat rose in his face, embarrassed to no-one but himself.

Bella pulled him close, put her lips to his ear, and whispered, 'Thank you!'

Sean's chest flooded with warmth, positivity, and emotion. Now he felt like the one who'd been healed. 'You're welcome.'

'You had us worried there for a minute. Glad to see you're all right,' Powell said, joining them. 'I hate to ruin this moment, but what's next, Sean? Senetep still has the Ark and we can't activate the beacon without it.'

'That's what he thinks.'

'What do you mean?'

'I haven't told anyone, but when I touched the Ark, something weird happened. I had a vision of Yonaguni, about how to get inside and activate the beacon. I'm not sure how, but the Ark's power changed me. It sounds weird, but... I think I'm the Ark now – the covenant between humanity and the Isharkute. The key to turning on the beacon.'

Everyone stared at him like he was crazy. Now he'd said it aloud, the truth sounded even more far-fetched.

'I hope I'm right. Otherwise, I'm going nuts!'

'You're not turning into a nut,' Nocao said dryly, scanning his body with a handheld scanner. Sean chuckled. 'But your cells have been charged at the molecular level, similar to the way the pharaoh's crown shared its energy upon the wearer. In this case, the effect appears to be permanent.'

'That's it! I can activate the beacon without the Ark. I just need to get to Yonaguni.'

'Then we'll get you there ASAP!' Powell said.

'Wait! Senetep still doesn't know where the beacon's hidden. If we go to Yonaguni now, we might just lead him straight to it. He can destroy it from the other side of the planet with a single missile. We need a diversion – something big enough get him off our tail.'

'You're right,' Powell said. 'What do you suggest?'

Sean paused, realising this was the moment his dad had been preparing him for. Every hurdle, every painful sacrifice all led to this. His destiny no longer felt like a burden. He was ready. 'We unite the world and face off against Senetep in one final battle. If we take all the Isharkute vessels and weapons from El Mirador and combine that with every military force we can gather, we can keep Senetep busy while we activate Yonaguni.'

'Sounds like you want to start a war!' Hazim said, squeezing through the group.

'Hazim!' Sean said, shaking his hand, realising they hadn't seen each other since escaping the first Isharkute attack at Giza.

'Good to see you alive and well, Sean,' Hazim said warmly. 'It's an ambitious plan, considering most governments are fractured or collapsed completely.'

'The world's a mess, Sean. We're literally hanging on by a thread,' Powell added.

'Isn't there a United Nations or something?'

'Not anymore.'

'That's not entirely true,' Hazim cut in. 'A small contingent of the UN was moved to a secret location in the northern hemisphere.'

'Really?' Powell said. 'That's news to me. Must've been above my rank and pay grade.'

'I won't reveal the location until we're there, but I can tell you it's cold...very cold,' Hazim said. 'Only a handful of leaders and military personnel were invited. When my uncle, General Mohammed Nejem, was killed on his return to Egypt, I was offered the invitation in his place, but I chose to stay behind. Those who accepted are humanity's designated survivors – our last line of defence in case the world falls apart. They're the closest thing we have to a UN, and hopefully they will have the resources to pull this plan together.'

'That's where we need to go,' Sean said.

'Agreed, but this vessel's not suitable for the journey. I'll reroute the pilots to the nearest base where we can swap vehicles.'

Sean nodded eagerly, feeling a burst of optimism.

'Okay, listen up!' Hazim called, rising to address the soldiers. 'This mission is now the most important thing happening on the planet, crucial to humanity's very survival. Everyone onboard will continue to the next destination after we change vessels. You're to protect Sean Livingstone and his friends with your lives. Nobody – I repeat *nobody*, except us – is to know about our passengers or final destination. Understood?'

A resounding 'Yes' echoed from every soldier, officer, and technician.

Hazim turned to Sean. 'You'd better get started on your speech to the UN.'

Sean felt a sudden burst of nervous butterflies. As the architect of the plan, it was falling upon him to convince the UN. The unanimous support from everyone onboard had given him a much-needed confidence boost. Hazim, Powell, Bella, and Arturo all believed in him...now he just needed to believe in himself.

After a quick changeover at a hidden military base in the Sahara, they were on their way. Their sleek new vessel was an Isharkute transport salvaged from El Mirador, capable of travelling the 5,000-kilometre journey to the northern hemisphere in less than an hour. Hazim kept the exact location a secret between himself and the pilots. Nocao spent the trip instructing the pilots and soldiers on Isharkute technology and weaponry.

Sean sat by himself, pen and notepad in hand, ready to start his speech. Nothing was coming to him. This was tougher than he thought it would be.

Bella sat next to him, looking ready for business. She'd changed out of her blood-drenched t-shirt and jeans and now wore camouflage army pants and a black t-shirt. 'Need some help?'

'Sure,' Sean said, noticing how full-of-life Bella seemed now. She was positively glowing. This wasn't the time to get distracted – he needed to focus. But all he could muster was a big blank. There was too much pressure, too much to explain. He had no idea where to start. 'I've never written a speech like this before.'

'You never did persuasive writing at school?'

'Yeah, but English wasn't really my thing. I was more into maths, science, history...'

'Don't worry, it's not that important. I suppose nobody's written a speech like this before.'

'What do you mean?'

'You're about to try and convince the governments of the world to put aside their differences, come together, and fight as one. In the history of the world, that's never happened.'

'Great! Knowing that just makes it so much easier,' Sean said with a sarcastic tone.

After a considered pause, Bella continued. 'Look, it doesn't need to be a long political speech or anything like that. Keep it simple. Say what you need to say to convince them.'

'Yeah, but where do I begin?'

'What about all that stuff you were talking about before? You know, how you're the covenant between humanity and the Isharkute. That sounded pretty good.'

'You believe it because you know everything we've been through. How do I prove it to them?'

'Start at the start.'

'That feels like ages ago.'

'I know, but you don't have to explain everything word-for-word. A list of bullet points will do.'

Sean sighed. 'It still doesn't make it easier. I was never good at last-minute homework, and this is like the hardest assignment ever. Geez, even the president of the United States has someone to write speeches for him. How are we supposed to compete with –'

'You don't. Don't overthink it. You convinced me, Arturo, Colonel Powell, Commander El-Amin... In fact, you've persuaded everyone you've met so far to believe in you – even General Maddock!'

Sean chuckled. 'I suppose when you put it like that...'

'Maybe think of it this way: What would your dad say if he was in your position?'

Sean thought about it for a moment. 'He'd state the facts to back up his argument without getting bogged down in details. He'd speak the truth...and he'd speak from his heart.'

Bella smiled. '*Bellisimo*. There you have it!'

Sean could finally see a connection between his chaotic thoughts. His story was filled with world-changing revelations, intense emotion, and visceral imagery that played in his mind like a crazy science fiction film. The foundations of his speech fell together faster than he could articulate. He had more than enough to say. 'I'm glad you're alive,' he blurted out.

Bella gave him a friendly punch on the arm. 'Duh, *stupido!* I'm glad I'm alive too.'

'That's not... Well, that's not what I meant to say,' Sean said, realising he was just blabbering. He knew what he wanted to say, but he was just unsure how to phrase it without sounding mushy or corny. His pulse quickened at the thought of opening his mouth again. His feelings weren't about to come out easily. 'I'm mean... I'm glad I met you, and...'

Bella stared deep into his eyes. The next couple of seconds seemed like an eternity.

'...I'd do anything to protect you.'

Her lips curled into a gentle smile and she leant forward, eyes closed. Sean did the same, heart pounding, their lips on the verge of touching...

'Here, put these on,' Hazim said, shoving a puffy cold-weather jacket between them, oblivious to their intimate moment.

'Thanks,' Bella said, winking at Sean as she pulled it on.

Sean snatched his jacket with a more exasperated 'Thanks.' This was the second time he'd almost kissed Bella, something he'd been waiting for since the last time they were interrupted. He put on the jacket with a sigh, feeling like their kiss was never meant to happen.

By the time he put some of his speech to paper, the outside landscape had changed dramatically. Sweeping African deserts and aqua-blue waters were far behind them. Stratospheric snow-capped peaks dropped into the deepest of fjords – giant grooves cut into the land by melting ice at the end of the last ice age. Brilliant white glaciers draped across the landscape, immense rivers of ice looked like they'd been frozen in place at a snap. They zoomed over a grey rocky coastline and headed out to sea.

Sean shivered.

'The jacket's meant to keep you warm,' Bella said, bumping his shoulder.

Sean chuckled, but it wasn't the sudden drop in temperature making him tremble – it was nerves of anticipation. It was ironic that everyone was now wearing a cold-weather jacket except for the one who needed it most, Nocao.

Sean collected a spare jacket and waited for Nocao to finish up an explanation about Isharkute shield systems to a group of enthralled soldiers and technicians.

'Here – the last time we went somewhere this cold, you wore a full protective suit,' Sean said, handing him the jacket.

'Yes, but Ramin's cryogenic chambers were at least ten degrees cooler than the current outside temperature.'

'It's gonna get a lot colder than this.'

'Then I'll wear two jackets,' Nocao said, pulling the jacket over his Isharkute bodysuit. He slipped his arms through the sleeves and stretched them out, assessing the result.

Sean smiled with mild amusement.

Nocao frowned. 'Something wrong?'

'No... Well, it's weird seeing you in human clothes.'

'Bulky,' Nocao said, squeezing the padding. He tried pulling the jacket together. 'Mine doesn't seem to close.'

'You need to do the zip up,' Sean said, starting it for him. 'Seals the jacket and keeps out the cold.'

Nocao pulled the zipper up and down. 'Effective device. I like the sound.'

'It's obviously not something we inherited from the Isharkute.'

'No. Humanity's devised many interesting solutions to problems without Isharkute help.'

'Yeah, we invented the zipper all on our own!'

Nocao laughed. 'Indeed! Humans grasp new ideas and technology with surprising ease. I've explained how Isharkute shield systems operate and they're already assessing the algorithms to disable Senetep's shields. Senetep's made a grave mistake underestimating humanity's potential – hopefully, Emperor Neberun won't make the same misjudgement.'

'If we get him here.'

'Once the beacon's activated, Neberun's arrival should be instantaneous.'

'I hope so, because once we start this war, there's no turning back.'

'Regardless, it's already started. You were lucky to escape Senetep's labyrinth in one piece.'

Sean twinged. A sharp pain shot down his back, reminding him of his horrible experience. 'I don't think your scan picked it up, but I didn't escape from Senetep in one piece.'

Nocao eyed him. 'Your wings?'

Sean nodded solemnly. 'He cut them off. I thought I'd be in more pain, but it's not too bad. I'm all right...except I can't fly.'

'Show me. Take off your jacket,' Nocao said, spinning him around.

'What? Right now?' Sean said, reluctantly removing his jacket. 'Can't you just see down my collar?'

Without warning, Nocao pulled up his shirt and examined his back. Embarrassed, Sean covered his pale skinny stomach and peeped around to see who was watching. Bella was talking to Arturo and hadn't noticed. *Thank God!*

Nocao prodded his back. 'Good.'

'Good!?' Sean replied. 'How's it good?'

'Senetep's incisions were clean. Your stumps have started healing and the buds of your new wings are forcing their way through the skin.'

'What?' Sean said, feeling the bumps over his shoulder. They tingled when he pressed them.

'Your implants were encoded with a specific genetic code, one that allows you to regrow severed limbs. The code was alien in origin but acts like the salamander and zebrafish species found on this planet. From the moment your wings were severed, stem cells formed within the wound. Within a few days, they'll be completely regenerated.'

'That's unbelievable! I thought I was just getting phantom pains.'

'Ramin was convinced you'd lose your wings in the first arena training, so he made sure they could regenerate on their own. I'm glad you proved him wrong.'

'Me too,' Sean replied. 'I just realised...I never thanked you for saving us from Senetep's missile. It was my fault. I never should've gone into the caves.'

'You did what you thought was right.'

'I should've listened to you. What if I make a mistake like that again? We mightn't be so lucky.'

'We all make mistakes. Trust in your friends. I'm an enemy and outsider to most of your people, but even when I was sitting on the bottom of the ocean, oxygen reserves dwindling, I held onto the faith that Carla would find me. We're in this together now, not just the two of us. Every human. Every Isharkute. Our survival depends on each other.'

Sean stood a little straighter and smiled. 'You're right.'

'We're here!' Hazim announced.

Their vessel veered sharply over an archipelago of barren, snow-covered islands. There were no signs of civilisation as far as Sean could see – just freezing wastelands and dark icy water. The governments had been clever to escape to such a cold and isolated location. It was the last place Senetep would care to look. They landed at the base of a mountain.

'Where's here?' Colonel Powell asked. 'Looks like we're in the middle of the Arctic.'

Hazim spoke loud enough for everyone to hear. 'We're a little over twelve hundred kilometres from the North Pole on the island of Spitsbergen in Norway. The UN has been moved here, into the Svalbard Global Seed Vault. We've landed as close as we can, but it's still a short walk from here to the entrance and doesn't get any warmer even on the inside, so make sure you're all suited up.'

The vessel door slid open, inviting a blast of chilly air inside.

The soldiers filed outside, semi-automatics poised to fire. Hazim forged a path across the shin-deep snow. Sean followed in his footsteps, with everyone trailing single file behind them. A rectangular concrete structure protruded from the frosty white hillside ahead, fronted by a short gangway leading to a pair of metal doors. Sean was surprised how small the vault entrance was, considering the millions of boxes of seeds that must have passed through its doors.

Hazim ignored the keypad and fingerprint scanner and pummelled on the door.

Sean was surprised there were no guards, not even a special knock to announce their arrival. Up here in the middle of nowhere, the last vestiges of human survival were surprisingly basic.

The door clunked from the inside and swung open, revealing a woman dressed in a white hooded jacket. She eyed them. 'Commander Hazim El-Amin?'

'Yes, we're all here.'

'Please, come inside,' she said, stepping back from the entrance. The Svalbard Seed Vault logo was embroidered on her jacket alongside her name: ASTRID NAEVERDAL. Sean guessed she was in her mid-forties, but it was hard to tell. The dark shadows under her eyes and beleaguered expression made her look older than she probably was.

Beyond the door, a platoon of heavily armed soldiers lined the concrete passage. Small badges on their jackets displayed their country's flag, indicating a diverse mix of nationalities: China, Japan, Korea, Russia, America, and Iraq were just a few of the ones Sean recognised.

There was a sudden commotion. Nocao entered the passage to a wall of guns pointed in his face.

'It's okay, he's on our side,' Hazim assured them.

'Please, put your weapons away,' Astrid said in a calming voice. She spoke fluent English with a thick Norwegian accent. 'Our visitors were expected, regardless of their race...or species.'

The soldiers lowered their weapons, but the tension hung heavy in the air.

'Welcome to Svalbard Global Seed Vault,' Astrid announced. 'I'm Astrid Naeverdal, former manager and newly appointed administrator to the Emergency United Nations. We've just been alerted to a new wave of Isharkute strikes happening across the world as I speak – and more powerful than anything we've seen so far. Understandably, everyone here's on edge.'

*It's our fault!* Sean thought. The timing wasn't coincidence. Senetep's attacks were a retribution for their escape from the labyrinth.

'Follow me, please,' Astrid said, striding down the passage to the next steel door. She keyed in a six-digit code and the door unlocked with a heavy *clunk*. One of the soldiers swung it open for everyone to pass.

The next concrete passage was longer and wider, boring deeper into the heart of the mountain.

'There's a bit of a walk and several doors before we reach the vaults,' Astrid said, keeping a brisk pace.

The temperature seemed to drop a degree with every step. The passage was lined with military officers, scientific personnel, leaders, and people from all over the world. Even though Sean understood every language being spoken, he didn't need his hybrid implant to translate the desperation and panic dominating their hushed conversations:

*There's no leadership...*

*Nobody knows what to do...*

*...no chance...we've already lost...*

*It's too late to fight back!*

Sean did his best to ignore their negativity. He needed to keep a positive focus.

'The three vaults were originally built to store seeds from all over the world, sort of like a global backup of our crops and agriculture,' Astrid said. 'Up until the Isharkute invasion, we'd only been using one of the vaults to store seeds.'

'Why'd you build the vaults inside this mountain?' Sean asked.

'We picked this location because of its unique ability to survive a global catastrophe. Even if every piece of ice on Earth melted, these vaults would remain above sea level. It's earthquake-proof, bomb-proof, and as many people have dubbed it...doomsday-proof.'

'That's about to be put to the test,' Bella whispered in Sean's ear.

'As we walk deeper into the mountain, you'll notice it's getting colder. That's because we're moving into the permafrost zone, where the surrounding ground stays naturally frozen all year round. So even if the power runs out and our coolant fails, the permafrost will protect the seeds at a constant minus five degrees.'

They approached the next pair of steel doors. A thin glistening layer of ice had crept over the handles and door frame, extending across the walls and overhead pipes like icing on a cake. Astrid keyed a code into the door lock and they proceeded into a T-shaped passage. Heavily armed soldiers were positioned every few paces, hands on weapons, alert and ready for action.

'These are the entrances to the three vaults,' Astrid said. 'Straight ahead is Vault No. 2: that's where we store the seeds at an additional minus eighteen degrees. Down the passage to the left, we've set up Vault No. 3 as a temporary command and communications centre to the outside world. The UN council is down at the opposite end of the passage, in Vault No. 1.'

'I hope you keep those vaults a little warmer than the seed vault,' Hazim said with an icy breath.

Astrid chuckled, stopping at the intersection of passages. 'Commander El-Amin, the UN council's asked for a single spokesperson to present your information. Everyone else will need to wait here with me.'

'Well, I'm afraid you're looking at the wrong person,' Hazim said.

'Who, then?' Astrid asked, looking straight past Sean to the rest of their group.

'Sean Livingstone is our spokesperson,' Hazim said, directing her attention to him.

Astrid gave Sean an incredulous look.

Sean couldn't help shivering. His stomach felt like it had just hit the ice-cold concrete floor.

'Okay...' Astrid said in an uncertain tone. 'They're waiting for you, Sean. Follow me.'

Sean couldn't move. His feet were frozen to the floor with a glacier-sized wave of doubt and apprehension. He never imagined he'd have to convince a room full of strangers without the support of his friends.

'You got us this far,' Powell said. 'Compared to what we've already been through, this should be a breeze.'

'Colonel Powell's right,' Bella added. 'You'll be fine.'

Sean nodded confidently and hurried after Astrid. As they neared the entrance to Vault No. 1, a cacophony of frustrated voices echoed through the semi-frozen doors.

Astrid gave him a sympathetic look. 'It's sounded like that since they went in there forty-eight hours ago. This is as far as I can go. I wish you the best of luck, Sean.'

'Thanks,' Sean said.

The soldiers yanked on the doors, cracking the layer of built-up ice off the hinges. Both men put their hips into the effort and the doors opened with a metallic creak.

Vault No. 1 was a vast rectangular cavity hollowed into the mountain. Stark LED lighting strips hung from the permafrost ceiling, creating pools of light over the gathering of diplomats. They stood huddled in groups, deep in conversation. There was no furniture or modern luxuries, just a long fold-out table for tea, coffee, and water. The basic amenities stood in contrast to the grandeur Sean associated with the United Nations building in New York. It was concerning that in just a matter of days, the most influential people on Earth were either dead or reduced to hiding in caves like this.

Sean slipped in unnoticed until the doors clanged shut behind him. The noise reverberated through the vault, immediately silencing the conversations. All heads turned his way.

'How'd you get in here?' asked someone with a British accent.

Sean couldn't tell who spoke. The sparse lighting turned the crowd into a foreboding wall of silhouettes, their shadowy faces obscured by high-collared jackets and hoods. Everyone seemed overly tall and imposing. 'My name's Sean Livingstone. I'm here to help.'

'You're just a child!' said a female voice.

'We were expecting Commander Hazim El-Amin,' shouted a man with a Middle Eastern accent. 'Where is he?'

'The commander's waiting outside,' Sean replied. 'I'm the designated spokesperson.'

'Is this a joke?' hollered another voice. 'Why would Hazim send you?'

'Because I have a plan to defeat Senetep.'

There was a predictable response of disgruntled mutterings and sniggers before another voice spoke up. 'Why should we believe you, Sean Livingstone?'

Sean wanted to take a nervous step back. His chest felt constricted, making it hard to breathe. The oppressive crowd were closing in around him and seemed to be sucking the oxygen out of the vault. He stood his ground, took a deep breath, and spoke up.

'I'm standing in the most secret, most heavily guarded place on Earth. How could I have made it this far, past all your armed soldiers, if I didn't have something important to say?'

A long silence followed.

Sean took their pause as a cue to continue. 'I was standing next to my dad when he discovered the first evidence of an Isharkute civilisation – an ancient door with strange symbols hidden beneath the Sphinx. At the time, we had no idea what opening it meant. We weren't just opening a door to our past, but also one to our future.'

'The Giza Plateau was ground zero for the first wave of explosions,' said another faceless voice. 'So it's true – we have Henry Livingstone to blame for all of this!'

'A lot of people want to blame my dad. I understand that. But the return of the Isharkute was inevitable. If we hadn't discovered the Hall of Records, then I wouldn't be standing here and humanity might not have had a chance at all.'

'What's the Hall of Records?' someone asked.

Sean sighed, suddenly realising the politics he was up against. 'I was hoping every country would've known about it by now. The hall contained an encyclopaedia of the universe – everything the Isharkute had learnt about, from other planets and alien species to their technology and hybrid programs. It was stored in an effort to assist all of humanity. I won't say who, but several governments were already salvaging that information... I guess they don't like to share.'

A chorus of raised voices erupted around him. Insults and accusations were punctuated with pointed fingers and raised fists. Any chance of a rational conversation had dissolved into chaos.

'S–H–U–T U–P!' Sean screamed.

The arguments died down enough for Sean to speak over the top.

'I can't believe it. Even in our darkest hour, you're still keeping secrets from each other. I don't have time to explain everything that's happened to me, but I can tell you what I've learnt: Our future is bigger than just this one planet. If humanity survives this step forward, we have a chance to explore the universe and expand our knowledge beyond our wildest dreams. But if we can't even talk to each other, how will we ever advance? We need to stop keeping secrets and put aside our differences. Eliminate our borders and prejudices. Humanity needs to speak as one.'

There was a prolonged silence, then someone cheered, 'Here, here!'

More conversations followed, some more heated than others. Sean allowed then to play out. After much back-and-forth, one voice spoke aloud. 'All right, Sean. Tell us what we should be doing.'

'There's only one way to stop Senetep, and that's by joining forces with those Isharkute who're likeminded about our survival.'

A few grumbles were quickly silenced by others in the group. 'Stop! Let him talk.'

'Senetep only represents a small portion of their race. I believe the greater majority would prefer to live alongside us, not destroy us. After all, the cure for their affliction's encoded in our DNA. They need us to survive... And right now, we need them to survive.'

'If this is true, why are they attacking us?' someone asked.

'Because the Isharkute who can help us aren't here yet. Thousands of years ago, they abandoned this planet to avoid an ice age. Senetep sabotaged their cryogenic chambers after they left, reprogramming their hibernation cycles so they'd never wake up. This allowed him to return with his own forces, assuming he'd eradicate us and keep the planet for himself.'

After more hushed conversations, one of the voices spoke up. 'How do we get the others here?'

Sean buzzed with excitement. He couldn't believe he'd almost convinced them. 'There's an ancient Isharkute beacon hidden under the ocean. It's designed to wake the fleet and bring them back to Earth. Senetep's been looking for it since he invaded because he knows once the fleet arrives, his reign of terror's over.'

'Tell us where to find it. We'll turn it on,' said someone.

'I'm the only one who can activate the beacon. It's encoded to respond to my DNA and nobody else's. But with Senetep looking for me, it's too risky – I could lead him straight to it. That's why I'm here... I need your help to bring the war to Senetep. If we coordinate a global attack, hit him all at once with everything we have, that should be a big enough diversion for me to turn it on.'

Further conversations followed with a noticeable shift in tone. The hostility and panic was gone. They weren't yelling at each other; instead, there was a general feeling of positivity and organisation. Their growing enthusiasm was infectious. Sean had given them a goal – something to bring them together despite their differences.

'Tell us what you need, Sean,' one voice said aloud. 'We're ready when you are!'

Sean bristled with pride. He'd never been more ready.

# CHAPTER 29

# Battle For The Ages

Senetep pulled his aching body into the command chair. Although safe inside his pyramid's private chamber, he'd paid a heavy toll for Azar's betrayal. Nefaro had been killed in the blast, along with most of his elite warriors. He would never have found his way out of the base's tunnels if not for Azar's surviving scientists, both of whom were now in pieces in his hybrid labs.

A collage of holograms materialised before him, each displaying a human city somewhere in the world. Half were under attack from his forces, the other half were the next targets. Senetep stared blankly at the images, trying to comprehend how he'd been beaten by the human meat he was meant to dominate.

The loss of Azar Hawati was of inconsequence. There were an abundance of humans to replace him, but it was Sean Livingstone for whom there was no substitute. The aggravatingly persistent child was his last link to the beacon and the only thing keeping him on this backwater planet. He couldn't risk Neberun's fleet being awakened, regardless of where he was in the galaxy. Sean had now escaped him three times: from their first meeting in his pyramid millennia before, then the Great Arena, and now the labyrinth. It was an unconscionable and embarrassing reality.

The entire world would pay for the child's insubordination.

One of the command crew sounded over the communications console. 'Overseer Senetep, what cities should we target next?'

'Destroy them all!' Senetep screamed.

He was in no mood to procrastinate. Time was running out on

every front. His ears were still ringing from the explosion in Azar's lab and his limbs seized with any strenuous exertion. The affliction was advancing quicker than before and the cold therapies he'd been using to slow the cellular degradation were less effective.

Senetep watched the cities crumble in a maelstrom of fire, laughing at the irony.

Earth was overflowing with a human cure, yet he couldn't bring himself to drink from that tainted cup. Humans were a slave race, a scrambled and dirty concoction of primate DNA mixed with his ancestors. His true cure lay in the *Spearhead of Creation*, the mythical vessel waiting for him at the edge of the universe.

An alert sounded. First Commander Vogran was returning empty-handed to the main docking bay. Now that Nefaro – the brains of his two commanders – was dead, it was time to tackle the Sean Livingstone problem head-on.

Senetep launched himself out of the chair with a groan. His body felt a thousand years old. Moving each leg was like dragging a heavy anchor. He hobbled over to the cold chamber, slumped inside, and adjusted the temperature controls to maximum coldness.

He gritted his teeth, stifling any chance of a scream.

The frigid air blasted him from all sides, locking every single muscle in a rock-hard spasm. The extreme cold was like being dipped in a bath of acid. Every single cell in his body felt like it was on fire – the most excruciating pain he'd ever experienced.

He was on the point of passing out when the cold air cut off and the door slid open.

Senetep staggered from the cold chamber and crashed to his hands and knees. He forced his eyelids open, breaking the seal of frozen tears. His chilled hands created frosty halos on the steel floor. The stabbing pains subsided and a soothing elasticity returned to his muscles. He stood up, wiping the icy condensation from his skin.

His mind was clear and focused, as if sharpened by a brisk arctic wind. He knew exactly what to do – it was time to wreak untold havoc.

Senetep stormed back into the main control room. His officers and technicians averted their eyes, knowing the wrong glance would incur his wrath.

'Prepare my annihilator!' he ordered. 'I'll coordinate the attacks from there. Inform Commander Vogran to meet me on the bridge.'

His ranking officers nodded and set straight to work.

Three annihilators were parked in the pyramid docking bay, the largest being his personal command vessel. It was the equivalent of a flying city, capable of transporting thousands of warriors and dozens of smaller vessels, and was armed with a powerful array of guns and canons. Most importantly, it was equipped with six tectonic missiles, enough to recreate the face of the Earth.

Vogran was already waiting on the bridge when he arrived. The burly commander stood tall and proud, but it was a thin veneer. Beads of sweat glistened across his forehead and his hands fidgeted anxiously behind his back. He paled in comparison to Ranatar, the best commander he'd ever had.

'With your other half gone, you're now twice as useless,' Senetep said.

Vogran nodded.

Senetep grunted. At least the commander was wise enough to keep his mouth shut. He strode past him and surveyed the expansive bridge. It was split across three tiered levels, stepping down to a massive floor-to-ceiling viewscreen. The assigned crew equalled half the normal numbers, with just enough pilots and officers to fly the vessel. It was a sober reminder of how stretched his resources were.

He stood in front of the viewscreen. Beyond the pyramid docking bay stood the smouldering remains of Cairo, glowing deep red against the smoke choking the night sky.

'Give me a list of ancient structures we haven't destroyed yet,' Senetep shouted to his crew.

Images appeared across the viewscreen. There were hundreds of potential locations, all of which shared similar characteristics: either not old enough, too dilapidated to be hiding anything, or clearly not

Isharkute in origin. 'Expand the scan to include subterranean and underwater structures.'

'That will take longer,' the crew member replied.

'I'm not going anywhere,' Senetep snapped.

'We've already destroyed most of their ancient sites,' Vogran said. 'I thought we were focusing on their cities and infrastructure.'

'And we'll continue to do so, but I want to find that beacon. It's hiding in something we overlooked. Our first wave of attacks only targeted the obvious land-based structures. We weren't diligent; we didn't dig deep enough.'

The results appeared onscreen. 'Compare our results with everything stored on the human internet. I want every location listed in front of me, no matter how small.'

Every archaeological site known to humanity was displayed with its given name. From the cloud-topping peaks of Machu Picchu in Peru to the sprawling subterranean city of Cappadocia in Turkey, anything that caught Senetep's eye was marked as a target. The scattered stone blocks of Puma Punku in Bolivia. The half-buried pillars of Göbekli Tepe in Turkey. The mysterious pyramid of Gunung Padang in the Philippines. One after another, Senetep added locations to the growing list.

'What kind of species is stupid enough to make their information so easily available?' Vogran asked.

'An ignorant one.'

Emergency sirens droned through the bridge.

'What now!?' Senetep growled.

'We're under attack!' cried one of the crew.

The list of ancient sites was replaced with a swarm of incoming vessels, human and Isharkute. Stingers and hunter-craft flew alongside F-15's, F-16's, F-22's, and heavily armed attack helicopters. Hundreds more hostiles emerged on the outskirts of Cairo, consisting of tanks, anti-aircraft guns, and rocket launchers.

'Shields are up! Pyramid guns locked and ready to fire,' yelled one of the crew.

'Finally, a proper fight,' Senetep seethed. 'Let's see how quickly we can squash this pathetic rebellion.'

'They're using our vessels against us,' Vogran said. 'Those stingers might be capable of penetrating our shields and taking out our pyramid guns.'

'You give this human scum too much credit. Piloting our vessels is one thing, but they don't have the intellect to decipher our shield technology.'

More hostiles emerged across the screen, illuminating the bridge in a blaze of red. Senetep twinged with apprehension. *What are these imbeciles up to?* The incoming hostiles all fired at once, engulfing his pyramid from every angle.

The pyramid guns fired back. Several targets disappeared, but it was a futile effort – there were too many. Senetep suddenly realised there was a grand, strategic plan behind this attack. Seventy-five per cent of the incoming barrage was going to hit at once. Fireballs erupted across the pyramid face, lighting up Cairo's cloud of smog. Violent shockwaves vibrated through the bridge and the crew glanced nervously at each other.

Walls of fire rolled over the docking bay entrance, held back for now by the pyramid's shields.

Senetep smirked at Vogran. 'See? I told you they'd never penetrate our shields.'

A succession of smaller explosions echoed through the pyramid, setting off a new whine of emergency sirens.

'Our shields are failing,' blurted one of the crew.

Vogran took a tentative step back.

'Onscreen!' Senetep barked. The pyramid defence systems filled the viewscreen. The glowing green shields flickered off one by one, exposing the outer walls and gun placements.

'How did they disable our shields?' Senetep screamed. 'Get them back up.'

The crew scrambled to rectify the situation, clamouring over each other, attempting to reinitialise the shield frequencies. The map lit up with a fresh wave of attacks.

Vogran stomped over to the crew. 'Get our shields up NOW!'

Military aircraft thundered past the docking bay and circled around to unleash a volley of rockets. Strafing fire spewed from the ground-based artillery like glowing embers caught in a gust of wind, all homing in on his pyramid. Seconds from impact.

Senetep braced himself.

The annihilator's shields activated just in time. Thunderous explosions tore through the pyramid, tearing off the outer walls and snapping the framework apart like twigs. Senetep stared in disbelief at the hologram showing a chain reaction of blasts cascading down through his pyramid, penetrating the core, snaking through the lower levels and incinerating every Isharkute not aboard the annihilators. His command centre, hybrid labs, and personal quarters with its life-giving cold chamber – all obliterated.

The fireballs burst into the docking bay, erupting from every vent and blasting panels off the walls. The shockwaves pushed the annihilators against each other with a scream of grinding hulls.

'Get us out of here!' Senetep cried.

Vogran pushed the pilot off his chair and took over. 'Give me full power!'

A wall of flames consumed the viewscreen. The hull creaked and popped with a sudden spike in temperature, turning the bridge into a giant oven. Their vessel lurched forward, dragging free of the other annihilators. They rammed through flaming debris as the docking bay collapsed around them. Bowed and melted beams smacked against the hull.

Senetep gritted his teeth so hard he heard one crack.

They shot from the conflagration and ascended high above Cairo. Vogran levelled their vessel and dragged the pilot back into his seat.

Senetep spat out the broken tooth and assessed the damage. The other two annihilators followed, their hulls glowing orange with heat. Behind them, his pyramid collapsed in a pyre of intense flames. He stared, numb with shock and disbelief. How had it come to this? How did the humans catch him off-guard?

Vogran approached. 'This isn't the only attack. They're happening all over the world.'

'Show me,' Senetep said in a dangerously low voice.

Images of more attacks appeared onscreen, the locations accompanied by their human-given names: London. Tokyo. New York. Paris. Sydney. Delhi. Mexico City. Berlin. On every continent there was a coordinated strike, the heaviest being in Cairo, against his capital. The humans were strategic and well-armed, their military vehicles supported by Isharkute vessels salvaged from the El Mirador pyramid.

There could only be one person behind such a daring and surprising plan – Sean Livingstone.

'Their attack seems ill-timed,' Vogran said. 'Their governments are scattered and their resources limited. Why would they attempt a pre-emptive strike when they know we can obliterate them? The timing makes no sense.'

Senetep faced him. 'You're wrong! It makes perfect sense.'

Vogran screwed up his face. 'How?'

'They're distracting us from their real intention.'

'Which is what?'

'Sean Livingstone's found a way to activate the beacon without the Ark.'

'Impossible!'

Senetep rounded on Vogran and clutched his muscular neck in a chokehold. 'Baboon-headed fool! This attack wouldn't be possible if you'd kept control of the El Mirador pyramid.'

Vogran's eyes bulged. His pale-blue complexion turned purple and he dropped to his knees, unable to breathe through his crushed windpipe.

'Fail me one more time and I won't let go,' Senetep said, releasing his grip.

Vogran sucked in a huge gulp of air.

'Give me a map of the Earth,' Senetep called to the crew.

Vogran staggered to his feet as a large hologram of the planet materialised between them.

'Now, show me an inventory of every global-range missile we have aboard our annihilators.'

A list of arsenal streamed alongside the globe. Senetep selected every tectonic missile, and then dragged them one by one onto Earth's major continents. 'Humans are like an annoying colony of fire ants, swarming and stinging us with their explosive venom. Inferior as they are, we don't have enough feet to stomp on them fast enough. There's only one effective method in dealing with this kind of pest.'

'What's that?' Vogran wheezed.

'Destroy the entire nest!'

'What about our warriors on the ground?' Vogran muttered. 'If we use every tectonic missile, there won't be a single rock left unturned.'

'Exactly! This way we don't need to find the beacon - it'll be destroyed automatically. Alert our forces to abandon ground positions and take to the air. I'm about to reshape the face of this planet.'

# — CHAPTER 30 —

# *Yonaguni*

Sean watched the events unfolding in Cairo with a feeling of incredulity. The strikes against the Isharkute were being streamed live from all over the world to the wall of flat screen monitors inside Vault 3's makeshift command centre. Senetep's pyramid collapsed in a tumultuous fireball that reached for the stars like a beacon of light and hope, a signal to the rest of the world to take up arms and fight as one. Sean was overcome with emotion. This was for his dad, and everyone who died and suffered at the hands of the Isharkute Overseer. Senetep's day of reckoning had come.

A cheer erupted from the packed crowd. Politicians, soldiers, scientists, and civilians stood together. Age, language, skin colour, and religious and political beliefs were forgotten barriers. Everyone was driven by a single goal: survival.

Sean enjoyed a few seconds of elation, ignoring the nagging fact that his mission was only half complete.

Bella and Arturo stood beside him, cheering at the images, caught up in the euphoria. Raucous applause thundered through the vault walls. Sean glanced up, half-expecting the permafrost ceiling to crack and cave in.

Nocao was the only quiet voice, busy watching the banks of computer screens at the back of the vault. Sean pushed through the crowd and joined him. 'What's wrong?'

'Senetep didn't just escape the pyramid with three intact annihilators,' Nocao said, pointing to the three large blips tracking across the screen. His finger traced ahead of the annihilators to another six blips speeding away in different directions.

'What are they?'

'Judging by their mass and trajectories, they could only be –'

'Tectonic missiles!' Sean said, his stomach going ice-cold.

Just one missile carried enough destructive force to send the Earth into an early ice age. Six missiles could reshape the world as they knew it. No continent would be left unscathed.

Sean turned to the unsuspecting crowd, their rapturous cheers now white noise to a hollow victory. 'What do we do?'

'Intercept and destroy the missiles in the air. They're ninety-five per cent less effective detonated in the atmosphere, but once they burrow into the ground –'

'Yeah, I get it – game over! How long have we got?'

'Since the missiles aren't travelling at full speed, I'd estimate two hours. Senetep still has forces on the ground. He's giving them time to evacuate.'

'What do we do?'

'I'll take the pilots I trained at El Mirador along with the stingers that escorted us here. They're the only vessels capable of catching them. Between the six of us, we should be able to bring down at least half of them.'

'Half of them!'

'Maybe more. It depends on your pilots.' Nocao said, pulling out a palm-sized crystal control tablet. 'I'll start plotting intercept courses for the stingers.'

Sean noticed the dark purple bruises colouring the top of Nocao's hand. He'd seen them before, littered across the pale bodies of the afflicted Isharkute deep in Ramin's cryogenic chambers. Bruising was a late-stage symptom, proceeded by loss of motor function and consciousness. 'How long have you had those bruises?'

Nocao glanced at his hand and continued keying in coordinates. 'Not long. It's nothing to worry about.'

'You're sick! Why didn't you tell me?'

'There's no time to worry about that now.'

'But you need treatment. There's enough human DNA in this room to make you a hundred cures.'

'Without proper labs and equipment, that's impossible.'

Sean couldn't believe his friend was shrugging off such a dangerous symptom. 'How long have you got, you know...until it gets worse?'

'Long enough. Now stop worrying and focus on your mission.'

Sean hated neglecting him in his time of need, but Nocao was right. They had less than two hours, after which they could focus on making him better. 'Okay. But as soon as this is over, you start on a cure.'

Nocao half-nodded, his concentration absorbed on the tablet.

'Promise?!' Sean said sternly.

Nocao looked up. 'I promise.'

Colonel Powell rushed into the vault and pushed through the crowd to join them. 'Sean, the Yonaguni team's assembled and ready to leave.'

'Great, but we've got a new problem,' Sean said.

'All right, but let's speak outside.'

Shortly after, they were assembled in the passage outside the vault. Sean, Nocao, and Powell were joined by Hazim, Bella, Arturo, and Carla, along with the five pilots for Nocao's stinger squadron. Comprising three men and two women, the youthful pilots were a mix of nationalities. Behind them stood a squad of ten soldiers, heavily laden with semi-automatic weapons and two hefty crates of scuba-diving gear – the same battle-hardened team that rescued them from Senetep's labyrinth and brought them to Svalbard's seed vault.

The door to Vault 3 was closed, so nobody could overhear their discussion. The muted cheers behind the vault door sounded more distant than ever. Between Sean, Nocao, and Powell, it took several minutes to explain everything, but it was simple: destroy Senetep's tectonic missiles and activate the beacon. Nocao would lead the squadron while Sean guided the soldiers into Yonaguni.

'Your human communications systems will struggle to keep

contact with our stingers from these vaults,' Nocao said. 'I'll set up a mobile command centre in the vessel heading to Yonaguni.'

'Okay!' Sean said, checking his watch. 'We've got less than two hours.'

'All right, let's go then!' Powell said.

Sean led everyone back to the surface. The soldiers guarding the main entrance pushed their shoulders against the doors, fighting back gale-force winds. The surrounding mountains and fjords had disappeared within a squall of ominous grey clouds. Their squad of Isharkute vessels was only a short walk away, but an incoming storm was about to beat them to the mark.

Sean tightened his collar and forged a path through the unspoiled snow. The wind howled across the tundra, whipping up sheets of loose snow that stung his face. His feet sank deeper with each step. There was no trail – their previous footsteps already lost beneath the featureless white landscape. It felt as if the entire world was pushing them back to the subterranean protection of the vaults, like a warning not to continue.

If Senetep's missiles did hit their marks, then Svalbard's seed vault was one of the few places on Earth that might survive the cataclysm.

By the time they reached the landing zone, a blizzard was upon them. Sean waved goodbye to the stinger pilots and they vanished into the whiteout. Visibility was down to a few paces. Shielding his eyes, Sean discovered his vessel's hull and the door opened automatically. He burst inside with a swirl of snow and helped the others find their way. The soldiers filed in and set down the crates. Hazim, Powell, and Arturo immediately began to sort out the scuba gear.

Nocao stumbled inside and sat in the pilot's seat. He opened a panel and swapped out a series of crystalline control shards. 'That should do it,' he said, closing the panel.

Six holographic screens materialised across the cabin's rear wall, live visual feeds from each stinger, just like a dashcam. For now, there wasn't much to see except sheets of snow. Each view was accompanied by long- and short-range scanners, vessel information, and biometric data for each pilot. Heart rates and other vital signs blipped across the screen.

'The pilots have nicknamed our squadron the Buzzbees,' Nocao said.

Bella laughed. '*Carino!*'

Sean smiled to himself. The name was surprisingly cute for such a critical mission.

'You can monitor our progress from these visual feeds,' Nocao said. 'I'll need someone to guide the Buzzbee pilots if something happens to me.'

'I can do that,' Carla said, holding up the Isharkute-to-English convertor crystal Henry left her. 'I have my magic wand.'

Nocao nodded. 'Of course.'

Sean noticed Nocao was holding his left hand close to his body, like he was protecting an injury. The bruising had extended over his wrist and his hand looked like it was trembling. He waited until Nocao finished explaining the controls to Carla before interrupting. 'I'm hoping it's just the cold weather making you shake.'

'Unfortunately not,' Nocao said.

'Can you fly with one hand?'

'It looks worse than it is. Once I'm holding on to a flight stick, I'll be fine.'

'Okay,' Sean said, not entirely convinced. 'Just shoot the missiles down, no crazy stuff. Be careful.'

'You too,' Nocao said, moving for the door.

'Hey!' Sean called after him. 'I almost forgot – turning on the beacon's only half our mission. What about sending the female DNA sample back in time to Nesuk? That was our original plan. Without it, he won't have the blueprint to manipulate our human DNA over the last ten thousand years.'

'I took a sample of Carla's DNA just after we awoke from our cryogenic sleep, remember. That information is still stored inside the main control panel in the Hall of Records, awaiting a power signal from the Ark. Once it's activated, the Ark will receive the data from the hall and automatically send the message.'

Sean nodded, then joined his hands in the Isharkute sign of the cosmos. Nocao returned the gesture with a steady left hand, giving Sean a modicum of confidence. If Nocao was even half the pilot he was before, he was more than capable. Nocao disappeared into the wall of snow and the vessel door closed behind him.

Seconds later they were ascending through gale-force winds, climbing to a safer altitude above the turbulent weather. Their vessel shook and shuddered in the violent gusts. Bella fell onto Sean and clung tightly. Arturo helped the soldiers stop the scuba gear from rolling all over the cabin.

They burst through the oppressive grey clouds into serene blue skies, the two extremes like heaven and hell.

Carla positioned herself in front of the displays and watched the Buzzbee squadron clear the storm. 'That's five Buzzbees, waiting on Nocao.'

Sean had a sudden sinking feeling. Nocao's video-feed showed him somewhere in the storm, his biometric data tipping into the red zone. 'Nocao, is everything all right?'

Nocao's stinger shot into the sky ahead and completed a flashy double loop before veering around to join them.

'Just making sure everything works okay,' Nocao said over the communicators. 'Adjusting your screens to monitor the tectonic missiles.'

Sean drew a sigh of relief.

A map of the Earth appeared between the Buzzbee screens. The six missiles were depicted by red flashing markers, creeping across the oceans and continents.

'Targeting now. Sending flight data to each Buzzbee,' Nocao said. 'Buzzbees, keep your stingers on autopilot until you're in range, then activate homing missiles. After that, it's up to you to fly yourselves to a safe distance before detonation.' Each pilot responded affirmatively. 'I'll take out the furthest missile first, then work my way back to help the nearest Buzzbee.'

'I'll keep you updated from here,' Carla finished.

All six stingers rocketed away in different directions, breaking the sound barrier with a thunderous clap and leaving vapour halos in their wake.

'All right, listen up!' Hazim said. 'We're flying to a higher altitude where we can travel at the equivalent of Mach twenty, around twenty-four thousand kilometres an hour. That should get us south of Japan and over the Ryukyu Islands region within the hour. Everyone diving at Yonaguni needs to be prepped and ready to drop.'

Sean sheepishly raised his hand. 'I've never scuba-dived before.'

'*Non c'e' problema*,' Arturo said. 'I can help you there.'

Colonel Powell emerged from the pilot's cabin. 'Good, because Sean's leading the dive team inside the structure. Aside from an unusually high number of sharks, our scans indicate the surrounding ocean's devoid of any Isharkute or human activity.'

'Sharks!' Sean blurted.

'Don't worry. They're mostly hammerheads.'

'Oh, great,' Sean sighed.

'*Non ti preoccupare!*' Arturo said, yanking a black wetsuit out of the crate. 'I've dived with them before. They're docile bottom feeders. They love eating stingrays, fish, octopus, crustaceans... We're too big and bony, *si?*' Arturo said, poking him in the ribs.

'I guess.' Sean laughed, taking the wetsuit.

He held it up, wondering how he was going to pull the tight-fitting wetsuit over his body. It looked about two sizes too small. He slipped off his shoes and copied Arturo and the soldiers, trying to give the impression he knew what he was doing. After an excessive amount of tugging and stretching, his legs squeezed through, then his torso, and finally his arms.

Arturo spent the rest of the trip explaining how to use the oxygen tank, mask, and every other detail he could cover in the short time. He spoke quickly, sliding back into Italian when his English wasn't fast enough. Sean struggled to keep up with the information. He got the main points, but couldn't stop thinking about how he was going to swim through the underwater structure. What if he got lost? Would he run out of air? He was beginning to wish Ramin had given him a pair of hybrid gills to go with his wings.

'Buzzbee 2's reached the first missile,' Carla called.

Sean joined the huddle around the screens. Nocao's voice sounded over the communications. 'Activate your heads-up targeting display, Buzzbee 2.'

'Activated!' the pilot confirmed.

'Once you have a target lock, fire, and then retreat to a safe distance.'

Everyone watched in silence as Buzzbee 2 closed in on the tectonic missile. The missile darted around the rocky mountain peaks, dipping lower each time, descending to a point where it could burrow into the Earth.

Sean held himself back from screaming 'Fire!'

Buzzbee 2's targeting scanner beeped erratically as the missile dipped in and out of lock. It finally hit the sweet spot and the pilot fired. The intercepting missile zoomed ahead and the pilot completed a sharp turn in the opposite direction.

*BOOM!*

The first missile disappeared off the map, leaving five to destroy. Everyone cheered. The shockwaves passed and Buzzbee 2's pilot righted her vessel, adjusting coordinates to assist the closest member of the squadron.

'Divers ready. We're coming up on Yonaguni Island now,' Powell shouted. 'Carla, activate the clear-hull tech so we can get a bird's-eye view.'

The floor rippled away beneath their feet. They were approaching Yonaguni's coastline on the westernmost tip of Japan. The island's rolling green hills met the ocean with an impressive shoreline of jagged cliffs and bright sandy beaches. From their altitude, they could see from one side of the island to the other. The picturesque landscape reminded Sean of Easter Island. They flew over the local airport, which stretched across a third of the island, then higher over the fields and mountains dominating the island's core, finally passing over the southern coastline to descend towards the ocean.

'Okay, this is it!' Hazim cried.

Sean felt an unnerving rush of butterflies. The soldiers pulled on their flippers and adjusted their masks. Arturo helped Sean fit his oxygen tank and breathing regulator. 'You're ready to dive.'

Their vessel stopped and hovered over the water. The side door slid open and cool sea air filled the cabin. Arturo handed Sean his flippers. He took them without looking, eyes transfixed on the ocean below, his mind racing.

'You think you can leave without saying goodbye?'

Sean was drawn from his thoughts to find Bella standing in front of him. 'I'm sorry...I –'

Bella grabbed his wetsuit collar and pulled him close. She kissed his lips before he could utter another word. The soldiers whistled and cheered. Bella pulled back, her eyes staring deep into his. 'Come back, no matter what.'

'No matter what,' Sean repeated confidently.

Arturo stepped between them. 'All right, all right. *Basta*, you two lovebirds.'

Sean stood at the edge of the open door with his back to the ocean. Arturo helped him fit his mask and regulator. Bella's kiss had cleared his mind and eased his doubts – he was ready to finish the mission. With a final wave, he dropped backwards into the water.

*       *       *

Senetep watched the tectonic missile vanish from the holographic map. It seemed too early for an impact – the missiles were meant to detonate after his forces had evacuated. He stared at the map, waiting for the shockwaves to ripple across the continent.

'Where's the explosion?'

He spun around, expecting a reply. None of the annihilator's bridge crew were brave enough to answer. Vogran took over one of the control consoles and assessed the data. 'The missile detonated five hundred kilometres before impact.'

'Why?'

'It was intercepted by a stinger... I'm tracking it now.'

'They're going after our missiles!' Senetep roared. 'Reprogram the missiles to detonate at their current position for maximum impact.'

He watched the final five missiles, expecting them to disappear at any moment. The seconds ticked by, but each missile tracked steadily across the hologram. There were no explosions – just silence from Vogran and the crew. 'Well?'

Vogran straightened up from the console, his face drawn with guilt. 'We can't override the missile coordinates. I encrypted their control shards before launch to prevent them from being altered by the enemy.'

'Send our nearest stinger squadrons to escort the missiles, then.'

'I can't,' Vogran replied in a nervous tone.

'Why not?!'

'The human offensive's taking up all our resources. Every country's attacking us at once. We don't have enough platoons or squadrons to spare.'

Images projected across the bridge viewscreen. Senetep's pyramid command centres were buckling under a relentless bombardment of human artillery. Some were caught in mid-flight, fending off fighter jets and missiles while attempting to redock with the orbiting motherships. The handful of Isharkute vessels being used against them were giving the humans an edge in what should have been a painless, one-sided war.

Senetep squirmed. His stranglehold on the puny world was loosening. Unbridled anger surged through his body, injecting his weakened muscles with a sudden burst of strength. He stormed across the bridge and backhanded Vogran with one almighty swipe.

The force cracked Vogran's cheekbone and sent him sprawling across the floor. Senetep leant over and grabbed him by his beard, forcing his heel upon Vogran's swollen cheek, ready to crush his face into pulp.

Several high-pitched alarms sounded.

Senetep glanced at the map in time to witness another four missiles vanish. One remained, ironically heading for his capital at Giza.

'Vogran!' Senetep groaned. 'Your failure is unconscionable.'

'I...can find...the beacon...' Vogran mumbled.

Senetep dropped him to the floor with disgust.

Vogran dragged himself back to the console. 'I can track the stingers backwards from their last position using their communications.' A series of yellow lines superimposed over the map, tracking back from the destroyed missiles to a location in the northern hemisphere. 'There were seven vessels to begin with, one for each six missiles, but the seventh vessel went in a completely different direction. It's stopped south of an island called Yonaguni.'

Senetep stared at the flashing yellow dot hovering over the ocean and the answer struck him like a blast of frigid air. That was the beacon!

'Set a course for Yonaguni. Send any platoons and squadrons we have in the area to that location. I don't care if they abandon their command vessels. Send them now!'

Vogran nodded. 'A squadron of hunter-craft and two hybrids transports are on their way. I've also sent every available vessel after the stinger intercepting our final missile.'

Senetep grunted. Vogran had saved himself for now, but was still a long way from proving why he should live beyond the day.

*    *    *

Boisterous cheers distorted through Sean's earpiece, hurting his ears. Their Buzzbee squadron had successfully destroyed five of the six tectonic missiles, with Nocao chasing the final one across the Sahara Desert. From the corner of his diving mask, he could see Arturo and the soldiers swimming alongside him. They all heard the news too. Arturo gave him a confident thumbs-up.

Sean returned the gesture.

So far, no sign of sharks. Sean kicked a little faster, worried their luck might run out. Indistinct, geometric shapes emerged from the depths below. The water visibility cleared, revealing a massive stone platform of flat terraces and different levels. The straight lines and right angles seemed too perfect to be a natural formation, looking more like the eroded foundations of an ancient city. Sean wondered how anyone could argue otherwise. Everything felt strangely familiar, but he wasn't sure where to find the entrance. There were no crevices or openings wide enough to offer a way inside the stone.

They swam over rectangular channels resembling paths and causeways, one of which ended in a conspicuous set of normal-sized stairs. There was a near-perfect triangular pool cut into the stone, and further along were a giant pair of star-shaped formations that previous divers had nicknamed the 'Turtles.'

The ocean suddenly became dark.

Sean caught sight of his shadow on the terrace below, merging with a large school of hammerhead sharks. His breath caught in his throat, his first instinct to dart back to the surface. The silent creatures descended around all them. Their distinctive hammer-shaped heads glided by, watching them with gentle and curious eyes, unperturbed by their human visitors.

Sean relaxed. The docile creatures weren't all that threatening and seemed more like a welcoming party, content to swim alongside them. He dove over the edge of a terrace and hovered in front of the giant moai-like face he'd seen in his vision.

Staring into the dark cavernous eyes, the path through Yonaguni flashed through his mind.

He needed to go deeper.

Sean spun around and kicked over a vertical drop-off. The sharks vanished into the ocean as he dove straight down, following the megalithic wall into the shadowy depths. At the very bottom was a small arch, just wide enough for one person. He swam between the rock walls, running his hand along the pitted stone, the space so tight his air cylinder scraped across the rock. He needed a clue. It was here somewhere. He closed his eyes and tried to visualise it, but the vision eluded him like a fading dream.

Arturo and the soldiers descended on either side of the arch.

Sean assessed every inch of the rock, forcing his fingers into the horizontal slits marking the walls. There had to be a mechanism or switch hiding somewhere. He dug into the sand and loose stones beneath him. Nothing. All he did was create a haze in the water, making it harder to see. He pushed off the bottom and struck his head on the arch.

'Mrgh!' he groaned, almost spitting out his regulator.

Sean rubbed his head and looked up. The stone lintel was covered in dark algae. He scratched some of it off and discovered something etched into the stone. He pulled a knife from his utility belt and scraped it clean. Chunks of algae and silt floated away, revealing an ancient handprint carved into the lintel. He placed his right hand upon the imprint. It was a perfect match. The outline came alive with a bright blue light and a loud *clunk* rumbled through the bedrock.

The soldiers yanked him clear of the arch and dragged him back. The vibrations reverberated across the seafloor like an earthquake.

Sean noticed movement to his left. Sandwiched between the natural bedrock and Yonaguni were two colossal stone slabs known as the 'Gateway Stones' and 'Twin Pillars.' A cloud of silt burst out from between them and the megaliths parted, revealing a circular black hole.

*That's it!* Sean screamed inside his head.

# CHAPTER 31

# The Beacon

Nocao disregarded his stinger's holographic map. It was easier to chase the tectonic missile by eye as it hugged the mountainous sand dunes of the Sahara Desert. The human pilots had done better than he'd expected, having eliminated five of the six missiles, and were now converging on his position to assist. Unfortunately, they'd never make it in time. He was alone with this missile. It was dropping in altitude and could dive into the ground at any second.

*BOOM!* The missile pounded through the tip of a dune and zipped around a rock ledge.

Nocao completed a sharp barrel roll to avoid the ledge, levelled out, and took one hand off the flight stick to activate his weapons targeting. He looked at his hand in shock. Without something firm to hold, his shakes were uncontrollable. He white-knuckled the flight stick with two hands and focused on the target, eyes flicking between the actual missile and the target lock.

He closed the gap, pushing his stinger to maximum speed.

Carla's voice sounded over the communicator. 'Nocao, I've picked up multiple enemies heading your way, matching speed and altitude. They keep disappearing off my maps – one second they're there, the next they're gone.'

Nocao eyed his scopes. The mysterious objects flashed up for a second, then vanished. 'I see them. They're stingers...scrambling their cloaking shields.'

'They're directly ahead of you.'

Nocao stared intensely at the missile, mimicking every deviation in its course. 'Can the other Buzzbees intercept them?'

'Not yet – they're a few minutes away. You should detour and catch up with the missile when you're safe. You're about to hit them dead on!'

'There's no time. I need to take this missile down now.'

'Nocao, you'll run out of time!' Bella interrupted. 'It's only one missile, let it go.'

'One missile that can destroy an entire continent... There's too many lives at stake.'

There was silence over the communicator.

Nocao replayed the comment in his head: *Too many lives at stake.* They weren't Isharkute lives he was talking about; they were human lives – people he'd never met. He was risking his life to save a species that he once looked upon as inferior and expendable.

'We won't distract you anymore,' Carla said. 'Good luck.'

The shadow of an approaching mountain loomed ahead. Several specks zipped over the summit and disappeared in the atmospheric haze.

The gap between his stinger and the missile had closed to a few metres.

Nocao teased his thumb over the trigger, waiting for the perfect lock.

The missile swerved left, right, and then settled in the middle of his windscreen.

This was it, time to fire...but something was wrong.

He glanced down at his thumb. It was seized over the trigger in a spasm, unable to press the button.

*        *        *

Sean led the way, kicking his flippers as hard as he could. Arturo and the soldiers were close behind, amphibious rifles in hand, mask-mounted LEDs gleaming through the depths. Sean peered up at the Yonaguni formation. They were about to swim inside its subterranean world – one that hadn't seen the light of day for over 10,000 years.

The entrance was a perfect circle, bored straight through the rock and wide enough for three people to swim side by side. The tunnel veered downwards on a steady 25-degree angle. Their LEDs bounced off the smooth walls, illuminating the darkness like car headlights.

Sean was breathing heavily into his regulator. Part nerves, part exhaustion, he was tiring faster than he expected. This was an intense workout. His arms and legs were burning, as though he'd been swimming for hours.

Fifty metres in, the tunnel abruptly ended.

Sean pushed against the stone. It wouldn't budge. There were no markings or handprints, nothing to indicate a way forward. It was a dead end. Arturo waved at Sean and pointed back up the tunnel. Their bubbles were bouncing along the ceiling and disappearing up a small square chute. The dark hole led straight up, barely wide enough for one person and impossible with the tanks on their backs.

Sean pointed up the chute with a flat hand indicating their new direction – one of the few diving signals Arturo had taught him.

Arturo returned the 'OK' signal, unclipped his oxygen tank, took a gulp of air from his regulator, and dropped his gear. He pointed to himself and held up three fingers, indicating the minutes he'd be gone. Swimming without a tank made Sean nervous, but it was the only option. Arturo disappeared up the claustrophobic chute with nothing but the final breath in his lungs.

Every passing second felt like an eternity. There was nothing they could do except wait and hope he made it back. Sean checked his dive watch. One minute gone. Free divers could hold their breath for up to five minutes or more, but the suspense was killing him.

A light emerged from the chute and Arturo swam out head first. He scooped up his regulator and took a breath of air, giving them the signal to swim up the chute.

Sean wanted to ask what was up there. How far did they need to swim? The limitations of communicating underwater were frustrating, but he trusted Arturo.

Sean unclipped his tank, took his last breath, and kicked his way inside the chute. His arms were outstretched ahead like he was diving, but it was too tight to complete a swimming stroke. He could only kick to propel himself. The tight, featureless chute continued straight up. It seemed never-ending. He kicked harder, suppressing the urge to take a breath, hoping the end was near.

The chute opened into a wide body of water illuminated by the yellow light of a glowstick left by Arturo. A couple more kicks brought him to the surface of a chamber. Sean gulped in the musty air and swam over to the only ledge. He dragged himself up, pulled off his flippers, and surveyed the square-shaped chamber. Ribbons of light from the pool rippled across the flat walls and ceiling. He cracked a new glowstick and threw it behind himself, revealing the outline of passage.

Arturo surfaced, then the soldiers one after another, until all twelve of them were assembled on the ledge. Sean fiddled with his earpiece, wondering why he was suddenly hearing crackling and popping instead of their vessel above. 'This isn't working properly.'

'The rock's causing interference,' the lead soldier said, tapping his earpiece.

Sean heard snippets of Carla's frantic voice. *Senetep's here... retreating... Look out...hybrids, warriors...in the water.* His heart skipped a beat. 'Did you guys hear that?'

Arturo and the soldiers returned grim-faced nods.

'Okay, we're setting up a defensive perimeter around this pool,' the lead soldier announced. 'I want two of you to go with Sean and Arturo.'

The glowstick in the pool suddenly vanished and the water went dark. Sean unclipped the LED torch from his dive belt and pointed the beam into the pool just in time to catch something slither out of the chute. 'Did anyone see that?'

The soldiers aimed their weapons at the pool.

Several tentacles shot out of the water and latched on to the chamber wall. They fanned out, pulling the bulbous head of a huge yellow octopus from the pool. The creature curled and suctioned its way up the wall, snuggling into the far corner against the ceiling, watching them like a hunter measuring its prey. The blue rings spotting its body pulsed like neon lights and reflected off the pool.

'Is that a hybrid?' one of the soldiers asked.

'Either that or the biggest blue-ringed octopus in the world,' Sean said.

From growing up in Australia, Sean knew how deadly they were. Usually no bigger than a person's hand, they were considered the most venomous marine animal in the world. A single bite contained enough venom to kill nearly thirty adults. Stretched to full length, this hybrid version of the blue-ringed octopus had to be at least ten feet tall. It watched them in an intelligent, unnerving manner.

'I know octopuses are smart,' Arturo whispered, 'but I've never seen one act like this before.'

'Why's it pulsing like that?' the lead soldier asked.

'It's a defensive reaction to being threatened.'

Sean could see it was more than a defensive reaction. The hybrid octopus was sending a message, one being answered from the pool.

Hundreds of tentacles emerged from the water, smothering the walls in a squirming mass of slimy glowing octopuses.

'Sean, what are you waiting for?' the lead soldier yelled. 'Go!'

Sean backed into the passage, unable to draw his eyes off the ghastly sight. Arturo and two of the soldiers followed. Sean turned his torch to the passage and rushed off. Within seconds, a deafening ring of bullets chased them down the passage. Desperate screams and frantic splashes sounded from the pool. Sean didn't look back. His wet feet slipped and skidded on the polished stone. The passage floor ascended sharply and suddenly disappeared. He stopped just in time, toes teetering over the edge.

'What's wrong?' Arturo said, almost knocking him into the void.

Sean shone his torch into the hole, illuminating the continuing passage several metres below. A blast of energy reverberated up the passage.

'That's not one of our weapons,' Arturo said.

'It's an Isharkute stave,' Sean said.

'Get down there. We'll cover you,' said one of their escorting soldiers.

Sean and Arturo lowered themselves into the passage, which continued straight on before branching off into five separate passages. The two on the left veered downwards, the middle straight ahead, while the right two sloped upwards.

'Which way now?' Arturo asked.

Sean tried to visualise the path from his vision. It was weird. All five routes seemed to beckon him forward – he wasn't feeling an urge to follow one over the other. He closed his eyes, but the harder he tried, the clearer it seemed. They were all correct!

'Move!' screamed the soldier, dropping down from the upper passage.

The remaining soldiers who had been guarding the first chamber followed, scrambling over the ledge as an energy bolt ricocheted above their heads. Sean and Arturo helped the soldiers to their feet.

'Look out!' cried one of the men, aiming at a yellow blob sliding down the wall.

The octopus unfurled its tentacles across the stone, moving with incredible speed, then bunched itself up and leapt off the wall. The soldier didn't even have time to shoot. It landed on his head and smothered his face, tentacles curling around his neck, blue rings pulsing brightly. His trigger finger seized, then his entire body locked stiff from the poisonous bite.

He was dead before his body hit the floor.

Sean turned his gaze from the horrible sight.

The higher passage was now a tangle of slithering luminous octopuses. The tip of an electrified stave appeared over the edge, highlighting a burly Isharkute. Sean gasped. An icy shiver raced down his back. It was Vogran, the commander who'd held him down while Nefaro cut off his wings. The octopuses slid aside as if Vogran was surrounded by an invisible barrier. He sized up Sean with a smirk, then tossed a flashing blue sphere into their passage. It bounced with a metallic clang along the floor.

'Watch out!' Sean screamed, leading the sprint into the central passage.

The explosion erupted behind him, scattering everyone into different passages. The blast lifted Sean off his feet and dumped him further down the passage.

'Arturo?' Sean gasped, clambering to his feet.

'I'm all right,' Arturo moaned, his faceless voice echoing from somewhere off the stone walls. 'Keep going. Don't come back for me.'

Warriors dropped into the passage and began hunting them down. Electrified staves swept through the haze for survivors. Sean clicked off his torch and backed up the passage, tiptoeing across the stone. Confident he was out of sight, he turned his torch back on and ran as fast as he could. Energy blasts and yelling echoed after him. The passage veered left and right, then finally straightened out, ending with a 10-metre-high arch into a cavernous void.

Sean pulled up just in time and stared, mouth agape in astonishment.

He was on a ledge positioned halfway up a circular chamber. His LED torch cast a dim spotlight on the adjacent wall, which was at least 50 metres away. In the centre of the chamber was a huge metal obelisk, rising a good four to five storeys from a tranquil pool of water. Soft blue lights illuminated the obelisk from deep in the pool. The metal-plated surface refracted the aquatic glow, casting iridescent bands of light around the roughly hewn chamber walls.

Sean's heart swelled with excitement. He'd found the beacon!

The chamber bore an uncanny resemblance to a modern-day nuclear missile silo, but this place wasn't designed to eliminate humanity in some futile atomic war. It would save it from destruction – providing he could turn it on.

The vision from the Ark flashed through his mind's eye. Somewhere nearby there was a stone plinth with an imprint of his hand. All he needed to do was touch it to activate the beacon.

He peered into the upper reaches of the chamber and spotted

a larger ledge on the far side, just below the rugged stone ceiling, then an opening to the control room. His heart sank. He couldn't reach it, not without flying. In his vision he'd circled the chamber once before entering, but without wings, that was impossible. There had to be another way. Maybe one of the other passages led to the control room.

Barefoot and unarmed, heading into the passages seemed suicidal, but his only hope was to slip past the enemy, make it back to the junction, and find another way. He froze against the wall, picturing the tentacled horrors awaiting him.

Just as he was about to push off, a flash of light caught his eye, coming from halfway down the chamber. One of the soldiers was standing on a lower ledge, gun pointed back the way he'd come, meaning the five passages led into the chamber at different levels. The soldier fired into the darkness, then scrambled off the ledge and along the chamber wall...apparently walking in midair!

*What the hell?* Sean thought, leaning over the edge for a clearer view.

His heart leapt with excitement.

Now he could see a thin niche spiralling up the chamber wall, starting at pool level, passing two ledges before his and rising past another two before reaching the control room. Less than twelve inches wide, the precarious niche was barely visible in the low light. No wonder he'd missed it. His Yonaguni vision was correct after all. Even without flying, by following the niche he'd circle the chamber once before entering the control room.

*Crack!* The soldier was shot down from the niche and splashed into the pool.

An Isharkute warrior appeared on the lowest ledge, then another on the ledge above. The dark passages behind them came alive with glowing blue rings, and a river of octopuses streamed from the arches, writhing over each other, dropping into the pool and smothering every inch of stone.

Heavy footfalls echoed down Sean's passage. He glanced up at the control room.

The upper ledges were still clear. This was his last chance.

He took a steadying breath and started up the perilous niche.

*     *     *

Nocao's twitchy thumb had cost him precious seconds. The tectonic missile had fallen out of target lock and Senetep's squadron of stingers were upon him. His cockpit blared with warning sirens and flashing lights, alerting him to a volley of incoming missiles. He cursed under his breath and pulled hard on the flight stick, veering sharply, leaving the tectonic missile to cruise across the desert.

He dipped lower and flew around the sand dunes, aiming his stinger at a colossal rocky plateau his map showed as the Guelta d'Archei, hoping to make it before the missiles struck.

'Whoa!' he cried, pulling up to avoid a caravan of camels, his hull virtually shaving the tallest camel's hump. 'Sorry about that.'

The missiles closed in, seconds away from impact...five...four...

Nocao rotated his stinger sideways and aimed for a crevice in the approaching cliff face. The gap was so tight it set off more onboard alarms which thought he was flying straight into a rock wall. He held steady, focusing on the impossibly thin sliver.

Three...two...one...

His stinger shot between the stone, swooshing the dust off the walls. The missiles attempted to follow, but the tight space proved too hard to auto-navigate. The blast tore through the mountain, collapsing the gap behind him. He kept ahead of the shockwave, zipping between the crumbling walls.

The ever-tightening space suddenly opened and he shot free with a cloud of dust.

The detour had led him into a canyon flanked by towering sandstone cliffs. Nestled between the shadows of these ancient rock faces was an oasis of pools teeming with hundreds of camels basking happily in the water. They raised their heads and grunted at the flying intruder.

Three stingers appeared on his map, flying high above the

plateau, tracking his vessel and waiting for him to exit. He plotted a course through the canyon and quickly realised he was about to run out of space.

He decelerated and the stingers slowed, matching his speed.

Nocao snickered. *Imbeciles! These are Senetep's best pilots?* He swiped up a hologram listing his onboard arsenal and selected the close-range targeting missiles, then yanked hard on the flight stick, good thumb poised on the trigger. His vessel went vertical and he rocketed out of the canyon, catching Senetep's pilots off-guard.

*Boom! Boom!*

He flew between the explosions, cheering all the way. 'Hah! You need to do better than that.'

The escaping stinger dove into the protection of the canyon as another three enemies appeared on his map, rising from the ravines behind him. *It's an ambush. I should've realised...I was the bait!*

Nocao dipped his stinger into the nearest chasm.

There was no sneaky crevice to save him from the fresh barrage of missiles this time, just the hope he could shake them off. His cockpit plunged into shadow as he plummeted between the cliffs. He leant his entire weight on the flight stick, veering on sharp angles, clearing the cliffs by centimetres.

A stinger appeared ahead, flashing in and out of the pockets of sunlight.

The missiles gained on him, sending his onboard alarms into a frenzy.

'Silence all warning systems,' Nocao howled.

Undistracted by technology, he could focus on what he knew how to do best: fly. Eyes locked on the vessel, he accelerated into its slipstream. The pilot swerved left and right, attempting to trick him down another gorge. Nocao stayed tight, glancing at the sensors.

The missiles were upon him...

*NOW!*

He cranked the thrusters to their limits and shoved the flight stick forward, ducking under the stinger. The missiles found a new target, obliterating the vessel above him.

Nocao sped around a corner into another ravine filled with camels. The sky went dark behind him. Rocks and debris flew high into the atmosphere and rained down around the helpless creatures.

'Sorry about that,' Nocao said, peering down at them.

'Nocao, it's Buzzbee 3,' said a friendly female voice. 'Are you still there?'

'Yes! I'd appreciate some assistance.'

'What do you need?'

'I've got three stingers tracking me. Follow my lead – I'll try and wear them out. Stay above the plateau, and when you have a good shot, take them out.'

'Copy that, we're on our way.'

Nocao breathed a sigh of relief. He needed help more than ever, his shakes now so bad that they were vibrating the flight stick. At this rate of deterioration, he'd be lucky to finish the mission with two hands. He checked the tectonic missile on the scanner. It was further away, becoming harder to catch with every wasted second.

Both hands locked on the flight stick, Nocao led Senetep's stingers on the trickiest route possible through the ravines. He skimmed over cliff ledges, dove into fissures, and rolled beneath the tightest overhangs. The enemy stuck with his vessel the whole way, making him feel like he was wearing himself out, not them.

His scanner showed a kilometre-long ravine coming up – the perfect place for an ambush. 'Okay, Buzzbees, here's your chance.'

'We're on it!' came Buzzbee 2's reply. 'Coming in over your position now.'

Senetep's stingers took the bait and followed him into the ravine, flying single file behind him. A bombardment of energy blasts rained down from the Buzzbees, shattering the sandstone cliffs. The trailing stingers were swallowed by the debris cloud and exploded. Their shockwaves bumped Nocao off course.

*That's too close!* Nocao thought, fighting to correct his stinger.

He scraped along a ledge, then bounced off another. He'd lost all control, barrelling full speed into a hard turn. An unforgiving wall of stone filled his windscreen.

*I won't make it!*

At the last second, Buzzbee 3 dove into the ravine and bumped him around the corner, saving him from destruction. He ricocheted along the cliff, spinning wildly, the outside world a disorienting blur. He hit the ground with a heavy *thud* and ground to a stop in an epic spray of sand and water.

Nocao ejected his stinger's shattered canopy and stood up.

He was back with the camels, having crash-landed right next to their drinking hole. The closest camel spat a mouthful of water at him and grunted.

Nocao wiped the watery spit from his chest. 'Fair enough. I'd feel the same way.'

Buzzbee 3 touched down next to the pool and the pilot jumped out. Nocao recognised her blue eyes and fair complexion. It was Captain Olivia Brasher, the same pilot who flew them out of Cairo in Maddock's Black Hawk helicopter. 'Once again, I'm in your debt.'

'That's two you owe me,' Olivia said with a smile. 'Glad to see you're okay.'

'You too, but I need your vessel.'

'She's all yours. Just don't forget to pick me up when you're done.'

'Indeed,' Nocao said, climbing into the cockpit. 'I hope you make better friends with the camels than I did.'

Olivia chuckled.

Moments later Nocao was flying high above the plateau, the Buzzbee squadron behind him. The tectonic missile was now 300 kilometres away. He checked the inventory of remaining missiles in this craft: nothing left. 'Buzzbees, do you have any missiles left?'

There was a distinct 'No!' from his squadron.

'Of course not,' Nocao grumbled. 'Accelerate to full speed – we're going to do this by sheer force.'

They accelerated across the boundless expanse of golden dunes.

Nocao watched the scanner.

One hundred kilometres to the missile...seventy-five...fifty...

He peered through the windscreen, expecting to see the speck materialise ahead. They cleared a ridge and came across a white sun-bleached salt plain. The missile appeared as a dark spot, shimmering in the heat. They had a clear, unobstructed path to intercept the missile. 'There it is!' Nocao hollered.

Plumes of dust swirled up from the path of the missile.

'It's on the final descent. We've got seconds before it hits –'

'What do we do?' Buzzbee 4 called back.

Nocao flicked open one of his dashboard panels and swapped out several crystal control cards. 'I'm rerouting power, dropping shields, putting everything into my thrusters. I'll get beneath it, slow it down, and force it up... Then help me push it into space.'

'We're ready,' Buzzbee 4 replied.

Nocao zoomed ahead of the squadron, aiming for the tightening space between the missile and salt plain. He took his trembling hand off the flight stick to improve his precision. He eased into the gap and pulled up. His hull met the missile with a *clunk*. Watching through his overhead canopy, he lifted the tip of the missile above the horizon and aimed for the open sky.

'Okay, Buzzbees, help me get rid of this thing.'

The squadron edged alongside the missile, their combined thrust forcing the missile straight up, through the ozone layer towards the upper stratosphere.

'Without shields, won't you break apart?' Buzzbee 2 asked.

'Keep holding –' Nocao said through clenched teeth.

Buzzbee 2 was right. He hadn't thought that far ahead. Bursts of superheated air rippled over his windscreen and the hull shuddered under the pressure. Nocao could feel the missile trying to right itself back to Earth, but he held tight, fighting the destructive behemoth. The blue sky darkened as the atmosphere thinned. The turbulence abated, giving way to a dazzling view of the Milky Way.

'Separate!' Nocao roared.

Their five stingers parted at the same time, leaving the missile to float away harmlessly. Nocao eased back into his seat and breathed a heavy sigh of relief.

'We did it!' announced Buzzbee 2. Everyone cheered.

Nocao listened to their cries of elation, taking a moment to appreciate the vibrancy and scope of the universe before them. There was still so much to explore – so much to share between humanity and the Isharkute. It filled him with the hope that Sean's message was on its way.

There was a blinding flash as the missile detonated in the silent vacuum of space.

The shockwave threw Nocao and the Buzzbees into a deadly spin back to Earth.

*     *     *

Sean pressed his back hard against the chamber wall, arms outstretched. His bare feet shuffled along the niche, toes gripping every deviation in the stone. There was nothing to grab on to if he lost his balance. A single slip and he'd end up hundreds of metres below, strangled and bitten in the pool of glowing blue-ringed octopuses.

He focused on the wall ahead and avoided looking down. *I can do this. Don't look down. Just two more arches to get past and I'm there.* The control room was three levels higher than his position, but he was only halfway to the first arch. His black wetsuit was the perfect camouflage against the dark rock, keeping him hidden from the warriors on the ledges below.

Gunfire and energy blasts echoed from the archway he was standing in moments before, followed by a bloodcurdling scream.

Sean glanced over his shoulder.

A soldier stumbled through the arch and toppled over the edge, clawing at the octopus smothering his head. Sean didn't wait to see his body hit water. He dug his feet into the niche and picked up the pace, scraping his exposed ankles along the stone.

Sean gritted his teeth and pressed on, suppressing the urge to grimace in pain.

Just a few metres to the arch.

He dove across the final gap and pulled himself into the shadows, tentatively touching his ankles. They were grazed raw and sticky with blood. Heavy footfalls echoed up the passage behind him. No time to rest. Sean crawled over to the niche and startled when a voice whispered out to him, 'Sean!'

Sean's heart leapt with excitement.

Arturo emerged from the shadows, panting heavily. He peered down at the obelisk and swirling pool of octopuses. 'Whoa! *Dio mio!* Is that the beacon?'

'Yeah.'

Arturo glanced back down the passage. 'They're not far behind me. Where do we go? This is a dead end.'

'It's not,' Sean said, pointing to the niche. 'There's a small ledge that goes all the way to the control room. If I get up there, I can turn on the beacon.'

The crackle of an electrified Isharkute stave echoed up the passage.

'They're almost here. Go!' Arturo said, forcing Sean on to the niche.

They edged out in opposite directions from the arch, pinning themselves against the wall. An Isharkute warrior stepped through the arch and peered over the edge, right between Sean and Arturo's petrified stares. The warrior sensed something and cocked his head towards Arturo. Before the warrior could react, Arturo grabbed his stave and yanked. The warrior lost his balance and tipped over, flailing all the way to the pool below.

Arturo leapt back onto the ledge with his new weapon. 'Keep going! I'll cover you.'

The warriors started firing at them from the lower levels.

Energy blasts erupted around the arch.

Sean ignored the sting of his ankles and forged ahead. No time to look back, let alone think. His heart was in his throat. Blasts ricocheted all around, disorienting him, threatening to throw him off balance. He closed his eyes to the chaos, letting his hands and feet guide him like a blind man. His toes and fingertips gripped every bump and crevice, guiding him along.

The pain in his ankles was excruciating. Just when the niche seemed like it would never end...

'Here! Give me your hand,' whispered a voice.

Sean opened his eyes to find himself within arm's reach of the next ledge and a soldier reaching for him. 'Thanks,' Sean said, jumping to safety. He found another two soldiers hidden in the shadow of the arch, providing covering fire.

'Can we go back that way?' Sean said, peering hopefully down the passage.

'No, it's full of coneheads and glowin' squids,' the soldier said, firing off several rounds into the lower chamber. 'Keep going, kid. We got you covered.'

Sean waited for a lull in the shooting and slipped onto the niche. His palms were extra sweaty and slippery this time. A torrent of energy blasts and gunfire filled the chamber. Sean dug his fingernails into the rock, clawing forward. He'd worked out how to move his feet without scraping his ankles as much.

'Faster!' screamed the soldier.

The three soldiers scrambled onto the niche behind him, their arch erupting with a swell of glowing blue-ringed octopuses.

'Don't stop, Sean! Keep going!' the soldier behind him cried.

Heart hammering, Sean pressed on. His surging adrenaline masked the pain. Another petrified scream was silenced. From the corner of his eye, Sean saw the trailing soldier fall off the ledge, covered in glowing octopuses. The creatures spread across the chamber wall, circling around them, closing in. *Don't look. Keep moving!* Sean thought as their pulsing rings filled his peripheral vision.

More energy blasts hit the wall beneath their feet.

The second soldier lost his balance and fell off, screaming all the way down to the pool. There were only two of them left now. Sean grazed himself along the wall, the back of his wetsuit catching and tearing on the rock. A tentacle curled across the niche in front of his foot. He couldn't risk kicking it off and quickly stepped over it. An intense tingling sensation shot up his spine and rippled through his shoulderblades. If only his wings were ready...

Five metres to go...four... He was so close, he could almost jump over the gap.

The octopuses were now hanging from the chamber ceiling, dangling their luminous tentacles like poisonous vines.

Three metres...two...

Sean leapt across the gap and caught the ledge. He pulled himself up and turned to help the soldier who'd previously helped him. The soldier was a good running-leap away from making the distance, but he tried anyway. Sean met his terrified gaze as he soared through the air towards him, octopuses launching after him, all seemingly in slow-motion. He was coming up short. Sean caught his hand, but it wasn't enough. The soldier missed the ledge and Sean fell to the floor with his weight, the only thing holding him from certain death. Sean slipped closer to the edge. He didn't have the strength to pull the soldier up.

The pulsing blue glow was all around them now.

'Let me go!' the soldier groaned.

Sean shook his head. 'No!' He couldn't let go. It wasn't in his nature. He dug deep, using every ounce of energy he had left. It worked! He dragged the soldier up to his armpits. A glimmer of hope filled the soldier's eyes, then...

*Bang!*

The ledge exploded, tossing Sean back in a fury of dust and shattered stone.

When he looked up, the soldier was gone. Beyond the smoking remains of the ledge stood Vogran, aiming at him from the arch across the chamber. Sean rolled aside as another shot tore through the stone and he crawled blindly around the corner.

Safe for the moment, Sean shook the dust off his face.

Ahead of him stretched a long passage. The far end opened into a chamber illuminated by a dim blue light. *That'd better not be more octopuses!*

He sprinted the length of the passage and skidded to a stop.

The chamber was the same as his vision, a large circular room dominated by an elevated pedestal in the centre. He hurried up the steps, heart pounding. Embedded into the top of the stone plinth was a plate-sized quartz crystal, pulsing like a heartbeat. Carved into the centre was the indentation of a human hand, the perfect fit for his own hand! It was hard to believe the chamber had been waiting thousands of years just for him, purposefully created to respond to his touch, his unique DNA sequence.

Sean held his hand hover over the indentation, awed by the gravity of the moment.

With a single touch, he was about to save the world and lead humanity beyond the confines of their planet into a universe of unprecedented knowledge and discovery. Not since human beings had travelled into space had there been such a jump in evolution. But unlike Neil Armstrong's first steps on the moon, which were televised to the entire world, this historic event only had one viewer: himself.

Vogran's heavy footfalls echoed down the passage, moments away from catching him.

Sean held his breath and placed his hand upon the crystal.

# CHAPTER 32

# A New World

Sean was consumed within an intense white light, suddenly weightless. There was no pain, no feeling at all. He couldn't tell if he was dead or alive; his senses were utterly consumed by the void. The light faded, revealing the control chamber beneath him, but he wasn't seeing it from his body, which was still standing at the pedestal with his hand locked to the crystal. He was hovering high above himself, near the ceiling. The chamber was transforming in shape and size. Megalithic stone blocks shifted up, down, and sideways like a giant three-dimensional slide puzzle, closing off the passage he'd taken moments before. Vogran was caught entering the chamber mid-stride, half of his body instantly crushed to nothing between the stones. His free arm went limp and dropped his weapon.

The chamber rotated 360 degrees and opened to overlook the beacon. The metal obelisk arose from the pool like a rocket preparing for take-off. The ceiling opened, but it wasn't water that poured in, it was sunshine. The entire Yonaguni structure had risen above the sea. Sean's perspective followed the tip of the beacon. From his vantage point, he could see Senetep's annihilator hovering nearby. A little further out, a fleet of military warships cut through the East China Sea – humanity's first united response from a new world.

A light brighter than the sun flashed across the ocean and Sean's consciousness was launched out of Earth's atmosphere into the depths of space. The beacon had activated.

Millions of alien worlds and galaxies whizzed by in a dizzying blur. He was travelling faster than the speed of light across the universe.

Neberun's fleet of motherships appeared from the shadow of a moon. His presence was drawn to the largest ship like a magnet, passing through the hull, weaving between thousands of Isharkute souls locked in their cryogenic chambers, right into the ship's core computer system.

His thoughts merged with the crystalline control shards. Sean finally understood: he was more than just the key to Yonaguni. His very consciousness was the message!

He could instantly see everything that happened to Neberun and his fleet since leaving Earth, but more than that, all his memories were instantly transferred into the Isharkute computer systems. They knew everything about him, every decision and sacrifice that led him to this point.

The last thing he sensed was the entire Isharkute race waking at once.

*     *     *

Senetep stared in disbelief at the beacon from the bridge of his annihilator, horrified and disgusted that it had come to this. He was out of options. Every onboard missile had been used to defend their vessel against the human uprising. His tectonic missiles had been picked off one by one. Vogran's platoon of warriors and hybrid cephalopods had failed to stop Sean Livingstone and his friends from activating the beacon. If he hadn't needed his annihilator for the next stage of his journey, he would have rammed it straight through Yonaguni.

'Overseer Senetep,' said one of the bridge crew. 'I've lost contact with First Commander Vogran.'

'Good!' Senetep said. 'He was useless to the end.'

'I'm monitoring multiple motherships arriving in orbit.'

The overhead hologram zoomed out from Yonaguni to display the entire planet. Dozens of disc-shaped motherships dropped out of light speed, instantaneously appearing in orbit over every continent. Emperor Neberun's gargantuan mothership arrived directly over their location and hovered in the daytime sky like a new moon.

*That was fast,* Senetep thought. Concerned mutterings and hushed words carried across the bridge. Seeds of doubt and fear were taking root amongst his crew, for they all knew if they were captured by Neberun's forces, it was instant execution. Their weakness was spreading like a virus and needed to be eradicated before it took hold.

Two of his bridge crew slipped away and made silently for the exit.

Senetep snatched a stave from one of his warriors and shot the fleeing pair in the back. 'Any more traitors?' he screamed, sweeping the weapon around to his crew.

Everyone froze at their posts, staring in horror at their crewmates slumped beside the exit.

'Those of you with questionable constitutions don't deserve a place on my vessel. Neberun and his human sympathisers have returned, but that doesn't change our objective.'

A brazen crew member spoke up. 'What's our objective?'

'The same as it's always been: to cure and purify our species.'

'We're running out of time. If we're not already sick with the affliction, we die by Neberun's hand or yours... Where's our future now?'

Senetep seethed at being questioned. Under normal circumstances, he would have killed the outspoken crew members where they stood, but he needed them to complete his next mission. First, he needed to regain their trust.

'Neberun would have you believe your future lives on this planet with these overbred primates, but it's not. Our future waits far beyond our homeworld, in the furthest reaches of the universe.'

'Where?' responded several crew members at once.

Senetep had kept his plans to locate the *Spearhead of Creation* a secret. For years, it was his private obsession. Many Isharkute would have called it ludicrous and insane – something that would have undermined his reputation and leadership. Even now, to prove the existence of the *Spearhead* uprooted the foundations of Isharkute creation beliefs and introduced a new way of thinking that even his crew would struggle to accept. But there was no time to delay his intentions any longer.

'With the *Spearhead of Creation*,' Senetep said.

A wall of stunned faces stared back at him. 'But the *Spearhead's* a myth!' someone shouted.

Senetep took a crystal control shard from his bracer and activated it, changing the overhead hologram to a map of the universe. The spiral path taken by the *Spearhead* traced its way through the stars, revealing his discovery.

'Myths are what you were taught to believe, but our ancestors had forgotten their true beginnings. My journey through time rewarded me with a vision, a reawakening – a single spiral pattern that became imprinted upon my mind. The path to the *Spearhead of Creation*.'

His revelation was met with silence and awe.

'As you can see, I've tracked the trajectory of a vessel that's been seeding the universe with life since the First Light. I know where to find it. With the *Spearhead* under our control, we can erase and recreate worlds as we please. And if we ever return to this insignificant rock, Emperor Neberun will be the one who kneels before us.'

There was a long silence...then a triumphant cheer resounded across the bridge.

Senetep smiled to himself. His future was just beginning.

*     *     *

Sean awoke with a start, lying on the Yonaguni platform in the shadow of the beacon. He picked himself up as Senetep's annihilator flew overhead and continued skyward, breaking through the upper atmosphere with a roar. There was a series of bright flashes as the vessel fought its way past Neberun's mothership before vanishing into space at light speed. Senetep had escaped Emperor Neberun for a second time, but now it was worse – he was on his way to find the *Spearhead of Creation*, a plan he'd proudly blabbed on about moments before cutting off Sean's wings.

Earth was safe for now, but if Senetep completed his mission, the entire universe was at risk.

Sean was a little disoriented from his whirlwind tour of the cosmos and took a moment to assess the change in his surroundings.

The control chamber had become part of a sprawling open platform encircling the beacon. The entire Yonaguni structure was now a symmetrically shaped monument sitting high above the sea. The lower third of the beacon surrounded it like an impenetrable seawall.

'Sean!' a voice cried.

Arturo emerged from the platform, waving excitedly. 'You did it!' He threw down his stave and raced over, arms open. They embraced. 'I thought I was going to be crushed.'

'What about the other soldiers?' Sean asked. 'Did they make it?'

'I haven't seen them. As soon as everything changed, the octopuses and Isharkute disappeared. All the passages moved around – I thought I'd never find my way out.'

Arturo noticed the mothership dominating the sky like a gigantic moon. 'Wow! *Che fico!* Look at that. Is that the Isharkute emperor?'

Sean nodded. 'Emperor Neberun.'

'That was fast!'

An Isharkute vessel swooped around the beacon and landed beside them. Bella bounded out the door and sprinted over. She smothered them with hugs and kisses, tears rolling down her cheeks. '*Grazie a Dio!* We didn't know if you were both dead or alive. When Senetep arrived, we had to leave. It was too dangerous. I feel so guilty –'

'It's okay. There's nothing you could have done against an annihilator,' Sean assured her.

'*Sì.* We had everything under control,' Arturo boasted.

Bella punched his arm. 'Not funny, Arty.'

Carla, Powell, and Hazim emerged from the vessel, all marvelling at the towering beacon. They congratulated Sean and Arturo, shaking hands and thanking each other.

'What about Nocao?' Sean asked. 'Did his squad destroy the missiles?'

'They did!' Carla said brightly.

An awkward pause followed. Powell and Hazim remained tight-lipped, adding nothing to her comment. Sean instantly knew something was wrong. The troubled expression in Carla's eyes only cemented his dire feeling.

'Unfortunately...we lost contact after they detonated the final missile,' Carla finished.

Bella wiped the happy tears from her eyes. Her smile faded.

Sean imagined the worst, but didn't allow himself to succumb to the panic. It was like a sixth sense telling him they were all right. 'Don't worry. They'll be here,' he said positively.

Bella perked up. 'You're right! They know where to find us.'

'I hope that's Emperor Neberun's welcoming party,' Powell said, pointing to the Isharkute vessel descending upon them.

Sean recognised the scarlet streamlined hull with its six landing arms. 'That's a royal ship – probably the Emperor.'

'Any royal protocols we need to acknowledge?' Hazim asked.

'Yeah, he's pretty old and cranky. Just keep quiet. Don't speak unless spoken to, and don't look him in the eye unless he speaks to you.'

'I thought we were on equal footing with the Isharkute now,' Powell said.

'I hope so, after everything we've done to help them. But the changes won't be instant. It'll take time for them to adjust. Last time they were on Earth, we were their slaves. For humanity, that was ten thousand years ago, but to them, it's only been a few days.'

'Doesn't sound overly promising, but I trust you know what you're doing.'

'We need to ease them into it, starting with Emperor Neberun.'

'I can't think of a better person to do that than you, Sean,' Hazim said. 'You singlehandedly convinced the UN to act – no small feat considering how defeated we were.'

'*Sí!* Of course he can do it,' Bella said, winking.

Sean was brimming with pride, feeling like he could take on the world. The royal vessel touched down on its six landing arms like a mechanical hybrid and the main door opened with a hiss, revealing the shadowy interior. Sean squinted to make out the tall heavy-set figure standing at the top of the gangway.

'Are we supposed to kneel or something?' Bella whispered.

'No, it's okay. Just stay behind me,' Sean said, stepping forward.

'Sean! My old friend,' bellowed a jubilant-sounding voice. 'You still risking your scrawny neck saving this backwater planet?'

Sean instantly recognised the boisterous tone.

Ramin stepped into the sunlight, a broad smile plastered between his chubby cheeks. He strode down the gangway, opulent, gold-laced robes flowing behind him – the perfect accoutrement to his unmatched ego. They greeted each other with the Isharkute sign of the cosmos, followed by a chest-crushing hug.

'It's good to see you too,' Sean said, sucking the air back into his lungs.

'You've made some new friends,' Ramin said, looking around.

Sean nodded, expecting someone to respond, but everyone kept quiet and nervously averted their gaze from Ramin. 'It's okay,' Sean said. 'This's my friend, Overseer Ramin. You're allowed to look at him... Don't worry, he's not the Emperor.'

'Well, not yet!' Ramin said with a laugh.

Sean chuckled. 'If it wasn't for Ramin, I wouldn't be standing here now.'

'What?! You haven't regaled them with tales of my magnificence yet?'

Sean faced his friends and rolled his eyes at Ramin's comment. 'Don't worry, you'll get used to his sense of humour.'

Ramin laughed away the remark, then furrowed his brow. 'I'm serious, Sean. Why don't they know about me? My exploits should be legendary by now.'

'I haven't had time to tell them,' Sean said defensively. 'In case you didn't realise, we've been busy saving both our species –'

'I'm joking, child,' Ramin interrupted. 'A tip I picked up from studying human customs: alleviate the tension of a first meeting with a little humour and lighthearted banter.'

Sean chuckled. 'You never spoke English before. Sounds like you've been speaking it for years.'

'Ten thousand five hundred years, to be exact. Every human dialect we salvaged from your laptop computer was integrated into our cryogenic chambers. We've been learning them while we slept.'

'What are you doing in a royal vessel?'

'After we evacuated Earth, Emperor Neberun appointed me to the position of Royal Consult. I've given away my title of Overseer and now report directly to the Emperor.'

'Then we're in good hands,' Sean said.

Ramin nodded earnestly. 'I'll do the best I can for your species. Emperor Neberun appreciates my insights into your human ways.'

A troupe of royal guards in gold-plated armour emerged from the vessel and formed lines on both sides of the gangway.

Sean's stomach tightened. He felt this could still go either way.

Emperor Neberun's tall gangly frame stepped into the light and sauntered down the gangway. He seemed even thinner than the last time Sean had seen him, more akin to a walking skeleton than a living being. His gold-laced red robes flapped behind him like the petals of a wilting flower barely clinging to their stem. The guards escorted their Emperor across the platform and formed a circle around Sean and his friends.

Neberun's pale-blue eyes focused on them with intensity, one side of his mouth curled upwards in a slight grin. Sean quickly realised the expression was a permanent fixture of his taut, mummified-looking skin. Neberun had lived centuries longer than his body intended.

Ramin stepped aside and bowed in reverence. Sean bowed as well, hoping everyone behind him was showing the same respect.

'Sean Livingstone,' Neberun said in a deep and powerful voice, 'raise your head to me.'

Sean obeyed.

'The last time we met, this world was on the brink of change... and here we stand again, facing another new beginning. History appears to be repeating itself.'

Sean nodded, wondering if he should speak. He had so much to say, but sensed Neberun already knew everything.

'There's no need to explain,' Neberun said, as if he'd just read his thoughts. 'When your conscious mind merged with our fleet, every Isharkute immediately saw what you'd done to save us. Without the foresight of your father and Nesuk to build this beacon, and the brave actions of your friends here, we were doomed to sleep for eternity in the shadow of a forgotten moon. For that, we are in your debt.'

Sean was giddy with relief. 'If you read my thoughts, then you know we have to stop Senetep.'

'Indeed, his quest to find the *Spearhead of Creation* is more than an attack against the Isharkute – it undermines our core beliefs. We regard the *Spearhead* as a divine being, the mythological creator of life that appeared after the First Light, a belief that's been embedded in Isharkute culture since the birth of our civilisation. To take that away from my people is to deprive them of their faith.'

'I understand,' Sean said. 'But with your arrival, humanity faces the same dilemma.'

'How so?'

'I'm probably not the best person to explain this,' Sean said, glancing over his shoulder at Bella. She widened her eyes at him as if to say *Who, me?*

'Why is that?' Neberun asked.

'Because I'm an atheist. I don't follow a religion...but my friend Bella does.'

Neberun raised his spindly finger and motioned Bella forward.

She stood beside Sean and took a nervous breath. 'I was brought up a Catholic. That means I believe in Jesus Christ, his crucifixion and resurrection...but I also learnt about other religions at school. There's more than four thousand around the world, which means ninety-five per cent of humanity follows a faith. As far as I know, none of them account for or explain the arrival of extraterrestrials. Just like the *Spearhead* undermines your belief system, the existence of the Isharkute places human religions into question.'

Neberun stared at Bella for a long time, and then finally responded. 'Regardless of our origins, we share one constant theme: the belief in a divine being or omnipotent power. In that respect, we aren't so different. We share similar questions about our place in the universe.'

'Sounds like the quest to stop Senetep from finding the *Spearhead* is a quest for all of us, to find a common universal belief,' Sean said.

Neberun nodded. 'Possibly. Tell me, Sean. If you have no religion, then what do you believe?'

Sean looked inwards and found a gaping hole of emptiness. What did he believe in? His spiritual self was an empty husk, a dried-up part of himself he'd ignored for too long. Emptiness had been eating him from the inside since the death of his mother, and had grown with the loss of William and his dad. He wasn't brought up in a religious family and had no faith to fall back on – nothing to guide him through the pain of losing his family.

'My dad taught me to believe in myself, but...'

'With him gone, you're wondering where you belong,' Neberun confirmed, as if reading his thoughts again. 'You're looking for a connection, a meaning to your life.'

Sean nodded solemnly. 'I don't have a religion, but I...I believe no-one is meant to be alone in the universe.'

'You'll belong somewhere again,' Bella said, squeezing his hand gently.

Sean brightened. Bella's affection poured life into his hungry soul, proving friendships could be just as strong as family.

Neberun noticed their connection. 'I see no need to look further than the two of you. Sean, you may be young in human years, but you're clearly an ambassador for your people. You and Bella will accompany Ramin to our homeworld. There you'll assist our scientists in perfecting the cure for our next generation of life-bearers. After that, you'll join my fleet in the hunt for Senetep.'

Bella glared at Sean, her eyes laced with terror and a hint of excitement. 'What? I have to go into space?'

Sean shrugged. 'This is the first I'm hearing about it.'

'Our situation is dire,' Neberun conceded.

'I thought once you had our DNA, you could make a cure.'

'Yes, we can rid ourselves of the affliction, but it's not proven to repair our process of procreation. When Senetep condemned us to our cryogenic chambers, he doomed the last generation of life-bearers on our homeworld to the affliction. Most died, even those put into stasis. Since then, no male Isharkute have entered hibernation and made the successful transformation into female form. We need living samples of male and female human DNA to keep our surviving nine females alive. They may be our last.'

Sean nodded. 'I understand. But what happens on Earth while we're gone?'

'My concerns that humanity was a warring, self-destructive species that could never unite have been proven wrong. For the first time in human history, your countries and governments have united for a common good - the first crucial step to ensure our cultures can work together.'

With those words, Sean finally realised he'd accomplished everything he'd set out to do. It was almost impossible to suppress his elation; he was bursting at the seams to cheer in victory.

'Commander El-Amin and Colonel Powell can coordinate the integration of my governing powers,' Neberun continued. 'In return for sharing your world, we will share our knowledge and technology. Humanity will expand beyond the confines of a single solar system.'

'Thank you,' Sean said.

'I'll give you and your friends time to say goodbye and await your presence on my vessel,' Neberun finished. He turned his stooped shoulders and returned to his vessel, looking more like a frail old man than the most powerful figure in the galaxy.

'Let's hurry this up,' Ramin said, clapping his hands. 'Finish the pleasantries - we don't want to keep our Esteemed Royalness waiting.'

'I understand why I have to go,' Sean said, 'but Bella has family. She can't just leave them.'

'*Sì!* I can take her place,' Carla said.

'Once the Emperor's spoken his will, it can't be changed,' Ramin said. 'It would be prudent not to disobey him, especially at such a crucial juncture for our species.'

'It's okay. He obviously picked me for a reason,' Bella interrupted, turning her attention to Sean. 'Besides, I can't let you go alone.'

'This is crazy!' Arturo said. 'You can't leave.'

Another Isharkute vessel whooshed overhead and landed on the platform. The gangway opened and a man and woman in their late forties warily emerged, both dishevelled and overwhelmed by their surroundings.

'Mama! Papa!' Bella screamed, racing over to them.

Sean was taken by surprise – it was Marco and Francesca Bonaforte! Arturo and Carla joined the joyous family reunion. Hugs, kisses, and tears flowed. Sean watched from a distance, his ache of emptiness returning, reminding him of his own parents. Then it dawned on him. *How did Marco and Francesca get here?* His hopes lifted. There was only one person who knew how to find Bella's parents and bring them here...Nocao.

His battle-weary friend limped onto the gangway, followed by all five pilots from the Buzzbee squadron.

Sean embraced Nocao with the warmth and familiarity of a lifelong friend. 'You did it!'

'I would've been here sooner, but we had a couple of important stops along the way,' Nocao said, nodding towards the joyous reunion.

Sean chuckled. 'I'm glad you did... Plus, your timing's perfect.'

They shared a quiet moment together, content to watch Powell, Hazim, and the Buzzbee pilots regale each other with their tales of daring and adventure. It had been too long since Sean had seen such unadulterated laughter and jubilation. He soaked it up, letting their cheerfulness wash over him. But his mind couldn't rest for long – not just for the dangers ahead, but for Bella. She looked so happy with her family. He'd do anything to save her from the pain of losing her parents again, a pain he was all too familiar with.

'Nocao!' Ramin boomed. He strode over to Nocao and made the sign of the cosmos. 'It pleases me to see you're still raising trouble with this young hero.'

'Ramin!' Nocao said, returning the gesture, admiring Ramin's regal robes. 'I see you've moved up in the Empire.'

'I've been appointed to the Royal Council and report directly to Emperor Neberun, but I can fill you in on more of my achievements during our journey.'

'What journey?' Nocao asked, looking perplexed.

Sean continued the conversation. 'The Emperor's asked me and Bella to return to your homeworld to save the last few female Isharkute. After that, we're going to hunt down Senetep before he reaches the *Spearhead of Creation*.'

'*The Spearhead of Creation?*' Nocao exclaimed.

'Just another thing we need to explain on the way.'

'Yes, you're coming with us,' Ramin said. 'Emperor Neberun will be eager to hear from you. We'll deal with your affliction during our journey.'

Sean felt a tap on the shoulder and turned around. Bella and Arturo were standing behind him, their parents between them. Francesca opened her arms to him. Sean looked around, uncertain how to respond. He'd never met Bella's mum, but she waited for him like a long-lost family member.

'Dear boy, come here,' Francesca said, throwing her arms around him in a crushing hug, a consistent Bonaforte trait. 'Thank you for everything. Bella, Arty, and Carla have told me some of what you've done.'

'That's okay...' Sean exhaled as she released him.

Marco shook Sean's hand with a warm, two-handed grip. 'Your father would be proud of you.'

'*Si,*' Carla added softly. Sean noticed the tears in her eyes. His dad's loss was still painful for both of them. She gave him a hug and kissed him on the cheek. 'If I'd married your dad, that would have made us family, but we already consider you family. No matter where you go in the universe, you'll always have a home with us.'

Sean looked around. The Bonafortes all nodded in agreement. The emptiness inside him was suddenly overflowing with love and contentment. He was ready to face the unexplored fringes of the universe, empowered by the knowledge he wasn't alone.

# A Note From Andrew D. Connell

Thank you for reading *Ark of the Gods*. Working as a self-published author, the success of my writing relies on you, the reader. Your reviews are the most effective way to introduce new readers to my books. If you enjoyed this book, please consider leaving a review on Amazon or your place of purchase. A simple sentence, or solitary one-word review is often enough, but if you're willing to write more I'd love to hear your thoughts.

Sean Livingstone's adventure continues in the third novel in the series, *The Spearhead of Creation*.

Subscribe to my monthly newsletter at *andrewdconnell.com* for the latest news and upcoming releases.

— Andrew D. Connell

# About The Author

Andrew Connell was born in Melbourne, Australia, in 1972. He studied film and television at the Victorian College of the Arts and has since worked as a writer, editor, and director of both short films and television programs. He has also written several award winning screenplays. Andrew lives in Melbourne with his wife and three children.

# Acknowledgements

As always, special thanks to my family for their love and support.

Proofreading by Susan Uttendorfsky.
adirondackediting.com

Cover artwork by Wayne Nichols.
wnichols.com

www.ingramcontent.com/pod-product-compliance
Lightning Source LLC
Chambersburg PA
CBHW051216120726
47905CB00004B/1139